978-1-8382720-5-0 (Paperback)
978-1-8382720-3-6 (eBook)

CHAPTER 1

Isadora POV

"Isadora Xxon," his voice chimes. The moment the lights flash in my eyes, I know it's over. The light blinds me; it takes a second for my eyes to refocus and make out the faint outlines of the stadium's audience again.

There's not a single thing I can do to get myself out of this situation. I feel the cameras shift to me. The faint buzz the monitors emit is audible, it's so quiet. The eyes of the thousands of people in the stadium peer into me, hawks watching prey. I lift myself out of my chair, gracefully. My heart is beating so fast I swear people around me can hear it.

I look down at the Prince adoringly as he continues, "Ability of Cryokinesis; would you allow this kingdom and me the privilege of taking my hand in marriage and becoming the Princess of Parten?"

There's nothing I can do. To reject the proposal is an act of treason. No one can or would deny this offer. Becoming the future Princess of Parten is a possibility I couldn't have imagined being offered to me a few months before.

The shifting silence in the stadium falls upon me. I realize that I've paused for too long, so I rush my words, blurting, "It would be an honor."

All my focus is poured into making sure my smile doesn't look fake. I have to convince all the people here, and the millions watching over the monitors, that I'm thrilled. I try to flutter my eyelashes slowly and control my heartrate.

Prince Lawrence smiles in acceptance. The sound of applause drowns in my ears as I sit back down. I tilt my head back and let my long brown hair brush against my chair.

It's Daymond's fault we had to attend this event. It's my brother's fault there was even a *possibility* of me being picked.

Even though we had planned to lie low after moving here a year ago, Daymond didn't follow through. Shortly after we settled in Parten, he got himself wrapped up in the royal military. It only took a few months and a couple of promotions—along with some slight persuasion from Daymond—for him to become a ranking general. I don't blame him; all he's done his whole life is train for the military. His brain is filled with strategies and brutal martial knowledge. He would have gone insane not having any way to use all his experience and education. Daymond is still impressively young for his position, at the age twenty-nine—ten years older than me.

If Daymond hadn't been so involved in the royals' affairs, I wouldn't have been considered for this honor.

When I glance back at the stage, I can see that Prince Lawrence is still smiling. He puts on a good front for everyone watching, like I'm trying to do. I wonder what it's like, pretending to be so thrilled when everyone knows this isn't your choice. Who Lawrence would marry has always been up to the royal council and his family, and they only ever select spouses from influential families. Daymond is my connection; and my ability to control and manipulate water in the form of ice didn't help me lay low at all.

Nowadays, there aren't many cryomancers in Parten. I've never even heard of any others, actually, besides my brother and me.

There aren't many powerful manipulators of *anything* in Parten anymore. It feels like every year, the kingdoms have been seeing manipulators of hair, dirt, wood, taste, color, fabric, and many other simpler abilities appear in greater numbers. They all have their uses, of course... but they're mundane. Boring.

I turn my attention back to the stage and watch as the oldest Prince stands. Alasdair doesn't seem fazed at all. I can't focus on his words as he asks some girl to be his future wife and Queen of Parten. There are too many thoughts spiraling in my head for me to hear anything clearly. I've only met the princes a handful of times. They were always friendly and kind to me. I don't know as much as I wish I did about them, but I trust Alasdair and his ability to rule. Compared to the princes in other kingdoms, he's going to be a gracious and lawful king.

Prince Alas, as he prefers to be called, stands up straight, with a slight smile on his face. His dark brown hair gleams in the light. It's a thick mane of wild hair tamed only by the coronet upon his head. His jawline is prominent, along with his stance as he starts to speak. He's everything you'd want a ruler to look like. His warm, fiery blue irises show a promising light behind them.

He's asked a girl named Trinity for her hand in marriage. I know very little about Trinity, only what I've heard in passing. Her parents are on the royal council and wield heavy influence there. She's a young public figure with a pretty face and the ability to control and manipulate light. She has black hair that reflects red in the sun. Her hooded eyes and diamond-cut face add to her petite, sweetheart figure.

She holds her head high and responds the same way I did: "It would be my honor." She gives everyone a small curtsy after. As nice as Trinity looks, she's an empty girl, which is precisely why they picked her. She's easy to control, and will most likely go along with whatever Alas wants. At least, that's what Daymond tells me. They probably picked me thinking the same thing. But Trinity will balance out Alas, who exudes power and control; he thrives off of it.

It's clear, as I watch the Princes, the kind of energy they're emitting. Alas is radiating heat, while Lawrence is ice-cold. Both Princes can control temperature, an ability I'd never seen or even heard of until I meet them. It's a rare type of manipulation. They can lower the temperature of a room. With a touch, they can freeze or burn anything, which works well when using metal weapons, especially when making them blazing hot. They can spiral heat and create waves in the air that take the breath from people. They can also manipulate someone's body temperature if they lay a hand on them. Technically, their Ability is known as Thermokrasis, after the Ancient Tongue's word for temperature, *thermokrasia*.

I would never mess with a thermomancer unless I was forced to.

Prince Alas returns to his seat as the applause dies down after his proposal. The crowd comes off just as thrilled as Alas. His back is perfectly arched to the throne. He sits beside his father, holding his head high.

The truth is, Alas is a little too young to be making this proposal. He should have had a few more years of learning before this; twenty-one is too early for a royal to get engaged. But the word I've gotten from Daymond is that the King is ill, very ill. He's been losing his sanity and consciousness, which is why the council is rushing Alas to take the throne soon.

At least it isn't Lawrence being rushed onto the throne. He won't have to become king. He's my age, nineteen. I'm sure he would have waited to get engaged, but it's a royal Parten tradition to do it at the same time as your siblings.

I do see the potential Lawrence has, but he isn't fit to rule the way Alas is. Lawrence appears younger than he is; his skin is so youthful and radiant. He always has an innocent, smug smile on his face, but I've heard his temper slips out quite often. I've never experienced it firsthand, but it's easy to see how he could turn on someone. His hair is a sandy blond that matches the style of Alas's, through Alas's hair is a much darker shade. Lawrence's eyes are as richly brown as the soil Parten is built on.

When I compare him to Alas, he looks unsteady and vulnerable. In his body language, I can see that he wants this to be over as much as I do. I whisper to Daymond, "What now?"

He sits still and silent. His face usually glows on days like this, but at the moment, it's pale. His golden aura was the one thing keeping me intact today, and now it's faded completely. His cerulean eyes are still shining as he continues to scan the crowd, though.

He doesn't seem to know what to do either.

Daymond faces forward as he finally tells me, "You understand and accept that this is happening. Stay calm. Don't let them think anything is wrong."

Daymond can get away with a poker face in the public's eyes; I'm not sure if I can. I continue to hold my head forward with a plastered-on smile. "Daymond," I plead. It's always Daymond who tells me what to do. He's the fixer, the soother, while I'm always the problem.

"What?" Daymond mutters at me, becoming increasingly frustrated with the situation. "What would you rather do?" We never get hissy at each other, but this moment is causing us both to break. "They'll be taking you to the palace any minute now. I'm sure I'll be summoned later, but you're on your own for now. You'll be fine. He might not have seen the broadcast."

I narrow my eyes at him; that's a lie, and he knows it. Of *course* he's seen it. He's seen me, and he'll be coming before we can do anything to stop him.

I stand up, looking at the royal official who has arrived to escort me out, just as Daymond said. I see the princes exiting the arena as well. Daymond meets my eyes as he reassures me, "We'll fix this."

CHAPTER 2

Isadora POV

E verything after the proposal goes by in a blur. The royal staff usher Trinity and I, along with a royal council member, into a small black car.

My glance toward Trinity falls short of understanding how she's feeling. There's only silence in the car. The rain is pouring down outside. Everyone in the vehicle has their attention focused on the rain thrashing against the windows. The thunder, I'm sure, is soothing to the weather and electricity controllers in Parten. The few of them left.

"Your rooms are set up," the advisor informs us. Her voice is misty, holding to the mood. "Tomorrow someone will be by to move your items from your home to the palace. You won't see the princes until then. Also, your families will start moving into the palace effective tomorrow. There will be a welcome ball in two days, which will only include the royal council and high-ranking families. Life at the palace will continue as it did before." Her voice gets shorter and more profound as she lets us know, "That means you two are not entitled to anything until your weddings. The wedding dates are not yet set, but I assume this will be settled in a few months. Stay in your rooms for the night, and get yourselves settled in."

The vehicle pulls up to the palace as the advisor finishes with, "Any questions?" My attention turns to Trinity as she opens her mouth. The advisor doesn't let her ask anything as the door of the car is pulled open. I catch a glimpse of Trinity's face changing as she tries to maintain her calm.

Quickly the advisor clicks her tongue and says, "Good. Follow me."

The palace holds its beauty even in this weather. It's several stories high, with towers extending upward on each corner and scattered small stairs giving the architecture the depth of an authentic castle. The structure is an old, brisk albicant white that morphs in places to a soft tan color. All accents of the castle are in a worn light-black and brown.

I've never really understood Parten Castle. Parten is a newer kingdom, newer in terms of centuries. Yet those missing hundreds of years make the castle feel less sacred. It's as if they built it to make it look much older than it is. But it does do its job of being pretentious.

There are several training rooms, dining rooms, council rooms, conference halls, and ballrooms inside the castle. The castle itself is elevated upon a small hill. Behind the castle is a jetway and buildings that house the soldiers and guards. I only know the castle's general layout, thanks to Daymond showing me around on past visits.

Parten Castle is deep in the kingdom's countryside. The nearest town is where the proposals took place, at least 40 minutes away.

We're quickly rushed inside to try to avoid the rain. I'm immediately escorted to a room on the second floor. Trinity has been separated from me, and is taken to hers.

I stand blankly in my new room. I take a second to scan my surroundings before realizing that there's nothing else for me to do except make myself comfortable. My feet ache as I take the pressure off them and collapse onto the large bed. I lay on the cloud-like softness while taking in the massive room for a few minutes, collecting my thoughts. The room is appealing, at least—much more space than my last one. There's a small living area, along with a fireplace right in front of the bed. The closet and bathroom are already stocked with anything I could ever need.

I sit up in the bed and let my feet dangle over the edge. Quickly enough, it all becomes far too boring in the room all alone. Ignoring the advisor's instructions, I stand and leave the room, hoping to find something new in the castle to pass the time until I get tired enough to sleep. Moving around may help me take my mind off things for a bit.

As I step into the hall, it's easy to tell that the number of guards is scarcer than usual. They must have all been working at the selection, and not at their regular posts. None of the few guards that I do pass stops me from walking around. I listen closely to the rain picking up outside again, and walk further down the hall. Parten doesn't usually get weather like this.

The hall is decked with chandeliers, decor fitting for royals, and a long-stretched carpet covering the center of the hall over the marble floors.

"Where are you going, Princess?" a voice asks me from behind. I turn around quickly, realizing that he's referring to me. A tall, lean guard stands in the middle of the hall. He raises an eyebrow with a friendly grin. He appears to be around my age, although his uniform shows that he's a captain, a position years past his age. His hand lifts the slightest bit, allowing me a glimpse of tattoos as his sleeves pull back a little.

"Want a tour?" he asks.

Alas POV

I toss my jacket over my arm, glad to finally be able to take it off. The medals pinned to the fabric clank against my cufflinks. The two guards at my side continue to walk with me, ready to escort me back to my room and get off their shift, I'm sure.

We turn the corner of the hallway, encountering the two people I most certainly did not expect to be out and about. Ryder, my least favorite Captain of the Guards, gives me a slight nod of the head as I greet them. "Isadora, glad to finally see you in the castle," I say quietly.

She smiles merrily, almost as if she's been caught in an act of something. Her eyes are bluer than I remember. They look like Daymond's, but lighter and brighter. Maybe their eyes are the exact same, but I just view them differently, because the only time I see Daymond is when he's yelling in the war room.

Do all cryomancers have blue eyes? Is that a genetic thing?

"It's a pleasure to see you, Prince Alas," she says, cutting off my thoughts. Lightning flashing through the windows at the end of the hall is followed all too quickly by a loud crack of thunder.

"I was just showing her back to her room," Ryder informs me.

I shake my head the slightest bit. "Well, that's no way to treat our new family. Isadora is perfectly fine to walk around as she wishes." If she's living in the castle now, there's no reason not to let her explore it. But it's interesting that when she was told to stay in her room, she went against the orders. A bit more insurgence than I would have pictured right off the bat.

Isadora parts her lips and softly says, "Thank you."

I nod, following her gaze as both she and Ryder suddenly gape at something over my shoulder. I whip my head around to see a woman racing down the hall. Her eyes meet mine, and she stops in her tracks. Her head fights between looking at the hallway on both sides of her, debating on where to go. Several guards come rushing after her.

She's wearing a guard uniform, but as one of the guards behind her yells, "Prince Alas, she's a traitor!" it's clear she's not on our side anymore.

My feet leave the ground swiftly as I drop my jacket and take off to intercept her in the middle of the hall. To my surprise, the woman starts to run towards me. I reach a hand to grab her. Her leg pushes out forward, sliding her on the ground and past my reach. She tumbles forward, her hands pushing her up from a dive roll. She lunges onward and, in the same motion, takes a knife from her pocket. Her other hand clasps Isadora's blouse, pulling her in to hold a knife to her throat.

I freeze, putting an arm out in a cautious stance, trying to de-escalate the situation. Ryder and all the guards in the hall stop moving altogether. We hear, all too clearly, Isadora's shallow breaths. Then, in a rapid motion, Isadora lifts her arm and elbows the girl right in the gut. The guard's hand with the knife pushes forward; Isadora takes her by the wrist and twists her arm. The woman drops the blade as Isadora kicks a leg at her back. The force pushes the woman to the ground, while Isadora continues to shove the traitor's arm forward; then she places a foot on the guard's back to keep her in place.

"Well, shit," Ryder says in unpleasant shock. He reaches for the woman to take hold of her other arm.

A flash of lighting blinds me for a second. Thunder rattles outside, shaking the hall. Another lightning bolt strikes outside the castle with a second wave of thunder. It's all too close. Then there's another strike.

I walk forward, past Isadora, and crouch down. I put a hand out, lifting the guardswoman's head up to look at me while Isadora continues to hold her down. "Your weather manipulation isn't going to do a single thing to this castle," I spit at the woman. Her face hardens as she exhales heavily. I drop my hand and stand up straight. This castle was built to withstand any weather, in case a manipulator of her caliber tried to attack.

Isadora's face is grave. I motion for the guards to take the false guard off the floor and into custody so Isadora can stop holding her down.

I no longer worry about Isadora; apparently, she can take care of herself. I really shouldn't have ever worried, especially with Daymond as her brother. He has definitely made sure she won't be taken down in a fight. Isadora didn't even have to pull her cryomancy tricks to get the knife off her neck.

"I'm sorry about that," I say to Isadora, as the other woman makes a grunting sound as she struggles in the background.

"What's going on?" Isadora asks to anyone who will answer, slowly recovering from the encounter.

I glare at the guards who hold the woman and snap, "Well? You heard her, what *is* going on?" I have no idea what's happening with this rogue guard.

"She's a spy, Prince Alas," one of the guards finally tells us.

I take a few steps closer to the women. She tries to launch herself forward at me, getting pulled back by the guards.

"Din Point?" I ask her, already knowing the answer. The woman doesn't make another move. She clenches her jaw, heat coming through her nose. I turn to face Isadora and say, "You don't need to be here for this part."

She doesn't move, making it clear she isn't planning on leaving the area. She only whispers to herself, "She's from Din Point." Her face turns a shade paler.

I nod, knowing that no other kingdom would send a spy. We've had more and more Din Point informants trying to breach the castle, trying to figure out what we're doing on our side of the war. And now it seems my guards have found another traitor in our mix. I thought we were clean of them.

I lift my hand, raising my body temperature. I hold my hand out, fingers in front of the spy. "Why are you here?"

She gives no answer. I shake my hand as a warning, but still, she remains silent.

I lay my hand on her shoulder; a hiss fills the air as her skin cooks. The woman screams. I do my best not to wince at the sound.

I lift my hand off her. Isadora shouldn't be seeing me do this, not when she's just arrived at the castle. Now all she's going to think is that we're riddled with traitors, and that I'm a prince who tortures people. I shouldn't even be doing this. This is not my duty as Prince. This is not my time to take these actions, and yet here I am.

"Why are you here?" I repeat. The weathermancer gives me nothing but silence and tears. I shake my hand out, giving it a second as I begin to cool off. I move the temperature on down to a deadly cold. A noxious blue color crawls over my skin. Cold added onto burns hurts far worse than just another burn. Her eyes widen: she knows what's coming.

I move my hand forward slowly. The spy cries, "No! No, please!"

"Neither of us wants this. I didn't want to burn you, and I certainly don't want to hear that scream again." I lower my hand, allowing it to go back to my normal temperature. "Answer my questions. Then we'll get a skin manipulator to fix your burn. If you don't talk, I'll take off the entire first layer of your skin and make sure no healer ever comes."

She gulps and replies, "I was sent to obtain information on the new princesses. That's all. That's all I know and all I was told to do, I swear."

Isadora shifts her weight forward, standing by my side now. I narrow my eyes. "Isadora and Trinity? That's what they wanted you to find out about?"

She nods heavily. I don't believe her, not a word of it. Why would she have put a knife to Isadora's throat if that were the case? She probably just sees Isadora and figures it to be a solid excuse. But I don't want to continue making her feel pain worse than I could ever endure. I step back and wave my hand. "Take her to a skin-mender for the burn. Then put her in a cell. Daymond is going to want to talk with her tomorrow; he's our specialist on Din Point. I'll revisit it in the morning with him."

I turn on my heel and place a hand on Isadora's back, walking her with me away from the scene. She glances over her shoulder, a shudder passing through her I try to lightly warm my hand to calm her down as she continues to have trembles.

"You shouldn't have had to deal with that," I say.

"Is that normal? Does Din Point cause this sort of problem in the castle often?" she asks, dismissing my words altogether.

"No. We haven't had a spy successfully gain access to our castle in over a year, though we've caught a few attempts. I turned over all the guards two years ago because of the concerns we had then. I make sure we check them regularly. This is something that should have never happened, especially if she was here to get information on you and Trinity, and not the war."

"Will you tell Trinity of this?" she asks.

I lower my hand and shake my head, "She doesn't need to know of it. Especially since both of you just got here a few hours ago."

"Have you spoken at all to her?"

"Aside from the one-sentence I said to her today, I haven't spoken to her since that ball a month ago."

"Oh," Isadora mouths. I can still feel her uneasiness. I note the way she walks so quickly, despite not knowing where we are going.

"Din Point isn't a threat here in the castle. That guard was a major error, and should have never happened. The war isn't in the castle, Isadora. I don't want you to feel unsafe here." She doesn't respond as we continue forward. I stop walking and finish it off. "I need to go have some words with people over what happened. Let me know if you need anything." I walk away from her before she gets a chance to respond.

This whole day has been a constant headache; and my stomach is already starting to turn from knowing that tomorrow, acting as future king, I'll probably have to burn that women's skin again for answers.

Lawrence POV

I probably shouldn't be doing this right now. But what else am I supposed to do? Sit in my room all night and just deal with what I'm thinking? No.

Especially not when I can just get up and talk to Isadora. At least, that's what I'm going to keep telling myself, since I'm already at her door. I knock lightly and wait a second until Isadora slowly opens the door.

"Lawrence, hello," she mutters, her voice a bit thin.

"Hi," I say lamely.

Her eyes are fixated on me, studying me. I don't know how to fill the void of silence.

Is she shorter than I remember? Or does she just not have heels on? Her hair is a much darker shade of brown than

I recalled. It seems to have changed from a sandy brown to a soft coppery brown.

Maybe I never really knew what she looked like. I've only met her three, maybe four times. She moves to the side, and I try to step into the room calmly. "How are you?"

I make my best attempt to read her face, but I get nothing. Maybe I've read the situation wrong, and she *does* hate me, and that's why I can't pin down her expression. Perhaps in the arena, she was just putting on a good face for the sake of royalty. Or maybe it's the fact that I'm unexpectedly at her door very late at night after a long, life-changing day. Her eyes do seem a bit hazed, her outfit much less put-together.

She glances over my shoulder. I should have told her there are no guards with me. I'm coming to her as myself, not as the prince. Isadora has never ever seen me out of the public eye.

"Not gonna lie, a bit overwhelmed," she says with a sign and overcompensating laugh.

"Overwhelmed?" I ask urgently.

Isadora smiles at me. Her whole face can light up a room. With her slightly faded freckles, she makes it look like she wants to know everything about the world. She has a manner that makes me want to tell her anything she wants to know, which is always a danger.

I try to stop my thoughts from derailing. I need to get over being flustered.

She continues, "About all this. About why I was selected. I wasn't briefed or even given a slight heads-up."

I can only try and offer an explanation. "I don't know who else they would have picked. You didn't see this coming?" She shakes her head. I need to reason with her. "I mean, I didn't pick you."

Immediately, she scoffs. Isadora moves to her bed, leaning on the front edge while crossing her arms.

That came off wrong, very wrong. "I didn't mean it like that!" I swear. "I'm just trying to say that Alas is the one who brought you up."

"Go on," she pries curiously. I have to keep track of my words. I have a habit of not being able to think around her.

"Well, he said you would make an excellent ruler. I assume he meant Queen, but the council interrupted his words differently. I mean, you're naturally gifted, and I thought we'd been friendly enough with each other. I didn't think it would be so dreadful."

Her eyes seem heavy; her stare is off on its own. This day has taken a toll on her, too.

"Your brother doesn't seem too captivated with Trinity," she notes.

"I agree. Obviously, Alas doesn't want to marry to her. She wasn't his choice. He knew it wasn't ever going to be his choice. It's still upsetting to him, though." I join Isadora and sit at the foot of her bed. She seems too casual around me. People aren't often casual around me. Maybe I'm not the first royal she's been around.

"Understandable."

"I shouldn't be here right now," I admit. My throat feels smoky and rough. It really isn't a big deal that I'm here. No one would care that much, but I was told not to speak to Isadora until the morning.

"You shouldn't be telling me that," she treads lightly.

"I know. I just needed to see what you were thinking. Your brother's reaction seemed incredibly uneasy."

"He didn't expect me to get engaged at nineteen," she states, looking at me like I'm an idiot, which is not how people ever look at me or *should* ever look at me.

"That's fair." I wasn't really expecting it either. I slide my hand into my jacket pocket. I pull out the ring with two diamonds and an azure, blueish stone of some sort, shining bright in the middle. I hold it out to her.

"Here's the ring... I'm not supposed to get it to you until later, but..." my voice trails away.

She takes the ring kindly and slides it onto her left ring finger. She flashes her hand out; we both check to see how it looks. It's gand, at least in my eyes. She retracts her hand and starts twirling the ring around with the fingers of her right hand, pondering something. Finally, she softly expresses, "You knew for days."

"I knew for weeks," I say. Isadora nods in response, accepting what she already knew.

"I should get some rest."

That's my cue to leave her. I get up from the bed slowly and walk to the door. I bid Isadora a goodnight with a solid hug—the first hug she's has ever given me. A hug where your hands wrap around the other person entirely, and you can feel their breathing for a second. A hug that we both probably needed.

I leave her room and shut the door fully behind me.

There were details hidden in her diction during that conversation. I just can't piece them together. I hear her quickly lock the door as I turn down the hall.

We all need some sleep.

CHAPTER 3

Isadora POV

I'm woken up far too early in the morning by a vicious knocking at the door. I jolt from my bed to unlock it. I've never seen the person at the door before, but he's in the Parten Castle uniform.

"Prince Lawrence will be here in ten, then your day starts." His tone isn't anywhere close to friendly, but maybe I'm just perceiving it wrong with it being this early.

"Thank you," I yawn. I shut the door swiftly and move to get dressed. I have no clue what today holds. I go as casual as I can. Within the closet are all sorts of outfits and stylish accessories that I would never wear on a daily basis. I quickly throw my hair up in the ponytail.

Lawrence is at my door in ten minutes, and not a second later. There's a quick greeting before we move down the hallway. Lawrence is also dressed casually, which means nothing significant should be happening today. His face is fuller this morning than last night. He has some color, some warmth to him. "Where to first?" I ask.

"Breakfast, thankfully, then whatever's on your schedule, I'm sure someone will be giving it to you soon."

This is the new normal, I suppose. "What does your day look like?"

Lawrence always seems like he has long and dragging days, from what Daymond has told me. "I believe that today I have some meetings with Alas about warfare; Daymond should be there. Then my all-time favorite," he voices sarcastically, "Council meetings."

"Do I attend them?"

"You get freedom after lunch. Unless, of course, you'd like to join me, but I don't see why anyone would. Unless you're Alas, and have an obsession with war-play."

I can't help but laugh.

I don't really mind the idea of being with Lawrence. He's charming and would be a wonderful husband if the circumstances were different. It's not him I'm worried about. It's the unsettling thought that the broadcast was shown everywhere, in every kingdom.

We arrive at the breakfast hall. I've never attended breakfast in the castle. Lawrence assures me, "Usually it's much more casual; today is just a celebration day of sorts."

In the room is an extremely long oak table that looks like it goes on for miles. There are two smaller tables on either side of it. It appears like anyone of importance is here, but it must just be who was able to attend. I don't see Daymond anywhere. Trinity and Alas are already seated, but don't seem excited. I wonder how their interaction went this morning. I wonder if Alas has already spoken with that guard from last night. I don't think he told Lawrence about what happened; he probably would have mentioned it by now.

At the head of the main table are the King and Queen. I didn't think the King got out much anymore.

Lawrence pulls out my chair for me directly across Trinity. He sits down across from Alas, and next to the Queen. Lawrence chirps, "Good morning," to the room as we sit down. Most people are all already seated. We must be just a few minutes late. Everyone is too engaged in their own conversations to care either way.

"Morning," Alas responds. "Great to see you, Isadora."

I nod to Alas as he turns back to the King in deep conversation. I wonder how late he was up last night dealing with the guard. I wonder if he noticed my reactions.

I start to listen in on their conversation.

"Where do you think they would get more troops up north? Din Point has no allies and no resources outside of their kingdom," the King makes known to Alas.

They're discussing the war, I assume. Din Point is north of Parten. It's a dying kingdom in chaos, and Parten has been in war with them for 58 years. It's not even a war anymore; it's just a constant fighting front that neither side choses to back out of. But in recent years, both kingdoms have started to get fed up; more serious advances are starting to happen, and the war is escalating rapidly.

"I don't think they're using all their resources yet. I'm waiting for their son to get into power and use them all," Alas says. confidently

The King sighs and says, "Their son is unmanageable."

"The Din Point prince? What's his name?" Trinity asks, surprisingly engaged.

"Prince Carac Cavinche, dear," the Queen informs her.

It feels like Alas needs to know everything, as he continues the questions. "Do you know if he has siblings?"

"A brother," Lawrence says jadedly.

"Actually, his brother died a while ago in a fire. It's just Carac now," I correct. They all give me a hard stare.

Alas' jaw is clenched as he listens. I don't think he knows too much about Din Point, aside from its martial aspects. Truthfully, no one in Parten knows that much about them. Din Point keeps its secrets close to its vest. It doesn't like their enemy kingdom to hear anything about them.

"Anyway," the King continues, "What are they supposed to do, use the snow and ice in the Caps as weapons? That's pointless." The king glances to me with a near-wince and adds, "No offense, Isadora."

I smile a bit in near-amusement as I ensure him, "None taken."

It would be pointless; there are no resources, no human life in the Caps. It's a snowy, frosted desert. And ice manipulators can use water to create and fight. The Caps corners Din Point into having no allies to the north of them.

"They can't get resources from Kindera. That kingdom is ruined now. A toxic wasteland," the King finishes.

I don't know much about the island of Kindera. The citizens are held there by an oppressed monarchy. In the past, the rulers started to consume and pollute their nation. People in Kindera have adapted over time to the conditions there. It's not comfortable, but they live. Anyone from another kingdom would die just setting foot there.

"I get it," Alas specifies, "but we won't get other any resources either. Vaddel has been in isolation for years, Oxidence doesn't want to be involved, and the Zenlands are Zen for a reason: they never form alliances, and always remain neutral. It's going to continue to be a push-and-pull war until we do something different."

"Save this for the meeting, Alas," the Queen says, instantly ending the discussion. Alas rolls his shoulders, his back clashing with his chair as he leans back.

The door of the dining hall is dramatically thrown open. A younger guard strolls into the hall with friends at his sides. I flinch at the sound, but no one else seems to care. I quickly realize that it's the guard captain who asked if I wanted a tour last night. Everyone goes back to eating. This must be a typical scene.

"Who is that?" I ask Lawrence quietly.

"That's Ryder, resident asshole if you're a guard. He's a plant-wielder and one of the captains."

Ryder walks to an open seat far down the table and smiles at the room. I mumble, "A floramancer? Seems like a character."

Alas answers, "Ryder is a refugee from Din Point; he arrived a few years ago. His already-large ego has only grown every day since he's been here."

"How did he get to be captain, then?"

Alas turns his attention away while answering, "Hell if I know." He's clearly over our conversation, and rises to exit with Trinity immediately after.

Lawrence follows Alas out, and I, of course, follow Lawrence as we leave the dining room. In the hall, Trinity becomes a different person. "Isadora? I heard your brother teaches you a lot of skills. How good are you at your ability?" she asks me.

Alas raises an eyebrow. He crosses his arms as he stares at his future wife.

"I can defend myself well enough," I try to answer politely, continuing to walk.

"Yeah, really?" I hear the challenge in her voice as she grabs Alas's arm. "How much time do we have?"

He winces at the touch. But then he lowers his guard and says, "Just a little before I have to be in a meeting."

"Isadora. Wanna spar for funsies?" She throws the challenge out in an annoying, whiny voice.

Lawrence chuckles to the side.

"I'm down if you are," I say. I can't tell why Trinity's bothering to ask me to spar, but it *has* been a while. I want to use my ability. If it's just for fun, this should be a quick and straightforward match. I still want to win, though.

We walk to the sparring room. Guards are everywhere. Lawrence hints to me, "You don't have to spar if you don't want to." It feels more like a suggestion than a statement.

"We have time to kill. What else are we going to do?"

He shrugs and nods while walking away. I turn and follow Trinity into the closed circle. It's drawn in the dirt and fenced in by a glass wall—a standard sparring circle. People start to look over and watch, while the princes seems mildly entertained.

A smile is the only thing exchanged between Trinity and I as we prepare. Since we didn't run in the same groups before now, I've never sparred with her. It's something I never thought I'd do. I hear the glass door automatically lock into place behind us. There are two marks on the floor as the starting positions. We each take a stance on one.

There's water in the room, at least a few meters away. I can always tell how close water is; it's like the warning of a storm coming that creates a tingly feeling in your fingers, a buzz that fills your body, never truly going away, just decreasing with distance. My body tells me where the water sits in the room: in bottles, bins and a pool nearby. I pick the bins, as they're closest.

I glance to the side, looking through the glass to see Lawrence and Alas standing firmly in place, their shoulders broad and collarbones arched. It's always nice to have a spectator watching and calling times. I guess Alas is taking that role today, as he yells, "Start!"

Once I hear his words, my instincts tell me to form a weapon as quickly as possible, but I have to remember this is a luxomancer, a light-wielder, I'm dealing with.

I turn my hands inward, feeling and pulling the water in the room.

Trinity races to the further side of the circle and turns the light outward, making her invisible. I watch the water flow over the circle, trickling in smoothly over the glass. The water starts to build up in the ring and forms a shallow pool. I catch the blank stares from people watching. I've made a makeshift reflection pool. Trinity can pull the light to hide, but she can't hide from the ripples in the water. Now I can see exactly where she is in the circle. It makes her ability useless, at least in the way she's using it.

To this point, I haven't even moved from the starting position. I jump out of the water, and when I land, I've formed ice to walk on. The thing most people forget is that many cryomancers can also control liquid water; we depend on the water molecules for manipulation.

Daymond, on the other hand, can't do what I can with ice manipulation. He has freezing—he can make anything turn to ice, even freeze it to its breaking point. He'd stand the best chance against Alas and Lawrence, as their heating ability wouldn't stand against him. I got the other side of the genetic coin, cryokinesis. It allows me to control water and freeze it, creating and manipulate ice however I please.

All my family's abilities are subsets of cryomancy that give us different skills to master.

My attention snaps back to Trinity as she dashes towards me. I watch the water ripple as she runs and push my hands out in front of me. I turn the water at her feet to ice, and freeze her in place. She panics as she unravels the light that hid her before and reflects it downward, in attempt to melt the ice. I make my way closer to her, casually strolling on my ice walkway. Water trickles up to my hands. I tense my ability, making the water turn solid, creating an ice dagger.

Trinity can't move, and now I have a weapon.

I stand a few inches above her on my walkway. I playfully rest the dagger right under her chin. I turn my head, looking at Alas with a raised eyebrow and a grin.

Alas yells, "Time," indicating that the sparring session is over.

I retract my dagger and drop it. I make all the ice dissolve back to water and have it retreat to its original location. This wasn't a real sparring session, but it was still fun.

When the ice melts away, Trinity stumbles back onto the floor. I offer her a hand up. To my surprise, she takes it. This wasn't anything personal. There aren't any hard feelings, thankfully.

"That ended a lot faster than I thought," Trinity muses, laughing if off.

"You asked for it, Trinity," Alas taunts as we walk out of the circle.

"Actually," Trinity says innocently, "Daymond asked for it."

"What?" I demand.

"Daymond asked me to get you to spar today. He knows it's been a while, and you wouldn't do it if a trainer asked."

I look at her blankly. I can't decide whether to be annoyed or not. She doesn't have to listen to Daymond—he has no pull over her—and Daymond has no business tricking me into sparring. And when would he have had time to talk to Trinity? I would probably have done it anyway if he'd asked me.

"Sounds like something Daymond would do," Lawrence says.

Alas leans an arm against me as we walk, a playful gesture. He tries to change to subject. "Just wait until you spar with one of us. *That* will be a show."

I counter, "You're so confident you'd win?"

"I am," he states, showing an attitude.

Lawrence glances at me, his face twisted.

"Don't you have a meeting to go to?" I ask Alas pointedly.

"I do. Lawrence, would you like to join me?" Alas asks, while turning his gaze away from me and lifting his arm.

Lawrence has to go to the meeting anyway... at least, I think he does.

"I was only asking because I wanted to see my brother," I let them know, since it came off as defensive.

"Oh," Lawrence says, "go for it. I think Daymond's on the third floor."

"Thanks." I start walking away from the group. I climb a floor, and get a servant to help me figure out where his room is. I've been dying to see it since the moment I arrived.

I knock on the door. After a few seconds, Daymond lets me in. I knew he'd been well taken care of, but this is far beyond what I expected. His room is even bigger than mine. He was supposed to start living in the castle grounds the moment he became general, so it makes sense he's living lavishly. There are still boxes and clutter all around the room; clearly, he still has plenty of unpacking to do.

"Isadora. How are you?" Daymond asks passive-aggressively.

"Stop," I snap.

"What?"

"Get to the point. I can see you have something to say."

Daymond pulls out a seat for me at a small conference table, and we both sit. He's getting ready to make a point, and immediately starts talking. "I've come to the conclusion that we should move."

"Again? We wouldn't be moving, we'd be running away," I state evenly.

"Then we run away. We need to leave now. It's unsafe for you here."

I fiddle with my engagement ring. I'd initiated this conversation by coming to his room, but I want it to end already. I'd just wanted to see him, not have this discussion. But I guess I knew he'd bring it up.

Daymond changes tactics, and tries to be light with the conversation. He suggests, "We could go to the Zenlands, or maybe Oxidence? I hear they have a nice military."

"I can't do that to you, make you start all over again."

"This isn't a game. There's no starting over once you lose. The only thing we're doing is advancing," Daymond says coldly.

"I'm aware of that, but here in the palace, the guards are the best of the best. The chances—"

Daymond cuts me off. "The chances are higher than ever. Your engagement has been shown everywhere. He's seen it. You don't get guards around your room until you marry Lawrence. I can't make that happen without raising questions. They don't care about his wife-to-be, they care about his *wife*. You've seen how many people come in and out of this castle."

"But if we leave now, he'll know we couldn't have gotten too far. The guards and security here make it the safest choice."

Daymond snaps, "Him not knowing our location is the safest choice!"

I lean back in the chair. "I'm content here. We've been too worried, you especially." I stand. "We'll deal with the issue *if* it occurs. For now, let's just lie low." I clearly convey the message that I want this conversation over.

I knew what I was walking into, but nonetheless, it didn't go as I'd wanted. I hug him tightly as I leave the room to reflect on the situation.

I meander down the hall, trying to kill time. As I wander, I come to a training room that's vacant of anyone who might bother me. People must have cleared out. I guess I can just practice solo. It will make my mind focus on technique, not my worries. I glance around the area, and find that the swimming pool is empty.

I decide to make use of the space and practice the creation of ice orbs. It's an essential skill for an ice controller to form a bubble of ice that allows breathing underwater.

I begin.

Alas POV

Isadora gasps when coming up for air. Her orb must have cracked, and by the looks of it, she's been at this for hours. I don't think she meant to get drenched, though; she's still in her day clothes. She peers at me with a slightly shocked expression.

"Enjoy the swim?" I ask. I offer a handout, and pull her out of the pool.

"Something like that," Isadora says, while looking around for a towel, I assume. I was just in here to grab a guard I needed to see, but he isn't in here and Isadora is, so the course of events has changed.

I shake my head at her and wave over a guard I barely know, but I do know he's an aeromancer. We exchange words too swiftly for Isadora to hear. Before she's aware of what's happening, a full wave of warm air hits her. Her feet tumble; I reach out and grab her arms before she falls into the pool.

She glances at both of us and mutters, "Thanks," now mostly dry.

I nod to him as a thank-you and release her arm. "Come on. We've got places to be," I tell her so we can leave the training room and talk. We don't have places to be, actually.

As we enter the corridor she asks, "How were your meetings?"

"Very good. I was debating the refugee program with my father."

"What was there to debate?"

I'm not sure what side she stands on, so I take caution in explaining it. "I'm against my father and brother on this one. I think we need to take as many refugees from Din Point as possible."

"Lawrence argues against you on that?" She asks. Her mouth opens, ready to say more, but she clamps it shut. She clearly wasn't expecting Lawrence to have a different opinion.

"He's for the refugees, but he wants a controlled number. He tells me that the people over there are rebels, and our kingdom comes first."

"They're rebels because they *have* to be. The rulers over there give them nothing. We should be taking anyone we can."

"I said the same thing. His response was to ask, where does it stop? Should we start to accept Kindera's people too?" I watch her eyes flicker with sadness. It clearly bothers her that Lawrence has taken such a stance. "You're arguing with the wrong person. Go talk to Lawrence about this."

"But really, can Lawrence stop you?"

"No. He wants to, though. Lawrence thinks everything I'll do as a ruler will fail." I probably shouldn't be telling her my issues, but it's refreshing to have someone new to talk to.

Suddenly she asks, "Alas, where are we going?" To this point, she has just been following my lead, focusing on the conversation, not the walk.

"Dinner." I don't think she realizes she was in the training room for hours. We're going to arrive to dinner early at this rate, so I slow down. With the slower pace, Isadora takes full advantage and begins to ask me more things.

"So, the ball tomorrow? What's that all about?"

"It's just for show, and to entertain the council. Personally, I think they just want an excuse to throw another party."

"So you're not excited about it?"

"If you knew my position, you wouldn't be either."

"What do you mean?"

"Well," I begin, "For me, this ball really means that instead of me getting the throne in a few years, it will be in a few months. My father is senile; he's lost his sense of direction, and frankly can't do anything that would have an impact. The whole council knows it, I know it, my mother knows it. And she doesn't want to rule anymore. She never liked it much, which I don't blame her for... hers was an arranged marriage, and she did a damn good job as Queen, but now all I think she really wants to do is live the rest of her life without the stress. I didn't expect either of them to be on the throne much longer, I just didn't know it would happen this quickly."

"If you're worried about being on the throne, you shouldn't be. You're perfectly fit for this role, and you know it."

I didn't know that Isadora supported me my ascension. I didn't have a clue that she actually liked my leadership enough to say it out loud. I give her a nod and continue, "It's just not a pretty situation. And it's not any help that Trinity will be on the throne with me. She doesn't want the throne *or* me, I assure you."

"You don't know," Isadora counters. It's easy for her to assume things. I would, too; Trinity plays things off very well. I've seen and been with her enough times in the castle to know her act. Each time I talk to her makes me more and more worried. "I think she's delighted with having some power, and with you," Isabella continues.

"You haven't seen the letters she writes to whoever she really wants to be with," I counter.

"Oh. I didn't know she did that."

"She does, and she thinks I also don't know."

"You don't say anything?" Isadora queries with a frown.

"There's no a point. I rat her out and she gets tried for treason, then what? They stick me with the next girl I don't want to be with. And that girl may be much worse. Trinity may want the power, but she doesn't want me." I stop myself from rambling; I'm saying more than I planned.

"You're fine with no one being with you?"

"I'm oversharing. This isn't anything you need to worry about." I quicken our pace.

"I like talking to you, Alas, as a friend, nothing political or strategic. You need people to talk to here, and so do I." She offers me a warm smile.

I nod to her and pull open the door to the dining room. This is going to be a long, tedious dinner.

CHAPTER 4

Isadora POV

I can tell you what everyone in the castle is doing. Trinity's busy making herself look perfect. Alas has a council meeting about the refugee program. It was smart of him to schedule it today. Everyone on the council will be eager to leave and get ready for the ball, making his vote more likely to get rushed and passed. Lawrence is elsewhere, taking care of some sort of communication laws. I didn't really listen when he told me where he was going. Daymond is most likely in a different meeting of some sort.

Which leaves me hours to get ready. I decide to walk a bit, wondering in my thoughts. I spend what feels like hours pacing the castle. It's almost empty. I barely see anyone in the halls except a few passing servants. There's an awful lot of preparation going into this one night.

Eventually, I mosey back to my room to get ready. The abundance of time allows for me to continue with my slow movements and extra care. I let in the maids who've been sent to do my makeup and hair. There's no way to send them away without being rude. They style my hair in perfect swirls. The makeup on my face is natural and light. I slip into my mazarine blue dress and let the maids leave to do their own thing. I move to my bed to wait, being careful not to mess up my look.

Finally, there's a knock at the door. I open it to see Lawrence dressed in his fancy suit, all ready for the evening.

As far as I can tell, we're 20 minutes late to the ball, but this is the time Lawrence wants to arrive. His steps are light and slow; no need to rush. No need for him to be on time.

I link arms with him. We both take a breath and prepare for a night full of fake smiles and people here more for the sake of showing that they were important enough to be invited than to enjoy the gathering. When the doors open, I can hear Alas speaking to the crowd. We enter right in the middle of his welcome speech, but there are so many exits and entrances that no one should notice us arriving late.

Once the welcome speech is over, we begin to make our way through the massive ballroom. We pass so many people, and I try to remember the faces and match them to an ability as Lawrence drags me along. One after another, Lawrence starts conversations I don't want to be a part of. But I smile sharply and try to act interested, to be polite.

Lawrence loves to talk with the council members. His diction changes with every conversation. He's trying to make allies in the council, to sway and show more members that he's a delight. And it works for him. Each conversation we walk away from leaves me wondering how much campaigning Lawrence does, and for what.

Lawrence turns as he concludes a conversation, and begins to walk us to another. I finally have a chance to take the lead. I grab his hand and pull us towards my brother. Once in range, Daymond reaches for my arm. I feel Lawrence get taken away by someone else for a conversation. Lawrence glances back at us with a questioning look. But the new person he's talking with leads him away, keeping him wrapped in a new conversation while Daymond and I walk away.

I turn to Daymond and give him a face that doesn't need the words to say, *What?*

Daymond looks in both directions. He quietly nags, "I don't have a good feeling right now. Something's wrong." The look in his eyes scares me more than his words.

I swallow the lump in my throat. "Why don't you ever have a good feeling?"

"You know something is off too."

I try to calm him. "Everything seems perfectly fine." I haven't noticed a single thing wrong with tonight. It's not the funnest ball I've ever been to, but it certainly isn't horrible.

"*Seems*," he repeats. "That always means something is wrong."

Daymond takes a deep breath through his nose, but before he can start talking again, music fills the room. It's the custom, as I was informed yesterday, to dance at these events. I make a pleading face as Daymond says, "Just keep your guard up," and walks away.

Lawrence quickly finds me. Alas and Trinity appear by our side. Lawrence grabs my hand and encircles my waist with the other arm, leading us in elegant circles around the room. The whole room feels like it's spinning into a downward spiral around me. I haven't practiced dancing in ages. Lawrence doesn't let his royal smile drop as he asks, "What was that about?"

"You know my family. We can be a little cautious sometimes."

His eyes tell me he wants to say something poetic in response, but instead, he continues the dance. I know he doesn't want to get into anything serious during the ball, least of all during this dance. "Have you been practicing?" he eventually decides to ask.

I laugh, "Sort of." I've been doing ballroom dancing for years. It always pays off in ways I don't expect.

Lawrence is the better of the princes at dancing; I can tell just from watching Alas on the other side of the room. His moves aren't as fluid as Lawrence's.

After the dance, Alas glides to the stage. The crowd instantly falls silent.

"People of Parten," he announces, "You know that in the next few weeks I'll have the honor of marrying my betrothed, Trinity. And with that, I hope to take the crown, with your blessing. This kingdom is at the peak of success." Applause echoes as he takes a breath. "But we still have struggles, we have a war, and I plan to do all in my power to fix it. I plan to do my best with my partner to make this kingdom a place you are proud to declare your home..." Alas continues his speech with the crowd enthralled. His voice drowns in my ears. I turn to see Lawrence's eyes on me. He laughs lightly.

"What?" I ask.

"His speech," he mutters. "I don't know what he's going for, but I don't think I like the warm approach."

"What would you rather have him say?"

"Be official and political. This ball is his first real public address. He should be making a powerful statement. I say we leave."

I shake my head. I want to listen to the rest of the speech; I want to see how Alas is going to conclude everything. But if Lawrence intends to leave, I'll go along with it for now.

Alas continues talking, but I can't focus on his words as Lawrence weaves us out of the crowd. I see everyone around me applauding. The speech is over.

We've beat the crowds, at least. Lawrence bids me a kiss on the cheek and parts ways with me in the hall that leads to my room. He's clearly preoccupied digesting Alas's words.

I need to get my mind straight, too.

On the one hand, I'm thrilled; the night went well, Daymond was wrong, Lawrence was benevolent, and everything seemed fine. But on the other hand, I need to know if Alas is okay. I want to know if he genuinely meant what he said about his future wife in his speech. I want to know if he'll carry through with his plans, or if it was just show for the public's sake.

I make my way down the ghosted hall to my quiet room while still pondering the speech. I take no caution when throwing open the door.

I close the door carelessly and slip my heels off.

A cold voice echoes before I can see where it's coming from, "Hello again, Isadora."

CHAPTER 5

Isadora POV

This is the last person I expected to be in my room. I can feel my heart sink as my breathing quickens. The best way to approach this is to be steady, but my thoughts are racing as my heartbeat consumes my chest, making the room feel rickety. I move my hand to the door handle. I don't move my body as my hand grasps it to open the door. It's stuck in place, locked in its frame, closed to keep me captive. I don't have time to evaluate the next move as the room rattles viciously around me.

Daymond's words echo in my head as I remember him telling me I have no protection or guards until I'm married. No one is coming to help me out of this one.

I feel his stare focus onto me, his deadly fingers not moving yet. This is a dangerous situation. simply because before me is a metallomancer, a metal controller. My hand is still gripping the door handle. I don't want to move; I don't want to say anything, I don't want to even breathe.

"Don't act like you forgot about me. It's barely been a year," he hisses. I know who he is. I wish I didn't.

Theo Shade stands in the room before me. His stance reflects his former career as a soldier, far more prepared to fight than I am. His tall, muscular frame and blond hair make him appear even deadlier. His power to control metal means that he can manipulate it in any way he wishes, which includes locking the door from across the room. I dart my eyes to him as a knife slips from his shirt pocket into thin air.

He takes a step closer to me. He speech is faint, yet cold. "Listen, I'm not supposed to hurt or harm you in any way." The way he moves the knife from the air to his hand and plays with it carelessly, and the way he said *not supposed to* as if it's a challenge, makes me test the door one last time. It won't open. Theo isn't much older than me, but his weapons experience is years ahead. They put him into the front lines of the war when he was barely a teenager. He was crafted to be a fighter.

"I'm guessing Carac wants to punish you himself," he hisses.

I take my hand off the door frame. My hair brushes to the side as I lock eyes with him. His face is without emotion.

Another step closer.

It's take action or be taken. The small stocks of water I have in my room, from moving, are my only saving grace. Theo's eyes remain locked on mine as the water trickles around his feet and glides to me.

"I'm under strict instruction from Carac not to harm you." He twirls the knife around his fingers. "But let's suppose you fall on my knife?" He glances down at the water. His expression slips; the water annoys him. He flinches up to face me again. "Accidents do happen," he breathes, his voice filled with menace.

My breaths start to stagger. I don't want to kill him. Theo may be working with Carac, but he shouldn't have to die. "Theo," I say trying to emulate calm, "You don't have to do any of this. We can both walk away."

"I want you dead, Isadora. You can beg all you want, but this is going to end with one of us dead either way. I promise. Those damn *accidents*."

In the flash of a second, Theo flings himself towards me and straightens the knife, aiming at my chest. I'm barely able move to the side in a dodging movement. The blade embeds itself in the door, not my chest. The water slows him down as I move. Theo uses mind over matter to use his other arm to create a new weapon out of the last. I lunge to the other side of the door, but as he jumps with me, he barely catches my wrist, just enough to grip it.

I pull both of our weights forward to land me on the bed. I twist his wrist backwards in the process. I lift my leg and kick him to release his hold on me. I hear his breath get knocked out, but he straggles forward and slices a significant cut on the side of my left leg.

As I make a movement away, flinging myself off the other side of the bed, he follows. From the corner of my eye, I catch his hand with the knife in it, aiming back at me. I swipe my hand to make a solid shield of ice and hold it in front of me. Before I can blink, the knife lodges in the ice rather than my neck.

My years of training to make a shield quickly have never been used until this moment. It was worth all the practice. He curves around it, and with the length of a big step takes hold of me again. I feel his hands wrap me in an arm-lock position. He keeps one hand around my chest, pulling me in.

Another knife has been formed, and he uses his other hand to rest it right under my neck. I can feel it cut into my skin just the slightest bit. "Your move, your funeral," he warns.

I use the water still on the floor to wrap around his ankle and climb midway up his calf. I turn it to ice. With his shock and moment of realization, I move out of his hold. The knife slides out of position to cut my neck, slicing my shoulder instead. I get one hand completely out of his hold. There are no thoughts running through my head, just instinct.

I swipe my hand down, just enough to construct a sword of ice and grasp it. In the same movement, I pull my arm back and plunge the sword into Theo's chest while he cuts my other arm. As the sword holds its place, Theo falls back into the water, making a splash.

His breathing starts to slow. Then it stops.

I drop to my knees. My hand moves to my arm to apply pressure on my wound. I hiss a breath of pain. It burns; everything starts to feel numb. The blood from my arm mixed with Theo's seeps into the water. It becomes a pool of blood. I scan around me, not processing the tears coming from my eyes.

It's a war scene.

A paper is crumbled in Theo's hand. I don't know when it got there, but I reach for it before the water makes it unreadable.

Theo knew what he was in for.
So should you.
Carac

I can't breathe. The ink on the note is enough to make me want to scream. This was planned. He wanted me to fight Theo and kill him. He *wanted* me to kill him. *He wanted me to kill him.*

If Theo committed himself to this knowing he would die, then he won't stay dead for long. I have no time to think. I grasp my arm, with blood streaming down it, and rush to the door. I twist the knob to unlock it; I t opens freely now that Theo isn't holding it shut. I almost trip over my feet as I rush down the hall as fast as possible. The guards stationed outside of Lawrence's room put their arms out and fling me back as I try to reach for the door. I gasp in pain hit as they my wounds.

"Lawrence!" I scream while managing to kick the door. "Lawrence!"

Lawrence POV

At this point, I only have a few hours to sleep. It's well into the night, and I'm going to have to wake up early for a meeting. I sigh into my room and undo my cuffs, ease myself down on the bed, and reach for my shoes as I hear a yell. Someone has screamed my name. I pause, looking around my room, and hear the shout again as a woman cries out, "Lawrence!"

There's immediately a kick at the door. I spring to my feet and lunge for the door, opening it to see Isadora on the other side. She breaks free of the guards for a second as I command evenly, "Let her go, now."

They instantly release her.

She looks awful. There's blood on her dress; her hair is wrecked. She has a weary cast to her frighteningly pale face. She's bleeding, too—a lot. I take her hand and slam the door behind us as we walk in the room. She removes her other hand from her arm, revealing another slash and allowing blood to trickle down her arm. The tips of her brown hair are dark from water and blood.

She stumbles, collapsing right on my floor. I can barely speak; there's too much going on with her. I manage to ask, "What the hell happened?"

She looks up at me with watery eyes. She puffs and puts a hand to her head as she tells me, "Lawrence… in my room… there's a body—you need to burn it."

I nearly asked her to repeat what she said, but it's clear she's disoriented and seriously injured. She might be in shock. "We need to get you wrapped up and to a medic."

"Burn the body!" she yells. I study her distressed face. She screams again: "Now!"

I have no time to ask her again for anything. I want to address the most immediate concern, but this isn't the time for me to ask questions. I race to the door and sprint out into the hallway. My feet won't move quick enough; nor will my mind process fast enough. I yell behind me, "I need a medic sent to my room ASAP, and double the guards. You hear me? No one goes in or out of my room except for that medic!" I can hear the guards scrambling to obey as I continue to run.

I arrive at Isadora's room and throw the door open. A body lies dead in the center of the room, an ice sword perfectly positioned in the middle of his body. A pool of blood surrounds him. I can't imagine what the hell happened here. I grab the closest paper I can see on her desk. I use my ability to heat the room, and primarily the paper, until it hits its ignition point and a fire starts. I let my hand hang close as the paper falls to the body on the floor.

Within seconds, the body is consumed by the flames.

Who did I just set on fire? I don't know what he did. I can't think of anything that provides a simple explanation. And why did I need to burn him?

I stand back and watch the flames do their job. Once he becomes charcoaled enough, I step back further. I survey the scene, and spot a small note by the door. The letter has a few droplets of blood and water on it. I pick it up to read what it says. Despite the fire dying down the room, I remain still and reread the letter at least five times before gathering any sort of information.

I have too many questions. My mind continues to flicker. I need answers.

Wrath and confusion mix in me: a hazardous pairing. I cool down the room; the fire will die out by itself, given all the water. I rush back to my room. As commanded, there are now six guards outside the door, and a medic just leaving. I walk straight past them; they wouldn't dare stop me from storming into my own room. Isadora sits drowsily on my couch, holding herself. The medic left a description card of what he did to her— mainly fixing the wounds and some bandages, but also plenty of painkillers that would put her to sleep for a few hours. I can tell they've already begun to take effect.

"Get some rest, then we can talk," I promise in a controlled voice while crumpling and burning the letter in my fist.

She nods without opening her eyes, and curls up tighter while drifting to sleep. I walk to my bed for a blanket, which I lay on top of her. I then take a seat at my desk and try to visualize my way through it all. Whoever I just burned obviously wasn't a friend of Isadora's. Evidently, something terrible existed between them, and she knows who he is because of the note. I just want answers, but I'm not going to take any of my confusion and irritation out on Isadora.

The wraps on her arms have bloodstains on them already. Her injures should heal in a week or so, but it will take much longer for her to be completely fine. I sit noiselessly for a few minutes, trying to reflect. Theres nothing more to contemplate that won't lead to more questions.

I glance at Isadora again; she's sound asleep. I stand and slowly push the door open. The guards seem on edge, too. I exchange some quick words with them to make sure they won't repeat a thing about Isadora or what they have seen. I don't even know what I'm protecting.

My mind is spinning like a hurricane. I need an explanation, but I won't get the truth from anyone else except Isadora. I go back into my room. I'm going have to wait for a few hours before getting my explanation.

CHAPTER 6

Isadora POV

I wake to a headache and a burning feeling all over my body. I pushed my ability far when fighting with Theo, and I'm paying for my actions now. I've never fought anyone to that extreme before. I look up to see Lawrence, who immediately notices that I'm awake. "How do you feel?" he asks. His voice is calm and unalarmed; I don't know how he's doing it.

I wonder how long I've been asleep. "Fine," I lie. I feel like shit.

I stand up slowly as Lawrence watches my every move. My eyes can't focus anywhere else but on him. He did so much for me last night, and I'm grateful for that, but I need to gather my thoughts. I walk to the door and place my hand on the handle as he says, "The guards won't let you leave." They move in front of me with serious faces.

"Lawrence, can you please tell them to let me out of here, then?"

He stands and walks to me. He tilts his head a little. "I'd like a word first, actually."

I blink slowly. I should've known it wouldn't be that easy to slip out. I shoot him a quick glance before looking back into the room. He's staring me down, and it's working. He takes a deep breath, trying to control the tension in the room.

"What?" I ask, standing with my arms crossed.

"*What?*" Lawrence scoffs. "You had me burn a dead man who was somehow in your room, stabbed with an *ice sword*." I don't say a word. He continues, "Who is Carac?"

He must have seen the note. I don't know how else he'd know that name. I don't even know where to start with explaining this one, or how to, or if I should.

"Why don't we just start with who you killed?" he prompts. He takes another deep breath and moves to stand in front of me.

"His name is Theo."

"Was," he corrects.

I straighten my back. Lawrence didn't need to say that. Whatever he's feeling, he's apparently going to take it out on me, and that's fair.

"He *was* a metallomancer," I grind out.

"Why was he here, and why did you have a battle in your room?"

"He wanted to kill me... or take me out of here... or... well, I didn't have much of a choice," I tell him. The guilt is still heavy in my stomach. I killed a man I knew for years in a matter of minutes. But Theo was prepared to die; this was a mission that held that possibility, for whatever purpose. It was kill or be killed. I don't know if I made the right decision.

"And Carac?"

"I really need to speak with my brother." I make a move towards the doors. I can tell Lawrence something after I talk to him. Daymond knows how to smooth things over. He's going to know what I should say.

"I don't have a problem with that, but I deserve to know."

He definitely deserves to know, but I can't function without a word of advice. "I'm not saying a word until I speak with Daymond."

He stares me down for another minute. I hold my ground. He finally raises his hands. "Fine, go on then." Thankfully, he knows my tone of voice meant business and lets me pass.

As soon as he agrees, I hurry to the door. The guards stand ready to take me down, but Lawrence calls from the room, "Let her pass," with a dismissive gesture.

I take the free pass and rush to my brother.

I enter Daymond's room without knocking. He's still awake, reading something that I imagine is for work. I don't have to say a word for him to know something is going on. "What's wrong?" he asks, standing up to reach for me.

I storm in to take a seat at the table. "Theo showed up in my room after the ball."

He clears his throat. "What did he do?"

"He was more of a messenger for Carac." I take a pause to breathe. "I killed him."

"You *what?*"

"I didn't have too much of a choice, I know it's awful, bu-"

Daymond stops pacing around the room to ask, "And the body?"

"That's where the issue lies. I had to get Lawrence involved to... dispose of it."

"You couldn't do that yourself?" Daymond snaps. He slams a hand on the table in frustration.

"I was bleeding out. I was nearly drained of my ability, and I was going to pass out from my injuries. That would have given him the perfect opportunity to kill me or drag me out of here unconscious."

"You could have pulled yourself together to get rid of the body!" Daymond shouts at me.

"I was drained! I panicked!"

"After *one* fight?" he hisses. I was drained too quickly; he's taught me better than this, and I failed again.

"I'm sorry," I say. "I've never had to fight someone like that. I made a mistake and panicked. I didn't know who to do, and I couldn't think—"

He shakes his head slightly. "Can't fix it now." His stare is full of disappointment. "What did you tell Lawrence?"

"Nothing yet. What *should* I tell him?"

Daymond says, almost hesitantly, "Nothing."

"He'll demand answers. I can't just say nothing."

Daymond stands still, tongue-tied. Finally, with his confidence rising, he orders, "Tell him the truth. Tell him our history. Nothing can be hidden forever; the lies will just get worse and worse. And what can he do? He has to care for you, at least a little."

I try to play the other side. "He could send me back. He could kick you out, too. And if that happens, Carac will be standing there waiting for us."

"Or, he could heighten security and protect the palace more. I don't see any other solution to this. He's already seen too much, and if we allow another opportunity, another 'accident' will happen, and we won't have an easy way out then."

"What if I just go back?" I blurt out in frustration at seeing my brother worry.

Daymond replies immediately, with fury in his voice, "*Go back?* Go back to Din Point, where they tried to *execute* you? Where Carac would send you to your death?"

"What if he didn't, if I went back? Then you could work here still, Daymond; everything in Parten would be fine. You'd be left alone."

"Do *not* talk like that!" Daymond yells. I flinch at the sound of his voice. "You are *not* going back. Don't ever say that again!"

I regret the words immediately. I realize my words have hurt Daymond, as he doesn't meet my eyes. I don't say anything. I move my hands to my head, trying to understand the options.

"You get to decide what you want to tell Lawrence," Daymond finally says. "You know him best."

I tilt my head up to look at my brother. "I'll tell him the truth." Daymond raises his eyebrows in shock, probably because

I listened to him. "I don't know how he'll react. If I can help it, I'll withhold it from Alas. The more people who find out, the worse it could get."

"Are you going there now?" Daymond asks. I can see him taking in my wounded arms.

"I can't avoid him."

"Be careful," Daymond warns as I leave the room.

Walking down the halls feels like a death sentence. As I walk, the walls start to cave in on my mind, as if they might collapse on me at any second. There's an eerie emptiness to the halls. I don't know the words to say to Lawrence. I know I want to tell him the truth, but how?

I guess I'll just spill my words out and hope it makes sense. I try to form the perfect sentences in my head, but they never come out right.

I arrive at Lawrence's quarters. The guards let me in immediately. I enter to see Lawrence reading a book to pass the time. I can't tell if he's actually focused on reading. I doubt it. "Figure out your story?" he asks me as I sit down next to him on the bed.

"Ask away," I tell him.

"Tell me everything."

Lawrence POV

"The man I killed was from Din Point. So is Carac, who sent the note, and so am I," Isadora starts her story.

"And Carac, he's the prince—"

She reads my mind too quickly and answers, "Yes. He's Prince Carac Cavinche of Din Point, and currently, the prince isn't very pleased with me."

"The prince sent an assassin for you? What the hell did you do?" I ask.

"He wasn't an assassin... more of a kidnapper. Which is a long story." She's trying to dodge this like it's nothing. There's no way I can let this story slide after waiting this long and burning a body for her.

I reply with the classic statement, "We have time."

Her eyes flutter around the room after I say that, as if she's trying to let me know she doesn't want to tell the story. Nonetheless she begins, "I was born in Din Point. My parents were royal advisors to the King and Queen. From the day I was born, I lived in the castle. I grew up with Carac as my only friend." She breaks eye contact with me and laces her hands together. "We did everything together: lessons, practice, anything fun. As I grew older, I had still never left the castle grounds. The only people I grew up with were Carac and the Shade family kids. The Shade family has a long history of being advisors to the Din Point court. The kids are Theo Shade—the one you burned in the room—his sister Castilla, and his two older brothers Zaven and Xeres. Castilla is now a raging aristocrat, who loves running a wrecked Din Point with her brothers. Growing up, it was Zaven and Xeres who really scared me. Zaven was the closest with Carac. They both found amusement in carrying out little acts of dirty work for the council. Zaven worked with the military and the guards around the castle to fuel chaos and his own power. Xeres... well, he just loved to benefit from the corruption of Din Point. He's always been wicked smart; I still somewhat admire his intelligence and drive."

The way she calmly tells the story drives me to absorb her words. She continues, "As I grew up, I was entirely in a bubble in the castle, and unaware of the tragedy outside it. But eventually, I was allowed out into the world and took in everything. I was torn apart over the condition of Din Point, and how I had been so oblivious to all of it. I then started to regularly go out and learn as much as I could, but in secret.

"Along with that happening, I also figured out why I had been raised as I had. I grew up proper and close to Carac because I was molded to be his wife, and he was raised alongside me to want such a union. We were built to be puppets by our families. Everyone knew it but me. Even Carac had an idea of what was happening. Beyond that, Carac even knew about how the devastated kingdom was functioning.

"I finally came into secret contact with several rebel groups, and eventually joined one. I was a mole inside the castle that no one suspected. I began working closely with the rebel group and became even closer to the Shade family and to Carac. This exposed me to so much about the kingdom's horrible state.

"It wasn't until a year after I met the rebels that I was informed of a protest that would be taking place in a central square. It was to be protest over the war and the increasing government neglect. I found out through the rebel group that they were terrified of something happening. They just wanted a peaceful protest, to make a statement that wouldn't be ignored. I did my digging, and Carac informed me that Zaven was going to kill the people at the protest. Even he had some resistance to Zaven's plan, but Zaven was older than us, and even with Carac being Prince, Zaven had more power due to his rank. Carac couldn't do anything, and he also loved his friendship with Zaven, so he turned a blind eye to it.

"The plan was to unfold after claims of the people starting the violence; then guards and military forces would arrive to exterminate all the protesters. It was to be a statement that protests by the people and open voices wouldn't work.

I immediately reported this to my group, and we started planning from there. Zaven was the head of this operation. He was the sole reason it was running, and the driving force behind it. Everyone else was listening to what he said to do.

"On the day of the planned riot, I set Zaven up. I remember the day it all went down like it was yesterday."

She pauses for a second, taking in a deep breath before continuing. "The day before the protest was when we would take our own action. I used the guards in the castle as my messengers, and led Zaven to the exact location my rebel group specified. The whole day, I made myself look busy. I also kept Carac busy, clueless to the fact that a raid was taking place Zaven walked right into the jaws of the trap that we'd laid out, along with several head guards. They raided a part of the castle where I'd purposely sent them. I don't know what the rebels did with Zaven and the guards—I don't think they killed them—but they took that opportunity and ran with it. No one has seen Zaven since the ambush. All hell broke loose in the castle afterward. I remember Carac losing his ever-loving shit that day. The attack Zaven had planned didn't happen, and it was a significant win of voice for the people. From that day on, I ceased all communications with the rebel group for a while, in hopes of hiding evidence of my connection.

"Eventually, a few weeks later, Xeres figured out I'd been a key player in setting up his brother. I don't know how he traced it back to me. But he figured it out, and he had evidence. I was immediately thrown in prison and scheduled for execution on several counts of treason."

She pauses again to gather her thoughts. I feel shock consume my body. If they hadn't caught onto her, Isadora could have eventually destroyed the Din Point Empire.

"Carac honestly wanted to kill me during that time. He screamed at me while I sat in a jail cell for weeks, rotting away. Even now I can understand his feelings of betrayal; I was supposed to be his wife, and for a while we really were in love with each other. But the fact that he knew what was going on from both sides and let the kingdom go to waste made me realize that every single way I had betrayed him was worth it. Sitting in that cell, knowing I was going to die soon, was torment. Yet being able to smile at Carac while he lost his mind gave me a sense of pride I'd never trade.

"With the help of my brother, I escaped the day before I was scheduled to be executed. My parents had already completely disowned me, but Daymond used everything he had to get us out of there. We ran away to the most remote part of Din Point, and lived there on the down-low for a while. We were found not long after. Soldiers ambushed us at our temporary home. Daymond was out that day for business, and ran for Parten. We had a contingency plan if the worse ever happened, but I was stuck in the house and couldn't follow through with my part.

"I remember clear as day the moment I was cornered by Carac in the house. He was a part of the team, because he wanted to personally get to me. I was completely cornered, and it was game over. But he just looked at me blankly and let me go.

"When no one was around, he looked me dead in the eyes and said, 'You have one chance: to run as far as you can from here, because after that, I'm going to continue to look for you. I'll continue this game of chase until I find you again. But right now, in this second, in return for our years in companionship, I'll let you run.'

"I bolted. After several days, I managed to finally meet up with my brother. We put our original escape plan into action. We fled here to Parten and started life over again, using some connections Daymond had here. And now, here I am."

My mind will not stop racing. All things she has been through, the amount of risk it took for her to do what she did: I'm astonished. Then my jaw drops. Daymond is from Din Point too; they were all the closest thing to royalty there. Isadora has lived a double life her whole life.

"I don't know... I don't know what to say," I tell her truthfully.

"I'm sorry, it's a lot to think about and process." She sounds empty. I sit in the silence, trying to soak up as many details as possible, letting my mind wrap around all she's told me.

"That's why I didn't want to be offered the position of princess. That's how he found me: the broadcast. He knows where I am now. It's over." Her voice was devoid of hope.

"It's not over. Nowhere close to it."

"He isn't going to stop. Carac is on a hunt; I don't think he'll ever stop. He has no limits, Lawrence. No hesitation, no morals, no end. Theo was just a warning. It's a game to him, and he doesn't ever lose."

"Then we double the guards and security; you'll be safe here. At the end of the day, you are in Parten and under my royal protection."

"It's not that easy—"

"Why didn't you tell me before?" I interrupt.

"Because Daymond insisted I didn't. He was sure you wouldn't want the trouble and would just send me back, but now… it was time to risk it and come clean."

I stretch out my arms and tilt my head. "Stay here. Get some sleep and let me see what I can do." I need to think about how to approach this so it will be successful in the long run. I need to keep her safe.

"You don't understand," Isadora insists.

"He isn't that powerful."

"Yes, he is. Don't you know what his ability is?" she asks, raising her brows.

"No," I admit, my voice gravelly with irritation.

"Carac controls death."

CHAPTER 7

Lawrence POV

"You can't control that!" I exclaim.

"Do you think I'm making this up? Carac can make anyone die in seconds, and then he can bring them back to life just as quickly. That's why I had you burn Theo."

I have no filter in my thoughts as I say, "That's impossible. No one can control death. That's a power only the gods get, not a moral prince." No wonder she's so terrified, if she honestly believes that.

"As long as a person's body is intact, Carac can bring them back from the dead without even a thought. Distance is a small matter. He can bring people back from the dead across kingdoms, but it would drain his power for the day. Without touching anyone, he can make maybe 20 people die before getting tired. But even then, with just the slightest touch, he can get through hundreds of deaths in a day. This is why people don't mess with Din Point. Once he becomes king, no one can stop him."

I have nothing to say at the moment. The information is getting shoved down my throat. I need a second opinion. Someone to help me level my thoughts. The only other person

I might even talk to is my brother. "I need a minute," I said, getting up.

"Where are you going?"

"To Alas' room."

"Oh no," she snaps, "You can't tell him."

Now I'm most defiantly going to tell him.

"What?" I mock. "If you get to speak with *your* brother, then I'll speak with mine—plus he's the only one who can enforce security without it having to get approved by Father."

She sits down, looking at her hands again. She mumbles, "I need to sleep." Her wounds and the conversation have obviously tired her out.

I storm to Alas' room. I knock harshly and wait a few minutes. It's completely slipped my mind until this point that it's the middle of the night, and my brother might be asleep. Alas squints his eyes with a frown as he opens the door for me. "We need to talk," I state from outside the room. He lets me inside.

After I retell the story, Alas reacts nearly identically to me. He expresses waves of astonishment, and then the connections run though his head. "How is she now?"

"I can't tell. She seems okay, a little shaken. Tired."

"We tell no one about this, understand?"

I raise my chin. "You don't have to tell me that. She didn't even want you to know. "

Alas rolls his eyes. His stance screams tired, moody, and overwhelmed.

I stand and cross my arms. "Alas, do you know what Carac's power is?" I had saved this bombshell for last.

His brows knitted together. "Well, I know the King and Queen are both holy-water controllers; therefore, he has to be one too."

I feel my face heat up as I shake my head slightly, wishing that was what it was.

"Well, what is he then?"

"He's a death controller," I inform him. "He can kill people with a touch—and resurrect them just as easily." I've digested what Isadora has said, and now believe her. She speaks the truth. I smile a smug little smile as I wait for his reaction as this sinks in.

"What?" Alas yells, whipping his hands up. "He's a crossbreed?!"

"What the hell is that?"

"It's when two people with the same power have a kid—for example, Carac—and the powers cross in a such way that they provide some unimaginable power. I haven't ever *heard* of true death controller, though. The only crossbreeds I know about can control the mind and time: but life and death? This guy is unstoppable." Alas seems almost impressed with Carac.

"I didn't know crossbreeds were a thing," I say, feeling a little defeated. I guess I'd hoped Alas would be able to counter the argument, and explain why a death controller isn't possible.

"It's rare," Alas assures me, "Incredibly rare. It's as if nature has to keep such powers under control."

"Death isn't something a human should ever control. Not that easily."

"No," Alas marvels, "It certainly isn't."

I almost felt guilty for dumping all this information on Alas at once. I can tell that additional questions are circling Alas' head.

"Isadora and I will push the wedding to an earlier date," I say, having just thought of the idea. Alas simply observes me. "The sooner the better, right?"

"You should do what you consider the right thing. Go check on her." This is his way of dismissing me. He needs time alone to process this. "And Lawrence, I know you trust Isadora, and I'd like to say I do too. But either way, we know now that she was a Din Point citizen, so until further notice, I'm not going to allow her in any council meetings. And I ask you to keep what you hear in them to yourself."

I hesitate a second before nodding. I hadn't even considered what he's implying. I don't get a chance to respond as I open the door and see Isadora walking down the hall. She blurts, "I couldn't wait." I understand; I felt the same waiting for her. It's pretty apparent, too, that we were just discussing her.

Alas, hearing her voice, comes to the door. "We need a plan."

I ask my brother, "Do we? We can't do anything major to retaliate."

"It's not like we're at peace with Din Point," Alas hisses back.

"What do you think?" Isadora asks to no one directly. Tonight is about listening; Isadora has to figure out what we want. She's playing the game as safely as she can.

I answer, "There isn't anything we can do. Let Carac make a drastic move."

"That won't be major?" Alas snaps.

"That's not what I'm trying to say." He's twisting my words. "He directed the attack on Isadora, but if we fight back, we'll just make him angrier."

Isadora interjects in agreement, "He's already pissed off."

"I'll get you guards. Until another move is made, we wait," Atlas says, while making eye contact with Isadora. He then turns to me and goads, "You tell her about your little idea?"

Oh, now pushing up the wedding irritates him.

"What idea?" Isadora asks.

I brush a hand through my hair. "I think we should have the wedding sooner."

"What!" she exclaims, and then calmly corrects herself. "Why?"

"It will let Carac know we aren't scared, and will gain you better protection. In the meantime, security will improve, quickly and incrementally as the dates approaches."

"You're egging him on."

"Yes. Let him strike."

CHAPTER 8

Isadora POV

Even though the wedding date has been moved up, we've been planning this wedding for what feels like an eternity. Thousands of little details and things that don't seem like they need consideration are discussed at painful length. Most of the time, it's just Trinity making calls on my behalf while Lawrence gives dismissive hand gestures to anything he doesn't like.

We finally get to take a break. I don't know how long this freedom away from the planning will last. I race out into the hallway to exercise my legs. It's a blessing to have a second without having to think about color choices and arguments over flowers.

In the hall, Alas catches up to me, "I knew you wouldn't like planning." He fixes his gaze on me.

"Is it that obvious?" I smile back at him.

"I finally have some free time, and now that I do, everyone is busy," he says. I shrug. "Do you have to go back to planning?"

"Are you really this bored?" I joke. I haven't ever seen what Alas does in his free time. I don't think he really gets any, and when he does, he must not know how to function.

"I'm just asking," he assures me.

"What are you thinking?"

"Training session," he says. "Training with me."

It's an open invitation to get out of planning for the next hour, at least. "Don't you have better things to do?"

Alas scoffs a bit. "I was asking to help *you* out."

"I didn't mean it like that. You're going to be king soon, right? I thought you'd have important things to do."

"I have time for this," he promises, deflecting the conversation back on me.

I hesitate for a second, thinking of my arm and the cuts that are just now starting to fully heal. But as long as Alas doesn't reopen the wounds, I should be fine. "Okay, I'm down."

"Yes!" he says, and starts walking toward the back lawn.

I follow behind him quickly. "Are we training outside?"

He nods and opens the door for me. I step out onto into the sunshine, onto the grassy lawn. Parten always has beautiful weather. It hasn't snowed or rained since I arrived; it's always sunny and fresh. As we walk, I notice several guards are outside working, or just simply walking around. It's a nice change of scenery.

"Okay," Alas invites while stretching his arms out, "ready for a light spar?"

"We're sparring? I thought we were just going to train," I say sharply.

"No, no, we both need a change of pace. We're sparring today." I've never sparred with Alas. I didn't think I'd get the chance to.

From a bench in the shade, the annoying Captain Ryder asks as he watches us, "My lady, you nervous about sparring with the Prince?" Ryder is sitting with a group of guards. I don't know what they're doing, but it doesn't seem like Ryder cares much. I don't answer, and he sasses, "You can spar with me if you want."

"You wouldn't last two seconds, Ryder," Alas chuckles. The other guards laugh with him.

"Hey, that's not fair, Your Highness," he complains.

"It's not that you're bad, Ryder. It's just that Isadora is really good," Alas explains, and turns to me. "Let's start this thing."

"Fine," Ryder hisses, "I'm going to spectate, then... Start!"

Alas and I move step-in-step. The most significant fact I've learned about thermomancers like Alas is that they don't need to pull any element to work their ability; they can use any resource and manipulate it to their advantage. The only physical weapon Alas has is a small sword secured to his belt, but he hasn't reached for it yet.

I call for water from the ground, and it comes. It's a fresh, earthy water, unlike the water I usual work with from bottles and stocks. I grip inward with my left hand, making the first attack, launching a spike of ice from the ground. Alas leaps over it before it can hit him. He moves forward, his hands out. He grabs my waist with his lead hand, and pulls us both to the ground. He starts to form a heat bubble around us. The air is soon too much for me to bear, and the oxygen begins to slip from my throat. I raise a leg to the side of him and, with all my force, flip us on our sides. Alas stares at me in shock at my movement.

I roll back and pull the water up to make a sword. In counter to my movement, Alas pulls his steel sword from its sheath. He stalks closer, and I feel heat radiate off his weapon. If that sword so much as touches my skin, it will leave third-degree burns.

I move my ice sword out a bit. Alas swings his red-hot sword, and the heat alone slices my ice sword in half. My mouth drops open as I drop the intact part of the sword. I'm now playing defense, and he's coming in for the attack. I push the water out of the ground at his feet and freeze it. He was already running, and the movement makes him tumble and fall to the ground. As soon as he hits the grass, I flow water over the wrist of his sword hand, freezing him in place. I dash over to him and form a dagger.

He heats his body and breaks the ice around his wrist. Before I can react, he sits up and grabs my ankle. With one sharp tug, Alas pulls me back to the ground, knocking the wind out of me even as I turn over and form an ice shield. Alas tosses a few heatwaves at it, obliterating it. He leaps forward and grabs my shoulders. His hands are burning hot.

"Time?" he asks. The heat is circling around me. I can't breathe anymore, and the heat from his hands on my shoulders is searing me. I nod quickly.

Instantly, I get a rush of air to my lungs. I tumble on the ground, pulling for water to cool myself off. I knew the Princes had a lot of training, but I didn't realize Alas was *this* good. I crouch a bit and lean back, trying to get myself normal again.

"Isadora," a voice calls. I look up to see Lawrence stepping around our mess on the lawn. I try to collect myself and stand, but I'm still out of breath. Alas stands still in his own silence.

"We can't have you hurt before the wedding," Lawrence jokes, standing over us.

Alas rolls his eyes at him. I smile in pain for a second before looking back at Alas. We can't help but burst into laughter.

I toss my hands up and giggle, "I hate those heatwaves."

Lawrence catches my hand in the air and pulls me to stand. "All the planning's done," he advises me.

I nod. It's time for me to go, I guess. I had my fun, and I think Alas did too.

I stand up and start to leave with Lawrence, then turn around and mouth, "Thank you," to Alas.

He smiles discreetly and nods.

CHAPTER 9

Isadora POV

A week and a day have passed, which means it's my wedding day—the only day when all I have to do is set aside my thoughts and go through the motions. But it's difficult to do that, as from the moment I wake up, my day is planned. I immediately get walked to breakfast.

Today, only Trinity joins me at the table. "Are you excited?" she asks me. Her eyes are crisp and bright. Her rosy dark-red hair is twirled into curls. Sharp-cut eyeliner covers her eyelids as she stares at me in excitement.

I twirl my rings around my finger. Trinity is more enthusiastic about today than I am—maybe because it means that her wedding will come sooner as well, and she will finally be queen. Then she can do anything she wants, really. I don't blame her.

I realize I'm taking too long to answer. I rattle with a shallow breath, "Yes."

Trinity continues, "I actually like the bridesmaid dresses." Because of Parten tradition, Trinity is my maid of honor.

"You seem to be in a good mood," I comment.

Trinity looks around at the empty room as she crosses her legs. "Today is your wedding day, Isadora. I expect the same response when *I* get married." It's an unspoken, now-spoken, rule I've been ignoring. Trinity should be my ally here. We need to stick together.

"I need to handle something," Trinity flutters. She gives me a smile that feels forced as she hurries from the room.

Nothing's forcing me to sit at this table alone. I clasp my hands behind my back and walk out of the room a few minutes after Trinity. She hasn't made it very far; she's stuck talking with Ryder in the hall. She's been taking care of a lot of things for me today; the least I can do is get her out of that conversation.

"Trinity," I call out from behind her. Ryder casts a glance at me, giving me a slight nod. He walks away from us both. Trinity turns around and drops a paper. I reach down to pick it up for her, but she snatches it from the ground before I can.

"I didn't see you there," Trinity says with a high-pitched laugh. She brushes her dress off, staring doe-eyed at me.

I caught them in the middle of something. I didn't know they knew each other; maybe that's how they wanted to keep it. I look at her hands. It connects with me quickly that this isn't just a paper, it's a letter. "I was right behind you," I say, realizing it's better not to ask about the letter. "Thank you for joining me at breakfast."

I walk away from her then. I don't know what they're doing, but it's not my business.

My mood doesn't get any better now that I've entered my room. The maids are already set up for me. I sit down on the vanity and let them do whatever they want with my appearance.

All my thoughts about today circle restlessly in my head. There are so many thoughts of how much easier this would have been if I had just married Carac. I face the mirror and watch them pin my hair up. If I *had* married Carac, I'd be queen of Din

Point soon. If I were queen of Din Point, maybe I could have changed things. I'd have a lot of power and sit on the throne—theoretically. I should have stuck it out in Din Point and waited until I was queen to fix things there in the long run. I jumped into fixing things too fast, and created this day instead.

Carac and I would have had a fine marriage. We would have been perfect on the throne together, with my balance to fix things. The only bad thing would have been the unhappiness that would still linger with a crown on my head. *But who really cares about happiness when there's power?* I try to tell myself. Besides, in reality, Carac probably wouldn't have let me do much.

My head is whirling. My actions turn rapid as the concern comes out of me while I get dressed. My motions are shallow and quick. The cycle of denial and frustration race through me, turning into regret. Lawrence isn't the love of my life, but marrying him is my best option. Carac isn't the love of my life either, yet he wanted a real marriage. It's like what Alas implied: being with someone you don't want when they want *you* is even worse than a mutual disregard for each other. But there's still this frustration in me that it ended up like this. I'm frustrated that I left my old life to end up in the same position. I'm frustrated that my brother gave up so much just to see me fall into another cycle of royalty.

But in my defense, if I had married Carac, I'd be part of a kingdom that's wicked to its people. I would have had to love a Prince who hates the world, and is glad to see it rot. There are pros and cons to each situation. All I'm listening to in my head are the cons.

After the maids deem me ready, Trinity enters the room, ending my regretful thoughts. "Your brother will walk you down the aisle. It's time to go," she says. Her eyes dart away from me as I walk down the hall with her. No one will leave my side, it seems, until I arrive at the wedding venue. Quickly, we're outside.

Just a few days ago, Alas and I had sparred out here. Daymond loops his arm around mine and keeps his head high. This is a big day for him, too.

Once we start walking down the aisle, everything becomes a blur.

A dark blush flushes my vision as my brother and I walk. The flowers are pink and orange and overflow the room; I don't even like them. A lot of pastels and plenty of people. The thing that is most vivid is Lawrence, standing at the end of the aisle. He's dressed to the nines in his royal dark-blue suit. Hair still messy, jaw slack, his posture upright. His colorful tie catches my eye; it makes me realize my dress isn't eccentric. I hate the thought of wearing the most basic wedding dress ever. I had always told Carac that if we were to marry, I wanted the most unique dress possible. But here I am in an all-white ball gown that floods down the aisle. I've worn it all day, and up until now I haven't given it a second thought. Now it weighs on me.

I keep walking down the aisle with my head held high, but now it's racing through my mind that nothing is the way I want it to be, and it's all my fault. I was the one who didn't take the wedding seriously because it felt fake. But even so, this will be my only wedding. This was my chance to plan and have it be mine, unique to me—and I walked away from preparing for it. Lawrence handled it all, and he did a fantastic job planning a wedding that would suit anyone else. It isn't his job to cater to what I want.

I glance to the sides. The rows are filled with people I don't even recognize. Barely any faces that I can pair with names. Council members and their families fill most of the front row.

I focus on Lawrence instead of the crowd while I walk. Trinity and three other girls I'm not close with are bridesmaids. It's a slap to the face, displaying just how political the wedding is; even my bridesmaids make a statement.

Alas is the best man; besides that, even Lawrence's groomsmen are cherry-picked.

I finally reach the end of the aisle and let go of my brother's arm. The man in the center between Lawrence and me starts to speak. The wedding takes its course. I don't pay much attention to the ceremony; it doesn't look like Lawrence does either. It feels too long to have any use besides carrying on a tradition. The only part where we have to take motion is when the words, "You may kiss the bride," are spoken.

Lawrence leans in and quickly kisses me.

It doesn't mean anything.

CHAPTER 10

Lawrence POV

The after-party has dragged on with smiles and shining eyes for hours. I can't count how many times I've heard the word *congratulations*. With everyone around us, I haven't gotten a single moment alone with Isadora. We've been ambushed with handshakes and questions about us that I'm doing my best to answer, and Isadora is doing her best to dodge.

The only two conversations that mattered to me tonight were my mother telling us congratulations, and Daymond wishing us the best.

Now that the party is finally dying out, we can exit. Isadora and I slowly walk down the empty hall. We have one room for tonight. As we enter the wedding suite, we glance at each other at the sight of one bed. It's big enough, though, that we can nearly avoid each other in it. We're like children. This isn't really anything personal; both of us just know what the boundaries are until we're in a different state of mind.

I roll up my sleeves and pop open a bottle of champagne for us to split. Isadora immediately goes to the closet and changes into comfy clothes. I do the same after. She collapses onto the bed.

"Are you okay?" I ask as she sits up. I hand her a glass of champagne.

"I'm... I'm great, honestly." She sounds genuine. "Just exhausted. How are you holding up?"

"I'm good. A bit stressed-out now, but otherwise great."

"What's got you stressed?"

"Well, now that we're married, there are a lot more responsibilities to handle. You're officially a princess now, which I know really isn't that big of a deal; what's mainly concerning me is the fact that Alas will be king soon."

She raises her eyebrows a bit. Curiously, she asks, "Well, hasn't that always been the plan?"

"Doesn't mean it's a good plan. I know you really like the idea of Alas being King, but I truly don't think it will go well."

"Why not?" she asks innocently.

"Alas has always been radical, and not the best when it comes to planning for the future. I feel things are in a vulnerable state these days. We've been at war with Din Point for years; something has to end it. I suspect something significant will happen soon. Given how long this has gone on and the constant tension between us and Din Point, there's no way it will end peacefully. Either they'll consume us, or we'll consume them. That will drastically affect every kingdom in the world. I think Alas will be an decent ruler, but I don't think he's the person we should have in charge when all that goes down."

She pauses for a minute, sipping her champagne. "I never thought about it like that."

"I don't think anyone has. I truly don't want Alas as ruler, nor my father if I'm completely honest; but there's nothing I can do except pray for the best."

"I'm sorry, Lawrence. You have a lot of ideas and opinions that I don't think anyone listens to," she tells me lightly.

I nod in return. I wasn't expecting Isadora to be so soft-spoken about what I just told her. I haven't really voiced it to anyone before, but she can grasp my ideas fully. We both finish our champagne in silence, mulling over my words and the day. I lay down on the other side of the bed and turn the light off.

I smile and whisper, "Goodnight, Isadora."

She rolls over and tells me, "Goodnight, Lawrence."

CHAPTER 11

Lawrence POV

Morning has arrived. I sit up in bed, and feel my mind ache as I think about last night. I took an odd turn and said too much to Isadora, without even running my mouth. I have a plan, and it will come to fruition one day; the only hindrance would be Isadora not supporting it.

She's still asleep, happily wrapped up in the blankets. I can worry about her once everything is in motion.

I stretch my arms wide and yawn into the room, then get up slowly as to not wake my wife. I stroll to the other side of the room before I see objects on the coffee table that weren't there last night. I go to the table and stare down at a perfectly folded letter. How did it get here? I'm positive that this document wasn't there before we went to bed.

It's addressed to Isadora. It's sealed with wax.

I don't want to wake her, but I want to know what's written on it. We're married now; married people open each other's letters all the time, right? I contemplate the letter for a few moments before picking it up and opening it.

Dear Isadora,

I hope you had the loveliest wedding. You looked stunning, and I'd love to discuss it with you later. I genuinely hope you enjoy the wedding gift; the necklace was made special. Now, normally, I would just hope you would wear the gift because of my wonderful taste in jewelry. But knowing that you don't like to listen to me, I recommend you leave it on... since it has spikes that are poisonous and will react if you try to take it off. I don't think you're that foolish.

It shouldn't be long till I see you in person.
Until then,
Carac.

My immediate response is to rush to Isadora. My footsteps are harsh enough to wake her quickly. Her eyes narrow as her mouth drops open in confusion. She places a hand on her head and mumbles, "Lawrence, what are you doing?" As she sits up, a sparking necklace dandles down, and a perfectly cut black diamond pendent lowers onto her neck. The black reflects the light coldly but radiantly.

Someone came into this room last night and placed the necklace around her neck without either of us noticing. The necklace couldn't have just magically appeared there. The letter was perfectly placed on the table. Whoever was here entered the room could have killed us both.

A chill trickles down my spine. My face heats red. I shout to the room, "Dammit!"

"What are you swearing about?" Isadora asks, her eyes widening.

"The guards," I say. "Oh, when I have a word with them for letting someone enter our room—!" I roar with such heat that my words slip together.

"What is it?" Isadora inquires, watching me yell.

I step closer, leaning over her. My hand motions to the pendent. I rasped, "This. This is what wrong."

Isadora grips the necklace, realizing it's there for the first time, as she's been disoriented from just waking. "...Did Carac do this?"

She knows the diamonds. The style. I don't know how else she could pick up on something that detailed otherwise.

I turn around to grab the note. I hear Isadora move; I turn to see her moving to take off the necklace. I spring back to her and catch her wrist as I yell, "No!"

She pulls back. I might have burned her wrist with my sudden reaction. I hold her wrist loosely, trying to take back my actions and cool them down.

"You can't take it off," I explain, handing her the letter.

CHAPTER 12

Lawrence POV

I call for a council meeting at once. There's no time to waste while we figure out this necklace issue, but the timing is implacable.

I don't want to see Alas at the moment. I don't want to see him and how he's carrying himself around the castle, like a god who does what he does just for the sake of making himself feel good. I have to disrupt some work in order to call for Daymond, which I'm sure will earn me some backlash later.

Isadora seems tired and disgusted at what the Prince of Death has done. That's what I have deemed him: the Prince of Death. And really, she has the right to be drained. Carac is hammering her with blows every chance he gets. I want him out of the picture, and for her to be able to breathe. For us all to have clear heads.

Eventually, after some time, everyone is ready to talk.

As soon as Isadora and I enter the room, Daymond demands, "What's wrong now?" with a dismissive face.

I don't know exactly what to say. I'm nonplussed by the necklace; what kind of a person does this? Isadora, although, appears levelheaded and steady as she takes a seat next to me. Her diction is typical as she starts to explain what happened, as if it were expected. Alas looks over at Isadora multiple times, either trying to catch her eye or to see how bad the necklace really is, but she only looks straight at her brother. After Isadora's explanation, Daymond stands and walks over to her. He grabs the necklace and starts to investigate it.

I can't stop looking at the damn thing. The way it silently absorbs the light in the room and grabs our attention. It's stunningly malicious.

"Get me some tweezers," Daymond orders. I stand up at the same time as Alas, and we both dash out to the task. I trail Alas quickly as we go to a servant and ask for a pair.

In a few minutes, we are back in the room with three different pairs for Daymond to use.

Daymond grabs the smallest pair and warns, "Don't move." Isadora tightens her posture. He fidgets with the pendent, rustling the tweezers around. After a moment, he pulls out a tiny piece of electronic hardware. It's small enough to have been hidden in the necklace successfully.

"Everything Carac does has a purpose," Daymond mutters, throwing the electronics piece on the table. The Xxons just look annoyed; this has to be the usual when dealing with Carac.

Alas sighs in disappointment. "A tracker." I'm irritated I didn't think of that first.

Daymond shakes his head and looks at the hardware. He finally picks it up off the table and puts it on the floor, where he crushes it under his foot. "That was the purpose, and they did a shitty job with it. Now the necklace is useless to him."

It makes sense, sort of, why he'd give her such a weird gift; but part of me feels like the purpose of it was just to dive us mad. The appearance of the necklace serves that purpose well. Carac could have directly placed a mini-pin or a million other things that would go unnoticed on Isadora, but he wanted *this*.

Alas turns his attention away from the table while asking, "Is there no way to get it off?"

"Not without killing Isadora," Daymond said, while placing a hand on her shoulder. "I checked, and he isn't bluffing on the spikes. I'll keep looking into it and see if I can find anything that will help." To his sister, he says, "He probably wants you to take it off so he can come in and bring you back."

Isadora chokes on her next breath. He *would* kill her just to make a statement.

"What if I melt the chain? Or heat up the whole pendent to melt the spikes? That might work," I suggest.

"I think if you break the chain, it will still activate. It's not a bad idea, but I don't want us doing anything, in case it backfires," Daymond tells me.

Isadora finally chimes in, "And now we wait."

Daymond nods in agreement. "There isn't something we can fight against, especially if we want to keep it on the down-low."

Alas counters him, "People will sense something is wrong. Too many witnesses, and they start to talk."

"Then let them talk," Daymond whispers.

"I will be king in fortnight; we can act then," Alas promises Isadora with a glance. She looks to the side. That doesn't mean anything to either of us.

I snap, "I'll be having words with the guards. It's their fault this happened."

"It's *not* their fault. Carac has ways of getting through things," Isadora says to me. She doesn't realize that it's literally their job to keep the castle secure, and that they've utterly failed.

She sees my face changing. I try to think of ways to counter her kindly. Instead, she changes the subject. "What was the use of a tracker? It's not like I'm leaving Parten."

"Direct location would be my guess, or just in case you try and run to a different kingdom," Daymond explains.

"Why would that be of any use?" I scold. "If he wanted to take you, he could have done so last night. It doesn't make sense."

Isadora quietly says, "Carac never makes sense. It's all a game to him."

CHAPTER 13

Isadora POV

The next few days continue as usual. Training has become a lot harder now that I'm working with Alas. It's become a daily workout for both of us. As hard as Daymond used to push, Alas pushes me harder. When I train with Alas, it's a double-edged sword; he's easily the best person to coach me, and the person I enjoy working with the most. But Lawrence would throw a fit if he found out. He doesn't like us doing things without him. Alas and I came to an agreement that it's better to keep our practices between us. Anytime Lawrence asks about my absence, my answer is that I'm training with my brother.

I'm not really lying. Alas is now my brother-in-law.

But as time goes along, everyone's becoming busier in the castle. Alas has a full schedule of pre-king duties. Lawrence spends all his free time with me; we're acting more and more like husband and wife. With our busy schedules, Alas and I have found that the only time we have to practice is right before dinner. We have just a few minutes to change in between, so we've gotten into the habit of racing to our rooms and making it in record time, usually two minutes early to the dining hall.

Today's no different; after lessons, we go in different directions. I'm speeding down the hall, not really wanting to be late to dinner—but I skid to a halt when Captain Ryder jumps right in front of me. He puts an arm out and leans against the wall, making me stop in my tracks.

"How is it, being a princess?" he drawls.

"A delight," I utter, trying to walk around him.

Ryder turns himself in front of me again. "What's your hurry?"

I take a second to breathe. If I'm late for dinner, it won't be the end of the world. But still, this is Ryder I'm talking to. "Is there something you need, Captain?"

"Just wondering why you train exclusively with Prince Alas. Your schedules are so different, and obviously, it's not an easy thing for either of you to arrange. And you keep it from Prince Lawrence."

"Alas is one of the best people to learn from."

"I could help train you. I've had a lot of experience," he says, swaying on his feet. "Plus, we get along so well."

"I've already altered my schedule to work with Alas, but I appreciate the offer." I again try to continue on my way.

"Excuses are all I'm hearing," he ridicules.

"Is that all?" I don't know why, but from the moment I entered this castle, Ryder has gotten under my skin way too easily.

"Why have you been avoiding me?" he asks abruptly.

"What?" I grumble. "I barely know you."

"You won't spar with me, you don't speak to me, we never hang out."

"I spar with Alas, and... look, I have to go," I say, storming past him.

I shake my head and go straight to my room. I'm already late, thanks to Ryder and his foolishness. I arrive in my room in a fluster and slam the door shut.

There's a noise in the room behind me.

As I turn around, I swear my fears are making me see things. Sitting on the couch, with a slight demonic grin and a laugh, is none other than Carac Cavinche.

CHAPTER 14

Isadora POV

T he Prince of Death has casually strolled into my room and made himself at home. I stare him in the eyes. His hazel-green eyes, with specks of jade in them, have a glow that makes you wonder how many people he's killed. His cunning smile makes you realize he's probably lost count. His dark hair frames his face with small, tight curls, rounding out his presence.

Perplexed whirlwinds rush through my body. Ambivalent undertones spill out as I roar, "What the hell are you doing here?"

I try to pull for water, but nothing comes. Carac is smart enough to not leave a weapon of any kind for me to use. He has the advantage. As always.

"It's been a while," Carac says, taking a stance in front of me.

I can't let him take another step closer. He lifts his foot, and my fight-or-flight reaction kicks in. I ball my fist and launch it at his face. Carac grabs my hand and jerks it down. I can feel the King's Ring that he wears press against my skin. "Isadora," he sighs, his voice too steady for comfort.

I feel my chest burn and my heart start to slow down. Carac is draining the life out of me. The only thing I can do is move my hand to my chest and grip my shirt. It burns; my head starts to spin. "Are you going to stop attacking me?" he asks. "I just want to talk, not fight."

It pains me more to nod in agreement, but I'll collapse at any second if I don't submit. Before I can use any of the strength Carac gives back to me, he grips my hands and pins me to the wall. Any movement I make causes him to slow down my heart. He's teasing death.

His alluring voice echoes in the room. "I missed you, just a little bit."

I raise a leg to kick Carac back, but before I can, my strength disappears again. I've been dealing with Carac for a long time, and have learned there is nothing I can do to stop the death controller.

He traces my collarbone until it meets with the necklace. "Do you like the gift?"

I stop fighting. "You did a shit job with the tracker." I flicker my eyes to his and spit, "You need to leave."

He raises an eyebrow at me in retaliation. "But I just arrived! And I've never been to Parten before. Want to show me around?"

"No," I say. I try to move my arms, to raise them, to stand, but he presses down firmly. "You said you wanted to talk," I gasp, "so start talking."

It's been months since I've last seen him. His face has grown fuller, a bit more prominent. And he's become leaner, less muscle and more tone.

"You didn't even try to cover up your tracks; it was sloppy. Did you think I wouldn't see the broadcast? You basically handed over your location to me."

"Is that why you came here, to mock me?"

"Shockingly, no, although I do know how much you like our banter." He releases his hold on me. I straighten my back, not making any movement to fight, but displaying my willingness to listen.

"I came to ask you if you wanted to come back home," he continues.

"So you can execute me?" I sputter in response to the surprising question.

A small frown crosses his face as he says, "I'll drop your charges."

"The people at court will throw a fit. Do you think they'll just let you do that?"

"They will. And even if they don't, I'll just kill you and then bring you back to life. That's technically a death sentence," he chirps, the frown disappearing.

I bite down on my lip; I don't want to laugh at his stupid death jokes right now. But he catches my reaction, my slight amusement, and presses forward. "Are you considering it?"

"No," I say immediately, but then mutter, "No... I don't know. I don't want to go back there, not with how it is right now, not when I'm, you know... married."

Carac tilts his head, his jaw clenching as he echoes, "Married to the brilliant Prince Lawrence... I'm starting to think you just manifest arranged marriages."

"You're a prick," I retaliate.

"Maybe, but I'm still one of the princes you were supposed to marry," he says with a shrug and a toss of the hands.

"You should go," I repeat.

Carac doesn't get the chance to come up with another snippy response, as the door opens and both our heads turn.

Lawrence POV

I stare at the clock in the back corner of the dining room. The ticks pass slowly while Alas sits next to me, tapping his foot. We both glance at the empty seat at the table.

More time passes, and the seat remains empty.

I declare under my breath to Alas, "It's been 15 minutes."

Alas gives me a slight nod and turns to my mother and Trinity, who are waiting impatiently too. He stands up and explains, "I'll be right back."

I throw my napkin on the table and calmly follow Alas out the door. The moment it shut behind us, the panic arises.

Alas suggests, "Check your room first. She could just be caught up getting ready in there."

I'm already walking to my room. If something is actually wrong, there's no time to be wasted. I'm overreacting, surely; she's just late for dinner. Nothing is wrong, probably, but I can't live with probably, not with all I know could be happening. Alas paces in front of me and opens the door. His uneasiness makes it swing open before I can even grab the handle.

There's a figure standing against Isadora. His power is what takes me by surprise. A cynical, sly presence radiates from him and overwhelms the room. The stranger casts a glance at us. The smile on his face says he really couldn't care less about our arrival.

Without missing a beat, Alas assesses the situation and creates a heatwave to launch at the stranger. Before the stranger can react, he trips to the side from the power behind the launch. He catches himself before he falls. Isadora tries her best to register what's just happened. Her head turns rapidly and she moves to the side, away from the stranger. She looks sick, but the color quickly returns to her face.

I hold back the urge that screams at me to burn the room to ashes. The man shoots himself back upright and offers a hand to Alas. "Ah. You must be the future king." Then he gives me just a slight glance, and twiddles his figures in a half-wave.

I move to stand besides Alas, becoming even more pissed-off by the gesture. My face turns stone-cold while the temperature in the room drops. He knows exactly what he's doing with his words, but is having too much fun with the jealousy seething in the room to care. He even has the audacity to laugh.

No one makes a move until. Carac brushes himself off and mocks, "Well, I'm Carac. A pleasure to meet you both." He mumbles as an aside, "Such a warm welcome." When no one moves, Carac continues, "I apologize on behalf of you two for interrupting." He glances at Isadora and says, "Now we'll just get back to our conversation."

Without thinking, I step forward to grip Carac by his collar and throw him into the wall. "Give me a reason why I shouldn't kill you right now," I hiss.

The room's temperature rises drastically with my actions, until it's uncomfortably warm; I'm going to burn him down. My hands heat his neck as I apply more warmth. He maintains a still face and doesn't move. He should be screaming from the heat by now.

"Because... I'd kill you... first," he calmly chokes out as my grip tightens. He's going to drop at any moment.

"Give him a second to talk," Isadora advises. I glare at her. She can't be serious. She pleads with me with a look. My chest starts to sink. I lower my hand from Carac's neck, not because I'm listening to Isadora, but because Carac is draining my strength. I've never felt the life leave me before. The room becomes fuzzy; my heart feels hazed by pins and needles.

Alas yells, "Are you serious? He's threatening us all!" He lashes an arm out. It doesn't matter, though, what they say or do; I'm dying.

When Alas has his arm out and exposed, Carac quickly grabs it. My body jolts up. I can breathe and think again. He isn't killing me anymore, he's going for Alas. Alas's eyes go wide; he made a grave mistake dropping his guard. The floor seems to sway under Alas's feet as he drops to the ground.

Isadora yells, "Carac!" as we watch Alas's face turn pale, the redness draining away.

Carac drops Alas to the floor, and steps over his body.

"You didn't!" Isadora shouts, flying closer to Carac. Carac smiles, nodding at her yelling. Before she can say anything further to him, Carac grabs her waist. I lunge forward with everything I have left.

Carac leans backward. He whispers to Isadora, "He's not dead, for your sake. I just slowed his heart down enough to make him unconscious. He'll be back soon." His wicked smile exposes his glee.

Isadora steadies her breathing. I stand, waiting for him to move, thinking of every painful way to kill him. I take a breath, "You dro—"

"Isadora," Carac says softly, "I'll speak with you later, but for now..." She passes out in Carac's arms. He sways her by the waist and sets her down gently on the bed. He's going to knock me out next, and there's no way I can stop it. I breathe out as he steps forward. Carac moves to the tea trolley in the room and pours himself a cup. He grabs another and, on his way to sit on the couch, hands it to me. Carac restfully takes a seat and a sip.

"Why does everyone seem to think I want to kill them? Maybe it's the title—*Prince of Death*. A bit too strong?" He looks up to me with a waiting face, as if I'm supposed to give him feedback. "Or not; maybe it's that people usually just assume the worse, and when the word *death* gets thrown around, they panic," Carac continues to lecture. He gestures for me to sit on the chair with him. Instead, I chuck my tea cup at him. In the nick of time, Carac shifts his head to the right and avoids the glass. It shatters behind him against the headboard.

Carac sighs, looking at the shattered cup. "I suppose you don't like me."

"To say the least."

Carac takes another sip and sets down his cup. I narrow my eyes at him as he asks, "Lawrence, may we talk?"

"Prince Lawrence," I correct him.

"Well then," he scoffs, "*Prince Lawrence*, I believe I need to take Isadora home."

"She'd love to tell you all the reasons you're wrong," I say with a glance to Isadora, who is still lying on the bed unconscious.

"A misunderstanding is all this is. No one was thinking when Isadora left, and I take fault for her leaving. But she's meant to be in Din Point. I can protec—"

"Currently, I'm trying to protect her from you!"

"And look at how well you're doing," Carac responses cruelly, with a gesture to Alas and Isadora. "You think she needs or really wants your protection? What do you possibly think is here for her that I can't offer? What is good for her here? You'll never be King, and she deserves the chance to rule. Imagine the good she can do for a kingdom; but because she's with you, she will never be nothing but a pawn in your political game."

I mask my uneven emotions and try to keep a poker face. Carac studies my reactions. He's watching every little glance I make, every breath and pursed lip.

"I can offer her freedom while you keep her stuck under your rule in this palace."

I snicker uncontrollably. "Your people are rebelling! You understand that, right? At least here, the people don't want their leaders dead."

"It's just a phase. Your kingdom is newer; your people will go through it soon." He casually brushes off the violence.

"I can offer her a choice, Carac. She can do whatever the hell she wants. If Isadora wanted to be with you, she would be. If you take her, you'll be taking her by force."

"I'm not taking her by force." He finishes his drink. "I could have done that by now. She'll return on her own. I just thought that by speaking to you, we could speed up the process."

My temper is rising. "You truly think she's ever going back there? After the hell you put her through? She was almost executed!" My voice isn't loud, but my diction speaks volumes. "She told me about you. I don't know you, Carac, but what I see now is a cruel, corrupted soul. You're trying to take away the one person I want here by my side. I need her here to support and rule with me. You have her lying unconscious while we discuss her future. Do you realize how *wrong* that is? I'll never understand how you arrived at such a morally gray state."

Carac stands stronger than before, his face colder; I've struck a nerve. "I'm going to walk out that door unharmed, and you can do nothing about it. When I return, I'll leave unharmed again—with Isadora. Keep living your petty little life here, Lawrence. I'm sure it'll get you far."

He rises from his seat and, just as he taunted, leaves the room—unharmed. I can barely stand. After a long moment, I can breathe freely again. My jaw unclenches and my fists open. I look at Isadora and Alas; they've started to regain consciousness.

Knowing they're okay, I blurt, "I'll be back in a moment," just loud enough for them to hear. I dash out into the hall, to find no sign of Carac.

CHAPTER 15

Alas POV

My body has shut down. My head is in a haze as I look around the room. Lawrence just left in a hurry. Carac is gone; he must have messed with Lawrence just as much as me, if not more. What the hell just happened?

Carac Cavinche was *in my home.*

He rendered me unconscious, and must have done so to Isadora, too. I sit up and pull myself together, then rise to my feet and move to the couch as Isadora sits up. My first words are a threat: "Once I'm king, we'll have his head on a platter." We just have to make it one more week before I can enact a solid plan.

Isadora looks at me with a blank, silent stare.

"How does one develop such joy in being a menace?" I ask her. Shaking her head, she moves over and sits down next to me. I no longer feel comfortable in the room; the thought of what could have happened consumes my mind. Carac had the opportunity to kill me; he knocked me out with a single touch. Isadora doesn't seem that worried—she must have been through this before. What an absurd thing to become used to!

"A lot happened. Different events here and there change a person. Everyone is shaped by their environment; he didn't have a good one," she says, after a deep sigh.

That's no explanation. "You grew up in Din Point, and you don't have an obsession or mindset to kill anyone in sight."

"I don't have the power to do that. No one does, except Carac. I'm not defending him, but I didn't grow up a prince and have to deal with such a position, with his power at hand."

"His position didn't do anything to him. It certainly didn't shape him to be a leader."

"Exactly," she says. "Should we check on Lawrence?"

"No, he said not to worry, and by now, I don't think we'd be able to find him. Lawrence needs to be alone. If he wanted us to come after him, I'd know. I respect his space."

"Carac wasn't going to be king, not originally," Isadora says in a hushed voice.

"What went so wrong for them to resort to Carac?" I ask.

Her face twists like she doesn't want to tell me. Maybe she doesn't; maybe she just feels like I need to know.

"No, I think they always wanted him to be next in line. A death controller as King? That's intimidating to everyone." Her tone shifts. "He had an older brother, Caspian."

"I didn't know," I admit. I vaguely remember her mentioning it at breakfast a while ago, but I haven't thought about it since.

"No one in Din Point talks about it. They cover it up well. But he was a beautiful person, from everything I remember and the stories I've been told. He died when we were younger; I think he was 12? There was a fire, and not everyone made it out. The royals blamed the fire on the rebel groups. They spun the story around."

"You don't think they did it," I say, implying a question with no real statement.

She sighs. "No, I think his parents killed him. I think it was an easy way to get Carac next in line. I've heard stories from both sides. I've seen the reports after. Daymond fully sides with me; he thinks it was even the king's idea. But Carac defends his parents and takes out any anger he still has about it on anyone but them."

"Carac couldn't have saved him? Why didn't he bring him back from the dead?"

"The bodies have to be intact for him to bring them back. Caspian was burned to ash. Also, Carac was only eight years old, and didn't fully know how to work his ability then. Trust me, if Carac could have saved him, he would have. I brought up the theory a few times to Carac about who killed Caspian. He lost his shit. We don't talk about it anymore."

I shift in my seat. I feel ill at the story. If Lawrence were to die, it would scar me for life. I wouldn't be able to function correctly. I can't imagine the havoc I'd cause if he were intentionally killed. As much as I despise the Din Point royals, no one deserves to die young. "We should go talk with Daymond," I redirect, cupping my hands together. It's time for me to end that conversation.

"He doesn't need to hear about it."

"Of course he does."

"Carac didn't hurt anyone. If Lawrence has some crucial information, then we should, but right now, it's better not to."

She's so still about it her composure frightens me.

I'm still unsettled. I won't show my feelings to Isadora, but the fact that Carac could knock me out, and there wasn't a single thing I could have done to change it, drives me mad. I whip my feet to the ground. "The one thing I don't understand is how he got in here. We have guards everywhere, well-trained guards; someone should have been alerted. No matter how many precautions we take, he still gets in seamlessly!"

"Are there any hidden passages in the castle?" Isadora asks.

"No, there can't be any; we have the original blueprints. They show nothing."

"Someone is helping him, then."

"I doubt it," I reply, looking around the room for a possible hidden entrance. "I know my people."

Isadora stretches her arms out and begins to speak, but before she gets the chance, the door is flung open and Lawrence blows into the room. He exclaims, "Neither of you seems to care that the prince of an enemy kingdom was here and threatened us all!" We both stare at him. His face is red, his hair frazzled. "Anyone?" he yells.

"Of course we care, but we can't do much right now," Isadora says, trying to calm everyone's nerves. "We don't even know if Carac threatened anyone. You have to explain what happened when we were unconscious."

"H-he didn't say much," Lawrence stammers. He pauses. Carac must have said a lot, but Lawrence wants to keep it to himself.

"What did he say?" Isadora asks firmly, seeing through his lie.

"Lies and bullshit… It doesn't matter. Carac just wanted to make a dramatic appearance."

I raise an eyebrow at him, and he shrugs. "What?" he snaps, and then rushes, "I'm just flustered, okay? I didn't know he could actually manipulate our bodies like that, to make us almost dead. I thought he was going to be a non-issue. He could have killed us all with a touch!"

I shake my head, leaning against the wall. "He's too young for that ability." If I had that much ability at his age, I'd have to make my best effort to even make someone unconscious with a single touch. I don't know how he functions; even if he *is* just three years younger than me, those three years make a difference. Lawrence would cause a hell of a lot of trouble if he had that ability—there's so much havoc he would wreak. A skill like that can change the world.

"We just have to wait a week until the coronation," Isadora says, cutting off my thoughts.

Lawrence rolls his eyes, his lips pressing together until he finally asks, "Yeah, and then what? What will you do to stop him then?"

I'm not ready for Lawrence to get so feisty so quickly. I respond, "I'll figure it out."

Lawrence breathes through his nose heavily. "Well, until you have even a *fragment* of a plan, stop saying that like it will fix everything."

He storms out of the room, and Isadora follows him to calm him down. Carac made him more riled up than I thought. I assumed I was the only one who got under his skin that easily. I wonder what actually transpired between them.

CHAPTER 16

Isadora POV

Carac whips my hand into his. I can see the sun reflecting on his eyes as he looks up to the sky. The sun makes his skin glow a bit more; his green eyes change to a lighter, fuller shade. It's a bright and sunny day. Din Point hasn't seen good weather like this in weeks.

Carac continues his thoughts as we stroll around the castle gardens. "I don't know, Isadora. Daymond seemed so purely frustrated at me when I saw him yesterday. I don't know what I did to piss him off that much."

I reassure him, "Daymond isn't frustrated with you. He told me he's just trying to solve issues that keep arising. He's going to keeping acting like this until he solves all the issues, you know? He's like that."

"Well then, I guess he'll be like this forever; there's no way he's going to solve anything here."

"Maybe, but it doesn't hurt for him to try." I pause to watch the servants work around the garden, tending to the lavish plants. Plant-menders really do create the most beautiful grounds. "But how did the council meeting go?"

His eyes stay mostly focused on me, with only an occasionally glance forward. He can't even take in the beauty of the gardens because he's *so stressed. He had to attend his first council meeting today; his father thinks it will start to prepare him for the throne.*

"Horrible. They do nothing in those meetings except bitch about our people and the war. I don't want to listen to that for the rest of my life."

"Once you're king, you can control the meetings," I tell him lightly.

He looks at me with a smile that's counterintuitive. "But here's the thing: I don't want that."

"Why not?" I ask him with a frown. This is the first time I've heard that he doesn't want the glory.

"Because, Isadora, there are too many horrific things happening in the kingdom, and we both know once I sit on the throne, they will all be pinned on me. The council will overrule anything we do that's useful," he says. He's starting to use the word we *in these sentences now instead of* I. *He continues, "And there's nothing we can do to change the council system. It's all a bunch of members who inherited the positions because of their ancestors, and no one wants to vote in new people. What am I supposed to do, kill them over it? Threaten all their lives? It will end a lot worse if I take that route."*

"Every kingdom has issues. Don't be so hard on yourself."

"This kingdom has far more issues than you know, a lot *more than you know."*

I just want him to be okay. If he doesn't want the throne, then he shouldn't have to take it. But he doesn't see how much potential he has. He can do a lot of good if he wants to. "It will get better," I promise. I don't know if it will, but things can't be that bad; he can't lose hope already.

"You don't understand," he says. I tilt my head. He stops walking and turns to me, swinging our hands. "I can't get out of this one."

"No one can control you like that. If you really want to, you can."

He pauses for a minute and rests a hand on his head. Then he softly tells me, "This is all a game, Isadora. Everyone is just playing it differently, and everyone has a different version of winning. The only goal I have right now is to not be a pawn in this game, and I'm failing at it. This king thing isn't the big picture, it's not winning the game, but maybe it's a step closer to understanding how to play." I remain silent; I don't know how to answer him on that. He leans in a bit closer. "For now, we should just not think about it."

I sigh lightly; he never wants to talk about these things. He scans my face as I look to the side. "Are you okay?" he asks.

I tear my eyes away from his and stare at the ground. "I'm just worried."

"Aren't you the one who just said we can fix all the issues? Why are you worried?"

"I'm worried about you. I'm worried you are—"

"Carac!" a voice yells a few meters away. I drop Carac's hand as I turn to see Zaven Shade walking along the path to meet us.

Carac smiles brightly at him. "What are you doing out? I didn't think I'd ever see you out on a sunny day," he jokes

"I'm looking for you, idiot," Zaven tells him. He glances at me for a second and says, "Hello, Isadora, sorry for interrupting."

"You're fine."

"You should come see this news report—I think you'll get a kick out of it," he says eagerly.

Carac gives me an unsure look. I nod a bit and tell him, "Go on," with a raised chin. Carac nods contentedly and walks off with Zaven.

I wanted to tell him I'm worried he's changing. I'm terrified he's losing his grip on himself, and that there are things going on that I don't know about.

Maybe I need to look into things myself if Carac isn't going to tell me anything.

CHAPTER 17

Isadora POV

Four days have passed since Carac's appearance.

Alas has been working on plans, preparing for his coronation and avoiding me. He's making sure his schedule is full, and it feels like he's planning it so he won't see me at all. I saw him yesterday for a split second, and all he said was, "I have so many ideas, all of which you won't like."

I didn't even get a second to respond or ask what the hell that meant. I know Alas is taking this seriously, not just because of me but because Carac is a political threat who's going to cause him a lot of trouble. Carac is going to jeopardize far more than just his own kingdom.

The more stories I tell Lawrence, the more he wants Carac off the throne. Lawrence is making himself busy too, running around doing anything he can. From politics to more public appearances, his schedule is packed. He's focusing on smiling to the people and telling them pretty things—anything to win their approval. With all these events, Lawrence also takes the liberty of dragging me out to every. Single. One. Trinity comes along with us sometimes, when she isn't busy working with Alas. She loves the attention. The people love her—as they should.

All that said, I have just a *bit* of free time. Today, Lawrence and I are going to use that time to rest and relax. We walk past the training room as Ryder runs out of it, directly to us.

"Isadora!" he exclaims. "You're just the person I needed to see today."

"Really?"

"Alas is sorry you can't train with him lately, so he asked me to train you, the absolute next best option! Care for a session today?"

"No he didn't," I say, with a tilted head. Great. Lawrence now knows I train with Alas, thanks to Ryder.

Ryder reaches in his pocket and pulls out a signed note. He hands it to me so I can see that it's for real. "Seems like something he would do," Lawrence mutters. He tells us, "I'll observe, if you want to do it real quick."

They both look at me, Ryder with eager eyes. There's no easy way to say no without looking like an idiot. "Sure," I mumble. There goes my free time.

"Great! You can be paired with my trainee, Lilah; she's a crystal controller, and a real prodigy."

Lawrence gives me a wince.

"Let's start, then," I answer. I thought I was going to work with Ryder; maybe this is better. But I don't know who the hell Lilah is. I've never sparred with a geomancer of any kind, though I figure they have to be pretty similar to a metal manipulator.

We start towards to the sparring circle; a woman, apparently Lilah, is already in her starting position. As I open the door, Lawrence puts a hand on my shoulder and whispers, "We can just walk out of this. Alas won't care if you don't train." His chest is out, while his brown eyes are gleaming with a prayer that I won't spar today.

I smile. "Practice never hurts." I refuse to back out of a challenge from Ryder. Plus, it's been a few days since I've sparred with anyone. I step into the circle. Lilah and I don't say a word to each other. She's tall, with silver hair, and looks like she's built to take out aggression on others. Much older than me. Her outfit is decked in crystals, and her jewelry is styled to hold as much crystal as possible.

I want to observe her more before we spar, but Ryder immediately yells, "Start!"

Lilah races to the other side of the circle. I move just as quickly, and pull out to the room for the water to come. It flows over the walls and to my side. I use the water to make an ice shield. From what I know, anyone who can control a solid substance has the instinct to create a weapon first. I'm correct in my thoughts, and learn Lilah doesn't like to play defense. She makes three crystal shards from her jewelry. I catch a flash of her eyes. She wastes no time and launches the daggers through the air towards me.

I lift my shield, and feel the impact as they all pierce the ice. I drop my shield and use my free hand to create a staff. It's a short, staggered, sharp piece of work. Lilah races closer, jumping to try and reach my weapon. She launches her foot up and makes a swing, trying to drop-kick it from my hands. I move back just enough to make her miss. A kick from a farther distance isn't as effective as a close one. In the time it takes her to kick, I have the chance to swing her leg out from under her. She falls to the ground. I stumble back but don't fall, which gives her time to stand back up.

Another dagger forms and darts at my head. I use my staff to deflect the knife.

Lilah sweeps her hand to the ground and collects two daggers that have fallen from her first attack. I morph my staff to be smaller, so I can get in closer. I throw a punch with my other hand. She dodges. She lunges for my arm with dagger in hand. No one is calling time. I wrap Lilah's wrist under my arms and keep it locked in.

She fights like Theo. They both only want to play offense and make sharp, quick advances, to make it a very aggressive fight.

Lilah changes her course of action and moves the dagger to my shoulder. If she has the intention of cutting me open, she could have. She just wants to show how close she is.

Pressure sinks into my skin. Pins and needles consume my throat. Lilah has turned her blade and applied pressure the necklace, causing it to break.

My body has no power. I fall back onto the ground and look up at Lilah, gasping. She doesn't know what's happening.

I hear a yell.

The room closes in. My conscience goes silent.

I'm gone.

CHAPTER 18

Alas POV

I'm late for my third meeting of the day by at least ten minutes. This day's going all wrong. No one seems to be where they should. I'm running amok. I glance into the sparring room. Maybe Trinity's in there. I have no clue where she is, but I need to find her. She should've been in the last meeting, and wasn't. I don't want her flaking out of the next one.

All I see is Lawrence. He throws his hands onto the sparring circle glass, and is screaming something. I lunge for the door. His face is hollowed out; he's staring into the abyss. I run into the room; they're all dead silent, except Lawrence. "Leave the room!" he roars to everyone.

"Lawrence," I call. He's looking at Isadora in the sparring circle. Some girl is holding her by the waist, trying to keep her off the ground, her eyes pleading to anyone who will look for help. "Lawrence!" I call again.

Someone on the other side of the room mumbles something. Lawrence turns to them and yells louder, "I said *leave!*"

His face is bright red His eyes have fallen short of any light. I walk to him, mortified by his appearance, and grab his arm. "What is this?"

"She's fucking dead, Alas! The necklace broke!"

His words suck the soul out of me. Lawrence races into the sparring circle; Ryder and I follow him in. The room is now empty besides us and the other girl. She pleads, "I don't know—I don't know what happened." Her hand is around Isadora, her grip loosening. I reach down to feel Isadora's wrist. There's no pulse. I lean down further, and move Isadora out of the girl's arms and lay her on my legs. "What the hell happened?" I snap at Ryder. "How did you *let* this happen? I asked for *you* to spar with her, not someone random!"

"I didn't know," Ryder says without a beat.

Lawrence is going to break; I can see it in his face. His mind goes blank when anything bad happens; he can't think when his emotions are running wild. I study the marks left on Isadora's neck from the necklace. I spot the pendent across the circle, lying on the ground, still glistening in the light.

"Lawrence," I say urgently, "Lawrence, it's okay."

"*Okay?* She's dead!" he wails at me, with the grief plain on his face.

"Carac has his ability. He can bring her back. Leave, please," I say to Ryder and the girl. I'll have words with Ryder later, when I'm calm enough to speak without anger. Lawrence stands up and wipes his eyes.

Once they're gone, Lawrence asks me, "Do we get Daymond?"

At the same time, I ponder, "Do we contact Carac?"

Lawrence takes a seat on the ground. "I have no clue. We could write Carac a letter…?"

"That will take too long."

Lawrence barks, "He's going to *want* something. I hope you realize that. I doubt that he would bring her back without expecting something."

We both soak in the silence. There's nothing more to say that can change anything, nothing we can do that will fix this.

After minutes of muteness, a huge breath unexpectedly comes from Isadora. She gasps for air like she's been held underwater for minutes. I wince and hold her side. She coughs out her lungs, then sits up and holds her chest. I croak, "You nearly gave me a heart attack!"

Meanwhile, Lawrence is saying a bunch of word along the lines of "You're alive!"

She's shaking her head while catching her breath. "What?" she asks after listening.

"I died?!" she exclaims, as if she's suddenly realized what has happened.

Lawrence asks, "You don't remember dying?"

She's still processing what she's being told. "I do, vaguely, but I've never been killed before." I watch her hand climb her neck, feeling for the necklace that's no longer there. "I *died.*"

Lawrence tells her, "You were dead for ten minutes." I was hoping for that time frame; however, it feels like hours have passed. He pushes himself up off the ground and shouts, "We have to do something!" His voice echoes off the walls.

"We have three days!" I counter.

"That doesn't mean anything!" he snaps. "I'm tired of hearing it!"

"*It means everything.* I have a plan, and I have ways to fix things. I just need to get past these three days."

I get up and leave the sparring room. I'm sick of Lawrence and his attitude. I'm sick of dealing with constant problems, and there's no way this one is going to go away.

I'm far down the hallway when Lawrence yells from the other end, "You have a plan?"

Isadora isn't behind him. She must have stayed back.

I keep walking; I don't even want to look at Lawrence. That doesn't stop him from continuing, "You didn't think it would be smart to tell us your grand plan?"

At this point, Lawrence has matched my pace and caught up to me in the hall. He gives me no room to ignore his comments. I take a breath; I try to speak cautiously, and not take my frustration out on him. "This isn't a good time to talk about it."

"You have no intention of telling us? We're more involved in this than you!"

"We?" I ask. "Isadora has every right to say that, but you don't." I lean close, and to repair my harsh words, say, "However, I have no problem telling you my ideas."

"Well, go on then." Lawrence glances around, making sure no one is in the halls with us.

I continue to walk while I speak to my brother. "The overall best plan is to form a peace treaty with Din Point, and then eliminate Carac."

"Correct me if I'm wrong," Lawrence says with a condescending smile, "but if you have a peace treaty with a kingdom, you can't go and kill the leader, yes?"

"Carac isn't in power yet, and *we* aren't going to kill him."

"They can sometimes trace assassins—you know that, right? That's not something we should risk doing."

"I plan to sponsor a rebel group. They've been trying to kill Carac for years, but they need more funding to be successful. We slide them money under the table and hope for the best. Worst case scenario, they fail and get themselves killed. We stay out of it."

"Okay," Lawrence agrees. "I see the appeal in the plan, but after Carac dies, who rises to power?"

"I haven't figured that out yet, but these rebel groups have people they favor. It would be hard to get someone worse."

Lawrence nods.

"My biggest goal is for us all to stop losing lives in this pointless war, a war started by people who are long gone, and to get the people in Din Point some serious help," I point out.

"Why can't we just fight to the end and take over Din Point?" Lawrence asks, playing devil's advocate. I know he doesn't want the war. Anything to do with war makes his skin burn and his head ache, but he's trying to argue all sides.

Nevertheless, I counter, "We can't win. If we had some allies, it could work, but there's no hope for that. I'm all for trying to win the war, but Din Point's army is double the size of ours. We have to end the war before they figure that out and know they can trample us."

"What about Vaddel?" Lawrence asks, "Their alliance would mean winning the war."

"Are you serious? Vaddel hasn't spoken to an outside kingdom in hundreds of years."

"But if we try hard enough, if we can get even a tenth of Vaddel's warriors, we could win!"

"You don't think I've thought about it? Over the centuries, hundreds of letters have been sent, alongside valuable items. We've gotten nothing in response."

"So, it's hopeless to continue the war?" Lawrence inquires, relieved.

"The only way for us to even, maybe, have the smallest, tiniest chance would be a major draft. That would ruin our economy and take people away from their homes. We'd be pulling in everyone—farmers, parents, doctors—and damaging ourselves at the same time Din Point would be attacking us. I don't want to do that. I don't think it would even work."

We arrive at my room, but I keep talking. "The best thing we can do is get rid of Carac after we make a treaty. Then we'll try our best to get them a leader with some sanity."

"So why didn't you tell us this before? It seems like a plausible plan."

I let Lawrence come inside my room. I shut the door behind him and admit, "Because of Isadora. I know she won't be supportive of us killing Carac."

"Isadora hates him. He killed her today! If anything, she'll want to help take him down."

"I don't think so." I watch Lawrence check out my room. It's been a while since he came in. It's a mess; maps everywhere, books flooding my table, a sword lying on the floor.

Lawrence has the same sword, I suddenly remember. It's tucked behind his door and wrapped up. A gift we each got from our father.

I let Lawrence walk around my room and look around as I keep talking. "You hear how she talks about him. He was her best friend, and practically her family until a year ago. As much as she hates him, I don't think she wants him dead. Isadora has asked for protection and defense. She's never once asked for us to get rid of Carac."

Lawrence knits in his brows. He hates everything I've said, but I know he's making sense of it. I can tell that he's annoyed that I have a plan. He's spent the last few days cursing about the fact that I'm not doing anything productive when, really, I'm running all over the place, making things happen.

He looks at me. I want a response, but he doesn't have one to give. Instead, I fill the space. "You should probably go be with her. After all, she just came back to life. Who knows what that does to a person?"

CHAPTER 19

Isadora POV

There's no way of stopping a smile from crossing my face as I look in the mirror. Today means so much to Alas. I can't think straight. The joy I feel for him is overwhelming every movement I make.

This is the one day that came sooner than expected, but we've all been looking forward to it. The only thing that's keeping me from completely losing control of my emotions is that I've been able to sleep in late and rest. I've also been able to dismiss the maids today and get ready myself. It's been a while since I got the opportunity to do my own makeup or even take care of myself, really. The room, and this energy from having a breather, are setting a tranquil tone as I paint my face. I move slowly to my closet and begin to get dressed. My outfit floods out like a waterfall catching wind. It's cut shorter in the front and waves its way longer behind me. The blue and white mix together to create an outfit I actually want to wear.

I move back to my vanity, really just to touch up and kill time as I wait to be taken to the carriage for the ceremony. Alas will have his wedding and coronation at the arena, for the public to watch and fawn over. It shouldn't be much longer until I have to go, but I have time to sit and think. Luckily, I don't have to participate in anything today. My marriage to Lawrence was what imbedded me into becoming a princess. I don't need to be crowned. Today is solely for Alas and Trinity.

I hear the door open slowly. I look in the mirror, ready to see a guard behind me.

Carac, of all people, paces into my room. I purse my lips and tilt my head back. Frustration vibrates through me. He's walking in and out of the castle like he owns the damned place. The way he thinks he can just stroll in here, especially after his bloody necklace *killed me*, makes me furious. He's a leader of the sole enemy of Parten, and he walks around here like it's his birthright—and everyone lets him. He has to have someone here working with him—or the guards are purely incompetent.

He shuts the door behind him and takes a seat on the edge of my bed. I swing my legs around the chair to face him. I'm not going to play any of his little games. Today is the first time in a while that I've felt calm, and I'm not letting him ruin it. I'm not going to let him drive me mad today. I clamp my mouth tightly shut and stare him down.

Carac raises an eyebrow at my steadiness. He wasn't expecting me to not do anything, I can tell it's a surprise. He sighs, "I'm not here to hurt you. I just want to talk."

"That's what you always say." I give him a sharp look.

"If you'll just have *one* conversation with me, I promise I won't do anything at today's ceremony, and I'll return home right after we talk."

"Okay," I say, glaring at him. If one short conversation with Carac is insurance that Alas won't be bothered today, I'll do it. He crosses his legs. There's something about me not reacting that's making him uncomfortable.

"Why did you do it?" Carac blurts. "Marry Lawrence? You were supposed to be with *me*, Isadora. You screwed yourself out of that, and now you're married to a prince of a kingdom we were born to hate."

"If I had married you, I would have been giving in to the command of terrible ruler. You were also the one who imprisoned me after the Zaven thing..."

His tone turns instantly more dangerous as he speaks out harshly, "Now you're exactly where you didn't want to be then! Married to someone you don't love, and a princess. The Zaven thing would have blown over with time!"

"And in that time, you would have executed me," I snap, still not over the memories. He would have seen me killed in that prison.

"You *really* think I would have executed you?" he asks me flatly, with no emotion.

"I was in that cell for a week," I grind out. "Xeres made it clear that I was going to die any day. I know I'd have been dead if I'd stayed. And then you hunted me for months."

"I wasn't going to kill y—"

I cut him off, "If you didn't kill me, then Xeres would have. Castilla would have. Theo, their parents, someone on the Din Point council would have found a way to kill me." I end that side of the conversation, my body aching at the thought of Zaven. I push forward to the other issue at hand: "Either way, if I stuck around in Din Point, I'd be married you, it would be real, and we would be sitting around waiting to take the throne and further fuel a council that was destroying the kingdom. This marriage I'm in now isn't real. You know that, and so does everyone else. I married Lawrence because he listens to me and promises to advance this kingdom. He cares, and he wants to do good. Look at yourself, Carac; Din Point is crumbling, and you plan to do nothing about it. Using your power for amusement is morally reprehensible." I'm breaking the serene setting I'd just created. My voice is still steady, but having to spell it out for Carac is infuriating, especially when he *knows* and can read exactly how I'm feeling.

Carac stands up. Immediately, I do the same and face him. I can't leave anything unprepared.

He looks me in the eye and asks, "You honestly think Lawrence doesn't want something? That he doesn't want a wife? That he won't want to hold you, or touch you or be with you? You married him, Isadora; he's going to use you to his advantage in time."

I step back, as the possibilities of this conversation flow over me. Lawrence hasn't wanted a thing from me, at least nothing Carac is talking about, but it dawns on me that Lawrence may have something going on that I've overlooked.

I've been staring off into the distance, which gives Carac time to step closer to me. I feel my throat close, feeling the way he looks at me. He's so wholesome in the moment, as if his intentions are for the best, as if the past has never happened. As if everything is gone, and it's just us. He's close enough for me to look up at him and feel his breath. It's been such a long time since I've felt I could trust him. Since I could stand this close to him and only feel my body aching to move in closer. There's a comfort in the discussion that's been absent from me for a long while. I feel his hand move to my waist.

He leans in and softly says, "Come back to Din Point with me. Come and be my queen. Change my mind about everything... Everything will change if you come back."

I choke as he leans in and softly kisses my lips. It's light and warm, a sensation I've missed and longed for. I place a hand on his chest and pull him in slightly before I push him back and create enough distance to speak, our faces still touching, our lips barely apart. "Make me want to come back," I plead to him.

I move my face back enough to look up and stare into his green eyes, which seem to have a light shining behind them. A light that he will never let anyone take, even if it shines from the wrong place.

"What do you want?" he asks, his voice husky.

"I want change; I want to live there and not fear for my life every moment. I want to see a change in our life, and the people's. To not see this downfall continue."

"I..." he pauses, lifting his chin, his jaw tightening, "I can't undo the downfall. I can't change the council, Isadora. That's not my job."

"That *is* your job. That's the *one thing* you'll be able to do when you become king."

His hands drop from my sides. The tension builds in his voice as he says, "*None* of this is my job. Din Point, the council, the people—none of them are my issues. My job is to make sure we make it out of this stupid political game with as few losses as possible." He steps a foot away from me and scoffs, "There is *so* much you don't understand. So many things are changing all around us, and Din Point is the least of my concerns out of all those. You're missing so many of the real issues, Isadora."

I swallow all the things I want to yell at him. I way I want to tell him off until there's nothing left of him. But instead I find a middle ground and say, "You asked me to come back. I told you what I wanted in order for me to do that, but you can't get past your own self-hatred and agenda to care—to even give a second's thought to the fact that you may not *like* your job, but you were born to be a king, and you are the one person who can fix this mess."

"I was *not* born to be a king," he insists. "The one thing I was born to be was in a team with you. And you can't even understand that, not even after all these years!"

"A year ago, I would have come running at your offer to take me back. I loved you, Carac, more than anyone in the word. But you've changed; you've slipped off the end of the rope, just like they wanted you to. And now you've lost hope of doing anything that would help the people of your nation. The only reason you came back to get me was so you could tell yourself it's okay to let your own people suffer, as long as you have someone who loves you."

"You want to help the people? Then come back and stop trying to do it in a kingdom you aren't even from," he says with bitter undertones.

"You wouldn't let me change a damn thing if I came back, would you?"

He nods his head, anger and pride showing through his gestures. "You'll come back at this point. I don't really care on what terms. You know I like challenges, so bring all you have, make it interesting."

"Go to hell," I spit before I even realize the words have left my lips.

He bites his lip inward before cocking his head and cracking his knuckles. He crosses his arms and says, "Fine. I'll go to hell, and I'll bring this kingdom and my own with me."

I turn away from Carac, and I hear him quickly walk out the door. I feel the breath come back to my lungs. Everything I've wanted to say to him came rolling out in that conversation. He's been using his obsession with me to compensate for his growing insecurity that he might be in the wrong. I felt myself falling for his words during the conversation, but at the end of the day, he's Carac, and that's what he does best.

Today is Coronation Day, and today promises hope: a hope that we've all been longing to see resurface. I rush down the halls, picking up the hem of my dress to avoid tripping. No guards have come to get me; that has to be because of Carac. Either way, I'm late, and Lawrence is most defiantly not. My heart is pounding, either from running or from the conversation Carac still replaying in my head.

"Where were you?" Lawrence complains.

"I'm so sorry," I say, trying to control the flustered tones, "I got caught up in getting ready."

"We had maids to help you be on time," he lectures, taking my hand and escorting me into the car.

"I excused the maids."

He glances at me as the car starts to move. He shakes his head slightly, but then just looks out the window. It isn't worth an argument to him. He doesn't say another word to me on the ride over to the stadium. Time passes much faster than expected. We arrive through the back entrance. I barely catch a glimpse of Alas through the passages. I had forgotten the insanity of Coronation Day. It's a day filled with advisors, skeptics, loyalists, haters, lovers, and royalists. The pressure he must be feeling... I can't even imagine, yet Alas looks the same. His hair is combed, teeth brushed and under-eyes gone, excluding calm. He always comes off as well put-together, which I'm sure is the goal, but his appearance never changes. Today he's wearing a suit with gold designs imbedded in it, with medals hanging from his chest. It has micro-tidbits of red and blue that weave through the fabric around his shoulders. As we pass, I see the light hit his eyes and make them glow.

The only thing that might be stressful for him is his father crowning him. It adds pressure to the day to make sure that the king is feeling well. The kingdom hasn't seen anything that indicates anything is wrong with King Rubeus, which is the idea. Alas and his mother want the king's legacy to about his rule, not his sickness.

Alas' mother will pass her crown down to Trinity. It's a whole new era of royals. With every little piece of the day flooding around, it adds tension to the room. Alas is unruffled, though. He isn't even nervous. I've told him it's okay to have some nerves—it's a sign of excitement—but as we pass, Alas is steady as a rock. He's talking to some officials without missing a beat. Maybe not having nerves is a sign of a good ruler.

Alas cuffs his sleeves in and takes a breath. He moves a hand to the back of his head and smiles brightly. He's ready to be king. He's the type of person who has everything figured out. The kind of person who plans out their sentences, down to the adjectives and pauses. The kind of person who's ready to change this kingdom.

Lawrence grabs my hand, making me follow him to our seats. Because we came so late, there's no time to say anything to anyone. We sit down in the front row, closest to the thrones on which they will be coronated. Where we're seated is a separate section on the side of the floor in the arena. Advisors are seated behind us, and behind them is everyone else. The arena is flooded with people; they have a large turnout, from what I can tell. The stadium must be at its compacity. But not everyone in the kingdom can attend the coronation, which is why the monitors buzz around us.

It's the same buzz I heard on the Day of Selection. The last time I was in this stadium, I was trembling with fear, scared of the future that was dangled in front of me. Now here I sit, Lawrence's hand warm in mine. The buzzing feeling tingles my soul with hope, and promises to make those fears go away forever.

I look around for Daymond, but he must be in his box high above the crowd. Voices continue to fog the sounds of the stadium until music hits our hears, telling us that the ceremony is starting. Alas walks out with his chin up, chest out, and shoulders back. Trinity walks by his side, gliding to her throne. They both beam with royalty and power. Alas surveys his the people with a glittering smile, and takes a seat on his throne with perfect posture.

Lawrence has told me the ceremony is long and extravagant. It's been a tradition since the creation of Parten. It starts when the former King and Queen give their speeches, serving as a promise for the new rulers.

Both Trinity and Alas take the oath that swears their allegiance to the kingdom and their intentions to do no wrong, to rule in the promise of discipline, axiom, and justice, to express mercy and value, along with power and poise. If only they made the Din Point leaders swear to that!

Finally, after the speeches and oaths, it's time to crown Alas and Trinity. The Queen crowns Trinity first, because she's getting married into royalty. This is also her wedding celebration. The Queen takes the crown slowly off her own head. It sparkles with jewels that are held in place by rose gold. The different shades of rose and pink crystals shine in the light and catch the eyes of everyone in the room. She lowers the crown onto Trinity's head. Trinity takes a seat back on her throne, the applause on hold, waiting for Alas to be crowned.

King Rubeus is clearly ready to get the crown off his head. It's finally lifted off. It's a radiant crown, the ultimate symbol of power. Alas holds his head up as the crown is placed on him. It takes shape in his hair flawlessly; he was born to wear that crown.

Alas is now *King* Alas. The stadium roars. Queen Trinity stands up as the celebration takes off.

I turn to Lawrence, but he's facing forward. He looks upon his bother with narrowed eyes. He watches his father award a nod of approval to Alas.

It's about time that Alas feels the weight of the crown.

CHAPTER 20

Alas POV

It's a week after the coronation, and I'm drained. I march the halls, trying to find Lawrence. I downright hate how massive the palace is, and the fact that I still get confused when walking around it. The first place I'm going to look for him is his room. I knock heavily on the door, and wait as Lawrence slowly opens it.

He looks me up and down and says, "You have a dent in your hair already."

I roll my eyes. He means from the crown I'm wearing. I shift it around; he's just making me worry already. I shake it off and say, "Din Point's King Argys just contacted me. He's willing to consider a peace treaty."

His face lights up. "That's great, Alas!"

"All of us will be attending dinner tonight with his council. They're flying in this evening."

"Isadora included?" he asks.

"Her presence was specifically requested."

"That means Carac is coming. We can't make her go."

I don't want to hear Lawrence's complaints; it's not my fault she has to go. It still twists my insides, though, to make her do so. "We need this treaty, Lawrence. She just has to make it through one night. Will you tell her?"

Lawrence glances at my hand. "Got the ring?" he leers, not responding to my question.

I'm wearing the King's Ring now; I got it after the ceremony. The public's sign of power is my crown, but anyone inside of the castle knows it's the King's Ring that signals the true power. They get a new crown every so often—the old ones are kept locked away—but the King's Ring has been around forever. It never gets replaced or changed out. Every kingdom's ruler has one. Even if a Queen leads a bloodline, she wears her kingdom's Ring. As long as you have the royal blood, you wear the Ring.

"Will you tell her?" I ask again.

Lawrence's attention bounces back. "I'll figure something out."

Isadora POV

The day continues as planned. I'm spending time with Lawrence as we attend to our schedules. The castle feels quieter, as things have fallen into order. With everything Alas and Trinity are planning, they're drowning in work.

Lawrence and I can't really help with any of it; we just get to do a few careless things.

As we walk through the halls, Lawrence turns to me with a red face. "Isadora..." he begins. I move to the side of the hall. He turns his diction to a more serious tone. "We, you have to attend a state dinner tonight."

"Okay," I say, dismissing his worry and starting to walk away. He grabs my arm. "With the Din Point royals."

"What?" I exclaim, while trying to maintain a low voice. "You're telling me *now?*"

"I'm sorry. I thought it would be better if you didn't have to worry about it all day. I just found out this morning." Lawrence has good intentions with bad excuses.

"It's fine," I reassure him. He did the right thing, as far as he knew how to. There's nothing I can do besides focus on the greater good... and it's not long until dinner. "I'm going to go get ready, then."

He allows me to leave. "I'll see you soon," he agrees, and walks the other way from me.

I storm down the hall, taking a sharp turn. My stomach drops as I see Trinity and Ryder share a quick kiss. A quick peck of a *passionate* kiss.

I retreat around the corner. They didn't see me. I lean against the wall, processing what I've just witnessed. It makes sense now; the letters, Ryder being a hell-raiser, their secret conversations. A while back, Alas even said he knew something was going on. I just didn't believe it.

Trinity is Queen. She's married and vowed to Alas. There's nothing I can do. Alas has made it clear before that he doesn't want to deal with the whole outbreak of accusing Trinity if his suspicions are right.

Ryder walks around the corner. He has a smile on his face as he notices me. He clearly doesn't know I saw anything. "You all right, Princess?" he taunts.

"Fine," I reply, and continue down the hall. I genuinely wish I hadn't seen anything.

CHAPTER 21

Isadora POV

Lawrence and I arrive not a second late or early to dinner. In the dining room, Alas and Trinity are already sitting at the head of the table.

I gaze upon Trinity and her perfect smile. All that fills my head is her scandal. Honestly, I can't even judge or think badly of her because of it. I kissed Carac. Maybe I didn't mean to, but I still did, when he came to me before the coronation.

The memories trample my thoughts. There's nothing I can do about it. Nothing I can do to take back what I did, and nothing I can say about Trinity if Alas just prefers to ignore it.

Alas' stare follows me. His eyes narrow; he's annoyed with something. He gestures to the seat to the left of Trinity. He commands, "Lawrence, you sit here." And then he points to the one on the left of that: "Isadora."

We take our seats. I notice how there are only a few chairs in the room. This is Alas' first political dinner without his parents. He doesn't have any advisors in the room, either. I watch him for a moment; he's well aware of every move he's made.

The room is highly decorated with fancy silverware and items of value as centerpieces. The table is large enough to fit double the seating it has been set for.

After a moment, the silence is broken by the door opening; this time it's the royal guests entering. They arrive with a few Din Point guards mixed with Parten guards as escorts; it adds safety for everyone. We all stand and shake hands with everyone in the room. Din Point's King is received first, and politely grips our hands. He doesn't look at me, even for a moment. I'm a part of his past he wishes to erase.

His Queen, Edisa, follows his movements, and sits down across from Lawrence. She has the most beautiful silver hair and a dress that flows, waving through with power. She glances to me, with a slight fake smile as a sign of our past. I can see that she secretly hates me; she wanted me dead just as much as everyone else, and probably more now. I remember how much I wanted to be her as a child. Now I'm disgusted by the thought.

There's already tension in the room, some that I've never really let go of and probably never will. The Din Point royals used me and Carac our whole lives. They locked me up, set a price tag on my head, and killed my parents after they slipped up in the council.

I wasn't even close with my parents growing up. They only had Daymond and I so that they could use us to their advantage. They brought us into the world and passed down their cryomancy... and that was all they did for us. They didn't raise me: Daymond did. But even if we weren't close, their executions show what they royals will do to keep the council under their control. They kill over small matters that they perceived as early rising threats.

If the mood in the room isn't already rough enough, Carac comes in with his usual style. He wears all black, with silver piping around his suit. His aesthetic is shadowy and contemporary colors. I stop breathing as Carac shakes Alas' hand. The stiffness in the room increases as he makes his way from Trinity to Lawrence. Carac then moves to me.

Instead of shaking my hand, Carac politely turns it over and gently kisses it; the temperature in the room rises just the slightest. I make eye contact with Carac, challenging his cunning stare. He has not a drop of fear in his eyes.

I glance at Alas, and hope he can make this dinner go faster.

The Din Point King, Argys, makes a point to change the focus of the center of attention as we all sit down.

Alas collects himself and sits. He and the visitors exchange the customary small talk about their flight and the weather as the food comes out. The dinner needs to be swift, before someone fouls it up. I only listen in on their conversation, holding back any comments or thoughts I have. This isn't the time for me to speak out; I can do that later, when it's just Alas and Trinity.

Carac manages to keep a straight face, and, on occasion, smirks at me.

Lawrence's hand grips mine under the table. It's a pure feeling of comfort to have him by my side. Carac watches everyone's movements, and duly notes Lawrence's.

They finally to talk about a treaty. It all seems swift enough, with Alas making remarks and them altering it to make things work. Meanwhile, Carac straightens his posture and shifts his attention to Lawrence. I don't want to pay such close attention to Carac, but he *makes* me want to. His first words of the night are, "Father, why don't you bring up the topic we discussed earlier?"

The king doesn't even look in Carac's direction, but moves the conversation in a different direction. "King Alas," Argys says kindly. "As we mentioned before, it's in our best interests to start the treaty off with a trade. Now, my proposal is for you to allow Princess Isadora to travel to Din Point—"

Lawrence inhales sharply. He looks at King Argys like he must be joking and says, "If you even think—"

Argys continues senselessly, "—for a few months. In return, we'll give you the most promising female influence possible for Lawrence to be with. Castilla Shade."

I feel Lawrence try to speak again. I grip his hand harshly and whisper so low only he can hear: "Don't say anything." I can take care of this in a much smoother manner than he can.

I gape at Carac in a near awe. He really *is* trying to give Castilla to Parten. She's nothing but pure trouble. Meanwhile, Alas gives the Din Point royals an empty, fake smile. "I will have to decline that offer," he says firmly.

"Even if it's in the best interests of your kingdom?" Queen Edisa counters.

Carac shifts to face me, quietly mouthing, "I'll make it interesting."

I prepare myself. If accepting this offer means a peace treaty, if it means stopping a war, I'll do it in a second. I have no problem going back to Din Point if it ends this war. I open my mouth to speak, but before I get a word out, Carac says, "Never mind; maybe, Father, you should try and trade a more concrete item."

I blink in relief. I was about to do the worst possible thing for myself, and give in. King Argys speaks again: "I see I've overstepped the boundaries. How about, instead, a trade of artifacts?"

Alas nods; he seems completely willing to trade now. "That sounds better."

Carac smiles with amusement stemming from this conversation. My head is reeling. If it had dragged on any longer, I'd be packing my bags, and Carac knows that.

"I recommend we change rooms to sign the treaty. Somewhere more official, with an opportunity to review things with our advisors," Alas announces, while standing up.

The dinner was just for the sake of being polite. Alas needs his council present to sign off on the treaty, and Din Point is sure to need the same.

The conversation moves to a boardroom where the entire advisory group waits. Alas rushes to his people, and Trinity starts to fill every one of them in on the conversation.

Lawrence and I sit down, but as we do, Carac struts over and asks, "Isadora, a word?"

I'm in a room filled with people; he can't do much to cause trouble. I agree to speak with him, and rise out of my chair. Lawrence stands up as I do, giving me a nod as if saying, *You aren't talking to him alone.* But before he can go with us, Alas snaps his fingers and beckons, "Lawrence, read this," while pointing to a document. Alas is only paying attention to this treaty, as he should.

There is so much commotion as they draft the treaty. I nod to Lawrence, and walk to the back of the room with Carac. We sit on two presidential chairs and watch the divided sides of the rooms get to work. He lowers his voice and keeps it quiet as he ponders, "You're welcome for earlier."

I have no reason to be surprised by him wanting to be dramatic. I brush myself off and hold it together. "For what?" I ask with fake charm.

Lawrence is now continuously glancing back at us, along with several advisors, watching our actions. There is no way they can hear us through the commotion of voices in the room.

The two sides keep going back and forward with negotiations, side offers, and positions being discussed. This is a horrible way to draft a document. Meanwhile, Carac leans back on his chair. "For changing the course of the agreement. I know you were about to open your mouth back there."

"You have no idea what I was going to say," I chastise. Carac is now acting as if our last conversation never happened. He always does this; he gets under people skin and starts arguments, only to later act as if they were nothing.

"Really?" he laughs a little, "You weren't going to agree to trade yourself for the treaty?"

He knows how to read my face, and is playing off it. "You have no class," I inform him.

Carac runs a hand through his thick, dark hair. "You have to admit I'm the best ever for stopping the trade."

I promptly tell him, "Other words come to mind."

Amused, he raises his eyes brows. "Such as?"

"Malicious, manipulative, annoying, lethal…" I stop myself as I realized he's enjoying me criticizing him in such a manner, and that I've said the words a little too loudly.

Lawrence continues to side-eye the two of us. and calls out, "Isadora, I need your opinion on this."

"Running back so fast?" Carac mocks as I start to stand. I lift a finger to Lawrence to signal him to wait a second. "I want to tell you something," Carac lightly says as I sit back down.

"Go on, then."

"I don't think you should have gotten on board with this treaty. I wish you would have talked to me before Alas called for this."

"I didn't know about Alas arranging this, or even about the dinner, until earlier today. Even if I had, I wouldn't have talked to you about it based off our last talk anyway."

"I think this is all a drastic mistake," he says with a grave voice.

"Why?"

"This treaty may produce a good outcome for Parten, but I think Din Point is going to suffer a major backlash."

"We're ending a war. This should be good for both sides."

"Din Point is going to get worse because of this. Ending the war is something we should have strived for, but in a different way."

"How would we have ended this war without a treaty?"

Carac leans back in the chair and taps his fingers on the armrest. While looking over the room, he softly says, "By eliminating Din Point. I'm not advocating for my kingdom to go away, but I think this is going to make everything worse for us. Neither Alas nor you has thought about the consequences of this."

"I don't see any negative ones," I reply harshly.

"Isadora," Lawrence again calls out.

Carac shakes his head a bit while rolling his shoulders back. "I was just giving you my opinion."

"Thanks. I'll talk to you soon, I'm sure."

I stand and walk away from him and his puzzling conversation. It could have gone a lot worse, but I really don't understand what he's trying to warn me about when he makes such vague statements.

I stroll over to Lawrence and read some of the verbiage as they're typing up things. Alas is in charge of all this mess, and he's doing his absolute best to control his worries. After what feels like hours of talking, they sign the treaty.

King Alas has just ended one of the most horrific wars in Parten's history.

CHAPTER 22

Isadora POV

I 've been keeping most things to myself, and they're starting to build up.

I haven't told my brother about any of my Carac interactions. They're out of the loop with most of my life at the moment. I'm sure Daymond guesses what's going on; he's filled in on most everything, and now he has some time to breathe with the war being over. Alas used Daymond's input when he decided to end the war. Daymond is the one who said we didn't have long until Din Point figured out that they could trample us if they wanted. But now, Daymond is out somewhere helping the troops get back home.

Alas, Trinity, and I went out in celebration the day after the treaty. We met the public and welcomed the troops coming home. My heart throbbed from the crowds being filled with smiles. The whole week was a pure moment. Lawrence stayed back from the celebrations to catch up on the work he's been putting off. With Lawrence so busy, I have more time to work with Trinity and Alas. And I have more time to do my own things, and even watch the monitor.

Monitors are scarce, and used for new reports only. They're usually displayed in public places or fancy businesses. Regular families in Parten don't typically own a monitor. I used to just read the paper like everyone else, but in the palace, we have monitors everywhere. I decide to hang out in Lawrence's room while he works. I sit against the couch and turn on the monitor.

A reporter from Din Point is on the screen. She's not the usual anti-Parten announcer.

Her voice is fragile. "As we speak, hundreds are on their way to prison. The trouble last night wasn't the fault of those returning, but the fault of our government."

I can't follow what's happening. My breath begins to shorten in worry. Who's being imprisoned?

Lawrence puts down his work and turns to watch it too. He moves to sit next to me, then grabs the controller and rewinds the broadcast.

We're now watching the start of the report. Already, the announcer looks terrible. She states, "The war with Parten ended just under two days ago, causing a horrifying effect." The reporter covers her mouth to keep from breaking down. She tries to breathe and collect herself.

Lawrence can't watch the pain on her face. Quietly, he mutters, "I don't understand."

The reporter continues, "Hundreds of thousands are being sent back home from the front lines, from what had been their only escape from what the kingdom has become. Thousands have no homes or families to return to. The list to enroll in the war has spiked in the last few years, but now their dreams of escape are lost. Soldiers are returning to severe unrest. Those with lost lives are living in chaos. As we speak, hundreds are on their way to prison. The trouble last night wasn't the fault of those returning, but the fault of our government."

I feel my eyes burning as I shut them to hide the tears that are forming.

The reporter is now rushing her words: "The government planned those fires, outbreaks, and attacks. It wasn't the returning soldiers' fault! The population is out of hand, and they needed an excuse to explode. They couldn't handle the waves of people returning."

The reporter slams her hands on her desk and yells, "Listen to me! Those being imprisoned are innocent! This was planned; hundreds of thousands will suffer in the next few weeks because of end of the war. Before, there was an escape for the disgruntled, and a way for the government to control the death count. Now they're doing it by turning everyone against each other! You have to join together, or they will continue to blame the innocent. The end has already started here if w—"

The screen goes black; static follows. I suspect it's not only the live feed that's dead.

I lean back. I stop breathing. I blink rapidly. My face turns red, and my throat begins to close. My chest goes hollow as my hands shake. I choke out, "We did more harm than good by ending the war!" My mind starts to waver. I can no longer think clearly through what I'd been warned of by Carac.

Lawrence's mouth twists; his expression closes off. "We saved people in *our* kingdom. Din Point has its own issues. Let them deal with them."

"We caused the end of the war. Din Point has issues, but now it's royal cruelty."

"Din Point has always had terrible rulers. We can't fix that."

I get up and pace, unable to stay still. This is a disaster on a multitude of levels.

"They reached out to us to stop the war before Alas even had a chance to. Th-they knew what they we-were doing," I stutter at Lawrence.

I storm out of the room and only hear the start of Lawrence's speech. The tears drip from my face as I rush through the halls away from him. My breathing closes off as I dash into my room and take out pen and paper. I rapidly write a letter and try to keep my body from shaking. The hurt in my heart is growing with every thought. Carac was right. He wanted to warn me this would happen. I didn't listen. Carac had good intentions, and I paid no attention to him.

My hand continues to tremble as I write the vicious note.

After a moment, I finish the letter and seal it with wax. I stand, and as I open the door, Alas is waiting for me. He reads my face, and lightly touches my shoulder. "Isadora?" he says gently. My lip trembles as I back up and move to hide the letter behind me. "Are you okay?" he asks, and shuts the door. I press my eyes together slowly. I breathe in deeply. "Isadora, I—." he says, taking the crown off his head.

"Did you watch that woman speak the words that probably got her killed?" I quiver, cutting him off.

"Isadora. I just—"

"Did you see the backlash?"

With loud, slamming words, Alas bellows, "Isadora, let me speak!"

I stand my ground with harsh eye contact. He moves his face to the side. "I'm sorry." He takes a seat and rubs his face. The crown drops from of his hands and slams onto the floor; the silvery sound rattles through the room. "I understand you personally know the people involved,. Th-that you're from Din Point, and so the events affect you more. More than most in Parten." He's flustered. He isn't speaking correctly. There's terror in him, too. He breaks his tone into a defeated voice, "I just—I did everything right. I ended a war that was wasting thousands of lives. I made sure we had peace. I got our soldiers home safe, and still…"

I hadn't considered that Alas didn't expect this either. All he wanted to do was good, and it backfired. He didn't sign the treaty with malicious

I take a deep breath and tell him, "It isn't your fault. Alas, you did what should have been done years ago. They just used you."

"People are dying, and the innocent are being thrown in prison. How is this better than the war?" It's no argument that things have always been worse in Din Point, but now the violence has increased.

I mumble, "Carac warned me this would happen." Alas looks up sharply. "I didn't realize what he meant."

"This is horrific."

"What are you going to do next?" I ask, because I don't know what to do to fix this. He doesn't have a response. I try to give him something to go off of: "If you sit back and watch and listen, it will only get worse. You did a good thing for the people you rule, and for most, that would be enough. Do what you can, Alas." I can't tell if I'm saying this to comfort him or myself.

"I need to speak with the council," he mutters.

I pick up the crown from the floor and hand it to him. He grasps it in his hands and turns to leave the room. I wait a few minutes before leaving myself. I need to mail my letter.

CHAPTER 23

Isadora POV

I'm slowly losing my grip on life. I can't take the small talk anymore. I can't take everyone around me trying to avoid the subject. Every meeting I go to with Lawrence, they focus on the good things in Parten. Din Point is never mentioned. My head is clouded with the decisions I've made in the last 48 hours. For better or for worse, I mailed that letter. Things need to change.

I leave the meeting early to try and get some alone time. I flee to my room to catch my breath. I just need a few minutes before the next meeting. I go to my room, unaccompanied; but as I enter, I realize I'm not alone. Casually drinking tea at my desk is Prince Carac, in the flesh. He barely casts a glance at me as I slam the door quickly. "It needs more decorations—quite a boring room," he comments while taking a sip. I take a breath and prepare for what he's going to say. Carac sets his cup down and crosses his arms. "If I recall correctly, you did invite me here?"

"Carac, your kingdom is falling apart."

"It's perfectly decent, thank you very much," he conveys. "It's just going through a phase. All kingdoms experience this era."

"You're imprisoning innocent people and making them turn on each other while discrediting any serious information."

"Ah yes, I, Carac Cavinche, am single-handedly ruining the kingdom," he barks sarcastically. "You think all this lies within my control? I tried to warn you. I won't even get power for at least a few more months. You lecturing me isn't setting up a good start."

"You're already wearing the King's Ring." Carac nods and plays around with the steel ring. I ask him, "When did that happen?"

"I wanted the Ring early, so I got it. Still doesn't mean anything."

He did always want that Ring. Growing up, it was the one thing he couldn't have; now, even before he gets the title, he wears it.

"You have no intention of fixing the kingdom?"

"Not planning on it," he says, and picks up his drink again.

"People are suffering!"

"Come back with me, then."

This is a constant cycle that keeps falling back on me. Carac wants me to think I can change everything with just my presence. "I don't want to go back there; the kingdom isn't falling apart because of me."

"It's not, but if you came back with me, maybe you could sway my thoughts to fix it."

"You said it yourself. You can't fix things right now," I counter. In the past, at least, he had said he was changing things; apparently those were just lies to appease me.

"No one can make a difference if they don't care." He calls for my answer, pausing for a second. Maybe he has a point in both of those sentences. I don't respond, pondering his intended points. He breaks the silence and croons, "Let's make a deal."

"I don't want to negotiate a trade after all of this."

"I thought you'd be willing to. I know you must be concerned about the safety of the princes and your brother." He grins slightly and takes a sip. "With a death controller getting in and out of the castle so easily…"

"You wouldn't dare touch them," I growl. He's playing this stupid game he's set up in a cruel way. He knows his words are striking me to the core. I don't think he would touch any of the people in this castle, but still, if he really wanted to play dirty, if he wanted to win, he would. I can't take that chance.

"I'm not going to threaten your relatives. I'll always leave your brother alone. But the royalty in this kingdom is still up for grabs."

I whisper, "You want me to join you in exchange for their safety?"

"I implied that, I think."

"You don't get to touch them, ever," I gasp, regretting the words as soon as I've said them.

"So, are we making a deal if you're negotiating?"

I knew deep down from the day of the broadcast that I was going to play into his hands somehow. "Here are my terms."

Carac rolls his eyes, and sarcastically says, "Oh, brilliant."

"You can never harm this royal family, ever. That includes Trinity. Nor can you hire anyone to do so."

Carac rephases my terms, "No harm to them directly or indirectly."

"In addition to that, leave Parten alone. And you have to *listen* to me. Just let me help with things; you don't have to do a thing. And you cannot execute me when I return."

Taking the final sips from his cup, Carac leers and says, "Well, that's a lot of leverage to hand over. I want something else."

I feel relief fill me for a moment. "Go on, then."

"I want five 'you musts'."

"What?" I scoff. What can that possibly mean?

"I want five times where I say, "You must,' and you have to do it."

"Nope."

"No deal… Four."

"Hell no."

"Three."

He wasn't going to go any lower than that, but I try. "Two."

He shakes his head. "I won't budge. Three."

I know well enough to stop and lock the number in. "Three, but they can't be anything that hurts others, nothing sexual, and nothing that would cause harm to Parten."

"Well, that ruins my three ideas," he sighs.

"That's my final offer."

Carac sets down his cup and offers his hand. "Then we have a deal."

I hesitate a second before concluding that this may be the best offer I can get out of Carac. I shake his hand firmly. Carac maybe a person with few morals, but the one thing that he is is a firm believer in is keeping his word.

My heart pounds as I accept; we have really made a deal. I tell myself that this is the best possible solution. Carac always has a plan; at least this one meets my needs, not just his.

"Shall we, then?" he says with a hand on the door.

"Now?" I question. Carac nods.

This is moving fast.

"I can have someone alert them that you went to Din Point. That way, they won't think you just disappeared."

I want to write them a letter so they would have an explanation of me leaving, but worse case, I can try and write from Din Point.

The more I think about leaving, a million questions pulse in my head. I have two options: regret my decision or start to mentally prepare.

After a second of hesitation, Carac opens the door. His face radiates pride as he speaks to me. "Coming?" His delivery is a question and a command at the same time.

CHAPTER 24

Isadora POV

Once in the hallway, I notice that there are no guards to be seen. The hall has cleared out. We walk down the hall a few feet when suddenly, Carac puts his arm out and pushes on the wall. The wall shifts to reveal a hidden pathway. Carac enters through the perfectly concealed doorway, and once I'm in there too, he seals it shut.

I'm baffled. I hesitate before asking, "A hidden passageway? The prints for the castle didn't show this."

"All castles have hidden passageways. You should know that. Back in Din Point, you knew them better than I did. Most of the time, they aren't in the castle's blueprints. You just have to look around. It seems neither you nor your princes have ever truly explored the place."

We walk down the passage; the only light shines from old electric torches that hang on the crumbling walls. We come to a stop, and Carac pushes forward again to reveal the end of the passage, which opens to the outside. He reaches into his jacket pocket and puts on a pair of black shades before moving forward.

We step right out onto the royal runways. There are two runways directly behind Parten Castle for jet transportation. Sitting on the nearest runway is Carac's jet. He got the beautiful custom black-and-silver aeroplane for his 16th birthday. Carac hands a piece of paper to one of the ladies working on the runway. She glances away, allowing Carac to enter his jet. I follow into the plane. Only Carac could pull off something like this. I wonder if he did this every time he's appeared.

Inside the jet, the two pilots are preparing for takeoff. Carac quickly exchanges words with them and moves to the middle of the plane. I follow. He takes a seat across from me. I watch out the window as we take off. "Ready to go home?" he asks.

"*Home*," I echo with a cold laugh.+

"It's where you were raised."

"Doesn't mean it's my home."

"You consider *this* home?" Carac asks as we look at the palace from the air. I know that Lawrence and Alas referred to Parten as my home, but neither kingdoms feel much like home anymore. He continues to push another harsh topic on me. "You think they'll come after you?"

I shake my head. "You won't let them come close enough to get me."

"No, I probably won't. And you know the second you leave, I'll break our deal. The only way to get out of Din Point and have the princes stay alive is if you kill me... And we both know that won't happen."

I've accepted my fate. He's right in everything he's threatening. "Are you scared of death?" I taunt him. I've never really figured out Carac's stance on death.

He turns his attention away from the window and looks directly at me. "I can't be scared of the very thing I am."

I have to rephrase my words carefully. "But are you scared of dying?"

I'm scared of dying. I'll never tell Carac that. But from everything I've seen, anyone who dies from Carac's touch, me included, feels nothing. There was nothing in my head when I was gone. I was only dead for ten minutes, but what if that's all there is after death?

He pursues his lips together and switches to a grin. "Death ain't shit but a new adventure. If you're scared, you're wasting your time on something you'll never be able to change." He has a point with his words. I didn't know what death really holds, but neither does he.

I ask him, "Is that what you really want? To continuously threaten the princes' lives? Do you want them dead?"

"I wanted you to stop being dramatic and come home. If I had to threaten the princes to show you that you needed to come home, then fine. But I don't have a preference on whether they live or die. Their life status is none of my business."

I need to change the subject to get things off my chest. "What's life going to look like for me there? Prison cell again?"

"I don't think the prison life would suit you well."

"Ah, pain and suffering then?" I say with a little laugh.

"What you call pain and suffering most would not. I don't plan for you to hate life in Din Point. Life will probably be like it was before."

Without thinking, I scoff and shake my head.

"I won't let anything bad happen to you there; you're not going to die," he says softly.

"Don't make promises you can't keep," I snap. Carac shifts uneasily. By accident, I've struck a nerve.

He vows, "I *can* keep that promise."

He hasn't even considered the fact that he isn't my only enemy in Din Point. "People in Din Point hate me, Carac. They hate you, too. Don't expect anything less."

The subject is too painful for him to keep looking at me. He stops talking to me for a while. The plane ride passes silently, the two of us deep in thought. A few hours of travel time only allows me to think and swallow up the possibilities of Din Point. I keep trying to think of what Lawrence and Alas are going to do once they see that I'm gone. Carac said he was going to have me back on whatever account, and he played his cards perfectly. I knew in time that it was going to come down to him hanging something over my head. And I would, of course, go back if it meant that princes wouldn't be touched by Carac. It's my fault in the first place that Carac even has an interest in Parten.

For a long time he just gazes out the window as time passes, never looking at me. Finally he sits up and redirects his attention to me. "The Prince's assassination attempts were comical."

"About time someone tried to kill you," I joke.

"He did a poor job covering his tracks."

"Who did?" I wasn't really paying attention to what he was saying, dismissing it as ego-boosting talk, but this is getting interesting.

Carac tilts his head at me. "Alas…?"

Maybe Alas kept something from me. I lean forward. "You think he did *what?*"

He smirks at me, realizing that, again, he knows something I don't. "Alas sponsored rebel groups to kill me. He paid at least seven different factions. Each one failed worse than the last."

"I didn't know." I had no clue Alas that was trying to kill Carac.

"Clearly," he states sarcastically. "I need to ask you a question."

"Go for it."

"Why did you ask me to come and get you now? What changed?"

"You warned me about what would happen if we signed the treaty. I don't know why what your intentions are, but I think you telling me alone shows that you know that something wrong is happening in your kingdom. When I saw the news broadcast with the reporter list everything that's gone wrong, I realized I'm doing nothing productive in Parten. I'm just sitting around and letting things pass me by. I think here, maybe, just *maybe*, we can do some good."

He rolls his eyes slightly, but nods.

Moments later, the plane starts to make its descent and finally lands in Din Point. Once we land, I take a deep breath, bracing myself to see the place I never wanted to return to.

The pilots exit without saying a word.

Carac gets out of his seat. He leaves the plane without looking back. I follow him out. Once I see the castle, my gut turns. I instantly regret the deal. Carac comes to my side and places a hand on my shoulder.

"Welcome back."

CHAPTER 25

Isadora POV

T he world shifts under me as I take my first steps towards the entrance to the castle, steps I haven't taken in a year. I pace the steps slowly as Carac walks far in front of me. I'm drowning in my thoughts. The waves are crashing over and over. Each time I try to breathe, it's as if my lungs are filling with water. I force myself up the stairs, filled with dread.

Din Point Castle is much older than Parten's. Originally brown, it's so worn down that it's now almost a dirty, musty, dark white. The tops of the castle, the details and curves, are a dark shade of blue, colors that seem to flow perfectly together, as there are so many windows and doors that you can barely see any jointing of things in the cluttered architecture. There are also many trees around the castle that feed into making the air feel fresh. The castle is placed in the center of a long, dense forest, but the plants around the castle grounds are keep in perfect condition. Two large, grassy lawns lie in the front and back of the castle, making it seem like an isle of perfection in a messy wilderness.

Once at the entrance, no one dares stop Carac. We're allowed to walk freely into the castle. I stare straight forward, ignoring the whispers that fill the halls. Every eye is watching us as we proceed deeper into the castle. I follow Carac. He doesn't once check to make sure that I'm obediently behind him. I could break away at any second, and it would take a while for him to notice. We pass Carac's old room; I stop and glance at the door. "It's still my room," Carac comments once he notices my staring. He continues down the hall a few meters and then says, "This is still *your* room."

Numbly, I enter. The inside is entirely different than it was before. My eyes widen as I look around, taking everything in. The walls are a different color, the furniture has been changed, yet it's still my room. Carac tries to initiate a conversation as I walk slowly around the room, but for the most part, I keep quiet.

One sentence snaps me to full attention: "I'm getting crowned in three weeks."

"I thought it wasn't until you were a few years older."

"I thought that, too."

"That's good, isn't it? Then you can start to make changes to the kingdom." My heart is flickering. I have to keep hoping that Carac isn't going use his power to go off the deep end.

"I have no desire to do that."

"Carac, you can—"

He cuts me off. "I don't want to. It's not my problem."

"It's your kingdom!" I thunder. If Carac takes the throne with this mindset, it will mean the worst scenario for so many people.

"Whatever," he says, annoyed. He brought this up. What did he expect me to say? He moves to the door and says dismissively, "I'm going to dinner."

"What am I supposed to do?"

"Want to come with me?"

"No."

"Then stay in your room." He slams the door. I let out a sigh. I have to get through to him before something drastic happens.

I go weak with all my thoughts, and wonder if there's still any hope left that Carac will hear me out.

CHAPTER 26

Lawrence POV

I f this meeting drags on any longer, I think I'll just get up and leave. They can't do anything to hold me here, and I have better things to do. It's only been half an hour, but this is driving me insane. I look around the large table; even Alas has turned gaze away. He's over this. He's been antsy the whole time. He keeps tapping his hand and shaking his leg. I don't know what's wrong with him. He hasn't stopped fidgeting; normally he can sit still for hours.

The old advisor from the council continues to lecture on. I don't even remember what his point is anymore.

"How do you possibly expect us to execute that?" Daymond asks harshly from across the room. I don't know what he's arguing, but if Daymond has to call you out like that, it's probably not a good idea. The old man turns his head to him and starts to ramble on. Daymond again says, "I don't think you're hearing yourself. This is not plausible. I know I'm not on the council, but what you're asking is ridiculous." The other council members in the room shift uneasily and start to whisper to each other.

Alas sits up and says abruptly, "I'm sorry, but I'm calling an end to this meeting." I give him a questioning glance. This meeting was supposed to have another hour left. People shake their heads and stand up to leave. Everyone begins to filter out the door.

I stand up swiftly. Alas states flatly, "Daymond, Lawrence, sit *down.*"

I turn around and sit in my chair. The final council member has left, and the door shuts behind him.

"I have things to do, King Alas," Daymond says coolly.

"Isadora is gone," Alas blurts. "I got word from a guard that Carac left a transmission claiming Isadora has gone back to Din Point with him. I had guards search the whole palace; she isn't on site. I even had someone collect jet records, and somehow a Din Point jet was on our turf just a few hours ago."

I lean inward toward the table. He can't be serious. Isadora would *never* go back there. I look at Daymond for his reaction.

"How can you have records of him having a whole fucking jet here, and not be able to catch him in the moment?" Daymond snaps at Alas. He has a good point.

"I don't know how he slipped by us all. I'm going to do some work on our guards, and trust me, there *will* be repercussions."

"Sh-she isn't gone," I stutter out. "There is no way she'd go back."

Alas looks just as frustrated as me as he says, "Lawrence, I've had people scour this palace up and down. I've done everything possible to try and see if she's still here. She's not. But I had one of our people in Din Point verify. She *is* there."

Daymond sits back in his seat. He places a hand to his chin and ponders. "She didn't go by choice, then; I know her well enough to say that. Carac must have held something over her head."

I now understand even better how strangely Carac's mind works. He probably didn't take her by force; Alas would have been told of aftermath of a fight. Carac always is a few steps ahead of us, and it shows how he doesn't even have to use his ability to get what he wants.

I can't stand him.

My thoughts are interrupted as Daymond stands quickly and starts to walk to the door.

"Where are you going?" Alas calls out to him.

"I'm going to confirm some things in Din Point, and try to get a letter to my little sister, who's being kept in a hell zone— because it's clear neither of you has a grip on what's happening in your own damned castle. I'm going to go do my job *and* yours." Daymond slams the door behind him. I look at Alas as he twists his palms into his eyes, trying to clear his head.

He admits, "I was told all this right before the meeting, and tried to think of how to tell you two." He looks up at me with an angry face. "This is all going wrong."

"What do we do? Do we go and get her back?"

"She must have gone for a reason... I hope. I don't think she'd just up and leave like Daymond said. I'm going to try and communicate with my people there and see what's going on. If Daymond gets word, I hope he'll fill us in. If we can take action, we will."

I shake my head. How could Carac get in here *again*? Why would Isadora leave? What is he holding over her head?

Alas gets up and leaves the room, his face full of resentment.

I can't move from the table. I need Isadora here. She's my sole ally in the castle, the one person that I'm supposed to be able to turn to.

And now she's gone.

CHAPTER 27

Isadora POV

My eyelids feel as heavy as lead weights as I open them. When I take in my surroundings, I immediately regret waking up. The room feels empty, and so does my chest. I could stay in bed all day; I could do nothing and let myself waste away right here in this bed. I indulge myself for a minute, then, knowing that reality must be faced, I force myself out of the bed. I force my legs to the floor and stand. I carefully look around and explore my room for a bit. As expected, there's nothing of any use here. If there's nothing in here, it won't hurt to check beyond the door. I open it lightly, and to my surprise, I'm able to walk right out. I'd fully expected to have been locked in. I'm immediately faced with an obscene number of guards, all in dark blue uniforms. There's a buzz in the hall, yet no one inspects me too carefully. They apparently aren't stationed to guard me.

From the other side of the hall, Carac walks towards me. The sea of guards parts down the center of the gallery as he passes them. I squint at him. As he approaches, I recognize a familiar face at his side. They're now close enough for conversation, but as I look, I can't believe who I'm seeing. "Ryder?" I ask, knowing that it's him. He smiles and casually brushes a hand through his hair. He stands in front of me wearing a Din Point uniform.

"Isadora, a pleasure to see you," he says cheerfully, then turns to Carac. This is the most proper I've ever heard his voice. He slants his head a bit at Carac and says, "I won the bet."

"Oh?" I remark unconsciously. I don't have enough clarity to form more than one-word sentences.

Carac reaches into his jacket pocket and hands Ryder a sack of gold coins.

"I thought you'd last longer in Parten, Isadora," Carac says. He's actually disappointed that I didn't stick it out longer, and he even bet on it!

"But," I say, trying to configure my speech, "But you're supposed to be in Parten." Ryder has so much going for him there. He has so much potential.

Ryder smirks at me, but he directs his comment to Carac. "You can explain this one."

They turn and continue their walk. I have to catch up and walk by their sides. Carac takes pleasure in explaining to me, "Ryder has always been a Din Point soldier. But then, about... two years ago?" Ryder nods to confirm. "As of two years ago, he was sent to Parten as a personal spy, and with some help, he worked his way up in the ranks."

Ryder adds in, "Ever wonder how Carac so seamlessly appeared in the palace?"

"She experienced the tunnels during her exit," Carac notes.

"But does she realize how much work it took to make sure that there was never a guard at their entrance and exit?" he continues, his voice filled with a light annoyance. "Or how on your first day in the castle, I had to use Trinity to get you to spar? Carac asked me to see how strong your ability was. Also, I had to have you spar with Lilah to get your necklace to break... I could go on." Ryder's diction is so different. His words are slowed to further his tone, and the sentence structure is off. He's no longer the careless asshole who roamed Parten Castle's halls and pissed me off. The number of things he's been doing for Carac that went unnoticed are insane.

"Applaud yourself another time, please," Carac commands.

Ryder instantly scoffs, but after a death glare from Carac, he quickly turns it into a cough.

"Are you staying here, then?" I croak, trying to wrap my head around Ryder as a spy.

"I'll return to Parten in a few hours. And now, I'll have to remove myself from this conversation, as I have business to attend to." Ryder walks away, and I quickly lose track of him among the other guards.

"I still don't understand how they didn't realize the passages existed. It doesn't make sense," I say, confused.

"Because we had the original blueprints of the castle removed, just as ours were lost long ago. They somehow just 'disappeared,' and were replaced by copies without tunnels."

Everything is slowly making more sense. The pieces of the puzzle are coming together, yet it's not entirely complete. It's clear now how much Din Point really interferes with Parten's affairs, and I'm starting to see how much Carac messed with me personally.

I still have more questions to ask him. "Can we discuss your kingdom?"

"Not now," Carac snaps. "All these guards here—they shouldn't even be in this hall now that I'm back..." His voice trails off. Then he straightens and yells, "Get out of here! Return to your posts!"

Quickly, most of the guards exit the hall. Carac rolls his eyes as he keeps walking. I walk by his side, not sure what else to do. We come upon the gardens; the memories I've attached to them fill me. The Din Point royal gardens are absolutely stunning.

Every flower you can imagine is here, protected by the glass surroundings. Grass hedges form stunning sculptures. A healthy glow fills the air, radiating from the vines and trees. The smell overcomes me. Flowers upon flowers fill my vision. Once we're entirely in the luscious greenhouse, I watch Carac raise his brows with a bored face as he walks along.

"What is it you wanted?" he asks. He's glancing all over the place, distracted by it all.

"To talk about the reason I came here."

"The reason you came here is so I don't kill Alas and Lawrence," he rasps while kicking a little dirt up with his foot. "Speaking of them, will they be coming for you soon?"

"I already said no."

"True love isn't that strong?" he mocks with a cold face.

I'm not going to explain how there was nothing like that among any of us, but the way he says it tells me he's being condescending. Carac can assume whatever he wants.

I continue with my previous wishes. "You need to do something, Carac. You'll be in power soon."

"The kingdom will be the exact same when I receive the crown."

"But you have the opportunity to fix things. You can at least try!" If I try hard enough to paint a picture of hope that appeals to Carac, it might just work.

"I owe these people nothing. They can keep living their miserable lives. I don't care to inflict anything horrible on them when I'm in power, but I'm most certainly not going to fix anything. The council has the real power here; I'm just going to be a figurehead."

"These are the people you rule! It's your job to fi—"

"It's not my job!" he yells at me, as he did before when I said the word *job*. He inhales deeply and looks around at the gardens. There's no one around.

I step closer to him and ask, "Why? Why do you hate these innocent people so much that you're willing to let them starve because of an unfair system your parents set up and control?"

Carac twists his face. His jaw is strong and clammed as he spits, "I didn't set up this fucked-up system, let that be clear," while he stops in front of some asters. "No one can make me fix anything."

"Bullshit," I counter, "No one is cruel for the fun of it."

"You don't get to ask these questions. You're here because I made a deal I'm already starting to regret. You don't get to annoy and provoke me for the sport of it. This is my kingdom, and like you said, I get the choice of how to rule it." I 've made him angry. His face has grown colder. His voice is strong and steady when he commands me, "Now, you should go."

Carac walks away from me and observes the flowers. He doesn't want to hear anything I have to say. He used to listen to me. He used to think my ideas and my brain were brilliant. I realize now *that* was all probably bullshit too. He starts to walk around again, and looks at the scenery. I follow at a bit of a distance. I just want him to try and bear with me, to really hear me. There has to be a reason for his actions. I think as we walk, and I come to a conclusion.

I hold my breath and step closer to him. I can't stop thinking about it, and finally burst out, "The fire that killed your brother wasn't started by the *people*."

He dips his head, turning away from the flowers. It's only day one, and I'm starting a war between us. I could be wrong about this approach, but it's the only thing left I can think to do.

"This isn't about that," he says. His tone matches his stony expression. He stares at me while crossing his arms.

"You can't blame them for the fire," I say weakly. This is a risky topic, and could prove to be extremely dangerous. But I can't back down from my thoughts yet.

"The fire took him away, Isadora. The people *caused* it. Later, the marriage they wanted between us drove you away from me. The ideas they poisoned you with was why you set up Zaven. The rebellion they caused was the reason I had to put you in prison. People will always be the cause of our fall. Society is what's ruling and destroying the world, not me. I'm just a guy with a title. They pin the blame of all the suffering on me when it's them creating and spreading lies. There are bigger things I have to worry about than this kingdom."

"What could possibly be bigger than this kingdom for you, Carac?"

I've hit the spot right on, but my jab goes deeper than I wanted. I have the urge to fire back harsh words, but what he said has made him vulnerable, his face taciturn. His words weren't perfect either, telling me they weren't planned. He didn't plan on this conversation at all, and neither did I.

He doesn't answer my question. "You can stay in your room for the next week. You're not to leave, because I need to have a clear head while this kingdom gets ruined."

I turn my back and rush away from him before he can see my eyes water. What he's said is an entirely new issue. It's clear that Carac thinks this isn't his responsibility—that just because he was born into royalty doesn't mean he has to try and use it correctly. It's a stark reminder that Carac is a product of his environment. His parents never cared about him. As far off the grid Carac is now, his parents let him slip, and they're worse. They killed his brother. They raised him with such venom. They sat back and watched the people in their kingdom suffer for years. They *inflicted* the suffering. The people in Din Point are different. They're struggling and getting worse because the royalty lets corruption spread, and even fosters it.

While Carac has a mindset to cause trouble, his parents are behind it. Not only that, but they created Carac. He's a product of tragedy, a corrupt monarchy, and a horrible environment. He was told and taught as a child to be a weapon. I don't know who started that fire, but his parents wanted Carac on the throne and wanted to use his ability. They wanted and needed his older brother gone, so they made him gone.

I have no way to prove my theory. Even if I could, nothing would change now.

I don't want to make excuses for Carac, but I wish he'd been raised differently. The way he talks and fights and questions authority shows that there was a chance for a different Carac to have been created. If he were born solely to be cruel, he would go along with the schemes with no questions asked; but there always seems to be a bit of hesitation.

Carac is just now starting to cause damage on his own—a different kind than anyone planned. His parents have lost their power over him, but they still watch him use his against the people.

I see the person inside of him dying in his own way, and I don't know if I can bring him back.

CHAPTER 28

Isadora POV

J ust as Carac warned me, I've spent the whole week trapped in my room. So much for the plane conversation, where he insisted I wouldn't be a prisoner. The only contact has been a servant who brings me food, and the one who cleans my room. Before our argument, the door was never locked. Carac is doing it now to get on my nerves, because I struck deep during our last conversation.

There have been no visits from Carac or even Ryder, which I almost expected. On top of that, there's been zero contact from Alas or Lawrence, not even anything from my brother. I don't know even if they've tried to contact me or take action. Most likely not. I don't blame them.

I sit at my desk, twiddling with a pen and writing nonsense that maybe, one day, will be useful. As I'm twirling the pen around my finger, I heard the door unlock from the outside. There's no knock or forewarning. The door flies open, causing me to drop the pen and stand abruptly to see who's entered. It's the first visit in seven days from someone who's not a servant. And the visitor isn't alone, either. Nor are they strangers, to my surprise.

Xeres and Castilla, the siblings of Theo and Zaven, have come for me. Theo and Zaven are dead because of me. From the dark looks they give me, this won't be a peaceful visit.

"Isadora," says the second eldest brother, Xeres. He's the tallest person I know. His lean figure haunts me often. His hair is the same bright blond as Theo's. Xeres is a harsh, quiet person with the deadly gift of controlling another person's body, the same ability Zaven had. He can use anyone to his own amusement, making them dance, jolt around, or worse. He can make anyone physically do anything. I was a victim of his boredom a few times while growing up. There's nothing like the physical torment he can put someone through. It's like the insides of your body trying to escape, only to be held back by the cage of your skin.

Not only does Xeres have a powerful ability, but he's wicked smart. Beyond smart—he's a genius. His mind is like a diamond: cold and harsh, but brilliant. Xeres usually keeps to himself, thinking and plotting. I honestly believe he's one of the most intelligent people I know, but that doesn't change the fact that he uses his abilities against anyone he can.

The hairs on my arms stand as they walk fully into the room. I bite my bottom lip, feeling a sensation of fearful nostalgia hit my mind.

"Haven't seen you since the day you took your pathetic life and fled the kingdom," Castilla says, anger lacing her words. Castilla has her own striking personality. She's the youngest of them all. and has the same ability Theo had to manipulate metal. Castilla is the sibling I know the least, but have heard the most about. She causes nothing but trouble for the people of Din Point, and relies on Xeres for everything.

It's clear they've come for a reason. As they pace around me, the sensation of death approaches. There's no water in the room for me to use. I'm left defenseless in a room with the two people who most want me dead.

Castilla says nastily, "But Theo saw you recently, and then you killed him."

I take a short breath. Castilla's words hit me like a punch to the stomach, reminding me of how I took a life. When Theo died, I barely considered his family. I was tormented enough by killing him that his people in Din Point hadn't entered my mind. "I'm so sorry," I apologize. I want to convey that I really mean what I'm saying, but it makes no difference to them.

Castilla advances closer as I back up to my bed. "I bet you are, you little—"

Xeres places a hand on Castilla's arm and draws her back. Castilla keeps going. "The day will come, Isadora, when Carac isn't here to protect you, or when we just get sick of waiting for that day. Until then, you can continue living your miserable life as his pet."

"I'm sorry," I plead. "I'd change that day if I could... but I had to protect myself."

Xeres growls, "Let's hope my morals develop enough that I can say the same when I end you."

I swallow and prepare to apologize, but they turn their backs to me before I get the chance, and abruptly leave the room.

CHAPTER 29

Isadora POV

Not even three days later, Carac comes to my room for a visit. I haven't gone anywhere, except once to walk around the gardens. Even then, I was immediately escorted back to my room. Carac wastes no time as he walks directly into my room. I'm sitting on my bed reading a book as he tumbles in. I give him a tentative glance, trying to decipher his mood. He sits down on the edge of the bed.

"I'm using my first 'you must' today," he states.

I shut my book. "What is it?"

"You just have to say yes," he commands while heading to the door. "That's all you have to do."

I stand up and follow him. At the door, Carac snaps and points into my room. A handful of maids enter. All privacy is lost as he exits. The maids start to work on me. I have to sit and think of everything he might make me say yes to today.

The maids make me look like a doll. The outfit is out of the ordinary; it's too extravagant. The dress they put me in is an assortment of red rose colors that fit me simply yet elegantly, and fluffs out at the waist. My hair has been tightly pulled and pinned up. I waste my time asking the maids questions they ignore.

After I'm done being primped and pampered, the maids rush me into the hall, where Carac arrives to meet me.

"What is this?" I ask, gripping my dress. Carac is well-dressed too, in a suit with a silver tie. He doesn't answer my questions as we start to walk. I know we're walking to the gardens. For what, a stroll?

As we arrive at the gardens, it's jam-packed with people. They fill the paths and plaza, crawling everywhere like ants. Everyone is busy; drinking, talking, enjoying the lush flower-filled area. Everyone of importance in Din Point is here. It's a beautiful scene; glass encases all the people holding any degree of power in Din Point.

And I'm just Carac's guest.

Carac is quick with his steps; he reaches down and grabs my hand. In any other situation, I would jerk away, but this is clearly not an event to create a scene at.

I see the King and Queen making conversation with several people. At another point, I can see Xeres and Castilla speaking with a few advisors. Their parents are here, too: Regime and Annica Shade. Annica is a body manipulator like Xeres and Zaven, and Regime is a metal manipulator, just as Theo was and Castilla is. They're just as deadly as their children, who they raised them with the encouragement to be cruel. I try to not look at the Shade family any further.

Even Ryder is here, talking with people and doing business.

It's clear that we've arrived late to the party. I keep pace with Carac as we pass more and more people. Everyone we walk by tries to speak with him, but he ignores them all. I'm pulled by his side until we stop near some rose bushes. Carac lets go of my hand and picks up a cup and fork from a waiter.

Carac proceeds to clink his glass. Instantly, the crowd quiets and directs their attention to us. He raises his glass up for a toast.

Once he's sure he has everyone's attention, he puts down the glass. Carac peers over the room and pronounces, "I am thrilled to see everyone gathered here today. I hope you enjoyed coming out. It offers me the most wonderful opportunity for a proposal." All the eyes in the room shifted to me as he continues, "Isadora Xxon, today I ask for your hand in marriage, to become my future wife and future queen of this kingdom. Would you do me the honor of accepting?"

I feel my head let go of all my thoughts as my breath shortens. The whole room watches me stumble, and barely manage to stammer, "Y-yes."

That was all I had to do: say yes.

The crowd cheers. Carac leans in and kisses me on the cheek. I'm frozen in my stance as the cameras flash. My only thought is, *This will be on the news. This will be seen by everyone. This will spread to Parten. This will be shown to Lawrence and Alas. My brother will see this.*

By the time we make it back to my room, my frustration is well built up. As soon as the door shuts behind us, I yell, "You're going to make me *marry* you?"

Carac walks around the room. He finds the whole thing amusing. His face breaks into a satisfied, smug smile. "That was always the plan."

"And your parents? Your advisors? Do they even care that you want to marry me, the traitor?"

"Unlike Parten, we don't do pitiful little selections for marriage. This was always the plan. They would not let you live here unless I made you my wife."

"You-you're—."

"Your marvelous, stunning, handsome fiancé?"

"Dangerous!"

"*Dangerous?*" he mocks. "I wasn't expecting that from your vocabulary."

"You are *dangerous*. There's no reason you should want me here this badly; you could have anyone in the whole kingdom to marry. People are suffering, and yet you're still focused on making my life a constant headache! You have no regard for anything except yourself, and whatever you deem fit for your life. That's the foundation that forms a dangerous leader—using your power for personal enjoyment!"

"Get over yourself," he says, not taking in or caring about anything I've said. "Stop acting like you're a hero for disagreeing with me. I may be dangerous, but I'm also the one making the calls, so you should watch how often you throw hissy fits."

"You're entitled and dangerous. You are not the sun, Carac; my life does not revolve around you," I jeer.

Carac moves in closer to me. I take a backstep in retreat, and feel my back collide with the door. He leans forward, placing a hand at my side, against the door.

"You're right, Isadora. I'm much too dark for that. I'm closer to a black hole, drawing you in no matter how hard to try to pull away." I feel my throat choke up, his stupidly calculating words preventing me from saying anything. He continues, "You didn't have to write me that letter and ask me to come to Parten. And you didn't have to make that deal with me; you know I wouldn't have killed the princes. That's not another issue I would have gotten myself into. But you did, and you came back. You agreed for whatever reason you don't want to tell yourself."

He leans even closer, his face nearing mine. I arch my back, my breaths getting closer together. His hand latches onto the door handle at our side.

"Just don't let me get bored, dear, and I won't have to use my *dangerous* power for my amusement." I close my eyes for a second, until I feel his breath on my face. "See you tomorrow," he says maliciously, as he opens the door with a smile and leaves my room.

My body releases the tension I was holding in. I wipe my hands across my face. My mind continues to jump around as I try to clear Carac from my mind.

I look down at my hand, at the new ring that takes the place of Lawrence's.

This is all getting more confusing and damning with every second.

CHAPTER 30

Isadora POV

I'm shaken awake by the rattle of the door slamming. I roll over to see Carac in the room. He doesn't hesitate to make a dramatic entrance even this early in the morning. Carac gives me no time to wake up as he says, "The wedding is tomorrow."

I glance at him with wary eyes. Sleep eluded me last night. I don't move from the safety of my bed. "It's been a day. Plus, we aren't getting married."

Carac is moving quicker than usual. He's doing the same thing Lawrence did before the wedding, except with worse jitters. "You have the ring, you said yes, it's happening."

"I'm married to Lawrence. I'm already a princess, I don't—"

"Yes, and you act like one, too. Look, I don't know how being married into royalty works logistically, but I can't really bring Lawrence here to get a divorce, so this marriage trumps that one in my books."

"Why the rush? Why so soon?" I ask.

"Because I'm also getting crowned this week."

I almost roll off the bed as I cry, "No way!"

"What do you want me to do? They moved it up."

"You are *not* ready to be King." I haven't had enough time to help Carac. This is all moving too fast. There's no way he can take the throne with no progress made for the better. Carac is going to avoid my influence as much as he possibly can. He's going to run this kingdom into the ground.

"You don't get a say in this," he taunts me.

"I don't get a say in anything," I correct him.

"Anyway, wedding tomorrow, be there."

CHAPTER 31

Isadora POV

Carac always told me how wrong weddings seemed to him. He used to swear it was a tradition that had no purpose, created by society. He didn't think people needed an event to declare their love. Yet today is our wedding day.

He used to say it was all too boring, even idiotic. The only reason he's making me marry him is to have a vow before the coronation. This is the only way I can become Queen of Din Point without causing a commotion.

He didn't even use another one of his "you musts." It would just be wasting a usage. I've already said yes. He played his hand wisely. It would be impossible to get out of this wedding without messing up everything, including my hopes of changing his mind.

It also bothers me how he used to complain how injudicious it is that he barely knows anyone at weddings. How it's all politics, and he never wants to pay attention to that. He used to promise that he'd have get us married in the simplest way possible. But now it doesn't matter what he used to say or what I currently think. He's going through with his plans despite everything.

This was a day I never thought would actually happen.

Even if, in reality, it means nothing except for a title, I'm still debating what it means to me. All I can do is think of ways to get Carac to change, or try to leave. I'm already considering and debating any ideas that can be built off this marriage.

Time is passing quickly now that the maids are done getting me ready.

It's time to get the wedding over with. This will be my second marriage in a year, and the second wedding I didn't expect. For some reason, though, this wedding feels less...awful. I won't ever admit it to Carac, but I feel more at ease today. With Lawrence, I forced myself commit to it. This ceremony I can blame on Carac for happening. The marriage is already giving me a bizarre comfort that I know isn't real. I can't do anything to stop it. It's better just to accept it.

The one thing I can shift my focus to is my dress. It's a fantasy of purple raining down; lavender, fuchsia, and violet. The beautiful, flowery fabric trails out behind me like a cape in the wind. Carac has commented about my clothing before. This time he picked it out, and I let him.

There's a knock on the door; a maid goes to answer it. I turn my head to see guards, who are ready to escort me to the wedding. I get up from the chair they got me ready in, and walk in the middle of the phalanx as we go to the gardens, where the wedding is happening. The doors to the greenhouse are opened for me, and I lift my head to see the wedding venue ahead of me.

I focus on the decorations. The flawless decorations and scenery. The temperature is perfect, controlled by the giant greenhouse. Natural flowers and vines drape over the seats and aisles. I don't see any cameras in the room; this thankfully won't be broadcasted. Even with all the people attending, it feels more protective and comfortable. I catch a glimpse of King Argys and Queen Edisa in the crowd; I don't look at them again. Even with all the negatives, I love this wedding. It would have been perfect if I weren't getting married to Carac in Din Point during this mess.

We skip all the traditional parts of a wedding, per Carac's request. All that matters is the "I dos." It's short and to the point. He's graceful as he accepts the vows. He softly speaks his words and slowly tells me, "I love you," in front of the crowd. I don't know if he means it, or if I do as I repeat it for the ceremony.

The rest of the ceremony is short.

It's all Carac needed.

CHAPTER 32

Isadora POV

I haven't seen Carac for days. There's been no word from him. It almost feels like a relief, but I'm restless and bored out of my mind in my isolation. I've come up with a million ways to help the kingdom, but I'm sentenced to my room, without a thing to do. If Carac would just let me speak to some advisors or anyone who would lend me an ear, maybe I could help.

I'm starting to learn why Daymond was so fed up in Din Point when he was trying to fix things. It's because no one here wants to listen, or even allow you to speak. So I'm sitting on my bed instead, reading another one of the few books that were left in my room, when the door opens.

I'm not expecting to see Xeres and Castilla at the door. They stand there with cutthroat eyes. I calmly hold my book and remain still. "Need something?" I wish.

"Came for a visit," says Castilla as they stroll farther into my room. I lower the book. There's so much metal in the room, Castilla could cut me open in seconds.

Xeres is solid in his motions. There's not a flicker of emotion to be seen. He turns to me like a panther stalking his prey. It's too late to do anything; he's not going to let me manipulate the water in the room.

I'm defenseless.

I have no control over the situation. I stand up straight. I hold the book in preparation to chuck it at Xeres. It's the only weapon at my disposal.

I look down, and lift my arm to throw the book. Before I can launch the book, my arm is held back by Xeres' ability. The book falls to the ground without even touching him. I lose all control of my body, and trip forward. I can't move my head to look up at Xeres and Castilla. I'm forced to stand there without the ability to speak.

"I think it's time to pay our respects to Theo," Castilla says, leaning forward. I'm forced to follow the two down the hall. We pass guard after guard; I can't say a word. My soul feels like it's getting shoved against a wall. I want to scream. I want to slam my head against the wall to escape my bodily prison.

Neither sibling says anything as we enter a small, empty event room. Chairs are stacked on dining tables. Barely any light shines in the place. It pairs with the freezing temperature.

Xeres and Castilla pull chairs out and sit, making me stand in front of them. I stand like a marionette in front of an audience of rabid children. Castilla sits back, watching Xeres move his hand up. I start to move around in rapid, pathetic motions. They become highly amused by jolting me around in swinging movements. I'm swayed around and around the room against my will. This is the most fun they can have with me as long as Carac is alive.

They chuckle as they make me spin, dance, and make a complete fool of myself.

It's all fun and games for them until Xeres gets caught up in his own laughter. I move to the top of a table in the room. He continues to spin me. My leg goes up in the air; then I feel my body flash into reality for a second as he loses his concentration. But my body is moving too fast; I can't stop myself as I fall to the side. I hit the ground., hard. My knees suffer the impact. I try to stop myself from falling over, but I'm now in the control of Xeres again.

I crash to the floor. Xeres and Castilla stop laughing for a moment.

The impact jolts my whole body. The fall isn't bad enough to break anything, but my cheek hits the chair and is sliced open. My knees are going to have severe bruises. Xeres rises from his seat. He ambles over me, not concerned in the least. Castilla calls from her chair, "Oh, just make her stand up."

Xeres plunges a hand down and grabs me by the collar of my shirt. He pulls me up to my feet by the neck. I let a hiss escape my throat as I catch my breath. Xeres spits in my face, "You tell no one about this. Tell them you fell. Got it?"

He lets go and shoves me away. I'm now free from his control. All the pain from the torment hits my body as becomes my own again. I turn to face him, wiping the blood off my check. "I swear when I get out of here, I will—"

"We both know you won't be leaving anytime soon. Your owner won't let that happen. You're the one who made this ugly, Isadora. I have the right to be angry with you. I have every right. I also have the ability to break your jaw in one snap if you say anything." My breathing has become more rigid. He continues, "I wouldn't be surprised if you went and told your precious husband about this. You always crawl back to him when things get messy."

I glance at Castilla and then back at Xeres. I pull myself to my feet as I stare him down. He wants me to fight back. He wants me to scream in his face, begging to break my mouth.

I start to walk out of the room. I yell back at Xeres, "Burn in hell." I don't once look back to see if they give a damn. I march right back to my room and collapse on the bed. I know I can take of myself, but this is just another reason I need to leave Din Point. The humiliation Xeres put me through today is enough for me to act on my own. I can't figure out where my emotions range. I was the cause of the loss of Zaven and Theo, their brothers. What they did today is just revenge. I can accept their anger, but I swear that it will never happen to me again.

CHAPTER 33

Isadora POV

B efore I can even ask why, before I can change and make myself presentable at the very least, I'm gripped by the arms and forced to walk down the hall by four guards. The guards only told me the royals wanted to see me in the Throne Room. The guards won't let go of me, even though I don't plan on running. If I really wanted to make a break for it, I doubt their hold would keep me in place long. I know I could make it pretty far down the hallway before they sounded an alarm and sent multiple guards chasing after me. By then there would be far too many guards upon me, and I wouldn't want to have to kill them all, even if I could. So I give in and walk in their hold, heading and Throne Room to face whatever's ahead.

The only thing even making me consider running for the halls is the fact that they said I'm headed to see the royals. If Carac wanted to see me, he would have just come to my room like usual. In private, he can say whatever he wants to me. He can torment me mentally and push me physically all he wants behind closed doors. But in the Throne Room, he has to watch his mouth and manners. It isn't his Throne Room to control yet.

Besides, my knees still ache, providing a constant reminder of what Xeres and Castilla pulled on me yesterday, and another reason I won't try to make a running break for it.

They walk me to the door of the Throne Room. The two guards in front, those not holding onto my arms, open the large, grand, marble door. It's meant to be intimidating. It's effective. The other two guards shove me forward. The door clicks shut behind me. I turned to the door, trying the handle to see if it will open for me. It's locked.

"Isadora," a voice purrs. I turn toward the dais. Two large, dark blue thrones, decked with gold lining, face out into the room. Only one chair is occupied: Queen Edisa, sits with her head leaning forward, drawing my attention. Gold decorates both sides of the thrones in the form of sculptures, and edges the shallow white stairs that lead up to where the two thrones sit. In other circumstances, I would appreciate the beauty of the room.

"Your Majesty," I respond, stepping few feet farther into the throne room. I never liked this place. Every single time I've been in it, I've felt at my most vulnerable.

The room has large, nicely decorated alcoves in the side walls, showing off the sources of the King's and Queen's power, as behind those holes are collections of holy water. The King and Queen of Din Point are holy-water manipulators, which is an entirely different and deadlier breed of water manipulator than me. They can only control water that's been blessed by the high priestesses in Vaddel. And since Vaddel is in complete isolation, they no longer produce holy water for the other kingdoms. The Din Point royals have some of the last holy-water stocks left in the communicating world. What's worse is the fact that no other water controllers can manipulate holy water. It's a special type of water even I can't control as an ice manipulator. So if they use it against me, try to drown me or shove the water over me, I can't stop them. The Queen could break those water seals and the water would come flowing into the room, and I couldn't push it away.

"You summoned me?" I ask her, growing increasingly uneasy with every passing second. Queen Edisa and I used to get along well. Key words: *Used to.*

When I was growing up in the castle, she was the best at grooming me for the palace lifestyle and making sure I did exactly as she pleased. She taught to do as the next ruler and council wanted me to do. She taught me how to sit, how to listen, and how to agree in all matters that Carac spoke about. If I had an issue with anything, it was for a private conversation, never something I should look to change on my own. That was all she ever shoved down my throat, but she did it repeatedly. She spent a lot of time with me, making sure those orders were engraved into my mind.

Daymond spent his life undoing what she told me. He's the reason that I can think for myself. He saved me from being her puppet, when even my parents encouraged it.

Ironically, I knew Edisa has never practiced what she preached. She was the one with the royal blood; the King had married into royalty. She was born into the kingdom's power, and uses it with the council at her beckoning hand. She knows her power and her reach.

When I was growing up, I wanted to be like her, even though she taught me to be the opposite. She spoke out in court, she manipulated the council to her favor, she controlled everyone in the castle to a large extent. In time, I realized that the power she'd gained and learned to control was actually quite impressive. It's the way she uses the power that's tragic. It was her rule, and that of her parents before her, that caused the downfall of a great kingdom. It was her blood line that made the monarchy oppressive. She's the one who has interlaced affairs within the council. She set up the council with members who will allow her to continue to control them when she steps off the throne. She tried to set me up to listen to her when I ascended to the throne, and planted seeds in Carac's head to get him to think exactly as she does. She wants Carac to think he's making his own decisions and his rulings, when really, she will have created his thoughts.

Her nimble, long fingers crash down on the arm of the throne, jarring my focus back to the room. Her hair, a dark silver, clashes with the outdated colors of the room. "I haven't had a chance to speak with you privately since you came back," she says, her voice echoing in the empty room. The high celling elongates the depth of the room, showing the distance between us. "Since my son brought you back and married you."

Memories rush into my head as I hear the tone in her voice. How her breath twists out, making the statement darkly filled with reprisal. That was how she spoke to me after I set up Zaven. Carac wasn't the only person who visited me in my cell. The Queen came to see me as well. When she came to speak with me during that week, she spoke entirely differently than Carac had. Carac was filled with anger and frustration created from hurt. Betrayal was all he was spewing about, and he had the right to. Even though I had done the just thing, I had still betrayed him to some extent.

But when the Queen talked to me, it was a vengeful anger, the type of anger that showed she was coming to punish me for what I had done. There were days when she told me how much she was going to enjoy seeing me die, and how much pleasure it was going to bring her to have Carac kill me. There were days when she would come simply to threaten Daymond, to say how he'd be killed next because of what I had done. It was her attacking every vulnerable spot I had, and taking a merciless pleasure in doing so.

And now here I am again, standing before her in the kingdom I never meant to return to, married to her son. I twist my wedding ring around, knowing she's watching my every movement.

She rises from her throne. She stalks down the stairs with slow, challenging steps. Her heels click against the marble floor. I plant my feet as she approaches. She comes close enough that barely a foot of space separates us. Her eyes lock onto mine, and hold our stare, neither one of us willing to back down.

Her hand reaches out and slowly lifts my chin to look at my more closely. I take in a sharp breath, not understanding how, in such an enormous room, I could suddenly feel so horrifyingly small.

"Such a waste of a pretty face," she says, letting only one finger lift my jaw. She then lowers her hands and clasps them behind her back. "Such a waste of a girl. Carac never should have brought you back. He should have finished the job the moment he saw you."

I say nothing in reply, because that's what she wants me to do. She wants me to feed into her and her distance. She tilts her head, realizing that I'm not going to respond to her words. She continues on, challenging, "I hear you are already planning to undermine the council."

I retort, "*Undermine* is a strong word."

She lets out a short, small breath of a laugh. A condescending grin comes over her face, telling me that she'll cut me over those words the first chance she gets, because I didn't deny my wish to overturn the council and get rid of the work she's done. The work that's preventing me from doing anything productive. The work that's the *one* thing she's relying on to keep her in power after Carac gets crowned.

"Don't get comfortable here, Isadora. And don't even start to think that the council is something you can touch. You can't. It will chew you up and spit you out before you can even start to undermine it."

"It's not that I *can't* touch the council, it's that you don't want me to," I say, before really realizing what I've hurled back at her.

Her eyes narrow, tongue clicking as she spits, "You have no power here."

My mind rattles, my tolerance going completely away. The guts I have left form the words, "Try and say that again to me in a week."

Her hand collides with my cheek in a harsh, quick slap. I move a hand up to feel where she's hit me. I scoff when I see her hand go back behind her back, clasping the other. My face already burns.

She turns from me and starts to walk back to her throne. "We'll see if you're even here in a week." She doesn't turn around as I stand there in shock, wishing I have something more I can throw at her. "That's all," she says, and waves a hand behind her while still walking.

I gulp down harsh breaths. This is her way of threatening me, of making sure I know that just because Carac wants me here doesn't mean she does. I knew she wouldn't just accept the fact that I'm back, but now I know it loud and clear that I'll need to watch my back.

I turn around and leave the room freely, the door now unlocked. I enter the hall knowing that this is her kingdom for now; these are her walls, these are her guards, and I'm the pawn, potentially getting sacrificed to the king and queen for the sake of the game.

But what she doesn't realize is that I'm the pawn that has almost made it to the other side of the board, and I'm just about to become a queen.

CHAPTER 34

Isadora POV

There is no frost outside, yet it's freezing. It rained last night, but the plants look darker, not greener. The sky is gloomy, and the birds are silent. I feel like the weight of my dress is going to drag me straight to hell. Midnight black fabric grips my skin. It's the pure silver that plaits the royal design that's making the dress so heavy.

The dress radiates power and wealth. My chest feels like a wind controller is dragging the breath out of me. Maybe one of the guards escorting me *is* a wind controller, or maybe I'm just overwhelmed. I brush my hand against my cheek. The cut is still red and in the healing process. When I last saw Carac, he glanced at the cut, but never addressed it. He either already knows how I got it, or doesn't care enough to ask.

I haven't seen him since; days have passed. No one is keeping me up to date on current events or the time. I can barely keep track of what day it is.

Everything was sprung on me when I woke up early this morning. The maids took over my room and got me ready so fast it was clear they wanted nothing to do with me.

Carac is followed by an army of his security as we meet in front of the entrance. He stops, grips his cuffs, and looks me over. "Gorgeous, drop-dead gorgeous," he chimes with a look at the doors we've stopped in front of. I give him a heavy eye-shut with a nod as a thank you. His outfit matches mine almost perfectly. He's in classic matte black, but his outfit has no embellishments. Carac's wicked aesthetic even matches the atmosphere today. I keep my face unaltered by his emotions.

"You don't look happy," he sighs. "That's fine; no need to smile. I'm sure some people would rather have a regal queen than a foolish, bubbly one." Carac twists his King's Ring, his prized possession that he shouldn't have gotten until today. It doesn't matter anymore.

"Your majesty, its time," says a timid guard from behind us.

"Fine," Carac says. He doesn't even wait for them to open the doors. He pushes the doors open himself. I walk by his side as we pass those already seated. Unlike Parten, coronations are private events in Din Point.

Carac doesn't spare a glance towards anyone while walking to the throne. He's extremely focused. I check every face in the room. Many of them were at the wedding. That doesn't matter; I still don't know who most of them are.

I sit down next to Carac in my chair. The King and Queen rise.

I'm crowned first. The Queen shimmers across the floor as she glides to me. She grabs my hand as I stand up. She grips it hard, almost in warning. I remember our conversation of several days ago. I don't want to associate myself with her, or recall her threats. I turn my cheek to the room as I lift my head high. Slowly, I recite the oath as the Queen lowers her crown onto my head. She gives me a cross squint of the eyes.

The world seems to shift just the slightest as the crown hits my temples. Black crystals point out from the base of the crown.

They're interwoven with black gems and diamonds; it looks messy enough to be expensive. If you look closely at the crown, you can spot the little details that were carefully crafted into its design. This crown is slightly smaller than Parten's Queen's. Din Point's crowns are more practical. They create crowns to be worn comfortably on a daily basis. It's light and airy as it sits on my head.

I lower myself onto my throne. I watch as the King stands. Carac is emotionless, while the King's misery is clear. He wasn't quite ready to be done with his power, and Carac isn't fully prepared to receive it.

The King grips the side of the crown with one hand and pulls it off his head. The crown is elegant, but doesn't shine in the light. It isn't meant to show off the wealth of Din Point; it's meant to show power. The jewels are mounted into the steel outer rim, unlike the Queen's crown, which uses the jewels to hold it together. Carac doesn't even stand up. He waits for his father to hand him the crown in a rapid motion. I look out to the people; their faces are horrified. Carac grabs the crown and slowly sets it upon his head. He shakes his head, just the slightest bit, making the crown sink down onto his hair. A small nod to his father makes him sit as Carac is proclaimed King of Din Point. He doesn't swear the oath, he doesn't stand, he doesn't do anything, and he's now King.

The King of Death, Carac Cavinche, is now on the Din Point throne.

CHAPTER 35

Isadora POV

A glow fills my room. Through the blinds a light shines, illuminating the room so brightly that it wakes me. I move my legs; they're cold against the sheets of my bed. I push a hand through my knotted hair, wondering what's going on. I'm still covered in blankets, feeling introverted inside, but I can feel an energy buzzing. Something in the atmosphere has changed.

I lift myself from the bed and move to open the blinds. Snow surrounds the castle, gleaming, reflecting the soft daylight. It falls harder every second, creating a concentrated power that covers the castle and outside grounds.

Din Point is the only kingdom that gets snow seasonally. Parten rarely ever has a change of weather, let alone snow. I haven't seen snow or ice that wasn't of my own manipulation in over a year. I don't even know if Lawrence or Alas have ever seen snowfall in their lives; I can't imagine. A warm, safe, nostalgic feeling enwraps me as I continue to watch the snowfall. In the distance, the forest behind the castle is becoming rich with frost. I can't see a single thing past the edge of the forest. The snow is falling ever faster. now

I've made up my mind; there's no way anyone is going to stop me from going outside. I race to my closet and don my snow boots. I add a light jacket.

I have to slow down. My pulse is racing too fast; but this is my element that fills the air. It's like a water controller going into the ocean, a fire controller seeing a burning building, a plant wielder in a garden. The snow makes everything feel complete in my world. Everything is right.

I push my door open and rush to the gardens. No guards stop me as I run.

The gardens thankfully connect to the outside through a small glass door in the back of the greenhouse. I pass the healthy vines and flowers that are safe from the snow. My hand goes to the door handle, and I open it quickly. A burst of cold air consumes me as I run outside, opening my arms to the snow. It falls onto my hair and clothes while I listen to the crunch of my boots beneath me. I walk around the back lawn of the castle. With every step, I kick up snow. Sheer happiness floods through me.

Back here, behind the gardens, I have plenty of space to play and create. There isn't a single guard around the backyard of the castle. I'm entirely alone out here. They must all be hiding from the cold. I wouldn't want to be out here either, if it weren't for my ability. I crack my knuckles in preparation to create. I've been deprived of snow for far too long, but now I face an unlimited supply. If I space my ability out, I can create for a few hours before becoming tired enough to stop. Without hesitation, I create ice sculptures, new weapons, walkways, and more beautiful creations. I manipulate the snow with ease.

The snow overpowers my vision, wrapping me in the near surroundings. The bright white snow makes shadows stand out. It creates an eerie distinction of what's around me. The sky is clouded in the storm; no sun is visible.

As I glance across the lawn, my eyes glimpse a faint shadow walking towards me. Xeres makes his way through the snow in a gray trench coat that's collecting snow by the second. I've been alone in the snow for an hour, but now he comes dragging along.

"If you've come to torment me more, I'd turn around if I were you. I have the advantage here," I say, moving toward him. I can take him in this environment, even though I'm tired of creating. The exhaustion won't stop me from fighting Xeres. He's becoming more visible the closer I get. I pull the snow up to create a beautiful sword in my hand. I let the edge scrape across the snow as I pace toward him.

"That's true," Xeres admits as he looks at the snow around us. If he makes any moves against me, I won't hesitate to use my ability. There's nothing to fear in a fight against him here. With the snow everywhere on the lawn, one move will allow me to impale Xeres without a second thought. "You should go inside," he says breathlessly. "Head directly to your room."

I laugh. "I'm not going anywhere."

"I would highly recommend you reconsider that."

I shake my head and turn away. He scolds from behind me, "I'm trying to do you a favor. It's going to get messy out here."

The way his voice bounces makes it unclear if his statement is a threat to me or someone else. Either way, I respond, "I'm not leaving anytime soon."

"Suit yourself." Xeres shivers, taking no pleasure in the snow. He observes our surroundings thoroughly. I cast a glance back to him; at any moment he's sure to make a move. I allow the sword I created to disintegrate into water that falls back into the snow. I place my hands into my pockets and watch the snow fall.

Xeres breathing hitches as he looks up at the sky again. His movement makes me look around too. The snow has slowed drastically. Before, it was descending at an average speed; now it's falling in slow motion.

I reach out and pinch a snowflake. I move it into the palm of my hand. It melts after a minute. The snow should have vanished in seconds upon contact with my skin.

Something's wrong.

I turn around, but the snow continues to fall thickly enough that I can't tell which direction is which. As my eyes move to Xeres, I notice he's looking over my shoulder. I turn to see what he's seeing. Another figure is walking towards us, now a few meters away and approaching fast.

A lady stares me down with a relaxed face. She's wearing a tight-fitting long-sleeve shirt with scales on one sleeve. They look like charcoal dragon claws that climb to her collar. The shirt flows out into a black skirt that matches her top. I've never seen such an outfit before. The stranger has straight red hair that's being pushed back by the snow. "Is Carac here?" she asks.

I glance at Xeres. Before he gets a word out, I myself reply with a heavy, brisk voice, "Um..." I need to think of an answer. I want to know who this lady is. "I don't think so."

"What's your name, dear?"

"Don't answer that," Xeres quickly commands from behind us.

"Xeres," she laughs, "I'm only curious."

"I don't care. You leave her out of this. She isn't involved," Xeres says. He's defending me. I can't keep switching my eyes between the both of them, so I watch the stranger.

"So he *is* here," the lady whispers. Xeres and I both turn around hastily to see Carac running toward us. His breathing is harsher than normal. There's no explanation for him to be outside unless he's here to explain who this woman is, or to face her down. He hates cold weather. His red face reflects the cold of the snow getting to him while he commands us, "Get inside."

I again try to see if Xeres has any guidance here, but they both look unsteady for once.

Carac loses any composure he has left and barks, "Isadora, get inside *now*."

The lady lifts her head in delight. She chirps, "You're Isadora? Carac, your wife is very pretty."

Carac exhales sharply. A cold cloud of air billows out of his mouth. You," he hisses at the lady, "You'd better get the hell out of here."

"It's too late, Carac. You can kill me and everyone else, but we were sent as a warning. I'm delighted to meet your wife. I think killing her will send an excellent message."

I gulp, but say nothing.

"How many are there?" he pants. She stands still; Carac walks up to her. "You *bitch*." He kicks the snow. "How many *are* there?" He takes her by the collar of her shirt. She gives no response, only a poisonous smile. "Fine," he snaps. The color leaves her face. She stops breathing. He releases his grip, and she falls to the ground.

Carac just killed her on the spot.

The snow now falls at its previous rate. Before I can say anything, a loud *BOOM* shatters the quiet. As I turn around, fire fills the snow's glow, allowing us to see a silhouette of the castle. An explosion just went off on the west side of the palace. I snap back to Carac. His face is paler than usual. He gasps out shallow breaths while brushing a hand through his hair.

The silence drowns in the sound of running. Steps are coming at us; there's no telling from what direction. Slowly, figures enter my field of vision. They surround Xeres, Carac, and I, a circle of shadows cornering us as we all take a stance in different directions.

"What's happening?" I ask.

"We're under attack."

"What do you want us to do?" Xeres asks, extending a hand in front of him.

"Fight," Carac breaths. The figures are closing in; unclear faces are attached to all of them. "I don't know how many there are. If I could kill them all at once, I wouldn't be asking for you to stay. Isadora, they're going to be gunning for you, so think fast."

"Now?" I ask quietly, ready to use my skills. If Carac is asking for assistance, this is going to be horrific.

"Now!" Carac yells as the figures spring into action. I see a glimpse of his feet dancing in the snow; he has no traction or balance. Carac has to conserve his energy if he's going to take down all the attackers he can.

He leaps forward, touching one attacker with each hand. It's the touch of death, literally. Each hand keeps moving in and out of the mass of attackers, taking them down in seconds. For each person Carac kills, it feels like three more appear. They wear dark colors, making them at least easier to see in the snow.

Each attacker has a different ability that can't be used fast enough before Carac takes their lives. He's literally talking down tens of them each minute.

I've lost track of Xeres since the fight started. Now, as I sprint into the fight, I can no longer see Carac in the snow. I'm at an advantage, literally in my element, making the snow stab up from the ground, taking out anyone who comes into my sight. The adrenaline and excitement of the battle take over my mind. I can't pause and ask who I'm fighting as I leap farther and farther away from my original starting point.

Twenty attackers later, and I've completely lost sight of my allies and the castle. I'm alone in a blizzard. I have to take anyone I see down, drawing any energy I have left. I pull up and grip two new ice daggers in my hands. I turn and slide, cutting and kicking anyone near. I multitask, taking them down while getting struck back every so often. Fire, metal, electricity, glass, air, and more all hit my skin and pierce me. My body continues to take the blows, but I start to feel my head become fuzzy. There's no stopping, even though every movement stings and cuts to the bone.

After a moment, I can breathe again. I'm surrounded by bloody snow and bodies. No more attackers appear. I can't see Xeres or Carac, even now that the snow has died down. It's still blinding when I try to see too far ahead. I must have drifted pretty far away from the others. I make myself run forward in a random direction. I have to check whether they need help, or if I can find anyone else. My legs are heavy; with every step, I feel they might give out. Even before Xeres met me on the lawn, I was drained from creating. But if I drop, anyone has the potential to find me and strike me down. I stand still in the snow; I need a minute to pray that I don't have to create anything else.

I hurry on, soon reaching the forest behind the castle. I continue to run into it, but there are no attackers to be seen. The trees are too tall to see their tops in the continuing snowfall.

As I lean over with my hands on my knees to breathe, the wind picks up and creates a hollow song all around me. I can't hear anything but the trees moving. Suddenly, a wave of heat rushes at my back. I turn to see a fire consuming the trees, and traveling fast. The destruction is jumping from one tree to another.

I turn and move as quickly as possible, focusing purely on running. Nothing else fills my brain. A tree root catches my foot, and I fall to my knees. They're still bruised from Xeres' torture; now the skin breaks open. This time the fall hurts much worse than before; I hiss through my teeth. The only movement I can make is to roll over on my back and huddle my knees to my chest and brace my arms. I curse aloud before I process a figure walking towards me. He stands high over me. I shuffle back through the dirty snow until my back meets with a rock, allowing me to press my weight against it and sit up. The man shakes his silver hair, which makes him look older than his face suggests. He plants his foot in front of me, digging in the ground firmly. His glare pours into my soul.

I reel at my surroundings. A circle of fire surrounds us. He isn't a fire controller. The emotionless stare he's holding tells me one thing: he's a wind manipulator, a dangerous kind of aeromancer. There's no light behind his eyes, nothing that fuels him except for emptiness and some unknown drive. He's the one who pushed the fire towards me, and now he's the one keeping it around us.

"You have no clue what's going on, do you?" he growls, taking a step closer. I hold my tongue. I can't get off the ground. "Yet you fight alongside him. Your ability is completely wasted on one so naïve."

"Who are you?" I manage to ask. The cold comforts my skin while I grip the snow. The attackers aren't from Din Point. They aren't a rebel group, either. He has an accent that isn't from anywhere near here.

"I'll offer you a choice. You can swap sides, help me burn this place to ashes, or you can stay here and burn to a crisp." His face is emotionless. He means everything he's saying. I need to know where he's from and what he's fighting for. The appeal to join them races in my head as the fires heat draws closer.

"You hesitated; therefore, you can stay here," he decides.

"Wait," I plead, but he turns his back on me and runs right into the fire, which parts as he enters and closes behind him.

The circle is now starting to close in on me. A burning branch falls near my leg as the trees burn. I huddle with my back to the rock. I have to escape the forest, but anything I create will melt in the fire. Any ice orb I could conceal myself in would get destroyed by the flames in minutes. There's only one thing I can think of, and it still has many risks. I have to pull from my surroundings. Any hope relies on the guess that a river or lake is close enough to draw from. The snow on the ground is giving me the time to pull for water.

Eventually, the water comes. It trickles in a small line to my hands. I make myself stand up and lean against the rock. I motion my hand up and force the water to shoot upward in a line that will destroy the flames for only a second. I jump through the cleared path, and continue to manipulate the water into a slim walkway.

The water barely holds. My skin is burning with every step. The water gets thicker as I follow it, making it safe to travel with less strength.

I come to a small lake in the forest. Nothing stops me as I jump right into it. My head dunks underwater. Every single cut, sting, and burn howls from the icy pain of the water.

I break the surface for air. There's no energy left in my body, but I need a ledge. The water streams into ice. I pull myself up to my creation and lie down. I'm stranded on an ice shield in the middle of this lake. The water is enough to keep me isolated from the flames.

The fire surrounds the lake, consuming the ancient trees.

I can't hold myself up any longer. My face meets the ice. The cold ensures protection; the flames will die down. My clothes are still drenched, but I can't keep my eyes open. Everything feels empty. A hollowness drags me down into sleep on the dense ice.

CHAPTER 36

Isadora POV

"What the hell are you doing?"

My hand slams against the ice. I open my eyes slowly to the frost around me. Every movement I make to sit up aches. My bones feel like icicles breaking with every motion. I sit crisscross, looking out to the lake. I'm still on the ice platform, still covered in scrapes, cuts, and burns. On the shore of the lake, Carac is shouting at me.

"Are you awake?" he yells again. His arms are crossed as he turns around to the group of guards behind him. "You can all go away. Now that you found her, after hours of looking!"

The guards quickly shuffle away into what's left of the forest. I peer at the trees behind Carac. They're burnt down, destroyed, far beyond recovery. The forest is only half burnt-down, though; someone must have stopped the fire before it consumed everything.

"Isadora," Carac echoes, "I know you can hear me!"

I blink heavily at him. Carac has so much explaining to do that I have no problem showing how pissed off I am. "What?!" I yell back. I stand up slowly on the ice. "What do you want?!"

"For you to come here. We have to get you fixed up." Carac looks over my cuts. There are so many. He, on the other hand, is barely touched. The only injury I can see is a cut on his neck. It's a long one that draws diagonally across, but isn't deep enough to kill him. It's just bad enough to stand out and look painful. Someone got awfully close to killing him.

"What happened?"

"I can't explain it from here." He sighs, with an anxious look. "The ice might break, you know." I don't move. "Isadora!" Carac bellows again.

I throw him a harsh stare, then jump on the ice forcefully. If it breaks, it breaks, and that's fine. I don't care anymore.

"Stop that," he calls.

I jump again.

"Isadora, cut it out!" He pauses for a second, and takes a deep breath. "At least come close so we don't have to yell everything."

"Fine." I shrug, creating ice as I step out on the water. It hurts to walk, but it hurts even more to produce. My skin is tight. My ability is still recovering. The freedom and spirit have been sucked out of me, but are in the process of coming back. I've never before used my ability so much. Not even close. There was never a reason to.

Alas's and Daymond's training was the only reason I didn't get myself killed out there.

"Tell me what happened," I demand at a comfortable distance. I still have enough water to separate me from Carac as he shivers in the snow.

He's wearing his crown. It makes his posture straighter and his face colder. I don't like the way it sits on his head.

"I had a whole team of guards looking for you. I was even out here looking for you. Why the hell were you in the forest? And how did you let so many people get past your guard that you got that many cuts?"

"Tell me who attacked us," I command.

"They set off a bomb in the castle's west wing. It's going to take months to repair, and money that I don't want to deal with. Did you know I have to deal with all that shit now? My first day as king, and already I have a fourth of the castle destroyed and an abundance of dead people on the lawn."

"Who caused that explosion? Who's dead on the lawn?"

My stomach drops as I think of how many people are, in fact, lying dead on the lawn. There are probably too many for me to count. I don't want to think about how many I killed alone.

"Come here. We can talk on the way to some meds." He's done with the weather and being uncomfortable.

I exhale, and create the last bit of ice I need to reach the shore. I just want to curl up on the ground and never get up. I want to bury myself in a snowdrift and never be seen again. His explanation, if he ever tells me, is going to reveal so many problems.

"Let me help," he pleads.

"I'm fine." I know he would carry me back if I let him.

"I'm in pain and didn't even use half of my energy. I know the feeling of being completely drained. Let me help," he insists.

"I'm not completely drained," I whisper. Why was he ever completely drained? How many people did he have to kill to get to that state?

He loops arms with me and takes some of the weight off. I hate being frail. I don't really want Carac to help, either, but I'm above being foolishly independent.

"Tell me what happened," I say. We walk through the ashes. Trees have been blackened to a crisp. The ground is covered with charcoal, alongside fallen branches.

"We got ambushed. A whole fleet of attackers."

"I want to know who, and why they came!"

"I can't tell you."

"You," I hiss while stepping wrong. "You can't keep this from me, not after I fought by your side. I'm part of the reason those people are gone, and I don't even know who they are."

"I'm thankful for your help, truly, but I think even without your assistance I could have gotten rid of them."

I scoff while stepping over a fallen tree. I look ahead; he's leading me in the wrong direction. I question, "Where are we going?"

"Just around the lawn. You don't need to see what's out there."

I lose my calm. "I am *queen*. You made me your queen, Carac; therefore, I have the right to know what's happening. I helped you, whether you admit it or not. I deserve to know!"

"It's not that I don't want to tell you," he explains as the castle comes into view. I can see where the explosion hit. The west side is torn inward and blackened on the edges. We walk on the path heading to the castle's side entrance. I don't see anyone lurking around. Any attacker is dead on the lawn, or long gone.

"Was anyone hurt in the explosion?" I ask. I lose sight of where it hit as we go through the iron-bound door.

"No. They wanted to hurt me, not anyone else."

"So I helped save your ass, and you still won't tell me anything!" I say angrily.

We walk into a room I don't even recognize. Inside is a medic who races to my attention.

"They wanted to kill you, too. You heard the lady; she commanded for you to be killed. We were both targets." Clearly, Carac doesn't care about the medic being in the room as he talks.

"Why did they want to kill me?"

He drops his shoulders and bows his head a bit. "Because they wanted to make a point to me. They want me to stop doing what I'm doing."

"What are you doing?"

"Trust me, I want to tell you."

"Then fucking tell me!"

"Oh," Carac chuckles a bit as he watches the medic do his work, "I so, so, *so* wish I could tell you. I wish I could have explained it all to you long ago. It's so unbelievably interesting," he purrs, enjoying having the advantage. "The information I have would make you question it all. You'd die to know, but I can't tell you. You're a liability, and if by some insane mishap you leave Din Point and see your princes again, I can't tell you. This information can never leave Din Point. I meant it when I said I have bigger issues to deal with than Din Point. These are those issues."

I purse my lips. "Do you even *know* what's happening? You looked shaken when you saw us outside. I bet you can't tell me because you don't know."

"I admit there's still a lot that doesn't make sense. But I've enough figured out to know what's happening."

"Does Xeres know?" I ask pointedly.

Carac laughs, "No. He might even know less than you. I spoke to him after; he's pretty shaken up."

"Is he hurt?"

"His ability allows him to attack at a distance. He doesn't even have a scratch."

"Want to tell me?" I plead again abruptly.

"We're not going to talk about this, or yesterday, ever again. So drop it," Carac orders, walking out of the room to take care of things.

I sit in the silence with the medic. It's the first time I know something essential that Carac doesn't.

CHAPTER 37

Isadora POV

I've asked at least ten people where Xeres is. No one has a solid answer. I search the halls everywhere for him. I've gone to his room, the sparring center, and the gardens. He isn't anywhere. Carac is too busy with the aftermath of the attack to place an order for me to stay in my room. As far as he knows, I'm the least of his worries.

The only place Xeres may be that I haven't looked yet is the library.

I love the library in Din Point Castle. It has an extremely large collection of books both new and old. There's a grand ceiling at least three stories high. It isn't musky, either, like Parten Castle's library. This one has several large windows and lots of natural light.

I walk in with downcast eyes. People are staring at me. My clothes are torn and in disarray. They have been drenched in water, frozen over, and now dried. I probably look like a disaster, but it doesn't matter right now. Sure enough, Xeres is in the back center of the library, sitting and poring over several books. I take the chair at the table across from him.

Xeres peers up to me with a pale face. "What do you know?" he asks.

"What makes you think I know anything?" I reply.

"You wouldn't be walking so confidently or even talking to me if you didn't."

"We should go somewhere else to talk."

He smiles a bit. It always feels like the world is going to end when he smiles. It's a sign of him always being five steps ahead of everyone. "I've manipulated the bodies of everyone around us so they can't hear anything."

I always marvel when I talk to Xeres. The way he speaks is so sharp and crisp. He knows how he wants to end a conversation before I say a single thing. As much as I hate him, he's brilliant. "Oh," I mouth.

"So, what do you think you know?"

"I'll cut to the chase, then. Carac says you weren't injured in the attack."

"I wasn't."

"I was though, so—"

"Clearly."

"So was Carac."

"And your point?" He's in a snappy mood.

"My point is, I don't think you fought in the attack. Not on our side, at least. Carac also said you know nothing about what's going on, but that's never true. You always know what's going on. You spoke with the women in black before Carac arrived. You warned me of the attack before it happened."

He lifts his head and brushes a hand through his light hair. "What do you think is happening?"

"I *know* that you're on their side. Whoever they are, you're with them."

His face remains still. He gives me no answer through his body language, instead asking, "If so, what are you going to do with that information?"

I wasn't expecting him to admit to it so readily. "I don't know," I whisper honestly.

"You're not the only one who wants Carac out of power, Isadora. As wrapped up as you and Carac are in feuding with each other, there are several things you both have missed. You want him gone; I do too, and so do my people. If you're smart, you'll keep everything, every single thing, to yourself."

I want to tell him that I actually want Carac in power, I just want him to use his power correctly. He's sitting on the throne and not making any moves; he's letting the council use him as a puppet. I want Carac in power so that maybe he'll actually do something. But I don't say that to Xeres. It's better for him to think I'm on the same page as him. "Who *are* your people?" I ask.

"The less you know, the better."

"But tell me, why? Why do you, of all people, want Carac gone? You've stood by him through everything."

"Everyone has their own motives for wanting him to perish. Carac knows too much about too many things."

"What does he know?"

"If I told you, I'd have to kill you," he mocks, though there might be some truth to his words. "Maybe once this is all over, you can know."

"Let me in on your secret. Tell me your goal and motives, and I can help."

"I don't think you have the guts to do anything, honestly. I think if I handed you poison for Carac, you would drink it yourself."

"That's not fair," I snap, not knowing if I agree with his statement or not.

"None of this is fair. If it were, we wouldn't be here. Here's how you can help: keep doing your part, and soon enough our paths will collide. What I can tell you is that many people here all want him gone for different reasons. Plenty want *you* gone too. Watch your back, Isadora." I gulp as he leans in close to me, "They can hear you now."

I stand up with my head full. I have plenty to think about.

CHAPTER 38

Lawrence POV

I cuff my sleeves up, placing the silver coin cufflinks into place to hold my outfit together. This isn't just any council meeting; therefore, this isn't just any outfit.

This meeting has been long-anticipated by nearly every official in the castle. Today we'll be casting votes for the final refugees law, the next year's council members, the trade and imports with Oxidence and Zenlands, and most importantly, the amount of ruling power that will be directly handed to Alas and Trinity.

I've been waiting for this meeting since the day Alas was crowned. The amount of power given to Alas and Trinity for this term is going to make or break things. In ten years, it will be voted on again, but this will the precedent for those future votes, and for the rest of Alas's rule.

The only negative thing about this meeting is that it's going to be long, tiresome, and very tedious, filled with long legal descriptions teeing up the voting. Only the highest council members get to cast a vote, along with me, Alas, Trinity, and, if she were here, Isadora. I'm sure the room will be buzzing with advisors, too, and my mother and father will also be present. My parents don't get a vote, but they still like to be involved in these things, for whatever reason.

Everyone who gets to vote will get to argue and make points during the debates. After that is the vote, and the act is passed and set to whatever the resolution is. Out of all the politics that take place in this Kingdom, Judgment Day is by far my favorite. I'm sure most of the kingdom is also sitting by waiting for the final results, which will be published tonight.

The handsome suit that was made for me today helps with the persona I'll have to project. I'm going to need to persuade the room in favor of whatever side I sit with. Alas and I disagree on nearly every single topic that will be voted on, and that will come through loud and clear. I 'll be taking a stance on every debate, except for the one about Alas and Trinity's power. I can't publicly go against my brother, so I won't partake in that debate. I'll be voting for Alas to get as little power as possible, though.

It doesn't matter if we're connected through blood or water, Alas doesn't deserve the power that he has a chance at. He's too aggressive and arrogant, and at times cares for the other kingdoms more than his own. Our kingdom will crumble in the next few years if the voting favors him. Worst-case scenario is they give him and Trinity override and majority vote; best- case scenario is that he gets the same voting power as a council member.

I walk down the hall with my head high, my crown in place and my thoughts aligned. The two guards walk with me at my side, minding their own business.

The meeting starts in 15 minutes, and it won't look good if I'm late.

As we walk, I see a group of guards running towards us— at least 20 of them. "Prince Lawrence," one of the guards puffs, "Please, come, there's an emergency."

I swallow and look at my watch. I have ten minutes. This had better be an actual emergency, and one that doesn't take up much of my time.

I don't have a chance to ask him what the emergency is as they start to run past me. I have no choice but to follow them. As I run, I take off my jacket and carry it by my side. We run through the halls and up the stairs to the top floor of the palace. I catch up to them and run alongside one of the guard captains. I continue to run with them until they all stop. I run a bit farther before I turn to look at them.

I glance at my watch; eight minutes until the meeting. "Where's the emergency?"

"In there," one of the guards says, and points to a door.

"Why the hell is everyone just standing around, then?" I demand. My hand clutches the door handle and I push it open. I feel a solid thump in the middle of my back, and I hit the ground. The door slams behind me. I turn on my side and bounce to me feet to look at the closed door behind me, dropping my jacket on the floor. I grasp the door handle; The door is locked. Outrage fills my throat as I bellow, "What the fuck are you doing?"

"Forgive us, Prince Lawrence," I hear a muffled voice reply form the other side of the door, "We're under strict orders to keep you in here for the day."

I feel my heartbeat increase rapidly as my head fills with red fury. "You let me out of this room right now!"

"We can't do that, Prince Lawrence."

"If you don't let me out of here immediately, I promise you that I will *ruin* you. I will make sure you never have the chance to serve as a guard or in the palace, much less anywhere else in Parten, for the rest of your life. Do you understand that?"

"We can't do that, Prince Lawrence," the same guard repeats.

I slam my hands on the door. I stand back a few feet and start to kick the door near the handle. I kick and kick, but the door isn't wood and is bolted in. There's no way sheer force is going to get me out.

I look at my watch. Five minutes until the meeting starts.

I kick the door again with all my strength; it doesn't even move.

"Who the hell set his up?" I yell at them.

"We can't tell you, Prince Lawrence," a guard replies sadly.

"I swear that if you let me out of here, I'll give you more than whatever you've been promised. I'll make sure that you get your reward in double."

"We can't take that offer, Prince Lawrence."

I slam my hands on the door once again. I turn around and look at the room. There are no windows; only a chair, some books, and a jug of water.

Nothing in here is going to help me. I kick my jacket to the side and place my hand on the door handle. I grasp it and try to cool it down to below the freezing point. If the door is cold, it might give me a better chance of getting it to give.

I kick it again and try every possible way to get it open. It doesn't work. I place my hands on the door against and heat it up to an extremely high temperature. Maybe I can melt it open. I try, and it doesn't work.

Whoever the hell set me up in here knew exactly what they were doing.

Alas POV

"Give it five more minutes," I say aloud to the room. I sit at the head of the table, with Trinity at my side. We both continue to look at the clock as the spectators and advisors in the room become increasingly antsy. I keep glancing at the door in hopes that Lawrence will run through it at any minute. He has to show up; he can't miss this.

"I think we have to start, dear," Trinity says, placing her hand on my wrist. I turn abruptly and look around the room again.

Where is Lawrence?

He promised everyone he was going to be here. This is the first time either of us can participate in one of these meetings, and the next one won't happen for ten more years.

My father sits in the spectator's section. He stands up and leans against the small divider that separates the meeting floor from the spectators. He gestures for me to come over. I stand up quietly as everyone continues to talk and dispute.

"Where is he?" I urgency ask my father.

"I don't know, but you have to start the meeting," he whispers.

"Lawrence needs to be here."

"He *should* be here, but he isn't. Start the meeting; there's not enough light in the day for this to go on forever. If he comes in late, then he can join in for the next vote and debate. I'll send guards out to look for him."

I purse my lips and shake my head. "This isn't right," I express to him.

"No, but you have to make difficult decisions as king."

I turn away and walk back to my position. I stand tall and call out to the room, "Sadly, we are missing the presence of our Princess Isadora," I announce. The room goes silent, and the attention turns to me. I see dismissive faces as the announcement spreads. Some of them don't want me to call Isadora our Princess while she's in Din Point, but it's too late to change what I said. I continue, "And Prince Lawrence. Either way, there are only so many hours in a day, and we must start the meeting."

Lawrence POV

I look down at my watch; the meeting has been going on for ten minutes. The introduction and first debate have already started. I grunt at the door while kick it and swear at the guards on the other side. "Tell me who the hell set this up!" I bark at them, my face hot, no doubt turning red.

I don't get an answer this time. I can still hear the sounds of guards moving around outside. Even if I get out of this room, I'm sure they will try to keep me here.

I look at the books on the table. If I burn them, it will do no good; the smoke will be stuck in this room, and there are no windows or good ventilation to let it out. I'll fuck myself over if I burn anything in the room. I look at the water in the vase. I can freeze it, but I'm not Isadora. I can't control it to form a shape that will be useful.

I continue to make more and more treats to the guards through the wall. No one answers.

I look at my watch again. Two and a half hours have passed, and I've made no progress in getting out of this room. I continue to search every single corner of the room and look for any fluke that will help me get out. There's nothing. Soon four hours have passed, and I've given up on getting out of this room.

I've started to read the books in the room and drink the water out of defeat. All this time has given me a chance to ponder who did this.

Carac had no reason to interfere with this meeting, and if he was going to, he should be messing with Alas, not me. Trinity also doesn't seem to have a strong enough motive to send me into the room; I don't think she'd be able to sway this many guards, either. Isadora is long gone, and she wouldn't do this to me anyway. If anything, she'd be stuck in this room with me if she were in Parten—or she'd be the person trying to get me out.

Alas has a reason. Alas has *every* reason to not want me at the council meeting. He and I disagree on everything that's being voted on today. I'm his biggest enemy when it comes to the refugee arguments, the trading with Oxidence and Zenlands, and even the military debates. I sit back in my chair, thinking on how my dear brother Alasdair has all the recourses needed to pull this off, too. He knows the guards well from working with them, and has the power to command them over me.

The rage builds in me as I stare at the door, knowing there's nothing I can do.

CHAPTER 39

Lawrence POV

The door clicks. I hear it move, making a small sound. I stand up and race to it. I place my hand on the deformed handle and pull. It opens for me with no problem.

There are no guards outside or in the hallway. No a single soul is around. I glance down at my watch and see that the meeting is well over. I've missed the entire thing.

I storm down the hallway, looking for any guard or answers. No one is on the top floor of the palace. I race down to the main floor and search the hallways. I rush into the meeting room. No one is in there except Alas. Everyone has cleared out: all advisors, guards, and spectators. His crown is in perfect shape, his dark brown hair cut and cleaned for the day. His is jacket off, since the meeting is over. He looks up and sees me. He stands up in a rush and calls out, "Lawrence!" I walk straight at him, my pace quickening.

When I get close enough to him I push my arms out, shoving him back.

"Lawrence!" he shouts again with a twisted, concerned face.

"That was *fucked up!*" I yell at him. "Do you really think I'm not going to do something about this?"

"What the hell are you talking about?" he snaps, pushing me back so I don't touch him again. "Lawrence, where were you?"

"You know where I was. I was locked in that damned room."

"I didn't lock you up anywhere. Father sent people out to try in find you. I delayed the meeting as long as I could, I'm sorry," he conveys. I don't know if I believe him.

"Who else would do that to me?" I yowl at him.

"I didn't do it! I'd never do that to you."

"Then who the fuck did?!" I bellow in anger.

"I did," someone says. Alas and I both twist our heads to look. Our father stands in the doorway, his head leaning forward as he closes the door behind him. My face hardens, and bewilderment flutters though me as I blurt, "What?!"

"*I* had the guards lock you in that room," he says emphatically. I stare blankly at my father and former king. His face doesn't change. He takes a few steps further into the room.

"What?" Alas repeats from behind me.

My father takes a seat at the other end of the room, at the large dusky oak table. "I made sure you missed the meeting, Lawrence."

"Wh-why would you do that?" I ask in shock.

"You would have come into this meeting and ruined it. I knew what you were going to say and how you were going to vote. The council and advisors were split on nearly every issue."

"You stopped me so that *my* side wouldn't pass any laws?" I say, my voice breaking.

Alas speaks up. "Laws and acts on both sides were passed. Lawrence should have been here to voice his opinion."

"Alas, Lawrence was arguing against everything you stand for."

"Not everything I stand for passed, and that's how it should be," he argues.

My father replies, "The ones that mattered got passed. I made sure of it."

"That doesn't make—" Alas tried to say, but Father's acid tone cuts him off.

"If Lawrence had been here, you wouldn't have gotten nearly as much power over the council. You would have been robbed of the power of the monarchy!"

"No, I *wouldn't* have. Lawrence would have helped me with that!" Alas yells while pressing his hands on the back of a chair. He's leaning forward, face becoming stern and filling with stress.

"Lawrence was going to vote against you on that issue," Father persists.

My heart flickers. I turn to look at Alas. He doesn't look at me; he keeps his eyes on at our father, but I can see his face change just an bit. I can't believe what I'm hearing. I clench my first and say unforgivingly, "You screwed me over. You screwed over everything I believe in! And for what? My ideas are just as valid as Alas's!"

"This is Alas's kingdom, not yours, Lawrence."

My mind turns hollow, empty of any love and faith I had in my father. "You don't mean that," I mutter brokenly.

"I do. You hold far too much power over this council, Lawrence. I did what I had to do."

I turn and blow past my father and out of the room. I slam the door behind me, not wanting to see their faces ever again. This kingdom is corrupt and going to shit. My father never deserved to rule, and he shouldn't even be here. Alas is going to take his ideas and be fueled by the laws that were passed today, and run this kingdom completely into the ground.

Alas POV

There is nothing I can say to my father to change what's happening. There is nothing I *want* to say to him. I walk straight past him as he calls out, "Alas, wait."

I dash out to the hall to Lawrence. My mind's going a million miles an hour as I see him. "You were going to vote against my rule?" I yell at him.

He stops in his tracks and turns. "Yes, I was," he states. His eyes are burning through his blue irises, shining with hatred.

"You want me to be a puppet, a figurehead? You want me to just sit on the throne and not get a single ruling past the council? That would strip you down to an advisor vote too, you realize that?"

"That's all I get anyway. You shouldn't have as much as they gave you... what was the final ruling, anyway?"

I pause for a minute. The words don't want to leave my lips. I tell him, "I can overrule any decisions, majority vote. That's how a king should rule!"

"That's how a good king should rule!" he roars. I can't look at him. I say nothing as he continues, "You're just like our father. He had overruling power, and he ruined things!"

"You may disagree with me on some laws, but you should never wish for the monarchy to lose its ruling power. I'm not even going to use the overruling ability unless I have to. I'm not like our father, but you can't run his name into the ground and say that he was a bad ruler. He was fair, and he did everything he could for this kingdom. He's sick, Lawrence! He's senile and fading more every day!"

"You think this is *fair*? You think silencing me was *fair*?" he questions, taking a step closer to me. My face is flushed. He doesn't mean what he's saying—he's angry, and rightfully so—but he cannot mean this.

"No! What he did was wrong! But you voting against me would have been the wrong choice too. You can have all the opinions against me that you want, and we could have had a wonderful debate, and some of the laws would have swayed the other way, but I cannot *believe* you would go against my rule!"

"You really don't see it?" he spits. "Our father made *thousands* of wrong decisions while on the throne, and you are just like him. He raised you to be him, and all I see for the future of this kingdom is failure. This kingdom is going to crumble under your rule."

"No, it will *not*!" I roar at him. "I'm a good ruler, Lawrence! I will *be* a good ruler. and I will do what is for the best of this kingdom! It wouldn't matter if it were anyone else on this throne, but it does because it's me. It's because *you're* not wearing this crown, isn't it?" I take the crown off my head and hold it out to him, "Take it. Will that make you feel better? Is that what you want me to say, that you'd make a better ruler? Because that's not true. You're not on the throne, nor will you be, and that's just fate."

He looks at the crown, then back up to my eyes. "I *would* be a better ruler. If Isadora were here right now, she'd tell you that too. Keep your crown while you can."

Lawrence turns on his heel and walks away from me. I have nothing more to say to him. He has betrayed me in every way. He's made it clear he hates me being on the throne, and that's something I'll remember. I always thought he was envious of the crown; now it's clear where he stands. He can continue to run amok under the table at this palace. I'm still his brother, even if he doesn't want that, and I will *not* use my power unfairly like my father did to get rid of him.

He will stand in this castle, and I will sit on the throne.

CHAPTER 40

Isadora POV

A week has passed since the attack. My cuts aren't totally gone, but thanks to some skin manipulators, they're far better. I still look scraggly, beat up, and tired. The only thing keeping me together is the fact that I've had the chance to get plenty of rest. Carac made sure of that by not allowing me to leave my room. I tried to leave every day, and every day the guards outside my room stopped me. I just want to be out of my room, but it isn't worth a big fight.

But there's a dinner tonight. All I know about tonight is that it's happening. Carac hasn't mentioned any details, but he did use another *you must*. His command was for me to act happy. For me to smile at the monitor, and seem thrilled with the marriage. It drives me mad to be as fake as everyone else in this palace, but it could be much, much worse.

Most of the time the maids take getting me ready is used to conceal my injures. They make my appearance very classy and clean. My gown is the most conservative thing I've worn in the form of a dress. It's plain, and my hair is simple. The only thing that stands out is the crown, but I can barely feel the weight of it on my head.

Everything seems to be normal. Maybe this is just another event.

Carac comes to the room. I inspect his outfit; reasonably simple. It's just another event, then. He doesn't say anything to me. I don't ask any questions.

This is also my first public appearance since the coronation. Once the doors open, cameras flood us from the press. Carac moves forward happily, smiling for the photos. He isn't sparing anyone a second thought.

Carac has a way with public appearances. He moves and smiles at the right times and makes everyone in the room forget about the terror in the kingdom. In seconds, he can turn from being carless and cold to warm and delightful. There are little things he does to forcibly change his moods. In daily conversations with me, he will drift in and out of his personas suddenly, too.

Carac reaches back and grabs my hand. He leads the way. "Do you want to sit?" he asks as we arrive at the table. "I can talk to the press on my own."

I'm a little shocked he isn't going to drag me around. "Sure, thank you." I never say anything in those conversations with the press anyway. Plus, my feet hurt.

Before I can ask him a question, he's gone and across the room.

For a few minutes, it honestly feels like not everything in Din Point is so horrible. Being married to Carac is still frustrating, but it isn't as much of a nightmare as I thought. Eventually, he's going to tell me about the attackers. And eventually he'll listen to my thoughts and change things. The longer I'm in Din Point, the more I can do.

I dine on a few bites of the cake on the table before I shove it away from me. It isn't good to eat their fancy things.

I turn to watch the crowd as familiar faces pass. The first person I see whom I know is the treacherous Ryder. He's flirting with a girl at another table. I wonder if he still has a thing with Trinity. Maybe he just switches personalities when he's in Din Point.

Xeres and Castilla are on the other side of the room. They look somewhat off. Castilla's eyes are sunken in her hollow face. But it's Xeres who has me confused. He's nearly shaking. His outfit is undone, nothing like his normal sophisticated look. A weak posture, along with his pale skin, makes me wonder if he's gotten himself too far into something. His condition is wretched; he looks like a walking corpse.

I immediately rise a bit from my seat and look for Carac. He's perfectly fine and talking with several people. Is Xeres going to try something tonight?

Suddenly, I feel lightheaded. My stomach curls; a sharp, shooting pain hits me. This isn't anything to do with my thoughts; this is a purely physical issue. I move my hand to my waist and try to apply some pressure to ease the pain. Carac is getting ready for his speech; I shouldn't tell him I'm feeling ill.

From a table away, Ryder stands. He moves over and takes a seat next to me. I try to not pay attend to him, and listen to Carac's speech as it starts. It's a small blessing that no one in the room will pay attention to me, as their minds are full listening to the speech.

Ryder inspects me. "Where did you get all those bruises and cuts?"

I shift my body away from him. My stomach is getting worse. I grumble softly, "It's not important."

Ryder looks to Carac on stage and whispers, "Did he do something?" I shake my head as he continues, "'Cause you can tell me. I'm on your side, if you want me to be…"

"No, no, he didn't do anything," I say. I'm struggling to think as the pain deepens.

"Did Xeres?"

"No," I say, flustered. "Ryder, I'm fine." But with my stomach tightening, I'm anything but fine at the moment.

"Okay. But if he lays hands on you, just cut them off." Ryder sits back, content with my answers. He brushes it off and chugs the rest of his drink.

I move forward and lean over my knees to try and stop the pain. I'm getting nauseous.

Ryder asks, "Are you okay?"

"My stomach," I quietly say. "I don't know what's happening."

"Do you want to leave for a minute? I can help slip you out for some air."

I nod, and he grabs my arm. We slowly and quietly begin to leave as Carac holds the center of attention in the room.

"My wife and your Queen share the same thinking," Carac articulates, and makes a gesture to me. "Isadora, dear."

Low, under his breath, Ryder whispers, "Just pretend you don't hear him."

I try to keep walking as Carac prompts, "Isadora."

"Don't," Ryder says. "I don't have a good feeling about this."

I turn around nevertheless. I made an agreement to be happy with him tonight. I have to listen, at least to an extent.

He motions for me to join him on stage. Ryder leaves my side as I walk up to him. I've missed the context of the speech, but still I walk on, smiling like I was told to.

Once in reach, Carac puts an arm out and wrap it around my waist, pulling me in close. His hand plays with my ring as he says, "As you know, we recently got married, but we have some more wonderful news to share with you." It seems the whole room is interested. I spot the camera broadcasting all this. "Currently, my wife, Isadora, is carrying our child and the future leader of Din Point. As the symptoms started early, we just couldn't bear to keep it a secret."

I have a hard time hearing any of the words he's saying, but I do understand that he just told the world I'm going to have a child. And that it's his.

I can't hold myself together any longer; I move my hand to my mouth. I veer away from the crowd. A lady at the side of the stage comes rushing at me with a bucket; once it's in my hands, I throw up in it.

I feel Carac's hand on my back, comforting me, but at the same time making everything worse.

After that, Carac finishes his speech and apologizes. He moves me off the stage and entirely out of the room. In the hall, what just happened sinks in. He told the world I was going to have his kid—a statement anyone could easily deny, but he added evidence. People in Parten and Din Point will have trouble denying it after seeing me throw up. I faintly recall him mentioning 'early symptoms' in his speech; he was referring to me when he said that.

I rush to my room with Carac on my trail. Once in the room, Carac takes off his jacket, throwing it on the chair. He moves out of the room and grabs me some water to help wash away the taste, smiling as he does.

"You think this is *funny?*" I say furiously while taking a drink.

"Slightly," he remarks. I take another sip and he says, "It was the cake."

I'm too angry to form clear sentences, "Yo-you!" I suck in a deep breath. Without thinking, I ruin my weapon by throwing the water in Carac's face. "Did you have a point?" I yell. "What's going to happen when I don't have a baby bump in a few months or weeks? Or when I don't have a kid in nine months?!"

Carac clenches his jaw and takes a second to collect himself. He's already going to get a towel for himself. He doesn't yell at me about the water. He wipes his face and starts to brush his shirt dry. "My point with all of this is that they were going to kill you. My parents told me that directly or indirectly, you'd die in a week."

My mouth clamps shut. He continues, "They hate you, Isadora. They wanted you dead, and they were going to do it despite my threats. The only thing I could figure out as insurance for you staying alive was this. They think you have something of value to them in you. They can't kill you, because then they kill Din Point's future leader. Under no conditions will they do that. I had to do this for your own good." My mouth is trembling. There's heat in my face. I don't even know how to react. He continues, "I haven't thought far ahead enough to nine months. We can say you had a miscarriage or something. We both know you aren't pregnant; we just need people to think you are."

Everything is a pure punch to the gut. This all goes far beyond me. This is horrible. Daymond will see the broadcast. Alas and Lawrence will see it, too. They will believe it. Carac doesn't have any sympathy for my relations with them. He couldn't care less about them. What Alas and Lawrence are thinking of me makes me want to tear myself apart. I don't care about everyone else's opinion, but it's the fact that the thoughts and opinions of the people I love are being manipulated that get me. I can't stop my emotions from breaking out. I look up at the ceiling in an effort to hold back my tears. After a minute I pull my face together; I won't cry in front of him. I breathe in and look forward.

"Looks like the mood swings are kicking in already," Carac jokes. It feels like every time he laughs, I'm getting dug deeper and deeper into to a grave. Everyone back home will think Carac has won me back. They'll think I want to be here. They probably think I left them for him.

"Please leave," I whisper.

"I was only joking," he says, a little defeated. He takes in my broken stare and explains, "I did this your own safety, so be mad at me all you want, but I'm the good guy here."

"Please," I say again. He nods and picks up his jacket.

"Isadora," he asked out to me.

"Please leave," I say, my voice breaking. He gives me one final plea of a look and then leaves my room.

The silence in the room consumes me. My thoughts start to attack again, and make my room a prison. I can't even make it to my bed. I just sink to the floor. I lean against the couch, curled up in my dress. I let myself embrace everything that's wrong in Din Point. Everything Carac has put me through and will put me though in the future. Tonight was horrific; the last few months have been torment. I let myself cry for everything I've been dragged through. Leaving Parten, Carac's proposal, Xeres' and Castilla's torment, the ambush, and now this. More and more things are piling up every day. I finally have to get my feelings out.

Eventually, I drift away from my thoughts and into a sleep that doesn't last long.

An hour past midnight, my door opens again. I've fallen asleep close enough to the door that the unlocking wakes me up.

I sit up. My eyes are burning. My face is wet. The dress feels old.

Drowsily, I look to see who's entering the room. The light from the hall reveals a face.

"Isadora," he says as I look up. "I'm going to die."

CHAPTER 41

Isadora POV

"What?" I yelp. My eyes take a second to adjust. I can now see Xeres in the doorway.

"I did something ungodly. Something went very wrong, and now Carac is going to kill me." His words come out as whispers, but translate into screams in the dark.

"What did you do?"

Xeres offers his hand. "I can't explain it to you. Not right now."

I grab his hand and pull myself up. "You think I'm going to help you without knowing what's going on? I can't save you if you don't tell me."

For a split second, Xeres grins. The moment flickers by quickly. "I'm not asking you to save me. I don't think you can." His words are rushed. Fear is taking control. "I just need your help. Please. You have the chance to make Carac... angry."

It's unsafe to make Carac angry. He gets flustered sometimes, annoyed a lot, but rarely angry. Anger in a pure form doesn't happen often in him, and it's hard to create in Carac.

Xeres read the doubt in my face. "Look, I know he's threatening, but the chaos caused will all fall on me. I'm the one who's going to die."

"What did you do to make him want to kill you so much?"

He glances around the room frantically. The person I knew before, the fierce, confident, resilient person, is gone entirely. The man standing in the room is terrified by a fear that Carac created. "We don't have much time," he whines, his voice cracking.

I have a burning ache in me from what Carac did to me. It gives me the fuel for revenge in any form. I don't like Xeres any more or less since the attack, but if it helps with a common cause, I'll agree. "Okay."

That's all Xeres needs to hear as he grabs my wrist and drags me out of the room. Turning swiftly around corners, Xeres somehow avoids all the guards. He's focused on staying out of sight. Nothing else matters. After twist and turns, we make it safely to Xeres' room. Once inside, he drops my arm. He glances ahead, out at the hall, before shutting the door only halfway.

"What do you need me to do?" I ask.

"Kill me," he says. My heart drops. "My plan is that it's quick and merciful. I'm going to take these pills." He moves and picks up a hand full of them. "They sedate me and I should overdose, so I'm going to be unconscious and dead in a few seconds. After that, I need you to stab me." He hands me a dagger. He points to his upper chest. "Right here."

"Xeres," I mumble in shock..

"I'd do it myself, but if I mess it up, then he can bring me back to life. I need to be gone for good. You have to do it right; you need to end me fully. He can bring back people with certain injures, but if you stab me in the heart, he can't."

"Xeres," I plead, "we can fix this. We can get you out of the castle if we try. We can escape this; you don't need to die."

"I do have to."

"We can get you off the grounds. You can leave and avoid him." My stomach aches. Xeres is a horrible person, but he isn't horrible to everyone. He's kind to some people who don't kill his siblings. He's too young to die. He has too great a gift to die.

"Isadora, I need you to do this."

I cry, "Please Xeres, we can—"

"Please," he begs, "Please. I chose you to do this because I don't have anyone else. Please, Isadora, I need you." My hand is shaking with the dagger in my grip. "Promise me that you'll make sure he can't bring me back."

"Xeres—"

"Promise me!" he yells.

My throat closes. My head goes dark. My words shake as I say, "I promise."

He immediately takes the handful of pills. "Take this," he says and hands me a ring. "It isn't much, but it could be useful."

I take the ring he gives me. I don't have a second to look at it as I shove it in my pocket. "Thank you," he says, and then closes his eyes.

I grab his hand and hold him tightly. His breathing slows. His body grows stiller. It only takes a few seconds for him to completely stop breathing. His grip loosens. I hear footsteps in the hall. I try to wait as long as I can to make sure Xeres is sedated and doesn't feel a thing.

I hear the door open, and stab Xeres in the chest. I drag the knife a little. He's gone forever.

My hand lets go of the dagger as I stagger back. Blood is oozing out of the wound. It feels like hours pass as I watch the color leave Xeres' face. I can't tear my eyes away. His lifeless face is set in place. Tears form in my eyes.

"*What. Did. You. Do?!*" Carac screams at me. His voice is ruthless. He really *did* want Xeres alive.

Carac is furious with both me and Xeres. I knew that Carac wanted Xeres alive for a reason. If I hadn't killed Xeres, thought, he would have suffered torture and more from Carac. Instead of a brutal death, Xeres died quickly. He died to keep his secrets in his head. My voice shakes as I look at Carac and say, "I killed him." There are pills on the floor. My dress has blood on it. Tears silently drip down my face. I stand in horror at my own actions. I throw the dagger to the floor in anguish.

Carac doesn't look at me. "Leave the room."

I pick my dress up and walk out. I'll let Carac take his anger out without my presence. Xeres has escaped Carac's wrath.

Carac has been outsmarted, a rare occasion for the Prince of Death.

CHAPTER 42

Isadora POV

I don't leave my room the next day. Or the day after that. Or today, so far. I'm going to have to see Carac eventually, but I plan on avoiding him for as long as possible.

I sit at my desk, writing, planning, and occasionally looking over the ring I was given by Xeres. Maybe it's an heirloom, or something he just saw personal value in. There's a red ruby in the center of the ring. A pure golden band keeps it in place.

What happened with Xeres is heart-wrenching. I have to try to remember that I wasn't the reason he died. I have to remind myself that he came to me. He wanted to die; he knew that before whatever he did.

My door opens quietly. Emotionless, Carac enters the room. "I want to train today."

"Train?" I know better than to take anything that easily. For Carac not to yell or scream or be angry at all about what happened. I can't even tell if I want to train with him.

"Did I stutter? Come on," Carac commands. There's more to this. If not, then I just want to fill the void of silence with questions.

With a gasping breath, I ask, "Why did you want to kill him?"

"There's nothing I can tell you."

"I know he knew about the attack h—"

"No, he didn't." Carac pauses. He takes in what I said. I've spoken too soon. A flicker of shock goes through his eyes before he ask, "How do you know?"

"I know more than that, but if you don't explain things to me, I'll keep it to myself." I'm sure I have something to hold over Carac now. Maybe nothing big, but he doesn't know that.

Carac holds the door open. He vows cheerfully, "I can figure everything out myself."

A wave of irritation passes through me as I follow Carac down the hall. He's going to have to tell me one day, but for now, that conversation is finished.

Carac turns the wrong way down the hall. We aren't going to the training room. Instead we walk outside to the lawn. It's freshly cut and cleared of any damage. It looks like nothing ever happened out here. I tilt my head at Carac. There's no reason to be outside. The training room in Din Point is three times the size of Parten's; it's stocked with rare items and specially made weapons. The only downside is that it's barely ever used.

"If we're training, why are we outside?" I ask.

"It's the first really sunny day in weeks. I wanted fresh air."

There are plenty of people on the lawn; many workers and guards and people just walking, enjoying the sun. I'm sure Carac wasn't planning to train today. He's dressed far too nicely and doesn't look bothered. He isn't wearing a suit, nothing extreme, but still, he's wearing a nice button-up shirt with a collar, slacks, and dress shoes.

"Want to warm up?" Carac asks, taking four hand blades out of his pocket. Why would he be carrying knives? Maybe it's a coincidence, but I find that hard to believe.

He offers two of the blades to me. Before I can throw them at anything, Carac rolls his shoulders back and takes aim. He launches the two daggers into a tree with barely a glance. They both land in the center of the trunk, right on top on each other, dead center.

I scoff under my breath. He's improved a lot since the last time I saw him do this. Before, Carac never really practiced regular training; he relied on his ability.

I realize there is water near us. I set down the daggers on the grass. I didn't want to just throw a knife. I make the water travel from the ground over to me. I create my own weapon. My dagger is sharp and strong enough to take hold in a tree. I throw my weapon and it hits perfectly next to Carac's. I stand back and smile at myself.

"Are you ready now?" Carac asks me mockingly.

"Who am I sparring with?"

Carac looks around the lawn. He motions to some guard far away. Then the star player comes out. "Ryder," Carac yells. Ryder steps away from his group of guards quickly, with a smile, like he's the Chosen One. "Are you feeling up to sparring?"

Ryder tilts his head in interest. "Always," he says.

"Go on, you two," Carac twiddles, nodding his head to the center of the lawn.

This is definitely an unfair advantage. Ryder is a floramancer, a plant controller, and this is a lawn filled with grass and other plants. I'm going to get pummeled.

Ryder looks at me with a half-smile; he's ready to play.

"Start!" Carac says happily.

I know that Ryder is immediately going in for an attack. I'm prepared, to an extent. First, I call for water to soak the ground. Soon, there's water all over the lawn. It's going to be hard to lose track of my resources now. This way, I can pull up and form a weapon at any moment; it's my new favorite trick. Through the mud and water, Ryder commands plants to rise up. Vines twist against each other, pulling their way to the sky. A vine latches onto my ankle. I form a handheld ice knife.

Ryder makes the vine tough, pulling me to the ground. My body hits hard, my head hitting the ground in whiplash. I quickly cut the vine so it can't drag me anymore. I stand before he can cage me in more vines, and dash to a new section of the lawn. I need to keep moving. I make another dagger from the water, and throw it at Ryder.

It cuts his arm as more plants start to form around me. It takes me a split second to realize that the plants are being creating from all sides. I leap into action and jump over the vines before they can enclose me. I land right next to Ryder, and use my force from the jump to grab his arms and push him to the ground. I twist my arms out to pin him there.

He turns violently and pushes me to ground. The arm I was holding is now pressed against my neck. Ryder doesn't move to control any plants. "Time?" he asks me.

I can't respond, so I make another sword in my hand. Ryder doesn't notice my weapons as he starts to make vines crawl over my legs. My waist gets pulled harder into the ground. I use my hand to sneak the sword up to his stomach. With one push, I can impale him. I wait and creep the sword to the middle of his chest. I want to win, but I don't actually want him to die. I slowly push the sword into his skin.

"And, time!" Carac yells from a distance.

Once he feels the sword, Ryder jumps off me quicker than light. He stands up and looks at his chest. It's slightly cut, not badly, but his shirt is starting to stain red.

Ryder shakes his shirt off and looks at Carac with a glare. "Isadora won," Carac says with a fake slow clap.

"What?" Ryder interjects. "I had her wrapped up! In a minute the vines would've cut off her breathing and I would've won."

"Do you think that bleeding on your chest is from nothing? Isadora had an ice sword right next to your heart. If she'd moved an inch inward, you would be impaled and dead. I ended the round before she kept pushing."

I'm thankful I was able succeed with my ability. While Carac speaks, I push the water back into the ground far enough that it won't get any muddier.

Ryder shake his head and starts to walk away. He's a lot smarter in combat than I thought. He's clearly annoyed that he didn't win, even if he did do an excellent job.

I'm sure Carac is going to have me fight someone new, but he doesn't call for anyone.

Instead he steps closer and rolls up his sleeves. "All right, now you can spar with me," he says, delighted in taking a stance.

I haven't sparred with Carac in years. No one really spars with him. It takes him actually wanting to win for a round to be over. He only spars with people to work on his hand-to-hand combat skills. I don't want to fight him. He's just going to mess around and take out some aggression. Regardless, I take a position and prepare to call back the water in the ground.

Carac stands casually. He leans back and declares, "Start."

In seconds, I have water surrounding me. I'm ready to from a proper weapon as soon as Carac advances. He makes no movement. He doesn't need to grab a weapon; he was born one. I wait until he takes a step, then form two daggers from my palms. Once I move closer to Carac, I hurl on, aiming for the ribs. With a lunge, Carac moves to the side. The dagger misses him. I know he has quick reactions, but that was better than expected. I'm annoyed and impressed simultaneously.

I'm going to have to use a different strategy. I throw the second dagger. Carac moves to the side, but before he lands, I make another blade and have it flying through the air. He tries to roll to the ground, but the dagger still cuts his shoulder. The blade rips through his shirt and into the skin. Standing with blood dripping down his arm. Carac's face shows pure annoyance. "I liked this shirt," he says with a dark laugh.

He takes a few steps closer to me. I've already turned the water into more weapons to use. I create a long sword. Before I'm close enough to do damage, I suddenly lose my strength. I use my free hand to brace my chest. My heart is giving out. I morph the sword into a cane. I lean on it to stand. The life is being draining from me. The last thing I see is Carac grinning, running his hand through his hair.

Then I'm gone.

CHAPTER 43

Isadora POV

"You killed me!" I yell once I'm finally alive and awake again.

"You deserved it," Carac yells back. He's midway through reading his book. He sit on his bed comfortably as I try to get my head back into real life. He's obviously brought me from the lawn to his room.

"You killed me!" I repeat. It's the first time Carac has ever killed me firsthand. It needs to be the last. "This is the second time I've died because of you! This is the second time I've died *in total*"

I try to lift myself up to stand, but there's too much comfort in laying on the couch. Carac doesn't even set down his book as he says, "And I brought you back both times. Really, you should be thanking me for bringing you back to life."

"See the issue here? Every time I die, it's *your fault!*"

"Get over it. Eventually you'll die and it won't be my fault. Then you'll want me to be there."

"How long was I out for?"

"Hmm," he pounders, "Around thirty-five minutes."

"Thirty-five! The longest I've seen was twenty minutes, and you had me out for longer than that?"

Carac brushed off his shoulder. "New personal best."

"You gambled your ability on my death?"

"I won the bet," he drags, raising an eyebrow.

"You're twisted."

"For challenging myself?"

"Just stop killing me. That's all I'm asking."

Carac slightly put down his book to reveal a dangerous smile.

"Carac?"

And then, for the second time today, he kills me.

CHAPTER 44

Isadora POV

"What the hell is wrong with you?!" I scream, after already yelling at Carac for a few minutes. I start to pace the room. Carac finally puts his book away.

"You were annoying me," he says, already bored.

"Therefore you killed me?"

"If you don't stop whining, I'll do it again."

"How many times can a person die?"

"So far, you're the only one I've saved three times."

"*Killed*," I correct. "*Killed* three times. How long was it this time?"

Carac crosses his arms. "Seventeen minutes."

"How many people have you killed this week? Aren't you bored killing people?"

"I don't know how many. That's not something I want to keep track of."

I think of Xeres and his death; that must have taken some toll on Carac. I think of Theo, too, how he died because of me. I don't know if Castilla is still alive. It will be an honest tragedy if all the Shade siblings are dead.

"What happened to Castilla?" I ask as the thoughts cross my mind.

Carac gets out of his bed and pours a cup of tea. "Dead. She was no use to me."

"You had to kill her, too?"

"Her and Xeres. I hope they burn in hell. Theo and Zaven were the only good ones in that family."

"What did Xeres and Castilla do to you?" I ask in disgust at his tone, but show a bit that I want to know.

"What did they do?" Carac snaps. "You didn't ask Xeres that before you killed him? Did you even have a reason to take his side?"

I go silent. I don't know what Xeres did. I don't even have the slight idea. "I killed him to keep what he knew with him. I truthfully don't know what he did or what he's protecting, but I know it's important, and I know it should be kept from you."

"You don't even know? You took his side *blindly?!*" He's angry at me, actually angry. I can hear the heat of his words. "He tortured us as kids! He wanted to tear you apart, and you took his side?"

"I was upset, and he was there. I didn't take his side; I just didn't take yours."

The anger is building in both of us. He has a point to what he's saying, but so do I. If Xeres was willing to ask for my help and fully admit he was in trouble, it means a lot.

Carac's face is growing colder. His voice is still not raised as he says, "You sided with him out of spite?"

"I sided with him because of you!" I finally cave in and yell. I lower my voice and tell him, "I sided with him because of everything you've done. Because you told people that I'm pregnant with your child that night. I know you think it was for my own good, but if it weren't for everything that I've been dragged through by you, you wouldn't have to tell such shitty lies in the first place."

"You're not having my child. You also don't know anyone in Din Point. Why do you really care what lies I tell them?"

"Because they will see it. My brother will see, and so will..." My voice drifts off.

"Because your stupid princes will see it, and because they'll think it's real and forget about you."

It feels selfish to even believe they still care. Alas and Lawrence think I changed my mind and slept with Carac and ran back to the old life I told them I despised. They think I'm over Parten and will move on. They *will* forget about me.

I don't want to give Carac anything more to feed off of. I get up from the couch swiftly and head for the door. "I need to go to my room." The thoughts in my head are building toward a breakdown. I refuse to break in front of him.

Carac stands up too, and reaches to block the door. "I'm not done with this conversation."

"Just let me leave," I say. My hand moves under his and grabs the door handle. He takes my wrist and moves it away from the door.

I'm on the verge of breaking. I want to leave before he sees me fall apart.

"I asked him, okay? I asked Xeres what he did. I asked *you*. Am I missing something major here? You're the reason Xeres killed himself." His face twists when I say that he killed himself. "That's right," I repeat. "He took pills and sedated himself to death. He asked me to end him so you wouldn't bring him back. But you're the reason he's dead. He was one of the smartest people in Din Point. Someone who was young and full of potential. You could have used him to do amazing things with his mind."

"He was a horrible person," he argues, still holding me in place.

"He was a kid when all that happened to us. We were all kids. None of us knew the extent of our power then. Xeres never truly hurt us, and what he did to me was because I killed his brother!" I can feel my face turning red. My emotions are tired and raw. "He was grieving for the loss of his brother."

"What did he do to you?" Carac asks softly while tracing over me with his eyes. He only now realizes there's something I didn't tell him.

"I didn't want to kill Theo!" I yell. I've reckoned with Theo's death only briefly. The thought of taking his life has been consuming me for days. All the people who died during the attack feel like a weight on my chest, sinking me down farther and farther, and Xeres was the final weight to drown me. I mumble, "I-I didn't want to."

"Calm down," Carac says softly. "What did Xeres do to you?"

"I need to leave. I need to leave this castle. I need to leave this disaster of a kingdom."

"You made a deal. It's okay, calm down, we can get through this."

I struggle, trying to free my arms. Carac continues to use his strength to hold me still, but I feel the anger draining from his grip.

I spiral down my thoughts. "They're going to forget about me. They're going to hate me. I hate myself for what I did." I never want to be like this in front of Carac. I never want to let him know he's gotten to me, but I'm flying through my thoughts and can't stop. "They already hate me, and Daymond is probably worried sick."

This is the first time I've allowed myself to talk about how much these thoughts are killing me. I've kept my mind busy, never letting it get to this point. Now, as I say it out loud, I can't stop my tears. Carac moves his hands to wrap me in a hug. I stop fighting and wrap my arms around him. He moves back to look at me. He still holds me close with one hand, the other moving to brush my hair back.

After a minute, I realize how this situation has me more vulnerable than I should be. I push Carac back in a slow motion.

The anger I have is wet. It's an anger that makes water in my eyes and my voice shake. I choke on my breath and the room becomes uneven. I can barely see through the tears. "None of this would be happening if it weren't for you and your obsession. You're the reason I'm stuck here, tearing myself apart over every little thing. I wanted to stay here, Carac. A part of me really wanted to come back and see that things where changing, but they aren't. I asked you to make me want to stay, and the only thing I've felt is a bigger urge to take back this deal."

Carac stands and takes my fury. His is a dry anger, and it's growing. His face turns cold. His voice becomes shaper than any weapon I could form. He speaks monotone, with filtered dialog, "You were born to live your life here, to be a team with me. You always said that, and now you want to forget about everything we've been through, everything we had going for us. You're the reason all this has happened. You understand that? You started this whole thing on your own. It would be better for all of them if you moved on and let them forget about you. Whatever you tell yourself about Xeres isn't true. You can tell yourself whatever you want to feel better, but we all know deep down it isn't true. After you kill people, you need to get over it, or life here will ruin you, and it's already started to."

I can't bear to fight with my words anymore. I move myself out of Carac's hold and he lets me. I turn to the door and walk out before he can drag me down any further.

CHAPTER 45

Isadora POV

I've spent the last day alone in my room, replaying Carac's words. Our argument has been ringing in my head for hours on end.

You're the reason all this has happened. You understand that? It would be better for all of them if you moved on and let them forget about you.

I can't tell myself it isn't true. I don't even want to leave my bed.

Rapidly, the realization that everything *is* my fault emerges; everything that's gone wrong in the last few years comes down to me. I'm the root of all these problems.

From my bed, I see a paper slide under the door. I stretch out my legs and walk to the door to see what it is.

It's a newspaper. I'm never given these in Din Point. Quickly I pick it up and start to read it. The headline on the paper makes my stomach twist.

Former Parten King Found Dead

I read the paper faster than I wanted to receive the information. The report says the old king died in his sleep, no injury and no struggle. Two reactions pulse through my head.

One, how are Alas and Lawrence? And two, did Carac have anything to do with this?

I look at the rest of the newspaper. There are new death counts in Din Point. The updated horrors roam under everyone's nose... or the updated horrors building under the noise.

I need to do what I can to save myself from Din Point, where I'm slowly wasting away. And I need to do something for the people living in this Kingdom, who are suffering the same fate. It's time for me to finally see how far I can push the limits in Din Point. I move to my desk and pick up pen and paper, and begin to write.

Dear King Alasdair,

I miss you and Lawrence greatly. And please tell Daymond I am fine.
I am terribly sorry for your loss. Your father was a brilliant king, and I see the resemblance you share with him every day.
On a different matter, I am writing to you in new terms and context at Din Point. I am worried about the information the press has portrayed in the past few weeks about me. Know that it is Carac's doing, and nearly everything you have seen was taken out of context and is a lie.
I need you to be ready for a change when the time comes, and I believe it will be soon. Perpetration of my newfounded idea is essential, and I am relying upon the fact that you still trust me enough to be on my side. Whatever communication outlets you have in Din Point, utilize them in these next weeks, as Carac's throne is becoming weaker. Also, disclose your information to your guards very carefully. Anything about Din Point or internal matters should be told only to essential people, as Din Point has spies working in Parten.

Best of wishes,
Isadora Xxon

The letter needs to be vague. If someone, by some fluke, were to learn of my true intentions, it could cause an uprising. I seal the letter shut with a wax seal to reinsure that when Alas receives it, it contains only my words. I need Alas to be on standby, and I'm hoping that he still has the smallest bit of faith in my words.

I rush into the halls. My door is unlocked, but it's only a matter of time before I get caught by Carac or someone else. I find a guard in the hall. "Could you direct me to Captain Ryder, please?" I ask her. She leads me down the hall to a conference room.

A meeting is just letting out. I grab Ryder by the arm and look around for Carac. He's nowhere in sight; he must not have been part of the meeting. "Ryder," I whisper as everyone else gets farther away from us. "Can you do me a favor?"

"Oh, hello," he says charmingly. "Depends on what it is."

"I know you're... working against Carac in some ways," I say.

His face lowers toward mine. "What do you mean?" he asks quietly.

"You wouldn't be doing everything you are to help Parten if you were fully on Din Point's side. I just need you to mail a letter. In return, I can get you any resources you might need in Parten."

"I'm not loyal to either side," he says bluntly. "I'm a free agent." He takes the letter out of my hand. "I'll mail this, but you must give me your word that you won't speak of my double-sided work to Carac."

"I give you my word."

He nods and happily walks away. It's a longshot, but if there's anyone who can get a letter back to Parten, it's Ryder. He's probably traveling back to Parten in a day or two.

CHAPTER 46

Alas POV

"Lawrence," I say sharply as I walk down the hall towards him. I motion for him to follow me. It's always like this now. No, "How was your day?" No, "Do you need help?" No questions about each other's work. Nothing except piercing looks and heated body language during council meetings. Ever since our fight, we've been avoiding each other and making life much harder than it needs to be. There have been small incidences here and there where we do things to undermine each other. Nothing major yet, really just petty actions that are still enough to get under each other's skin.

I tried to talk to him again about what happened, and to apologize for what Father did to him—because it truly wasn't fair. It was a cruel thing our father did, and I'm honestly sorry on his behalf for it. But Lawrence walked away before I could even get a word out. And because he has given me nothing but silence to work with, I've spent days thinking of what he planned to do to me. He was going to auction off my power to the council so that I would indeed become their puppet, just the face of the throne.

That's something a brother should never, ever do. Especially when he's just as much a royal as I am.

Really, I think he's detached himself from the royalty side of his power. He no longer shows up to many meetings, he doesn't join Mother, Trinity, and I at dinners, he doesn't speak to anyone except for those he has to. And worse of all, I think he's taken what Father did and engraved it in his head as who our father was.

At the funeral, when the air was filled with sorrow, and my mother was sobbing in the crowd, when I was trying my best not to break down in front of everyone who attended, Lawrence did nothing. There were hundreds of people there: council members, guards, staff, loyalists who all came and wept over our father. Thousands of tears were shed. And then there was Lawrence, who stared down at the coffin with a stone-cold face.

He didn't show distress or mourning even for a second. Anyone at the funeral could have argued that it was his way of coping and holding in what he was feeling. But I know Lawrence; I know that he couldn't have kept such emotions inside of him if he'd had them. I know that if he were truly grieving, he would have been crashing down on the ground of the cemetery and crying enough tears to water the place into a flood. But instead he was still, numb.

I left the funeral early because I could no longer stand there breaking down while my brother did nothing. When I left the funeral, I felt my throat collapse inwards and my skin start to shake, and the tremors have not stopped since.

But he has not changed. Lawrence should have forgiven him. Lawrence should put everything behind him, and realize that he's dead.

Our father is dead.

He's dead, and there's not a single thing I can do about it. The one person who should be able to understand what I'm going through won't talk to me.

I shake my head and continue to walk down the hall. I listen to make sure Lawrence is following me. I walk us right into a meeting room where Daymond is already waiting. "King Alas," he says and then adds, "Prince Lawrence, I hope you brought me here for something other than just talk."

I hold up a letter creased between my fingers and say, "A letter from Isadora." I take a seat and watch carefully as Lawrence grabs a chair closer to Daymond than to me. I slide the letter across the table and into Daymond's hands. Lawrence gets out of his seat and stands over Daymond to read it.

"A letter to you?" Lawrence asks. I can hear the addition to that sentence in his voice. The part that's thinking of how she wrote a letter to me, and not to him.

"Yes, and from the writing, I don't think she's gotten a single one of our letters," I add, with my voice holding much more sternness than normal.

After a moment of reading, Daymond, without looking up, admits, "I didn't write her any letters."

Lawrence stands up straight and casts me a glance as a response to Daymond's statement. I feel my gut tighten a bit. I've written Isadora several letters, and I know Lawrence has too. But Daymond, her brother, hasn't sent a single word to her.

Lawrence sits back down in his chair and says what I'm thinking. "You didn't write her at all?"

"What was am I supposed to say? Congrats on the marriage? The child?" It's almost too silent as we wait for him to continue. "Carac is playing some game with her over there, and I'm not here for it. He went and got my sister pregnant and made her Queen of Din Point. That's everything and more that I didn't want for her, and worked my whole life to stop. Next time I see Carac, fucking Prince of Death or not, I'm shoving a dagger through his chest. So no, I didn't write her. Because I don't trust a single thing over there. She said in the letter that Carac is manipulating what we're seeing in the press. Whatever the hell you sent her, I guarantee Carac has read it. And until I get a letter like this directly from her, I'm not listening to a single broadcast or word that I hear from Din Point. I would never send a letter, because I know it would be compromised."

I clench my hand onto the arm of the chair. Daymond has never, not once, spoken to me of what he thinks of Isadora being in Din Point again. I've tried to use him as a resource, but he's always said that Isadora is playing out something, and that he's not interfering until he has to or until Isadora asks him to. This letter from her shows all of us that if she needed help earlier, she probably would have figured out a way to communicate it.

My voice increases in austerity. "I didn't send anything in a letter that I wouldn't want someone else reading. I'm not that thoughtless or carless, Daymond. And this says that Din Point has people working here in Parten. Now, I know the people in my council inside and out, but I don't know everyone in the guards and the military. And Isadora pointed them out specifically. So I'm ordering you to check your people again, because whatever you're doing, they probably know."

"My people are secure, King Alas. I'll check them again if you wish. And we both need to start getting people ready in Din Point. If Carac's throne is growing weaker, then Isadora, I hope, is going to take advantage of that, and we need to be ready," Daymond says. He takes the letter I gave him and shoves it into his pocket. He stands up and says dismissively, "I need to get to work on this." He leaves the room; Lawrence stands as he does.

"Lawrence," I call out again. He exhales heavily, and drops his shoulder while turning around. "Stay a second."

He walks back into the room, flaring his hands out slightly while mockingly saying, "Yes, Your Majesty."

"Sit down," I order, trying to ignore his hostile attitude. He pulls out his seat from before and resentfully sits in it. I study him for a moment, taking note of the way he refuses to look at me until I make him. The way he sits and crosses his arms to show he that wants nothing to do with me. After a moment of me not saying anything, he blurts, "Yes?"

"Stop acting like this," are the first words I can think to say.

"Oh, apologies. I didn't realize my attitude was a royal issue."

"Stop acting like this, Lawrence. Fix what you're doing, and pull yourself together. You need to start coming to court meetings again; whether you like it or not, you have duties to attend to. Mother isn't going to get on your case for this because she's dealing with so many other things, but I'm telling you—no, I am *commanding* you that you need to go back to doing your duties. You're a royal, not just someone living in this castle, and you need to get it together."

"Why don't you just cast me out then, huh? Kick me out of the kingdom, throw me in a prison. Really, you can do whatever the hell you want with your overruling power. So do it, Alas. If you're that annoyed with me, do something."

"Cut it out, Lawrence," I snap. "You're not the only one dealing with difficult things here. But you *are* the only one taking people down with you because of it."

"Fuck you, Alas," he snaps back while jerking his head forward. My shoulders tighten as I raise an eyebrow in anger. I don't open my mouth. He wants a fight to break out, and I won't feed into his ways. He shouts at me, "You don't get to tell me to fix my attitude! I get no fucking say in court meetings! You think anyone listens to someone who missed Judgment Day? You think my *one* vote makes any difference? And you have no right to say that I'm not the only one dealing with things. My wife—my wife!—is out there married to the king of an enemy kingdom and is going to have his child! So fuck you and your throne."

I lunge out of my chair and stand in front of him.

"Do not *ever* speak to me like that again, or I'll use my overriding power to make sure you never get to say another word to anyone in this castle. We shouldn't be enemies; we shouldn't be yelling at each other like this, and I shouldn't have to watch my back from my own brother. You're going through a lot of things, but it does *not* give you an excuse to ignore everything that's happening right now. You're still a prince; you still have a vote, and that can do a lot of things in this court. Get your shit together so that when Isadora *does* come back, she doesn't have to clean up the mess you made for both yourself and her in the court."

He shoves past me and walks out of the room. The door slams shut behind him.

I rest my hands on the table, taking in deep breaths to try and cool down from the conversation. Lawrence is running amok in the castle, and I'm on my last strand of patience with him about it.

CHAPTER 47

Isadora POV

It's been a few days since my argument with Carac. Weve both had time to think about that we said. I'm still frustrated about everything he yelled at me. I'm sure he feels the same way. I've been trying to avoid him, but I have to see him tonight for a dinner. My presence was requested.

The maids arrive at my room and make me up to look the part. I know nothing about the dinner, aside from the clothes I'm dressed in. Based on their informal nature, it can't be anything super-important. I get styled in a short emerald-colored dress with slashed sleeves. While getting ready, I think about all the ways to make sure I don't get into another argument with Carac tonight. I need to formulate a plan to both get out of here and get Carac to listen. Not pissing him off is a good step in that direction.

Carac catches up with me in the hall. All he tells me is, "This dinner is with Annica and Regime Shade, parents of Xeres, Castilla, Zaven, and Theo. They're both high directors for the advisors and requested this dinner." I'm shocked that Carac even agreed to this. He continues, "I have no clue what they want. I'm doing this because they have trade connections in Oxidence, and

I'm not willing to lose that." As I expected, he makes no mention of our last encounter.

My skin crawls as we enter the room. They're both already there, and look ready for business. Their eyes stare us down. Their faces are sharp. I can tell nothing is going to be skipped over.

I sit down across from Regime. He looks just like Theo; lean, yet full in the face. Theo and Zaven showed such a resemblance to him. He's a metal controller too. I feel sick. Annica is even scarier than Regime. Her jawline is crisp. At any given moment, she could kill someone and not even blink an eye; she appears more than ready for it.

Xeres was just like her in that way. They share the same ability; both are body snatchers. Well... Xeres *was*. I try to tell myself there's no reason to be scared. Carac is here, but at this point he's lost all his morals. He could and might just feed me to them. If anyone's neck is on the line, it's mine.

I keep looking at Carac as I sit down. He carries himself like an untouchable god, and I want nothing more than to be an atheist. He's so high and mighty in the presence of people who are still suffering from such a brutal loss.

The dinner table is only set for us four. All the hopes I have of distracting myself with other people are lost. There aren't even any guards in the room to take charge if someone goes for my head.

"King Carac, we haven't spoken to you since the wedding," Annica begins.

Carac maintains a straight face. He inquires, "It's been that long?"

"Suppose so." Regime's voice is foul and old. "What have you been up to?"

Such obscene pleasantry; I'm waiting for their assault. Carac beckons for it. "What did you want to discuss?"

Annica and Regime don't address me at all; all conversation is directed at Carac. It's as if I'm invisible to the discussion. For once, I'm perfectly fine with that. They don't even cast a glance my way, but they both look power-hungry as they focus on Carac, who is responsible for several of their children's deaths. It's unfathomable to me how they can kiss up to him after what he did. Even if you take Xeres and Theo out of the conversation, Carac killed Castilla, no question.

It's an intense game.

Annica's guard drops for a second. She lowers her head while Regime continues to speak: "I think you know."

"Why don't you tell me anyway?" Carac asks, the portrait of innocence.

Her eyes dart up in a treacherous motion. She spits venom at Carac: "You killed our daughter and son. You murdered them." She casts a glance at me. "We know Theo was sent on a suicide mission."

Carac doesn't react. His mouth is pursed. He can barely mumble out the words, "I... can't move."

I gulp. This is not the dinner I was expecting. The table starts to rattle as the metal on it shakes. I grip the arms of my chair.

Cholericly, Carac hisses, "I. Will. End. You. Both."

Then, in a split second, Regime clenches his talons, causing all the silverware on the table to leap together and coalesce into a sharp sword. In the same motion, he launches the weapon into Carac's chest. It happens before I can even blink.

Carac's eyes widen. Before, his face was so powerful; now it's stripped bare. He takes a deep breath, clutching at his wound. Regime uses his ability to pull the sword out of Carac's chest. It leaves an exposed gash that's rapidly bleeding out. Carac takes a staggering breath; he struggles to take another.

Annica stands up and stares me dead in the eyes. "Run," she orders.

Regime rises beside her. "The guards are busy for now. Run!"

I'm frozen in my chair from the shock. My heart races in my chest. My thoughts move twice as fast.

I look at Carac.

I can save him. I can *try* to save him.

I can pull the liquid in the room and try to kill Annica and Regime. My skills might be better than theirs, especially with easy access to water. But I won't catch them off guard; they're more than ready to fight. Still, my ability is well-trained; I've had plenty of practice in the past few weeks. I can try and end their lives quickly. Then I can take Carac to a medic.

I watch the blood color his white shirt red. His breathing is decreasing rapidly, becoming shallow. He's fading out. He must not be able to kill them as he's dying.

I can try to save him.

But now the King who controls death is on the brink of it, and for the first time in his life, he can't stop it.

"I said *run!*" Regime screams at me, echoing his wife. I look at Carac's body.

And I run.

I pick up the hem of my dress in a mist of panic and dash though the halls. As they said, there are no guards. No one is stopping me from running. I run like there's no tomorrow. I finally get to the back of the castle, where there's an exit. I kick off my shoes. I race down the marble stairs until I'm faced with the vast, snow-covered lawn. The snow coats my bare feet while my breath grows shorter. I keep running, straight ahead.

Voices from behind me start to fill my ears. There are guards yelling out to me, searching for me. I just let the one person who could stop them from killing me die.

I let Carac die.

I know from the previous ambush that there's a lake behind the castle. I can feel water somewhere in the trees as I leap over ashed branches.

The yelling is getting closer. I approach the murky body of water and dive right in. I swim to the center, and with all my strength, form an ice orb around me. The orb is half-full of water, but there's enough air to last me a few hours.

I sink to the bottom of the lake, the yolk in an egg of ice. I can't hear the yelling now.

My crown unravels in my hair. My dress is soaked with water. Nothing seems to be intact anymore. I rip the crown out of my hair and hold it in my hand. I brace my knees to my chest.

There's no light at the bottom of the lake.

There's nothing I can do anymore.

I made a choice, the wrong choice, and there's nothing I can do to undo it.

Carac is dead.

CHAPTER 48

Isadora POV

I wake up surrounded by water. I gasp for air, but the only thing I inhale is water. I have no clue how much time has passed, or where I am. My breath is gone entirely. My lungs burn from inhaling water. I reach my arms out around me, feeling for anything. My orb must have fallen apart and left me stranded at the bottom of the lake.

I must have been able to stay awake only for a few hours before the tears and exhaustion dragged me into a heavy sleep. There's barely any energy left in me. With as much strength as possible, I kick upward and soon breach the surface. Finally, I can take a deep breath. I turn in circles, looking around, and see the shore. I swim the small distance to land. I can't stop from collapsing onto my hands and knees on the sandy, muddy shore of the lake.

I start to cough up water. My hair falls over my face, dripping over my eyes. I crawl farther out of the water and grip the sand, staring down at the shore.

A pair of boots walks into my view. It's too dark to see anything clearly. I can only make out the silhouette of boots. I follow the shoes up to see the butt of the weapon heading directly at my head. It knocks me out completely.

CHAPTER 49

Isadora POV

This time, I wake up to the sound of a crash around me. My first instinct tells me to move my hands, but I find them tied to the arms of a seat. I survey the scene rapidly. I'm not in a room; I'm on an aircraft. There are multiple seats, each filled with a soldier of some sort. This gives me two main questions. First, the soldiers aren't wearing Parten or Din Point uniforms, nor do I recognize any of them. The colors they're wearing aren't a combination I've seen before. So who are they?

Second question: why are we on a plane?

Again, I try to move my arms, but they're tied down well. The solider next to me says, "Don't bother." His voice isn't harsh; it has a soothing affect. Even seated, I can tell he's tall, and he looks awfully strong. I don't really want to cause trouble with him. His eyes are green and bright; they complement his dark skin and dark-brown hair.

The uniforms are so different from any I've seen before. I continue to look at the clothes, loose and cut for warm weather. Maybe they aren't even soldiers. But they're so muscular and built that if they aren't soldiers, that makes it even stranger. All of them are wearing the same thing, except for the man next to me; his outfit is fancier, tailored to fit him perfectly. A leader, maybe. I finally speak up: "Where am I?" My throat burns as I speak. It must be from the water I inhaled.

"On a jet," he says. His voice leads everyone else in the plane to follow our conversation.

"Who are you?".

"*Who are you?*" he replies. I really don't want to answer that.

"Where are we going?" I continue. I'm not really expecting an answer at this point.

"See for yourself," he responds, and looks out the window. I try my best to move forward, but through the window I can only see the runway we're descending toward.

I try to call for water. I sense they have lots of it on the plane, in bottles. The jet hits the ground harshly; we all shift in our seats. The soldiers don't even move at the sight of a trickle of water crawling toward on the floor. I get one touch of it in my hands and immediately push it away. The water has sent a shock through my body.

I look around in confusion, but no one seems surprised or to care; they're watching me fumble. I slowly called the water back to me. Another touch, and I yell, "Ouch!"

"Done with your water games?" the tall man asks.

A soldier sitting across from him speaks. "It's *her*, sir."

What's that supposed to mean? I lean forward in my chair, my arms still tied tight.

The soldier from before, sitting next to me, replies in a sarcastic tone, "You think? You men head out of here."

After his command, the soldiers flood out of the jet, leaving just him and I. He takes out a knife. I raise my head, inhaling. I'm ready for him to use the knife on me at this point.

He moves quickly to cut the ropes that hold me to the chair. "You aren't a prisoner… yet," he says.

I gape at him in confusion. He starts to walk, so I stand and follow. As I get to my feet, I feel my headache renew. I lift a hand to my forehead; pain spears my temples. I push on as he leads us out of the plane. His face doesn't change. I need to figure out where I am.

"You're an electromancer, yes?" I ask him as I descend the steps. The only reason I can think of for the water shocking me is that he charged it with electricity.

He peers down at me and scoffs, "There are many kinds of electromancer. That's too vague an assumption."

"Well then, correct me," I say, eyeing the desert I'm walking onto.

"The ability I possess is electrokinesis. Controlling and absorbing electric fields."

"My apologies," I say. No one really cares about the specifics of an ability nowadays; I wonder why he does.

"Well, it's the same as when someone calls you a hydromancer or 'ice controller.' Speaking of that, what's the proper name for your ability?"

"Cryokinesis, giv—"

He cuts me off while we walk in the sand, "I understand; the ability to control snow, ice, and other forms of water."

"Sure… Where are we?" I try to slide my inquiry in again. I can now see a few cars in the near distance.

He brushes off my question. "Does your brother have the exact same ability?"

I haven't been asked that in years; no one ever notices a difference in ice controller abilities. "No," I tell him cheerfully. "He has a freezing ability."

"Could you explain that in further depth, please?"

"Basically, he can lower the energy in the atoms of any substance to freezing temperatures… and how do you know I have a brother?"

He turns to me with a small smirk. "We have a small drive ahead."

The other soldiers are already in the cars. They're not normal cars. They're small, but with no doors or real metal to close us in. Each is an open carriage, with only seats and a wheel. He hops in the car and motions for me to as well.

"What's your name?" I ask.

"Drítan," he says, and then abruptly slams on the gas. My head gets launched into the back of my seat. I grip onto the rail for dear life as we drive thought the desert. His laughter only increases with the speed. After a few minutes, the terrain changes from desert to tropics. In a matter of seconds, we're surrounded by a dense, wet rainforest. I sit up and look around at the trees, having a hard time understanding how the environment has changed so quickly.

We drive up to a secluded house in the forest. The building is old stone, covered in plants and surrounded by wildlife. I rest my head against the seat back. I breathe out harshly and lay my hands in my lap. My mind flickers to Carac. The way his body lost its color after Regime stabbed him. How all I did was run. I did exactly what they wanted me to. I should have tried to save him. I should have done something, anything, except run.

My head jolts forward as Drítan stops the car and turns it off. He hops out comes around the vehicle, and offers a hand for me to hold onto. I take it as I jump out and look around. Under my feet I feel mud compacting; it must have recently rained heavily. The mud doesn't hit my bare feet, though; I'm wearing tennis shoes that someone put me on me while I was unconscious. I think back to my discarded high heels, and the scene I ran from. I turn my eyes to something else to try and focus on the present. "Are you going to tell me where we are now?" I ask as we enter the building. It's a very open; it makes it difficult to tell what's outside and what's in. This structure is like nothing I've ever seen before.

He stops in his tracks, turns to me, and says, "Kindera."

My heart skips a beat. He watches my expression change to one of sheer horror. Then he walks on. I race up to him. "No, no, no. If this is Kindera, I should be dead! The air here..." I look around at the jungle I'm in. "The environment is supposed to be toxic to anyone who isn't native."

"*She* will explain it to you," he says as we approach a door.

"She? What the hell is going on?"

"*She* is the ruler of this kingdom. Probably the deadliest of us all." He places a hand on the doorknob. "My best advice is not to look *Her* in the eye, say nothing stupid, and most importantly, know that if you make one wrong move, *She* will ruin you."

His expression has completely changed. His formerly lighthearted face is now solid and straight. He makes it clear that this is a life-or-death matter. He opens the door. I walk in, as it shuts only halfway behind me. I keep my head down.

A cheerful voice fills the room. "Isadora Xxon! It's about time we met."

I take her words as an opportunity to look up.

Before me stands a small girl, maybe five feet tall on her tiptoes. She's beautiful, but very young. She seems too young to be some terrifying ruler. Her face is round and not yet fully developed, her hair tied up and braided with golden clasps, her eyes a sharp and gorgeous green.

Green like Carac's eyes. I feel my body start to go numb at the thought.

The girl looks me up and down and then asks, "What did he say to you?" in a harsh tone. The girl speeds to the door and opens it. All I can hear in the hall is laughter.

I try to focus on what's happening.

"What did you tell this girl?" she yells down the hall.

Drítan responds as he walks into the room, "Was she terrified?" He laughs. Back is the cocky, confident Drítan.

"Sit down, you jerk," she hisses to him. "I should have sent Hector to get her."

Drítan moves to the conference table on one side of the room. He sits down and throws his feet up. "Hector sucks at this stuff, and you know it."

I finally take notice of the room we're in. It's much more modern than the rest of the building. It's enclosed fully and has a monitor attached to the wall.

The girl gestures to me. "I'm Era, and I apologize for my idiot brother. Why don't you take a seat?"

I move to the table. "I think I deserve answers now."

Era nods and takes a seat across from me. "That's fair. I can start off by welcoming you to Kindera."

"Kindera is a wasteland. This isn't Kindera."

She sighs. "Kindera isn't really a wasteland. Truly, it's the opposite. I assume you saw a few different climates on your way here. Those allow us to produce anything we need on this single island. We have the highest population of weather and terrain manipulators in the world. With their help, we're able to grow anything we need. The island is suited for our manipulators, and that made us see that there's no reason to share our wealth with the other kingdoms. We stopped trading with the others a while ago. With all these factors in play, and our small population, it became obvious we could lose our island if we weren't careful. Other kingdoms would invade us and take over Kindera for their own benefit. So our grandparents masterfully created the legend that Kindera is a toxic wasteland. Ever since, no kingdom has dared to look into the island out of fear that they might be harmed in the process."

I sit on the edge on my seat; this can't be true. "So, you're really the queen?"

"That's the one thing my brother didn't lie about. Currently, I'm in charge of Kindera, but unlike Parten, we have a democratic monarchy."

I'm thrilled to hear that a kingdom has had some success with a democratic monarchy. "If you don't mind me asking, how old are you?"

"Sixteen, not much younger than you, but young enough for concern. I understand. But I've been raised my whole life for this position. As you can tell, my brother is older than me. Our parents were recently killed, and we inherited the ruling positions. I had the option to rule or turn it all over to our government."

"And are you an electricity manipulator as well?"

"Yes. I assume my brother told you about that?"

"He showed me," I say vaguely. I have to process this information, but a million questions continue to race in my head. "Why am I here?" I ask her next.

Era grabs a remote and turns on the monitor in the room. The news comes on, with red letters flashing on the bottom of the screen. "Current reports indicate the former king of Din Point will step up and retake power after the murder of King Carac Cavinche," states the news reader. "Authorities are still looking into the murder, but King Carac's parents have told us it was a stab wound caused by Carac's wife, Isadora Xxon. After the incident, she was able to escape, and currently has four tags on her head."

I watch the news in shock; it all makes sense now. They blamed the murder of Carac on *me*. They let me run as if I were trying to flee from the scene of the crime.

With all this running around and being held captive on an island, I haven't had time to think too in-depth about Carac really being dead. In my head, it's as if I just ran away from him again. My eyes water and my face heats up as I sit and think about it for a second. Carac is truly dead. I try to not change my breathing as both siblings sit and observe me react.

I watch rest of the broadcast, blinking heavily. The other part of the report that shocks me is the fact that they've put four tags on my head. Regular crimes get one tag, murders get two, rebel groups and terrorists get three... and apparently, I get four for killing the Prince of Death.

I didn't kill him, but I let him die.

I guess I'm just as guilty as the Shades are.

The camera changes scenes to a crowd rioting outside Din Point Castle, and guards gathering weapons. Era turns the monitor off before I can see the rest.

"You, Isadora, have quite a few people after you." I quickly locate all the water in the room. I prepare for them to try to turn me in and take the rewards. "But we both had a common issue: Carac."

I mutter under my breath, "Who didn't?" My eyes start to burn with guilt.

Drítan turns to me and says, "A month ago, our parents went to Din Point with a proposal to open our first trade route in years. Din Point slaughtered them."

"I'm sorry for your loss," I softly say. I don't see grief in Drítan's eyes. He's past the stage of sadness, and on to revenge.

Era rests a hand on the table. "We want to offer Parten our resources to invade and take out Din Point."

I want to jump out of my seat, but calmly hold myself down. I nod. Era continues, "We are prepared to offer you our services, but on the condition, if we succeed, that we get half the kingdom's land."

"You want half the land? What good would that do you? You just said this island is perfect, didn't you? Why change now?"

Drítan steps in, "For trading purposes, we want a mainland port. We want to be back on the mainland."

Era, with the slightest bit of sass, states, "I think half is very generous, considering that our army is one of the best in the world."

"No one knows anything about your army. You're the only one claiming it's good."

"Because we haven't had to use our army."

"Yes, because you've been in hiding for decades. What's an army without experience?"

Era pauses for a second before countering, "We can get Oxidence soldiers too."

"And what will you offer them? Part of your half of the land?"

"Oxidence will join us on different terms. They're one of the few countries that knows of Kindera's current state, and they owe us a favor."

I raise my chin. "I think you're overstepping the line with asking for half, because it's clear this isn't an offer for help, but you silently begging for it." Era glances to her brother, exchanging a mental conversation. I continue, "My best guess is that Din Point found out about Kindera's true state when your parents thought they could trade with them. Din Point doesn't trade, and they don't allow for negotiations. I'm guessing they saw a kingdom with no allies and great resources. If your parents did walk away without a deal, Din Point probably took no mercy. So you're left with either fighting off an invasion or taking down Din Point before they attack. And I know that Oxidence will take no chances of becoming involved in an ongoing war. They won't support you if you try to fight alone. Your forces simply aren't big enough to stop Din Point, and you'll lose the island and probably be killed. You need Parten's help to get Oxidence to join, so together, we can remove Din Point from the board before they can remove you. Correct?" Era clenches her jaw and nods. "Well then, I think it would be better for you to just ask Parten to help, looking for nothing in return."

"We brought you here because you killed Carac, and you're the best chance we have at making Din Point fall. You're not a negotiator; you're our go-between with Parten," the Queen states. I want to correct Era and tell her I wasn't the one who killed Carac, but she's thankful for my service. Best to keep myself viewed as an asset. Era continues, "We need you to sway the princes without revealing Kindera's true nature, to see if they'll join us."

"How do you expect me to convey that to them if I can't tell them the truth about Kindera? Besides, King Alas is under the impression that we would need Vaddel to take down Din Point."

Drítan chimes in, "I guess that's for you to figure out. We're on a time limit here."

Era asks, "Do you understand the conditions?"

"Perfectly," I reply, though I'm still trying to process everything.

Era has no issue making herself clear. "If you betray us and reveal the truth about Kindera without Parten meeting our terms, then I'll have no problem ending you. Isadora, you just killed the one person stopping anyone from doing that, giving me an opportunity that I will gladly take if this goes wrong... Drítan, take her back to Parten."

He nods. I stand; we walk back the same way we came, and again enter the 'car.' Drítan drives a little slower this time. It gives me the chance to speak with him. "Why did you turn down Kindera's throne?"

"You've see how things are for everyone in that position. They hate it; they have all this pressure on them. It's awful. I didn't want to drown in that, but she embraces it. Era, for some reason, loves all that political stuff. She wanted to take it all upon herself, so I let her. She rescued me from a life I would hate."

"I'm so sorry about your parents," I say again.

"It's in the past." It may be, but I can still hear the sullenness in his words. He asks, "It's been a while since you were in Parten?"

"Just over a month, but it feels like longer."

"Any time away from home is long."

I look around at the desert as we leave the jungle and enter the dunes. Drítan informs me, "The tradition is for visitors to go on a run here. It's a scenic trail that passes through several different environments, just a mile or so... maybe when you come back, you can experience it."

We arrive at the runway. This time, a smaller plane waits for us. Drítan leads me to it. "This is my private plane; I'll be giving you the ride back. When you need to contact us, just write. We have a few post lines in Parten Castle. Give the letters to one of these people." He writes three names down on a slip of paper and hands it me.

We get in the plane; there's barely enough room for three people. On one wall is a small mirror, and I look into it. I haven't seen myself in the past few days. There are some minor cuts on my face, along with scratches. There's a large bruise on my forehead that blends into my hairline. It's a sudden reminder of what happened at the lake.

Once the plane is in the air, I ask Drítan, "Why did you feel the need to knock me out at Din Point?"

He doesn't look back, but it's as if he can see my expression, "Is that what happened to you? We didn't know. All we saw when we arrived was you being carried away unconscious by some Din Point soldiers. We took you from there, and only used the hand ties until we were sure it was you and you weren't going to try and fight us."

"How did you know I'd be out there?" I ask, thinking of what would have happened if they hadn't found me. I'd probably be dead by now.

"Because we got word a while ago that Carac was going to die soon."

"What!?" I exclaim.

Drítan takes a second to think through his answer. "Someone wrote a letter."

"From Parten?"

"No, it was from somebody in Din Point."

"Who?" I ask.

Drítan goes quiet for a second. "I think he's a guard captain... I'm not sure, though, honestly... hold your next questions," he commands as he pushes a button. A slight static sound fills the cabin. He takes a breath and then calmly says, "Parton Control, Plane 208 requesting permission to land."

"Plane 208, Parton Control. Who specifically is requesting permission to land?" a voice responds.

I lean forward and say, "Isadora Xxon."

After a few seconds of dead silence, there's a response: "Permission granted."

I let out a breath of relief. I'm finally going back home.

CHAPTER 50

Isadora POV

Before Drítan can even unbuckle himself, I'm out of the plane. Several guards are waiting for me at the runway, along with King Alas. They stand in formal formation, not looking very welcoming. Regardless, I don't hesitate to walk straight to Alas and hug him.

I feel his arms take me in as he says softly, "I missed you." I immediately feel better just from his touch. I let go long enough for Alas's eyes to turn and look at the plane. "Who is this?" Alas asks, turning slightly.

Drítan smiles a bit. "Just dropping Isadora off." Drítan rips his attention away from Alas and says to me, "Well be in touch." He turns away from us both and struts back to his plane.

Alas doesn't ask me anything right away; he just looks into my eyes, trying to see silent answers. "Where is Daymond?" I ask him.

"Inside. None of us knew you were coming."

The guards follow behind us as we enter Parten Castle. From the looks of everything and everyone in the halls, it doesn't seem like much has changed. Alas asks me again, "Who was that? We had a whole group of guards looking for you in Din Point."

"You got my letter?" I ask in shock. I thought Ryder had given my letter to Drítan rather than Alas. Did a different captain of the guards in Din Point send Kindera a letter? Or is Ryder trading information to everyone, having written the Kindera royals a separate letter?

"Yes, and beyond your letter, we had confirmation that Carac was going to die that night. But who gave you the ride?"

"A Din Point rebel group," I lie, while wondering again how so many people knew Carac was going to die.

Alas stops and stares at me for moment. I arch my back while standing tall and make straight eye contact with him. He wants to see if I'll break, but I make it clear I'm not going to say anything more. If Alas can't see the confidence emanating from me, he's blind.

He tilts his head to the side. "That isn't a Din Point plane, and certainly not a rebel one. It was small yet fancy, wealthy, and decked out; royal. And I know it for sure isn't from Parten."

I forget sometimes that Alas knows more about this stuff than anyone else. We keep walking through the halls. I silently try to show Alas that I can't tell him anything more about the plane. He shakes his head a little. He doesn't ask anything further. Neither of us wants our first conversation to be an argument.

We walk into a sitting room, and I quickly understand that I will not be seeing my brother until after I talk with the princes of Parten.

Lawrence doesn't even get up from his seat. Instead, he waits for us to sit down and then begins, "What the hell happened to your head?"

I again become self-conscious of the giant bruise on my forehead as I tell him, "A Din Point guard got me."

He leans back, content with my answer. But he pushes, "You want to start explaining the rest of it?"

He looks different. His face is thinner, his skin sallower than before. There are bags under his eyes that weren't there when I left. His posture is straighter and his hair cut shorter. Alas looks the exact same as when I left, but Lawrence has changed in many noticeable ways.

Alas asks another question instead of letting me respond to Lawrence's. "Let's start with why you left in the first place."

"Carac was holding something over my head. I made a deal."

"What was the deal?" Lawrence asks.

"That's irrelevant. The point is, I made a deal, I kept my end of it, and now I'm back."

Lawrence's expression is cold. He places the glasses on the table and lets me call for water to fill my glass. "And in your time away, you got married and supposedly pregnant?"

I choke on the water. I had almost forgotten Carac did that. After clearing my throat, I say calmly, "I told you in the letter. He did everything possible to manipulate my public image."

Alas asks, "So you're not having his child?"

"No!" I exclaim.

Lawrence twists his mouth. "We *saw* the broadcast."

"That was food poisoning, I promise. The King and Queen of Din Point wanted me dead, so Carac staged a pregnancy and my illness to make sure they wouldn't kill me or kill their heir."

Alas seems content with that answer, but then he asks, "But you did actually get married?"

I try to discreetly slip the ring off my figure and into my pocket, but Lawrence watches my every movement. "I don't care what 'officially' happened, I am *not* married to Carac."

"Then are *we* still married?" Lawrence asks. The room falls silent. We all glance at each other, making guesses with our own thoughts.

I finally answer truthfully, "I don't know."

"That's not the biggest issue right now. We can deal with that whole mess later," Alas declares.

Lawrence shrugs and raise his eyebrows in annoyance. "Well, then," he clears his throat and asks, "How did you kill him?"

"I didn't kill him," I correct him. It feels so good to finally say that to someone else, not just myself.

Alas turns to me; he doesn't seem to comprehend my words. "What do you mean, you didn't kill him?"

"Exactly what I said. I didn't kill him."

"Then we have to clear that up with the public. Everyone thinks you did."

Lawrence has a different thought process and asks, "Who killed him?"

I respond to them both, "Theo Shade's parents." Then I wonder aloud, "What does the public think about the murder?"

"From what I heard, it's nearly all positive. You killed an enemy king personally responsible for hundreds of deaths and for putting his kingdom in a deadly state of jeopardy. The real issue is that you killed the king of a kingdom we just became allies with. I don't doubt that King Argys will declare war because of this."

I take a second to think and say, "Then you have to let them think I killed him."

Both Lawrence and Alas shout, "What!?"

I try to use this conversation as an opportunity. If Din Point and Parten go to war again, it could be a way of ensuring the people of Din Point revolt, and mark the perfect time to end the partnership with our new allies. We'd just need time to create the perfect plan. "What if we do go to war again?" I ask.

"Are you insane? We just ended that horrid war!" Lawrence hisses.

"What if we get enough allies? We could annihilate Din Point."

"What are you getting at, Isadora?" Lawrence snaps.

I bite my lip. This isn't a conversation that Lawrence should be present for if he's just going to say no. I give up for the moment. "Fine, never mind."

Alas glances at me. He knows that I'm holding something back. He'll get it out of me later, but for now he asks, "Why did they kill him?"

"Theo had three siblings, as you know, and about a week ago the other two died. One committed suicide, and the other one Carac just killed. Carac was a link to all their deaths, and I think it was just pure revenge by their parents."

"So we have no chance of becoming allies with them. The murder wasn't for the greater good?" Alas ponders, already thinking of possible benefits.

"These aren't people you want as allies."

"Why did Xeres kill himself?"

"I don't exactly know. He came to me frantic, late at night. We weren't friends, so for him to ask for my help was major. He wanted to withhold some information from Carac, so he decided he needed to be ended. I agreed to help him because from what I can tell, Carac really did need the information."

"What information?" Lawrence interrupts.

"I don't know," I admit. "I'm just as much in the dark as you are." Neither of them says anything. "Anyway, I helped him. Xeres wouldn't have gotten himself into that position unless it was something worth protecting. It all intertwines with an ambush and bombing that took place at Din Point Castle a few weeks ago. Xeres was heavily involved with that attack. I know he had to be working with the attackers. I helped Carac in the ambush because one of the attackers said she wanted to kill me. Honestly, I shouldn't have fought; I still don't know the whole story, and it was a mistake to take action. But Xeres died to protect something along the lines of all of that."

"So suicide was the only answer?" Lawrence asks, aghast.

"Xeres made it seem like he had no chance to escape. I understand why he needed my help for it. If Carac had gotten to him after, he probably would have brought him back to life, tortured him to death, brought him back to life again, and then continued the cycle. Either way, the whole situation is tragic. He was too young to die; he was barely twenty-one."

"If he was protecting something, we need to look into that," Lawrence says, clapping his hands together.

"I agree... I just... I don't know, it still bothers me. The way he acted that night, it didn't seem like he was ready to die."

Alas asks, "What about the other sibling?"

"I never hear a word from Castilla, but Carac killed her after Xeres died. He said she was of no use to him."

"That's something we need to look into, but for now we're going to table it," Alas says, trying to get to another point off his chest. "Carac's dead, so we won't be getting any real answers."

"Do you think Xeres' parents had anything to do with the attack?" Lawrence continues; he isn't ready to drop this conversation.

"Carac wouldn't have let them live if they did," I say with a glance at Alas. He doesn't want to look at me.

Lawrence sits back and jokes, "You don't think I could find another necromancer to bring him back to life, do you?"

Alas and I don't laugh. Alas turns his head to him and barks, "Why the hell would you want to bring him back? Are you insane? This is the man who—"

Lawrence blurts, "I was joking! Calm down. I only meant that we could find out what happened with Xeres."

"No one can bring him back anyway," Alas says without a blink.

"Why?" I ask, "Hypothetically, another death controller could, easily."

"You didn't see it?" Alas asks. Lawrence and I both stare blankly back at him. "His body isn't intact anymore. The place where they were prepping his body for the funeral burned down. It destroyed a few other bodies too, and killed two workers."

Everything goes blank in my head. The room turns fuzzy. I've been dealing with the thought of Carac dying ever since it happened; but, deep in my soul, I figured he's just been waiting for the right time to come back to life. I never, ever thought he'd stay dead. Now he's really gone. I can't look at either of them as Lawrence says, "Are you serious? That means both princes of Din Point were killed by fire."

He's referring to Caspian and Carac. They're both dead. *Carac is dead* is all I can hear in my head. Carac is gone. There is nothing I can do to reverse this.

A shiver goes through me as Lawrence mentions the fires. I get up from my chair and tell them, "I'm going to talk with my brother." I need to leave the room.

"I have a few more questions," Lawrence calls.

"You can ask them later," I snap, and leave the room before he can argue with me and see the tears in my eyes.

CHAPTER 51

Isadora POV

T he eyes of the guards drag on me as I pass through the halls. I don't rush as I let the tears roll down my face. I don't have the energy to run. The thoughts of Carac being dead drain everything positive from my mind. Even as much as I wanted to change him, and begged for him to leave me alone, I never wanted him to die. Carac still had a chance to amend his ways, to do good; he was just starting his reign.

We're all just kids, and these kingdoms are wrecking us and claiming our souls.

I continue to walk, my feelings gripping my heart. As I turn the corner of the main hall, I see my brother a few meters away, and he sees me. I quickly wipe my face dry as best I can while I run up to him. Immediate confusion crosses his face as he walks into me for a hug. He embraces me in the most perfect and comforting way for a few minutes; then I step back, and he grabs my arms.

"You're back," Daymond says with a stern voice. "You're back from Din Point, where you got married and pregnant."

"It's good to see you, too," I say almost sarcastically, trying to twist out of his grip. He doesn't seem to notice my red face; if he does, he just doesn't say anything.

"You'd better start telling me everything," he says as we start to walk. We stroll the castle grounds, and I try to fill him in on every single detail I can from Din Point. I tell him the stories, I inform him of Carac's death and the plans he had, how the council is, the people, the security, the guards, the food, the weather, the Shade family, and more.

After a long conversation, my voice grows more serious. Daymond raises his eyebrows in surprise as my diction grows harsher. I say, "What I tell you now is strictly between us."

Daymond gives me a small nod and sharply replies, "Okay."

"I mean it. If this gets out, it could put a lot of people in jeopardy."

"I won't say a word."

I believe him. I say quickly, "Kindera isn't a wasteland, and they're going to help Parten in a war that shouldn't last long, because they have ties with Oxidence."

For the first time in his life, Daymond looks confused. He then spins out a million questions to me. I do my best to answer every single one, and once he seems to understand all aspects, he's quiet and I can see him processing it all.

"I'm telling you this so you can start getting ready. Just prepare in your head and plant the seeds for an attack," I explain.

"I appreciate it," Daymond assures me. "I'm glad to have you back."

CHAPTER 52

Isadora POV

I walk lightly down the hallway, hoping to make it to my room. Maybe I'll even pass by Alas's room to try and talk to him a bit about the plans. I need to think quickly about how to approach Alas with my ideas. There's no easy way to spring it all on him.

As I stride down the hall, approaching the training room, Lawrence races up to me. "There you are. We need to talk." As he speaks, a group of guards come down the hall, just leaving the training room. "Alas asked me to…"

He notices me staring. My facial expression can't help but change as my eyes widen in shock. Ryder is among the crowd of guards. Ryder has spotted me, too.

"Just give me a second," I tell him, and start to speed-walk. Lawrence lets me go. I feel him watch me until I'm mixed into the sea of guards. From the other side of the group, Ryder turns around and hurries away from me. I increase my speed. Both of us are trying not to run; we don't want to attract attention. I weave my way through the group of guards, keeping an eye on Ryder as he starts to run.

I can't waste any more time. My walk turns into a full-on sprint. I catch up to Ryder just before he enters the training room, reaching out to grab him by the collar of his uniform. I'm just able to grasp the fabric of his shirt and yank him back.

I pull him around a few feet as I look for a place to talk. I feel him push forward, trying to get out of my grip. I go for the nearest door. Whether people are in this room or not, I'm not taking the chance of him escaping my hold. I turn and shove us both into the room, then spin around and put myself in front of the door. I scan the room to realize it's a tiny closet.

I tell him, "We need to have a quick chat."

"There are easier ways to get me alone, you know," he mocks, with a tiny grin pulling at the side of his mouth. I shake my head to clear my thoughts as he continues, "What are you going to do, kill me? Turn me in to King Alas?"

"No," I snap.

"Why not?" Ryder winces without thinking.

I say softly, "I know you did a lot more to help than just mail my letter. You helped kill Carac."

His smile disappears, and his eyes grow narrow as he leans back. He states flatly, "I don't know what you're talking about." With a glance to the side, he twists the question. "Didn't you kill him?"

"You know damn well I didn't. There were no guards in the castle when I left. There were no guards outside either, until I started to run away, and you're the only one who could make that happen."

Ryder shifts his weight and stops talking. I continue, "There was a letter sent to Kindera, too—sent before his murder. My letter was sealed in wax, and Alas told me today he got it, seal intact. I know you couldn't have read it, because then the seal would have been broken, and Alas wouldn't have trusted it. There had to be a separate letter sent to Kinder, and I think you sent it."

"What do you want?" Ryder spits, flustered. His deflecting my question tells me that I'm correct in guessing that he sent the letter to Kindera.

"You know what's going to happen soon. I can tell you right now that Parten has allies that Din Point hasn't considered. If this war breaks out, it's going to be Parten winning this time."

"Din Point is a lot stronger now that Carac is dead."

"You helped with his murder because you saw flaws in him. I need you to be my ears in Din Point, just like Carac had you working here."

"What do you have to offer? You've already promised me safety in Parten for delivering the letter."

"That isn't what I promised, exactly, but here's what I can offer now: When this is all over and Parten is in power, I can offer you greater power. I can offer you a position far higher than Captain of the Guards."

He glances down at the floor and considers for a few seconds. "Okay," he finally says, sticking his hands in his pockets. "I'll take that offer."

I know he's power-hungry, and a hungry dog is never loyal.

"One more thing," I say, grasping the door handle. "What happened with Xeres?"

His eyebrows rise and he admits, "I know just as much as you do."

"That's rarely true."

"I wish I knew. Carac taunted me with that information constantly, but he never told me shit about why Xeres died." I believe him. Carac wouldn't have told Ryder if he knew he was a sellout.

I give Ryder a nod and open the door. We go our separate ways.

Ryder is a traitor all the way around. I'm not going to tell him anything that he can use in Din Point's favor, but I can hope he can work things for my side.

Just as I leave the closet, Lawrence greets me in the hall. He bites his lip and approaches me. I turn to check that Ryder is still walking away. I barely see his back as he turns a corner. When I face forward, Lawrence stands barely a foot away. "All I have to tell you is that Alas wants you not to make any public appearances. The general public can't know you're in Parten or the palace," he declares.

I nod, and for a split second look him over. His posture is better, his voice stronger. He knows what he wants from me. Something's changed in both of us when I was gone.

"What were you doing with Ryder?" he asks.

"Just talking," I say quietly as we start to walk. He gives me a questioning look. "I promise. It was nothing important."

He doesn't have anything else to say to me, and I don't have anything else to say to him. It's the first time we both don't know what to say.

I part ways from him in the hall, and go to start thinking about how to talk to Alas. I have to convince Alas to going to war with Din Point again, and it's not going to be easy. I know he loves the idea of war and all the mythos behind it, the glory it holds, the promises and skill that prevail; but he doesn't like death. No one wants innocent lives to be lost, but with everything comes a sacrifice.

We can take Din Point out, though, once and for all. We can help all the people living there; in the long term, this will save millions of lives.

I let myself into my room. Nothing has changed; not even a paper on my desk has been moved. A slight wave of comfort flows over me. If they thought I was gone forever, and if they had given up hope on me when I was in Din Point, they surely would have packed up my room. But I can see that they didn't even look though my things. Although the last time I was here was a month ago, I remember how the room looked when I was last in it. The couch cushions were messy, and the blanket that usually sits on the edge of my bed was left on my desk chair because I'd been writing that day. There were two water bottles on my nightstand, and I told myself that I was going to throw them away before a maid had to. The tea trolley was in the center of the room, where Carac had poured himself a drink.

Now that I'm back, I can see that everything is just the same. I shut the door behind me and place my hands on the tea trolley to push it back to its place against the wall. I can feel the cold metal against the palms of my hand as my grip tightens on the bar of the trolley. I stare down at the trolley, seeing how the cups of tea are uneven and one is missing. It must have been the cup that Carac drank out of. That was when he sat so casually in my room, mocking the decorations and having ideas in his head about making a deal. I move my eyes to look at the coffee table in front of the couch. There's a single cup on the table. I can see that there's still some tea sitting coldly in the cup, scummed over with mold. As he drank that cup of tea, we had just started to talk about me going back to Din Point. I remember the hatred that filled my body when I spoke to him, and how he'd come to my room because I'd asked him too. I... I had asked him to come and speak with me, so that hopefully we could fix things in Din Point.

He wouldn't have bothered me if I hadn't asked for him to come, if I hadn't asked for his help, if he hadn't tolerated me and listened to my thoughts spiraling as I bitched about everything he'd ever done.

But now it doesn't matter. I won't ever get to tell him all the things I wish I had said in that conversation. I won't ever get to yell at him again, and have that adrenaline rush though me when he argues back and I feel the heat of the conversation rise. I won't ever get that fluttery feeling in my chest as I roll my eyes after one of his comments and turn my face so that he can't see my small grin. I won't ever get to tell him how much

I still loved and cared for him, even when he drove me mad. I won't ever get to tell him that I'm sorry about everything I've done to him.

I didn't think that those would ever be the words to came to my mind after he died, but that's what I'd tell him.

That I'm sorry.

I'm sorry for us not being able to communicate. I'm sorry I didn't try to talk to you about the things that were going wrong. I'm sorry that I left Din Point because I truly thought you hated me, and when you let me run for my life and told everyone I had escaped again, that I still felt hatred for you in my heart. And I'm sorry I was horrible to you when you just wanted to protect me at times; and even when I screamed and told you that I despised you, you didn't retaliate. I'm sorry that at times, I thought of ways to undermine you and even accepted the thought that Xeres was going to kill you and that it would be for the better.

I'm sorry.

The words spiral though my mind as I think of everything that could have gone differently and how I could have saved him and given us both the chance to fix things.

His eyes flash though my mind. His eyes when they were going lifeless, and his shirt was turning crimson and I had the chance to save him. He was the Prince of Death. He was supposed to have total control, and it was taken from him.

I release my hand from the cruel, cold trolley and back away. I stare at the trolley that still sits in the middle of the room, and realize I can't bring myself to move it. Instead, I sit on the edge of my bed and stare at the trolley until I can't stare anymore, and the sobs and yelps of pain take over.

CHAPTER 53

Isadora POV

I wake up breathing in air more harshly than my body wants to. Cold sweats and chills take over my body as I grip my bedsheets. I start to cough heavily, unable to escape the nightmare still gripping my thoughts. I feel around in the darkness, trying to find anything that can bring me back. Anything at all.

But the thoughts don't seem to stop; the vision of it won't leave my mind completely. My body, without my mind even able to process it, carries me to the bathroom. I throw up in the toilet and take some deep breaths, slowly feeling the shifting of my mind slowing. And then I repeat them. Over and over, until there is nothing left in me.

I curl my knees up to my chest, and feel the cold wall hit my back and my feet clutch the bathroom floor.

My throat starts to tighten again, and I can no longer see out of my watering eyes. I can't breathe at all. I continue in my terror for what feels like hours, a never-ending cycle that's been filling my head constantly, never leaving me alone. I clutch the skin of my arms, nails digging deep. Eventually, the pain brings me back enough to process what happened, what has been happening every night since Carac died. What I haven't mentioned to anyone, but what their stares always press a bit of a question about.

I put my hands flat on the floor to center myself in the bathroom. I crawl one hand up to the top of the vanity, and use it to pull myself upright, my legs feeling as brittle as old bones. I turn the water on and lean down to get some in my mouth and clear away the wretched taste. After several cycles of rinsing, I look up into the mirror above the sink. My hands are shaking as I turn off the water.

I don't even understand who I'm looking at. Detachment from myself becomes more and more intense every moment. I want to see the person I was a year and a half ago, the person who would have done what I did. But instead I see the person I am—the horrific, disloyal, and terrifying person I am. The person who let all those people die on the lawn at Din Point. The person who killed Theo. The person who shoved a dagger through the chest of Xeres.

The person who let her other half die.

I am that person.

Before I even comprehend what I'm doing, my fist smashes into the mirror. The sound of empty shattering collapses in my ears. Immediate pain travels through my hand as I pull it back, realizing what I've done. I inhale sharply as I feel blood trickling over my hand. I take a step back in anger at myself.

I walk out of the bathroom while trying to piece together even one solid thought. My other hand trails along the wall. I finally find the light switch. The light floods into my eyes harshly, causing me to shut them in agony. I open them slowly to see that my knuckles took most of the impact of my punch, and were badly sliced by the mirror shards.

Blood starts to drip onto the carpet. I look around and find a discarded shirt on my desk, and try to wrap it over my hand. I can't move my hand without pain shooting through it.

I walk to my door and open it quickly. In a daze, I pace slowly down the hallway. The pain starts to fade, and a numbness comes over me, all too quickly. My eyes start to fill with tears again, which stream silently down my face as I take the stairs. I get to the door that I didn't even realize I was walking toward. I release my hold on my wrapped-up hand and knock faintly.

After a minute, Daymond opens the door. He takes a moment to collect himself before realizing that it's me standing there. "He's dead," I say, my voice breaking.

Daymond's face falls as he softly says, "I know," as if he were just waiting for me to say it. He then looks down to see the shirt wrapped around my hand, strained bright red. His eyes widen. The sight wakes him up, but I don't have the emotion to care about my hand anymore.

"What happened?" he asks me loudly while putting a hand on my back and forcing me into the room. I don't response or realize that he's moved me to a chair. "Isadora," he says, the word passing through my mind without any understanding. I feel his hand touching the fabric of the bloodstained shirt, moving it to examine my hand. I stare straight ahead, still unable to stop the tears from coming down.

He walks away for a moment and comes back with some material I don't look at. He removes the remains of fabric and mirror and starts to clean the cuts on my hand. Pain stays constant with me; I'm not quite sure if it's coming from my hand or my heart. It fades together.

Eventually, a distant tone comes from Daymond. "Isadora." It brings me back to the moment. I don't know how long it's been. I look down as Daymond turns my hand over. There are bandages over sections of my hand. "Just one stitch, not a big one, but several cuts."

I move my head and meet his eyes for a moment. He continues to look up at me; he must have been kneeling on the ground the whole time he was fixing what I had done to myself.

My lip twitches as I say, "I didn't mean to."

His other hand comes onto mine, cupping it in a light hold. "I know," he echoes from before.

"I let him die," I cry, defeated. This time Daymond doesn't respond; he didn't know. No one knows what really happened in that room. I told Alas and Lawrence that I didn't kill him, but I never told any of them that I let him die. "Right in front of me. They stabbed him, and I didn't try to save him. I let him die."

His face goes soft, and his eyes plead in secondhand pain. He remains silent. I'm not looking for him to try to ease what happened or offer answers, because there are none.

"And now he's gone. There isn't anything I can do to fix this," I announce to the room. Daymond's hands leave mine and move to stand me up as he takes me into a hug. A flat hand goes up and down my back to try and add some comfort. "I can't bring him back," I wail.

Daymond's hand comes to the back of my head, lightly pushing me into his chest as I continue to cry. He hugs me tightly as he whispers, "It's okay."

CHAPTER 54

Isadora POV

I'm taking today slowly. I didn't get much sleep last night, and I don't think I'll be getting much for a while. Beyond that, I've spent the whole morning in my room thinking of everything I need to say before I go to speak with Alas. I've prepared for the conversation, but there are still so many ways it can go wrong.

I shove myself out of my room and walk the desolate hallways. As I take the route to Alas's room, and catch him just leaving. My head aches, my face still burning a bit. Alas keeps walking forward and says dismissively, "Isadora," as a form of hello.

"I need to have a word with you," I mutter.

He tries to politely tell me, "I'm a little busy at the moment." He doesn't stop walking. It forces me to turn and walk with him as I talk.

"Alas, it's important. I think you need to hear something."

He stops for a moment. I follow his eyes as they look over my face. He doesn't say anything about my puffy eyes and dry mouth and instead asks, "Is it important enough for me to miss this council meeting?"

"I just…" I try to think if this is the right time. I'm not sure how long this conversation will be delayed if I don't talk to him about it now. "I just think you need to speak with me. It's important enough for you to be a few minutes late."

He takes a second before sighing, "All right." He turns around, and we walk back to his room. He opens the door for me and we go inside. Alas shuts the door swiftly and takes a seat in his lounge chair. I sit across from him at the coffee table. I glance down at the table; it's covered in maps and papers.

I've been staring at the table too long, and he's letting me.

I begin the conversation, "During my time at Din Point, I saw what a true mess the kingdom is. The people are suffering—"

"I know that," he says, looking displeased that he's late to a meeting just to hear me to say that.

I continue anyway. "Right now, the government is a mess too. They don't have anything together and are scrambling to figure out who will take Carac's place. They aren't in order, and won't be for a while. Now is the perfect time to attack. I know you just ended a war."

"A long, terrible war," Alas pitches in.

"A war that could have been ended a long time ago." I hear what I've said, and realize I phrased that last sentence very poorly. I correct myself, "I don't mean to discredit you. That was a major accomplishment, ending the war, but Din Point is still out there. The regime is still corrupt and hurting its own people, and won't stop. The situation will never change if they stay untouched. We have to get involved."

Alas answers, "I completely agree, but how? We couldn't take them down in the last war. Their military is far better than we thought."

"If we get allies, then we *can* take them down."

"*If* we get allies. That's just the first issue. No kingdom will get involved. Kindera isn't an option, Vaddel is solitary, Oxidence doesn't want to get involved, and the Zenlanders are always peaceful." Alas clearly has thought about this. "And that's just the first issue. If we do get allies, then they'll want part of the land, or something else in return for their help. That could lead to a whole different conflict of who gets how much land, who comes out on top, who sends the most troops. No one will want to give up land. We would owe people favors that cou—"

I cut off his ramble. "Hypothetically, if you had allies who didn't want any land, and have good militaries, would you declare war?"

"Of course!" Alas says, captivated by the idea. "There wouldn't even be a war. In just a few weeks, we could hypothetically launch one attack that overpowers Din Point. It would be one for the history books—an invasion that saved millions. Not only that, we'd expand Parten."

I'm in shock upon realizing that he actually wants war. It makes sense, but I'd planned on him needing much more convincing. He shakes his head and stands up, stating, "But that won't happen, so we have to find a different way to help the people of Din Point."

"But it *could* happen."

He laughs and says, "I think I can still make my meeting on time." And with that, he leaves the room.

After a minute alone with my thoughts, I get up and leave the room as well. I go right to my room and a letter to Drítan. I need to inform him that Alas is on board with taking down Din Point. I also need to reassure him that I've kept their secrets, but Alas needs to know everything if he's going to attack with them.

I need them to all meet, and for Alas to understand what Kindera is hiding from the Kingdoms.

CHAPTER 55

Isadora POV

Sooner than I expect, just two days later, I receive a letter back from Drítan. It's more threatening than I expect, but they do trust me enough to fly Alas to Kindera. Either that, or they're confident that they can kill us both if the meeting goes bad.

This gives me just one day to convince Alas to clear his schedule tomorrow and fly with me to an unknown place to meet with unknown people.

The only time I'll get a chance to speak with Alas is between meetings, and I'm going to use every second of that time. I haven't gone to a meeting since I returned; it just doesn't feel right anymore. As far as I've heard, Lawrence hasn't gone to many council meetings either. I'm not sure what made him stop, but he doesn't bother showing up to many things nowadays. At least that means he won't be right by my side when I talk to Alas.

I'm swaying on the tips on my feet as I wait for the current meeting to end. I press my back again the wall across from the door, hoping to calm my nerves. A few minutes later, and the council room door opens. I stand up straight and greet Alas.

"What is it now?" he asks as soon as he sees me. I guide him to the side of the hall. There are fewer guards around, and more room to talk now that Carac isn't a threat.

"I have a gift for you, and also I'm sort of pulling a favor," I say with a smile.

He hesitates. "What do you need?"

"That guy who dropped me off when I came back from Din Point has just gotten a huge import of old war books from Vaddel. He's offered to let me to go see them, and I want you to come with me. You'll enjoy them much more than I will. He's stationed right at the edge of our shore."

"Our shore? His plane isn't from Parten."

"He's not from Parten, but as far as I know, this is where he's stationed right now. He's from," I have to calculate my response for a split second, "he's from Oxidence." I'm hoping I've used the right lure.

"That sounds amazing, really. I'd be honored to go with you. How did he get these books? How many books? Which war—?"

I can't let him ask too many questions and find a loophole in my lies. "I don't know that much about it. I just want to see them in person. The issue is that he's having them moved to the Oxidence Museum in two days, so if we're going to see them, we need to go tomorrow."

"Tomorrow? All day?" he asks. "Do we need to fly there, then?"

"Yes, unless we want to spend a day or two traveling." I really hope he agrees to flying. There's no way to get to Kindera in under a day without flying. According to Era, a ship ride to Kindera takes three to four days, even on a large ship. I doubt anyone from Parten even travels to Kindera, so we 'd have to set up a whole boat and map the course, all of which would take a long time to plan. Plus, setting that up wouldn't even make sense in supporting my lie.

"I have to move a lot of things around for that to work. You're sure it's worth going? I mean, I hold Vaddel in high esteem for military training, but are these books anything we don't already have copies of and have seen before?"

"He made it seem like there's a reason he's trying to keep the books on the down-low. He doesn't want people to know how rare they are. You don't have to go. I mean…"

His face turns startled, scared of missing an opportunity. "No, no, I'll go. Just give me some grace if we can't stay that long."

"We don't have to stay long at all." I know I have a much better chance of him liking the idea if it doesn't take too much of his precious time.

"Morning, then, is when we'll depart. I think I can manage that." His face is still uneasy, but I can see the curiosity in his eyes.

"Perfect. Thank you, Alas."

"No, thank you for the invite." He rushes away from the conversation and scurries away down the hall.

We could be gone for days; he really needs to clear his schedule. I let out a sigh of relief as he moves out of my vision. Slowly but surely, we're making progress.

CHAPTER 56

Isadora POV

My hands won't stop shaking every time I look at Alas. I have to clench my hands together to keep myself still and remain calm enough to function. I can feel my face heating up; maybe it's from the jacket I'm wearing, coupled with the hot sun hitting the pavement of the jet runway that's heating me up, or maybe it's just my nerves. I do have a short-sleeve shirt on under the jacket that I'll be able to shed to help me with the heat in Kindera, but Alas checked the weather for the Parten coast and told me to dress warm. I know very well that we're going to be in a humid jungle soon, yet I need to maintain my ruse. I did thankfully remember to steal one of Lawrence's T-shirts, because I know that soon Alas is going to be steaming in his long-sleeve wool shirt and jacket. Hopefully he hasn't wondered why I have a small backpack on that's only holding clothing. He seems to be lost in his own thoughts.

I hate keeping things from him, but there was no way in the world that Alas would go to Kindera if he knew what was going on, and there's no way Drítan would let him come if *he* knew what was going on.

There are hundreds of ways this could go wrong. Alas could freak out, he could declare war on Kindera, he could kill Drítan and Era, or they could kill us. I know the possibility of the worse is small, but still there's chance of disaster.

Alas walks with me on the runway. He's dressed casually and somehow looks warm and fit, while also looking shiny and clueless. "Inner kingdom trip, should be a few hours of flight time, hopefully the plane is small and quick."

I nod slowly. We watch Drítan's plane land away some distance from us. It takes a few minutes for Drítan to get out and greet us. I watch Alas raise his eyebrows the slight bit, and press his teeth together in concern. "Oh, it's *this* mysterious friend," Alas says. His smile has gone away as he mumbles to himself, "I don't know how to feel about this friend."

Drítan is close enough to talk with us now. He extends a hand to Alas. "I'm Drítan. A pleasure to officially meet you, King Alas."

Alas replies with a smile, but I can hear the fake undertones in his diction. "The pleasure is all mine. Good to see you again."

Drítan just gives me a slight tilt of the head as we start to walk to the plane.

On the way Alas says to Drítan, "I have a few questions."

"Let's wait until we board," Drítan tells him. I see a slight twist in Alas' face. He isn't used to people dismissing him like that.

Alas continues to give me very uneasy glances as I put my small backpack up in a compartment and settle into my seat. We buckle ourselves into the leather seats of the jet. I catch the faces of the pilots as they go into the cockpit. They're not anyone I recognize from my first time on a Kinderan jet.

The door seals, and Alas again tries to ask some questions. He's seated next to me by the window, and Drítan sits facing us and across from me. Poor Alas is trying his best to be friendly with his conversation. "Isadora tells me you're from Oxidence?"

The jet jolts us a bit as it moves forward, and in a few seconds, we're starting our ascent.

As we hear the wheels of the plane pull in and the castle and town of Parten become smaller in the distance, Drítan responds, "Actually, I'm from Kindera."

Alas can't fully conceal his expression as his eyes look to me for an explanation.

The plane is far enough in the air that even if Alas majorly freaks out, he can't do anything to stop the flight. I don't think he knows how to fly a plane, and even if he does, it will be difficult to get into the cockpit. His leg is restless as he realizes that things aren't what he was told. I feel my stomach twist, knowing that I've directly lied to him. I had no other way of making this work if I didn't lie to him; Drítan told me to not say a word until Alas got to Kindera, but it's still something I never wanted to do to such an honest man.

"Tell me where we're going," he commands me. There's no longer any sense of security for any of us.

"Kindera," Drítan says.

"Turn the plane around," he orders without emotion. Neither Drítan nor I say a thing in response.

I can see the bewilderment and the horror overwhelming him as he looks at me with wide eyes. "No. I'm not going to Kindera." He unbuckles himself and stands up in the jet. He gestures toward me. "You can't go to Kindera. No one can go to Kindera. We'll die!"

I try to calm him down with a sympathetic voice. I plead for him to hear me through his thoughts. "Alas, it's okay i—"

"Are you trying to kill me?" he yells, his hand pushing up toward the ceiling of the plane as if it's a coffin he's trying to escape. Then he glares at Drítan and back to me. "Are *you* from Kindera?"

"No, Alas—"

"Is that why you're okay with this? Because I'll die and you won't? After everything I've done for you—"

"Alas, shut up and listen!" I yell. I can't think straight while he's panicking. Alas never panics, and I shouldn't be panicking, but he's making me anxious with his tone. I take a deep breath in and say flatly, "We *are* going to Kindera, and you *won't* die."

"Are you stupid?" he hisses with urgency. "Kindera's air will kill us! Don't you know that?!"

"The air is fine!" I yell back. Both our voices are raising as we argue. "Kindera has been lying to all of us for generations! The air is *fine* there. We're going to meet with their Queen so they can help us with Din Point. You said we could take over Din Point if we only could get enough forces, and these are the allies you want and need."

"They're tricking you, Isadora! You should know better than to trust people like this. Turn the plane around." Alas lunges to the cockpit door. He bangs his hand against the door. "Turn the plane around! That's an order!" he yells at the door. After he gets no response, he turns back to us and glares with an insistent face.

"Alas, please calm down and have a little faith. You're causing an uproar over nothing. I promise you that if it's deadly, I would have died. I've been to Kindera and the air is fine." I want to say something more to get through to him, but it will do no good. All I can do it look at Alas and his pissed-off expression. He never shows his uneasiness, and now he's exposed and vulnerable.

Drítan finally speaks up, and with almost a laugh he says, "Now that you're done with that meltdown, my full title is Prince Drítan of Kindera."

I can see Alas become uncomfortable as he takes the crown off his head and sets it down on an empty seat. He returns to his own chair and glares at me furiously. I know he has no reason to trust Drítan, but surely, he must have a little faith in me.

Alas settles into his seat. He doesn't look at me or Drítan for the rest of the flight. Instead, he buries his head in his hands. Drítan and I engage in conversation to try and calm Alas down, but he doesn't say anything else to us.

Eventually, the plane lands, and Alas immediately stands. "Don't open the door," he orders me.

I sigh as we watch the pilot leave the cockpit and open the plane's door. Alas looks around with panic, then slowly takes a breath and realizes he isn't dead. Drítan gets out of the plane first. I peer back at Alas and take a step forward; as I do, he grabs my hand. "You know this isn't right," he mutters to me.

I know the fear he's experiencing, I had felt it too when I first came to Kindera. All he needs to see is the climate changes and the jungle-covered castle. Then he'll know that this isn't any other kingdom, and that the "toxic air" is a remarkable cover up for this treasure of an island.

I wrap my hand over his, grab my bag, and walk us both out of the plane. I practically have to drag Alas out. I feel his feet sink as we step onto the sand. I watch Alas staring everything in sight. I take the backpack off and give him the T-shirt I was carrying in it.

"Put this on," I say. He looks at me blankly. "We're passing through a desert and then into a humid jungle. I know you're a temperature controller, but you're going to hate being dressed in wool in a jungle."

I take my jacket off as Alas takes his sweater off and hands it to me. I shove both articles of clothing into my bag as he puts his new shirt on, and we walk to the open-air car Drítan is already sitting in. We silently get into the car, and Drítan starts to drive.

The only sounds we hear are the gears grinding and the wheels turning. After a few minutes of driving, we enter the jungle. My eyes are on Alas as I watch for his reaction. His eyes fill with curiosity as he looks behind us to see the desert we've left behind fading into the distance. The lush jungle flies past us, and I catch Alas relaxing his shoulders. He's now accepting that Kindera's tricked him, just like the rest of us.

Just as when I first visited, we pull up to their vine-covered stone palace. Queen Era is waiting for us at the main entrance, with two soldiers flanking her. Alas jumps out of the car, and Era offers her hand. Alas accepts. "King Alasdair of Parten," he says, introducing himself and shaking her hand. Drítan and I get out of the car and stand behind Alas.

I look at Drítan, and he makes eye contact with me. He grins.

"Queen Era of Kindera," she responds gracefully.

Alas has the same reaction I did. I know he must be dying to ask questions, but as we enter the palace, he only glances back at me and my smug look. "This is real?" Alas asks everyone. "This is truly Kindera?"

"Indeed it is," Era says, and explains to Alas why the true nature of Kindera has been a secret long kept from the outside world. Alas marvels at the story and brilliance of it all. But when it comes to the part when Era explains how her and Drítan's parents died, he goes cold. I can see his eyes darken with empathy and sympathy.

Quickly, Drítan changes the conversation. We begin discussing Din Point in further depth and move into a meeting room.

As we sit down, Alas stops and looks at me. "*Hypothetical,* right?" he taunts, alluding to our earlier conversations in Parten.

"Right," I say, as the conversation launches fully into how Parten and Kindera can ally to take over Din Point. The full day turns into us four talking and bouncing ideas back and forth. We both have one common goal, and that's to get rid of the Din Point royals—for good. Era mentions Oxidence and how they will join Parten in the attack, to bring our numbers high enough to outweigh Din Point's. Close to the end of the day, I ask the room, "Would you be comfortable with us talking to our military leaders and council so we can start to formulate a plan?"

Era doesn't skip a beat as she responds, "The more people you tell, the more the chance of Din Point hearing about this increases. We want to take our time and plan out every situation before a whiff of the word *war* is heard. We absolutely need to have the upper hand."

Alas contemplates her words, and then says, "I want to speak with the Oxidence leaders. Once I hear it directly from them that we have their troops, we can decide how to proceed with our plans. If everything goes smoothly after that, I recommend you let us tell select council members and generals about the plans."

I agree with Alas. He's always had a way of getting the perfect outcome he desires in meetings. I ask, "How soon can we get the Oxidence leaders here?"

Drítan answers, "I imagine within a day. I can write to them right now." He excuses himself and leaves the room.

Era smiles, pleased with the conversation. "You can stay here for the night if you'd like," she offers.

I let Alas answer: "Better than traveling back for such a short time. I'll need to write a few letters to take care of my absence." He gets up and follows after Drítan.

I sit across from Era, almost in disbelief that everything is working out; if it continues to go as planned, we'll start to work on strategies very soon.

It will come together in time.

Hopefully, a short amount of time.

CHAPTER 57

Alas POV

I've been up for an hour or so, and it took me nearly all that time before I finally convinced Drítan to take me and Isadora on the scenic hike that's custom to Kindera. It only took me so long to convince him because he doesn't think it's right to go to Isadora's room, in case she's still asleep. I told him that she'll sleep the whole day unless we wake her.

I suspect she just didn't sleep well. Drítan and Era put us in separate guest rooms in the palace. The rooms are smaller than we're used to, and full of plants and greenery. It was pretty humid last night, which didn't affect me since I can lower the temperature in the room. But I'm sure it made it hard to sleep for Isadora, since she likes the cold weather more. It's not ideal, but fine for a few nights.

I watch from a few feet away as Drítan knocks on Isadora's door. After a moment, the door opens and Drítan says, "I'd like you and Alas to go on the hike I mentioned before. The one with the different climates; it displays our natural heritage, and Alas thinks you'll like it." He marvels at her for a second and then laughs. "Did you just wake up?"

I walk over to the door and stand behind him. I tease, "She most definitely just woke up."

Drítan turns to me and cheerfully scoffs, "It's almost noon!"

"I told you," I say.

Isadora glares at both of us and snaps, "Give me five."

She shuts the door on us. Drítan and I pass the time with conversation, and five minutes later Isadora opens the door dressed for a hike. with her hair tied up and shoes laced tightly.

Isadora and I follow Drítan outside. I can see she's dragging, still trying to wake up completely. I warm the rest of the coffee I've been drinking and give it to her to hopefully help. She thanks me, and drinks it as we walk deep into the jungle., stopping after about 500 yards. In front of us are five paths.

We both wait for Drítan's instructions. He begins, "We can take any path you'd like. None are very long; they're each around a mile, and all end up at the same place."

I raise an eyebrow and ask, "What's the fastest time?"

I see Isadora shake her head and look to the ground. I know this is supposed to be a calming experience, but Drítan, mirroring my face, shows he's up for a challenge. "I don't know," he admits. "But I doubt you can beat *my* time."

"I think I'll put up a fair fight," I say, raising my head a bit more.

Drítan gazes at Isadora, who hasn't said a word, and teases, "A mile too long for you, Princess?"

I'm not sure how to react when he calls her Princess. She was crowned as a Princess in Parten, and as Queen in Din Point, but still her title is up in the air.

"I'm gonna kick your ass at this," she replies with a smile.

"Pick your path," Drítan replies, and gestures at the five routes.

She rolls her neck and walks to the path on the far left. I know she isn't in the mood to race, but she won't let us show her up.

I take my pick next, going to the path in the middle. Drítan takes his place on the one to my left.

I can't even remember the last time I went on a run. Hopefully, I'll be the one to win while I still can take in my surroundings.

Drítan takes his running position and says, "Ready." He squints to us quickly. "Set." Then he looks ahead and yells, "Go!"

I leap forward. The mud slides under my feet as I take my first few leaps onto the path. It's dense with trees and brightly colored plants, but there's no time to look at the marvelous flora closely. So much for a nice hike to see the sights! I keep pushing forward and let the distant noise of the palace fade behind me.

The environment grades into a temperate forest. Shorter trees than in the jungle, along with rocks and grass, fill the area around the pathway. I feel the wind flow through my hair as the temperate climate leaves just as quick as it came. As I run, my skin becomes damp and covered in small drizzles of snow. I don't even remember the last time I touched snow or saw it collected on the ground. It doesn't snow in Parten very often, and I almost never go outside when it does. It's a stimulating coldness that tempts me to raise the temperature around me to get back that secure, warm temperature I'm constantly creating.

For a second, I pause and look at the snow falling around me. I lift a hand up and follow a snowflake as it descents to the ground. But before I can stop and admire the snow any longer, I remember I'm participating in a race that I intend to win.

I pick up my feet and continue to run. The snow starts to lessen, and the trees turn from frosted to a warm, colorful combination. The crunch of leaves under my feet fills my ears as I marvel at the scene. It reminds me of fall in Parten, that special time of year when the leaves are an array of different colors and the weather is a brisk coolness that makes it enjoyable to be outside without getting too warm.

I can barely believe that any of this is true. How is it possible that Kindera kept this big a secret all these years?

Finally, the environment changes for the last time, becoming a sandy desert. It's much harder to run in the sand, as it slips under my shoes and makes me sink farther into the ground, giving me less traction.

My mind goes from pure concentration to defeat as I see Drítan waiting for me at the end. "You beat me?" I ask while catching my breath. He definitely had a home-field advantage.

"Barely. I just got here," he says, breathing in slowly and deeply.

"Is Isadora still running?" I ask, puzzled that she isn't here already.

"I guess so." We both stare at her path.

A few minutes pass, and she still isn't here. She's a good runner, even better than me at times; she shouldn't be taking this long.

"Should we go check?" Drítan asks.

"We just need to let her walk down the path," I say, with a bit of concern filling my head.

After a few more minutes go by, I give up waiting and start to walk down her path. Drítan and I slowly follow it, giving me the chance to take in the climates without a rush, trying to calm my rising concern.

I bet Isadora just stopped in the snowy climate and is playing around with her ability.

But as we walk through the snow, I don't even see footprints. The snow wouldn't have covered them that fast. She hasn't even been here. I don't express a word of my worries to Drítan as we trail farther down the path, but my heart is racing. Now we're in the jungle climate again, and I still don't see her. Drítan and I stop for a second as I hear a sound coming from a small pond a few meters to the side of the trial.

We both rush over and see Isadora in the pond, coming up for air. She breathes in heavily and looks around the jungle intently. Her eyes are wide as I walk to the edge of the pond and stand on the rocks above her. I look down and ask her, "What *are* you doing?"

She stares blankly at me and Drítan, then dives back under the water.

Drítan says in confusion, "Is she okay?"

I don't know how to answer but assure him, "She can swim very well."

After a minute, she comes back up for air. Drítan asks, "What the hell are you doing, Princess?"

She gulps, "Isn't it obvious? Swimming." She takes a lap around in the pound.

I explain in utter confusion, "It's been nearly ten minutes since we ended our runs. We thought something happened to you."

"It's been that long?" she asks, swimming closer to the edge of the pond. "I must have lost track of time. Do you want to come swim?"

"No," I snap. "Come on out."

Isadora sighs and starts to climb on the rocks, but before she's out, Drítan runs and jumps into the water. Isadora pushes off the rocks and laughs as she heads back out.

I'm not sure if I'm seeing things right anymore. They both continue to swim. I have a war to plan, and they're swimming. I have lives at stake, and they're splashing water around. I'm beyond worried about the faith of the kingdoms, and they're laughing and swimming!

"Are you coming, or what?" Isadora says to me.

"The Oxidence leaders aren't going to be here until later tonight, not until dinner," Drítan argues to my annoyed look.

I look down and to the side, then slowly walk down the rocks to sit by the water. "I don't want to swim right now," I respond.

"Fine," Isadora says while she makes a wave of water hit Drítan. He splashes back with his hands and dives under the water.

I don't understand why Isadora decided *now* would be a good time to go swimming. She was just as worried as I am about the planning. She's still wearing all her day clothes, and I can even see through the water that she has her shoes on.

I sigh and sit back against the rock.

I'll let them have their fun while they can.

CHAPTER 58

Alas POV

I just got word that the Queen of Oxidence has arrived, and despite working through my thoughts all day, I'm not fully ready. I calmly pace from my room to the dining room. I need to make sure that nothing, absolutely nothing, goes wrong in this meeting.

In the span of two days, I will have met two kingdom leaders whom neither my father nor grandfather has. This is the start of a whole new era.

I meet Isadora in the hall, and we walk side-by-side. I just saw her a little bit ago, when we were in my room talking about the points we wanted to bring up during this dinner. It helped to hear her input and put my thoughts into words. Usually, I'd talk things out with Trinity and listen to her input, but she's not here. Now that the ideas are in my head about taking over Din Point, there's no way I won't let the plans go through. We're in this together, and we'll finish this together.

"I know the majority of the council will be on board with us. Trinity will support it as well, but the one person who'll give us a hard time will be Lawrence," I say, picking up the conversation where we left off. We came to an agreement earlier that we'll go home tomorrow, and Isadora will tell Lawrence.

"He just dislikes war more than the average person, but I agree he's going to put up quite a fight over this," she says. I don't think we should tell him anything ahead of time, so that he won't make a scene in front of the council before a meeting. I'll just have Isadora tell him, while I tell the council separately.

"He also thinks I'm irrational, too self-centered, power-hungry, not a forward thinker... I could go on..." My voice fades out.

"No he doesn't."

"You haven't seen him and I talk recently. I can't even breathe without him getting manic. I can't imagine how much of a fit he's going to throw when he finds out you only told *me* about Kindera." I take a pause, and then spark a question: "How did you even know about Kindera?" I've had so much introduced to me I hadn't thought about asking her this until now.

"When I was leaving Din Point, I met Drítan on accident. Well, he sort of found me," she quips. She hasn't looked at me this whole conversation. Her weight is shifting on her feet, and her diction is snappier than normal.

I take in her attitude. "What's the matter?" I ask.

"Nothing. Nothing's wrong."

"Don't tell me, then. Fine," I say. I know her better then to take "nothing" as an answer, but I have bigger things to worry about than her mood right now.

We finally get to the dining room, and I open the door for Isadora. Already in the room are Drítan and Era, and a handsome woman whom I can only guess to be the Queen of Oxidence. She's old; her hair has turned gray, and her face tells me that she's seen the world and isn't impressed. Her skin is wrinkled, and I wonder why she keeps it that way when she's a dermamancer. From private briefings, I know her personal ability is to manipulate skin at all levels. Not only could she change how her skin looks if she wanted, but she can also help people heal from gash wounds, burns, and similar skin injuries— even acne. I once met a skin manipulator who told me that he'd changed his appearance so much that he no longer remembered what he originally looked like; maybe that's why she keeps herself authentic. From the little I've learned from my briefings, I also know her name is Galen.

She looks me and Isadora up and down, and then, with a voice much bigger than she is, says, "So I'm meeting a king who ended a war, and a queen who's about to start one."

I knew this dinner wasn't going to be an easy one, but damn, based off that greeting, we're in for it.

Isadora takes a seat across from Queen Galen, and I sit down next to her, across from Queen Era. I glance at Drítan as he sits in the seat next to Isadora, looking awfully serious.

"I'm not a queen anymore," Isadora says primly.

Queen Galen doesn't hesitate as she tells Isadora, "You were crowned in Parten as a princess, but you were also made a queen in Din Point. Queen trumps Princess, and they cannot cast away your title just because your husband died. As far as I'm concerned, you have every right to say whether Din Point is surrendering or going to war. The royals may not listen to you, but the people might."

"Is that how you want to do it? Parten can't break its treaty without revealing that they might break a treaty with other kingdoms, so you want to use me to declare war?" Isadora asks the Queen.

Queen Era responds, "I don't see a better option."

I marvel at the conversation between the three queens. One is so young she looks like a child, and the one sitting next to her looks like she was alive when Parten was founded. The third queen has helped ruled more kingdoms than they have, albeit accidentally.

For the entire dinner, almost all we talk about are the plans for Din Point, though I ask Queen Galen any questions that come to my mind, even some about Oxidence. How is the weather, how did she rise to power, how is the food? I never expected to meet anyone from Oxidence, and now I have the opportunity to speak with the Queen. I'm not going to waste a minute of this dinner. And apparently neither is she, as all her answers are short and to the point.

I hear side conversations start up as Drítan compliments Isadora's necklace. I watch as she tucks the necklace , which has a ring looped in a chain, under her shirt and softly says, "Thanks."

I need to wrap things up so that no more irrelevant conversations intrude. Towards the end of the evening I make the statement, "I think everything we've planned here is promising, and I know it can work if we fine-tune it to perfection. But if I'm going to go to war again, I need some documented form of an alliance with both of your kingdoms." The worse thing that could happen would be Parten and Din Point going to war, and then Kindera and Oxidence backing out. That would be devastating to us all.

"I understand," Queen Galen agrees. "I'll sign whatever you need, but like you, I need to discuss this with my council before lifting a pen. We'll reconvene in two days. Is that enough time for you all?"

"It will be," I answer. I don't want to keep Queen Galen waiting.

CHAPTER 59

Isadora POV

Alas just *had* to make us leave Kindera before the crack of dawn. I know he needs time with his council, but this is far too early for my taste. As we drive to the desert runway, I can feel the brisk breeze off the sand; it's cool, as it hasn't yet had enough sunlight to get overly hot.

We hop out of the car, and Alas parts with some kind words to Drítan as he climbs onto the plane. Drítan told us last night he wouldn't be traveling with us to Parten, but promised to have his finest pilots fly us back. As Alas gets on the plane, Drítan quickly moves in front of me. I don't move, and give him a confused smile. Quickly, with authority, he states, "We have a lot on the line here."

I gulp and reply, "I know we do."

"I know what I saw," he says.

"And what will you do about it?" I ask, holding back any sign of emotion.

"Pray you don't screw us all." He stands to the side. I pass him and walk straight to the plane. "Have a good flight," he calls.

"Thanks," I mutter, afraid that he may do something irrational.

CHAPTER 60

Isadora POV

"**I**f Lawrence gives you any trouble, tell him to come talk to me," Alas tells me as we walk down the halls of Parten Castle. He prepped me the whole flight back from Kindera on talking to Lawrence about the war. I have to speak to Lawrence, while he takes the easy path and presents the information and ideas to the council. At the end of the day, Alas has the final say and can declare war at any second, but the process will go much smoother if he gets the council's approval.

He gives me a slight nod. I know he's worried about the meeting, but I'm far more concerned about telling Lawrence. I know he isn't going to agree with any of this, I just don't know to what extent. But what can he do, really?

"I'll be fine," I say to him as we part ways in the hall. Lawrence's room is just down the hall from where Alas's council meeting is taking place. We aren't wasting any time.

I knock on Lawrence's door. I sway back and forward on my heels, trying not to show that I'm nervous. Lawrence quickly opens the door and looks annoyed as I enter his room. "Back from your 'day' trip with Alas?" he snarks while sitting down on the couch. I'm sure that he, just like everyone else, he has a lot of questions about why Alas and I were gone so long.

"That's what I'm here to talk to you about," I say with a smile. With Lawrence acting so weird in the last few days, I have to make sure this goes smoothly. "Parten is going to declare war on Din Point again in a few weeks," I blurt. I don't think there's any way to ease into this conversation.

"Did Alas say this?" he asks, raising his head, "because Alas is wrong."

"It isn't just him. We have powerful allies now."

"Who?" He crosses his arms abruptly while shutting down his expression.

"Kindera. It isn't a wasteland, Lawrence. That was all a scheme for their protection." I don't want to explain this whole situation again. I feel like I've told it too many times now. I continue, "And Oxidence has agreed to help."

"This is bullshit! We can't go to war again. We just finished one!" Lawrence says, raising his voice. He doesn't even mention the fact that I just revealed that Kindera is a hidden nation. His mind is far too focused on Alas and the potential war. I give him a second to catch his breath; I can practically feel his heart jumping out of his chest.

"Lawrence, this is the right thing to do. A little war, basically just one battle, will end hundreds of years' worth of suffering in Din Point."

"Din Point isn't our issue to worry about! We are *Parten.* Our people are happy, and *that* is what matters. You and Alas are blind not to understand that another war is going to raise hell." Lawrence stands up to meet me.

"We aren't doing a draft. We'll make it through this successfully with the soldiers we have. You don't have to agree with it, but it's what's happening. Plans are already in motion."

Lawrence shakes his head, his eyes becoming slits. "You don't understand," he grinds out through his teeth. "This isn't going to work." His face is turning harsh, the temperature in the room rising. "Isadora," he says while looking around the room, "I need you to believe me."

"I value your opinion, Lawrence, but a lot of powerful people have thought this through." My emotions can no play a part in this conversation. This is strictly political, not personal.

"Do you trust me? Will you keep what I tell you between us?" Lawrence asks me quickly.

"Lawrence, what is it?"

"Will you?"

"Yes, fine. Whatever will calm you down," I say to him.

He grabs my hands and sits me down. His gaze meets my eyes, full of precision. "Alas is too violent. He always tried to push rash strategies on the council when we were younger, and he does it now. What he wants, this war, it's wrong. He can't lead with this mindset. He can't lead very well at all, just like our father. We all know how terribly that went."

I can see Lawrence getting worked up, but what he's telling me goes far beyond this moment. The truth is, his father wasn't a bad king. And Lawrence told me before how much he hates the idea of Alas on the throne. This issue he has with Alas is deep-rooted and has been growing for a long time.

"He will run this kingdom into the ground. First Din Point, then who? The Zenlands? He can't be in control of that much power. He won't stop, and if we cave in to letting him take down Din Point, it will lead to much worse."

"There's nothing you can do," I say, trying to contain his thoughts. What he's saying has value, but not enough solid facts, and I don't believe that Alas will want anything more after this war. I can't tell where Lawrence is getting these ideas from; jealousy, fantasies of personal gain, or pure fear that he's been holding in for too long?

"We can lead," he says tersely, "you and I. I need you to trust *me* more than *him*, and lead Parten with me. I'm not saying we kill him, we just take—

"Lawrence," I whisper. I clench my teeth. I can't do what he wants me to do. I can't take his side on this one. Alas is king. I'm shocked at how deep his hatred seems to run.

"Don't you understand what I'm asking you? Trust me for once! Let me take control for once. I've been hinting this to you for a long time. Now I need you to come through with me. Your whole philosophy is to do the best thing for this kingdom, and *we* can do that. Not Alas!"

"You're insane," I finally snap. "He's your brother, and you're talking about ruining him!" I stand up quickly. Lawrence grabs my hands and stands up too.

"I need you to do this! Just work with me to get rid of him. We can keep the peace!" he yells at me.

"Get it through your head that I support this war! I support Alas! *He* is our king, not you! What you propose would be treason, the worst kind of betrayal!"

Lawrence tightens his grip on me. The temperature in the room has risen to the point that I'm starting to sweat. His anger shows through the redness in his checks. He grinds out, "You don't know what you're saying."

I swallow my breath and firmly say, "I'm on Alas's side."

That's the breaking point for Lawrence. He looks around the room and then back at me as his emotions flip. "You're always on his side! You won't listen to me! Tell me that I didn't just waste all of my time and energy by telling you this!" he shouts at me. I try to take my hand back from him, but he grips my wrist harder.

"Listen to yourself, Lawrence! This is insane!" I don't want to betray Lawrence or Alas, but with everything Lawrence is saying, I'm going to end up betraying one of them. This isn't the Lawrence I married. This isn't the Lawrence I trust. This is someone else. I quickly blurt, "It wasn't his idea! I'm the one who persuaded him to go to war!"

"*Do you understand what is happening?!*" Lawrence screams. "You have no clue how long I've been working on this! You don't even understand the position I just offered you! You can't see how you're in the wrong here!"

I finally jerk my hand away from him and back away. Lawrence has the upper hand here. His voice is getting louder, and the room is turning against me as the heat rises.

"You just ruined *everything*," he says, and reaches for my hand again. He grabs my wrist and burns my skin. I leap away, and stand on the other side of the table. I call for water in the room; this is going to get messy. and I don't want it to.

The temperature in the room increases. My heart is rapidly beating as I look at him with wide eyes, sweat beading on my brow. He's about to try to end me over this.

He lunges forward. I run to the door and rush out of the room. If I'm going to have to fight back at all, it's not going to be in a room that Lawrence is already flooding with heat. I breath in the cool air in the hall; Lawrence had better just stay in the room and cool off.

I hurry away from the room as the hall now starts to heat up. I glance at the guards in the hall, who all start to back away. It's apparent no one wants a part of this. I turn to see Lawrence stepping into the hall with a sword in his hand. Pure shock has already hit me in several waves, but seeing Lawrence with a weapon raised against me hits me especially hard. He's going to try to kill me with that sword. He's done with asking me to be on his side, and has now proclaimed me the enemy. He wants Alas gone, and me as well.

I quickly drag water close to me and make three daggers in defense. Calmly, I say, "Lawrence, are you serious?" I glance at the sword. "If you put that down and calm yourself, we can both walk away and act like this never happened. We can talk it out."

I don't think I can follow through with acting like this never happened, but I don't want Lawrence to do this. This has all escalated too fast. There's no reason why what I said to him should have instigated this much chaos.

"I stand by everything I said. You let me down. *You* are the reason that everything I've done is ruined." He moves closer. I step back. "It's over for either you or for me," he says, quickening his pace and heading straight at me with the sword raised. I don't want to fight Lawrence, but I'm not going to let him attack me without defending myself.

He swings the burning sword, and the flat strikes my raised arms. My skin hisses, seared, and I react by swinging an ice-knife that barely cuts his shoulder. I move in closer to Lawrence, and with one hand I slide the dagger into his arm, while with my other I try to grab the hilt of the sword. I struggle with his hands, and eventually knock the sword to the floor. With a swift kick, I send the sword clattering down the hall. Lawrence grabs my arm and leaves deep burns ruthless enough to make me shout in pain. I flinch away from his touch. Then my husband kicks me in the chest; I stumble back, trying to catch myself. The impact isn't enough to send me to the floor.

My hands are ice-cold. I motion for the water kept in the hall for this very purpose to glide closer to us and across Lawrence's feet. With one hand I swing for a punch; it barely scrapes the side of his head.

He reaches out and shoves me to the floor.

"I've been working on this for years, and I threw it all away in one conversation! You were the last step to making this work!" he roars.

He throws a punch at me. I twist my head to the side, and his knuckles hit the stone. The rage he's built up his whole life is storming down on me.

I feel all the coldness disappear as Lawrence heats me up. I roll to the side and stand up, just in the nick of time. I move inward and cut his arm as he blurts out in pure, blazing anger, "I killed my father for this!"

My hand starts to shake, even as the shock nearly makes my mind goes blank. *He killed his father for the throne?* I thought the king died from his illness; everyone thinks that. Or they did, until he admitted it in front of an audience. My breath whooshes out. He's ready to kill Alas too, and even me. He's been planning to get Alas out of his way this whole time.

I create a spear of ice and take aim at his head.

Just then Alas and his advisors finally arrive, summoned by a guard who's witnessed the fight. I glance at Alas as the spear I throw ruins a painting on the wall, missing Lawrence's head by inches as he runs.

"What the hell is—" Alas shouts at Lawrence as turns to create a heat bubble that closes in on me. Lawrence moves in closer as I lose my breath. He swipes an ice dagger from the ground that I'd previously made and lost. He launches the blade at me, and it sinks home in the lower left side of my stomach. I freeze up in reaction and grip my side, then pull my hand back and form ice razors. I hurl four of them at Lawrence as I see Alas running down the hall toward us. One strikes deep in Lawrence's leg. He looks at his brother and then at me before turning and running down the hall as fast as he can manage.

I watch him turn the corner in the direction opposite Alas. Alas doesn't chase after Lawrence; instead he runs to me. "Go," I scream at Alas, "Go get him, and take guards with you!"

Alas looks at the members of the council as they watch the commotion. Then he bolts down the hall after Lawrence in full speed, his guards following.

I try to breathe in, slowly.

I pace a few feet while studying the members of the council. They don't know what to do besides stay out of the way. Or maybe they're just in shock; I think I am.

I'm tempted to melt the ice-knife back to water, but I know better than to remove it; that would allow more blood to flow. Instead, I make it colder and harder so it's less likely to melt, then slowly lower myself to the ground and lie down.

Ryder comes into my field of view and leans down to me. He rips a part of my shirt off to see the wound fully before deciding to wrap cloth around it. He leaves the dagger in as I remain as still as I can. I try to lighten the situation with a comment: "If you wanted to take my shirt off, this really isn't the time." He doesn't laugh. Ryder should have laughed at that; this must be pretty bad.

"Who did this?" he asks while assessing the dagger's location.

"Lawrence," I breathe. He moves his hand. He pulls the dagger out abruptly. He's careful and precise and doesn't hurt anything further. I inhale sharply. By now there are multiple guards around us. Thankfully, one is a dermamancer, like Queen Galen. he leans over me and presses a hand to the wound.

"Lawrence? Fucking Prince Boy?" he asks, looking at me like I'm a liar.

All I can say is, "Yep."

CHAPTER 61

Isadora POV

"Lawrence is gone," Alas says, panting as he jogs down the hall, followed by a swarm of guards. He stops next to me, looking at Ryder. My stab wound has been taken care of by an excellent skin manipulator and Ryder, but it's still going to slow me down for a few days. Ryder and the skin mender are standing by my side, inspecting my other injures.

"What happened?" Alas asks. Everyone's eyes are drawn to me. It's still fuzzy in my head, as if this is all a terrible nightmare. Everything escalated so quickly. Lawrence pressed so much information on me at once. I don't want to believe that everything he said was true, but there's no reason for Lawrence to lie about his intentions, then attack to protect them.

I glance around at everyone who's listening. I tell Alas, "I don't... I don't know if you want to talk about it here. With everyone."

Ryder looks at me with a stern face. He follows alongside me and Alas as we move into the now-empty council room. I move very gingerly, the pain still fresh. I take a seat and rest myself. I don't care if Ryder sticks around anymore; this information is going to a terrible effect on Alas.

"Lawrence..." I have to pause in between words to make sure that I say everything to the best of my knowledge and don't overstep or imply anything. "I broke the news to Lawrence about the war and being allies with Kindera and Oxidence. His emotions..." I explain the whole conversation I had with Lawrence to them. I don't gloss over anything we said. I explain it step-by-step: when he increased his movements, when he heated up the room. I tell them everything.

Alas doesn't make eye contact with me once. His face grows paler, his eyes showing betrayal as his mouth twists down. Ryder asks questions. He helps push the conversation forward by saying what Alas probably wants to. But finally I have to say the hardest thing: "I cut his arm a bit and stepped closer to him. Then he said, 'I killed my father for this'. "

Alas's head lifts, and his eyes meets mine. He inhales deeply while uncrossing his arms, and walks straight out of the room. My breathing hitches as I watch him leave. I run a hand over my face. "I-I shouldn't have told him. He should have had something left of his brother that was good." I gulp, "It's his *brother*."

"You couldn't have *not* told him. You did everything right, as far as I can tell," Ryder reassures me. I reach for the door, but before I open it, Ryder calls out, "Don't go. He's going to be extremely and justifiably upset about this for a long time, and honestly, I think he needs to figure it out alone. There is nothing more you can say."

"He needs someone to lean on."

"Maybe, but I don't think that can be you right now."

I slowly lower my hand. If Lawrence really did kill their father, it changes a lot of things. If he did plot against Alas, that shakes everything we know about him. I also need some time to figure out my thoughts on all on this.

Nothing makes sense anymore, and it won't for a while.

CHAPTER 62

Isadora POV

I wake up to the familiar sound of someone knocking on my door. I'm not expecting Alas to be the one on the other side as I open the door and meet his eyes. I let him into my room.

He isn't wearing his crown. He isn't dressed like a king; he looks less than himself. His eyes look sunken. "I didn't get a chance to tell you what the council agreed to yesterday," he says while taking a seat.

I cross my arms as I feel chills spreading over my skin. When I take a step to sit down, sharp pains shoots through my stomach. The spot where Lawrence stabbed me is still hurting. The skin menders did everything they could, but it's still very sensitive and sore.

"They're on board with the plans, but they advised that it happen sooner rather than later. While Din Point is in disarray, it will be easier to attack. The goal is for us to strike in a month's time, if we get the final words from Kindera and Oxidence."

"That's amazing, it really is," I say. I need to address yesterday somehow. I have to see how he's holding up. "Alas, about Lawrence…"

Alas whispers defensively, "I don't know what you want me to say."

"I just want to see how you're doing."

"Badly. He was my brother, Isadora." He shakes his head and snaps at himself, "He still is."

"I know. Did you send any guards out to try and find him? He couldn't have gotten far."

"No. The only thing that really changes around here is that we have someone to blame for my father's death. If he even did it." Alas is talking so fast, his words are blending together. "And I don't want to say that he did it. So, I'm not putting tags on his head and I'm not sending a guard hunt out for him."

I can only nod in response. I don't know to say. It's like Ryder told me: there's nothing I can do to fix what's happening.

"I think he did it," Alas admits quietly, even as his voice breaks. "I don't know why he would run and leave everything behind if he's innocent. And I don't know why you'd make up anything like this." He clasp his hands together and looks up at the ceiling. "That's what's pissing me off. No matter how I look at this, he's in the wrong. No matter how I read the situation or how I interpret what I saw, your words add up." I wait for him to continue. He stammers out, "I-I want you to be wrong. I want you to be a liar. And you're not." I bite my tongue. "I wish it were different. I wish that you were the one I'm angry at. I wish *you* had betrayed me, not my very own blood. Maybe it's wrong to wish that, but I do. I wish it so badly."

I can't even be mad at him. I don't have one angry bone in my body towards him. Everything I can see in Alas is pure sadness. I wish what he said a little bit too; it would be better if I were wrong and Lawrence hadn't done what he said he had.

"I'm sorry," Alas whispers.

"So am I."

"We're leaving for Kindera tomorrow morning."

CHAPTER 63

Isadora POV

War rooms scare the shit out of messengers. War rooms should scare anyone who isn't supposed to be there. The war room in Kindera is no different. It's crowded. Not just your normal room with lots of people; war rooms are crowded with very important and powerful people. It's loud, too; everyone is opinionated, and because it's so busy, often everyone raises their voices to be heard.

It's also just frightening to think about what's happening in this room. The kingdom leaders and generals are all in this one room, trying to figure out how we're going to attack and destroy Din Point.

You can't repeat anything to the general public that you overhear in the war room. Everything is strictly off-limits to talk about, which is why kingdoms only allow their most trusted messengers in the room.

I watch, from the other side of the room, as a messenger scurries through the crowd of people. Poor guy; he just needs to deliver the one letter I see in his hand. I glance to the side, at the corner of the room Queens Era and Galen discuss finances and a few moral standings they have different opinions on. In the other corner of the room, Drítan is completely consumed with talking to some Parten leaders about ways to get Kindera's troops to the mainland.

Everywhere in the room are small tables for people to take a sit and discuss. But there's not even close to enough room for everyone to be seated. People are standing around the room and leaning against walls to have conversations. I don't think Kindera has ever had this many visitors.

The war room in Kindera is far more frantic than any other I've experienced. I've only been in a few from talking with Daymond when he worked in Din Point. The reason for it being so chaotic is because we only have a little over a week to plan this attack. Usually kingdoms would have months to plan, maybe more if they were lucky.

The messenger takes a deep breath and launches himself into the center of the room. I can't imagine his job. It's not like you can ask people where someone is. You can't even ask anyone to move out of the way. You could be asking a general or someone who has run out of patience, and you defiantly don't want to piss them off.

I turn back to the table where I'm seated. In the middle of the room is the war board. Most of the generals and colonels are seated at a large oak table in front of it, discussing and arguing the attack. There's one large map spread across the board, and figurines that represent thousands of troops scattered through it. I sit on the end of the table directly across from Daymond, who is at the other head. He stands over his seat with his hands pressed on the table. He yells at any move he disagrees with. Daymond is not a nice person when he's in a war room. I've never seen him in action before; it's amazing, terrifying.

Daymond has been given a lot of power by King Alas recently, and is using it to the best of his ability. Alas made him

High General of Parten's military, which means no one can give him military orders anymore except for Alas himself.

Alas sits in the middle-left side of the table, observing everything going down and very strongly giving his opinions when he thinks they're is needed. People stand behind us at the table and watch the work.

One of Kindera's Majors moves a bunch of figures to the north, which causes Daymond to throw his hands up while he lectures, "You go there, they'll get pummeled by the straight lines, and die. Are you serious? Are you trying to waste my time? Who taught you these idiotic..."

I lose track of what my brother is saying as the messenger I saw before comes to my side. He hands me the letter and quickly adds with a frantic tone, "They said it's very urgent."

I bid him a short, "Thank you," while I inspect the letter. The red wax seal on the front is still intact, which gives me some hope that no one has read it.

I wasn't expecting a letter from anyone, yet alone an urgent one.

I open it carefully and read the words rapidly. From across the table, Daymond has finished his lecture, and I can feel his eyes on me. I finish reading and lower the letter. I make direct eye contact with Daymond. His attention is totally focused on me. "What is it?" he asks.

People are talking too loud for us to communicate. I slowly shake my head. Fear has overtaken me as I try to tell him with my eyes that something is wrong.

"What is it?" Daymond asks me again. I open my mouth to speak. When no one gets quieter, Daymond slams his hands on the table and draws the attention to himself. *"What* does it *say?"* he demands. The whole table follows where he's looking and turns to me.

I glance quickly at Alas as he leans back in his chair. His look makes my throat close, and I forget for a second how to form words. I turn back at Daymond to get my head straight.

"Lawrence is in Din Point. He told them everything he knows. They're going to declare war on us tomorrow."

"*Prince* Lawrence?" someone yells. A officer says, "He doesn't even know the royals there," at the same time as another person questions, "How did he even get there without us knowing?"

Twelve other people start a commotion, all at the same time, and the news spreads like fire through the room. I force myself to concentrate on Alas. He stares straight forward, intensely peering down at the war board with his hands clasps together. He hasn't made a single movement since I read out the letter.

Daymond once again commands the rooms and asks, "Who wrote you the letter? Do we even know if your source is valid?"

"Our current captain of the guards, Ryder," I say. I'm nervous that Ryder could very well be lying, but I have to take his words as if they are serious.

"How would he know?" someone asks me.

I hesitantly reveal the situation. "When I was in Din Point, I learned that Ryder had been working as a double agent for Carac. I confronted him when I came back to Parten, and once again he flipped sides. He has been updating me on things in Din Point ever since."

Alas snaps his head up from his stare in shock. It just hits him that someone close to him in his circle of guards has been spying on him for years, and he had no clue.

"How confident in Ryder are you?" Daymond asks me already uneasy about it.

"80%-ish," I choke out.

"Oh for crying out loud," an Oxidence general says while hurling a paper on the table and throwing his hands in the air. "We don't even know if it's true."

Daymond shakes his head while tapping his hands on the table. Another commotion runs through the room while Queens Galen and Era come over to the table to be caught up.

Daymond again takes the floor with a heated voice. "Anyone who has any connections in Din Point, write to them now, we'll get more solid confirmation in a few hours. If we're lucky. If we aren't, we still need to start moving troops now. Either way, this is starting this week. Doesn't matter who declares war first anymore. If they don't declare anything by mid-day tomorrow, we'll start moving troops and get this started. This is not a war, this will not turn into a war, this is an attack that will end with Din Point's royals gone. Our element of surprise may be gone, but our mission remains the same."

The room is mute for a few seconds. People are processing the information that has been revealed to them, commanded to them. If anyone has a better plan, they're not speaking up. No one knows how to even begin to fix this.

After a few seconds, people scurry back into action. Letters are being written; people are dashing out of the room with fury and determination.

Tomorrow, everything changes, for better or for worse.

CHAPTER 64

Isadora POV

here's no time for rest when a battle is near. As 3am hits, I'm given no choice but to wake up in the middle of the Parten woods. Yesterday we flew back to Parten and set up camp right on the border of Parten and Din Point. The capital of Din Point, where the palace sits, is only a few miles north of us.

I step outside of my white tent. All I can see are the outlines of our tents in the forest, ranked in orderly rows. Every tent hosts soldiers, and there are only more troops on the way. The sun hasn't yet risen, and all I can see is the campground with the faint lights coming from corners of the grounds. I watch the dim outlines of soldiers moving around the camp like an infestation. They're working, training, and worse of all, waiting. I can feel the anticipation in the still air.

I speak to a Parten Lieutenant Colonel. He tells me that no letters have come back, which means that there is no confirmation of Din Point declaring war. Din Point is either doing a really good job of intercepting our communications, or we're doing a terrible job of communicating. I talk to the Colonel as long as

I can, taking in every bit of information that he has to give. He tells me that he's sure Din Point will know of our position soon. As dense as the forest is, we're still sitting ducks. The white tents stand out against the trees, and it will only take one slip-up for us to be exposed. Assuming they don't know we're here already.

I leave the conversation with the lieutenant colonel as I see Alas walking through the camp. From a distance, he seems fine. But as I get closer, I see that he's paler than normal. His eyes are drooping a bit. I bet he hasn't slept in the last two days. His face is hollow, flushed of emotion and solely focused on the battle. Yet he still gives off the impression to everyone that he is the leader they not only want to lead this battle, but *need* to lead them.

I reach him and stand by his side as he watches over the soldiers. "Good morning," he greets me.

"Did you get any sleep?" I ask him, already knowing the answer.

"Yes," he responds. A lie.

We stand in silence for a while, listening to the quiet hum of conversation in the air, the way that the leaves rustle constantly with everyone walking around, noting how the birds have stopped chirping and the darkness is becoming fainter as dawn approaches.

"Isadora," he says quietly. "Do you think Lawrence is in really Din Point?"

I shiver as I take a breath of the morning air. "I don't know... he... he doesn't think he's in the wrong here. He may fight on their side."

Alas nods slowly, his head still raised high. "If he *is* in Din Point, if he really did mean everything he said, then I shouldn't try to save him, right?" The internal conflict that fills his mind spreads across his face as he clenches his jaw. This is his only brother, his best friend from birth, whom he may now have to fight against. I always imagined the iconic brotherly duo working together during this battle. I know Alas imagined it like that as well.

I can't tell him what to do, but if it were Daymond on the other side, even if he'd done what Lawrence has, I would try to save him. I would drop everything for him; I would let him kill me before I laid a harming hand on him.

"Do what you think is just. Do whatever you think is right," I tell him vaguely.

My head turns to another tent in the forest as footsteps crunch the leaves beneath us. Daymond walks out of his tent, making a furious gesture. He scans the area before spotting us, then marches directly over. "You were right. We just got a declaration of war a few minutes ago," he tells me while handing Alas a slip of paper.

I can feel Alas's heart racing. This declaration means that Ryder's warning was true, and that Din Point most likely already knows we're at the border. "If we don't attack soon, they'll meet us here. Then it will be us defending Parten, not playing offense," Daymond growls.

"We aren't ready," I point out. "We need three or four more days for the Kinderan troops to get here."

"I know!" Daymond scowls at me. "We're short a third of our troops. Our allies are useless if they're not here!"

Kinder has to travel by sea, and their large troopships don't move as quickly as we'd hoped. They won't get here for three days, maybe even four.

"Did you send our planes? We can fly some here and try to—"

Daymond cuts off the king. "I already ordered that, but most of them are already on boats, so I moved our air usage to the Oxidence soldiers."

I feel the world collapsing all around us. This was supposed to be a flawless battle, a swift victory, and now everything we've created and planned may be ruined.

"We need to work out a revised plan, and quickly. Be in the main tent in ten minutes," Daymond commands. He storms off into the camp again.

Daymond is our best general; he's *the* general who is supposed to carry us through this. Yet no matter what he does, no matter the strategies he might create, we could still be in grave trouble.

I choke in frustration and put my hands my head. Alas starts to walk off away.

This is a train wreck.

CHAPTER 65

Alas POV

I walk straight past the two guards protecting the large Chantilly-undertone white tent. Isadora trails behind me. All the other leaders of this disaster are already sitting around the large circular table when we enter.

I look at Era. She's barely breathing. I try to give her a reassuring look. She's far too young to be wrapped up in all this.

Isadora enters the tent, and I see her look at Era with the same expression I used. Then she turns her attention to Drítan. I can practically see the fumes of frustration rising from him. His eyes dart away as he glances all the over the place. His jitters show; he has no way of concealing his thoughts. They're clear in his every movement.

Queen Galen is sitting as regal as always, keeping her head up and sharp.

The other commanders at the table are radiating anger, just as Daymond is. I sit down across from Daymond, Isadora following my movements.

"If we don't get troops here before tomorrow evening, then we won't have the numbers or the time to attack with success,"

Queen Galen says. It feel like everyone just wants to talk about the issue, not solve it. I roll my head on my shoulders. I'm fed up with the conversations and Kindera.

"If we don't get them, we should still attack," some Oxidence general says.

Daymond nods. "It won't be pretty, and it might not work, but we can't let them attack us and go for our capital. Alas, if you're here, that gives them the opportunity to cut us off at the roots if they get to the palace. We need to play offense here, not and never defense."

Daymond is completely right. Maybe I should be at the castle with Trinity, so that if the worst-case scenario happens, we'll have more protection there. But I don't want to be the king who commands his troops from afar on a pretty throne. This isn't a war I'll ask anyone to fight if I'm not at their side. I trust Trinity to make the right decisions if she has to. She's just as prepared and ready for this battle as I am. She will hold the castle steady.

Drítan sighs. He tears his gaze away from us and looks up at the celling of the tent.

"There's no easy way to win," someone in the room mutters.

"I don't want to hear complaining," I snap. I slam my hands onto the table. The mood for bitching and bickering is rising in all of us. I don't wany anyone feeding into it verbally. The only thing *I* want to complain about is how I want to reverse time, back to the exact moment I made the decision to fight this war. The thought that my brother would still be by my side, that I wouldn't be worried sick about my own kingdom and wouldn't have this need to win a hopeless battle if I had just chosen not to fight, burns in my mind.

But if I command no complaining, then I'll follow that order as well.

I glance to the side of the tent as I detect a flicker of motion. My eyes no longer want to stare at the war board. Outside,

I see the silhouette of a guard thrown to the ground. I sit up immediately, and listen. In the woods I detect an odd new silence, and the spread of confusion. The background mutter of people and speaking moving outside has stopped.

I can only faintly hear the crush of boots outside as they march closer.

No one is listening or even paying attention to what's happening as they continue to argue. I start to stand up as the curtain of the tent is drawn back forcefully.

The personification of death strolls into the room. The breath of everyone, especially me, is stolen. Drítan rises slowly to his feet. Meanwhile, Daymond draws his sword as he processes who is standing in front of us. Me? I lean forward and grip the table. I'm ready to fight if he dares to make a move.

"Hello, everyone. I'm here to save your asses," declares the Prince of Death, Carac Cavinche.

CHAPTER 66

Isadora POV

Not a single person in the room knows what to do. Everyone is on their feet, ready to fight. I turn to Alas, who is barely able to stand. His hands grip the table, knuckles turning white. Even I'm not sure what to think as Carac stares at the room like a hero risen from the dead, forgetting that he died a villain.

"What did you do?" is all I'm able to say as a response to his entrance. Everyone turns their attention to me. They slowly start to realize that I'm the only one still calm. They start to piece together assumptions as their faces turn cold.

"Isadora," Daymond angrily beseeches me. He doesn't want to wait for answers.

Simultaneously, Alas grinds out, "You're not dead." The way he says it makes it feel like it's not a threat, but almost a relief.

Drítan forces his chair behind him as he marches to the side of the table. He walks right up to Carac. "I don't give a fuck why or how you're here, but this time I'm going to kill you and make sure you stay dead," Drítan barks.

Carac doesn't blink as Drítan tries to stare him down. I don't think there's anything anyone can do to faze him. Carac responds by simply slowing down Drítan's heart rate so that he can't do anything except focus on living.

Drítan twists his body as he reaches for the table. He grasps the wood, holding it tightly, trying to remain standing.

"You can threaten me all you want later," Carac says charmingly. "Isadora, a word?"

"No." I ask him again, "What did you do?"

Carac tilts his head a bit while scanning the room. He seems a little perplexed, as am I, that someone hasn't thrown a knife at his head yet. He looks at Queen Galen and asks, "Who is this? Why is she wearing a crown?"

For whatever Godforsaken reason, a general plays into Carac's game and whispers to him, "Queen Galen of Oxidence."

The Queen looks absolutely confused and horrified at the situation. As old as she is, I don't think she's ever met Carac or knows of his ability.

Carac nods politely. "A pleasure to meet you, ma'am. I'm the formerly dead former king of Din Point." He chuckles a bit at himself, showing he's in control and that he thinks the whole thing is amusing.

"Carac," I snap.

"Ah, right, yes, what did I do? Well, I got you troops to use." I hear Daymond put his weapon away, and a few of the other generals calm themselves. As soon as Carac says that, they nearly forget who he is and the fact that he's risen from the dead.

"Where did you get them?" I ask.

"They're from Vaddel," he says casually while righting Drítan's chair and sitting in it.

Era looks at the Prince of Death sitting next to her, then at me. Her eyes are watering with doubt and hatred. I lean my head toward her, trying to convey that I didn't mean for this to happen. She thinks I've betrayed her—and parts of me have.

I turn my focus back to Carac. I can talk to Era after this is all figured out. I tell him, "I don't believe you."

"You can go outside and look for yourself; there are thousands of them," Carac says, while lifting his hand to give a fluttery gesture at the door.

I don't get up to investigate just yet. Instead, I check everyone in the room again. Then I take the necklace I'm wearing off and toss it to Carac. He catches it with calm grace. He takes the King's Ring off the chain and slides it back onto his finger.

"What *is* this?" Daymond hisses at me.

"This is Carac trying to prove he still has a heart, even after he died," I say, while starting to explain what happened when we were last in Kindera.

I launch myself forward, starting my run down the scenic path. The traction under my feet is treacherous as the slippery mud collects under my tennis shoes. Running is something I've always excelled at, but the humidity, mud, and terrain are making it a challenge.

Still, I push forward, flying past the jungle, the vines, the colorful surroundings.

I feel my breathing starting to increase a bit. Then I hear a faint call: "Isadora." I halt and frantically look around at the jungle. I know that voice.

I turn and see him standing on a large, rocky ledge that juts out over a pond a few meters away. I force myself to stand perfectly still, trying to catch my breath as I look him. My eyes water as I take a few steps closer. My mind must be deceiving me.

Standing in Kindera, fully alive, is Carac Cavinche.

I race forward and wrap myself arms around Carac. I feel his body in my arms, solid and real. I grip the fabric of his shirt, intertwining it in my fingers. His arms come around me, and he embraces me tightly. My hands can't feel enough of him. My mind can barely grasp the idea that he's actually alive. Too many emotions collide my mind at once as I look up at his face. His green eyes look at me—eyes that I didn't ever think I would miss this much.

"Don't look so surprised," he says to me; I feel the slight laugh in his chest. I can't comprehend him speaking, living. He's like a ghost whispering in my mind.

"How… how are you here?" I whimper as a few tears slide down my face.

His hands move from hugging me to cupping my chin. His thumbs wipe the tears off my cheeks as he says lightly, "You didn't really think I'd let those assholes kill me permanently? And that easily?"

The things I want to say won't come out of my mouth. I continue to trace his face with my eyes, taking in every little detail: The faded bags under his eyes, the cheekbones that cut inward, the dark hair that flows slightly over his forehead. Not a hair out of place. I move my arms around his neck and pull him against me again, tightly. I need to feel his touch; I need to accept that he's really alive.

"Don't cry anymore," he snaps with a cunning and sharpness lacing his words. The tone I always associate with his voice. I let go of him and take a step back.

I choke out, "You died. I saw you stop breathing, I saw you die." My breathing becomes jagged with shock. An uncontrollable shiver is taking me over.

"I knew they were going to try to kill me. It was the perfect time for me to slip out of Din Point, and it worked like a charm."

"But you died. I saw you die!"

He puts a hand on my shoulder and says, "That's because I did. But here's the thing, lovely. The Prince of Death never stays dead for long. I knew that if I died, I'd come back."

"Your body was burned!" I pant.

He smiles just a bit and quips, "I staged that. I died and was out for a while, and when I woke up, a couple of idiots were trying to take my body apart in the morgue. I lit the place up and walked away clean."

The question spits out of my mouth like fire. "How did you know you'd come back?"

"Xeres thought me that new trick," he admits, bitterness in his voice. "Xeres killed you?" I ask without a second thought.

He glances to the side, tearing his eyes away from me, before answering, "Xeres did a lot of things you don't need to know about."

My mind flickers back to the night that Xeres died, and how he said he'd done something ungodly. That night must have been the night he tried to kill Carac, and since Carac had never died before, he couldn't possibly have known Carac would come back from the dead.

"I'm so sorry," I plead, with more hot tears streaming down my face. "You let them kill me," he says without any sorrow in his face. "You left me to die."

My throat closes up as I tear my eyes away from him. There are too many thoughts flooding my mind to think straight. "I'm so sorry, Carac." I have no excuses to make and nothing to say that will make what I did right. I'm in the wrong here.

After a moment in silence he finally says, "I hope you are." He takes in my torments for a minute before telling me, "Truthfully, I bet my whole plan on the fact that you'd betray me."

Immediately I ask him, "And what was your plan? Why would you do this? Why would you die and let me think you were dead?"

"Why would you let them kill me? If you're so concerned, so upset about this, why let them kill me in the first place?" he barks. My mouth clamps shut. I want to say that I thought then that I would feel some relief in my mind, knowing I had done what needed to be done, and that Carac would leave my mind in peace. Yet after he died, the only thing in my bitter, regretful thoughts was him. How I let the one person I needed in my life, even filled with horrors as he was, die. How I stood silently, my loyalty nonexistent, spineless, and let him die.

Carac turns his head away and continues, "I have nothing holding me to Din Point anymore. I needed to get out of that place as quickly as I could after Xeres killed me. I learned that I could stage my own death. It was the perfect opportunity, the perfect chance to leave without anyone knowing and coming after me."

"Why would you want to leave Din Point?"

I can see his face harden, but he's already thought about how to answer the question. "A lot of things have happened that I can't explain to you right now. I had been working and devoting myself to something larger than anyone could comprehend, and Xeres burned everything I had discovered and planned for a year. Everything that could have led me to the answers. Not only that, but he tried to kill me over what I had learned. When you killed him, you took all the answers down with him." He clenches his fist and then continues, "There are things I've learned that can never be erased from my mind. It brought me to the point where I realized that Din Point isn't my home. I wanted out of that fucked-up kingdom. There are so many things, Isadora, that are far beyond you and me."

"Like-like what?" I stammer.

"There's not enough time now for me to tell you now, but trust me, when I tell you what Xeres and Zaven were hiding, you won't want to miss out."

"Carac, I—"

He cuts me off and states boldly, "I want and need Din Point, as we know it, gone just as much as you do, if not more. And I need you on my side."

"Carac, I'm so sorry for what I did. I know there's nothing I can say to fix what has happened."

He places his other hand on my shoulder and looks me dead in the eyes. "There are things I did that I wish I could undo. I know that's the case for both of us. There is nothing you can say now to fix that, but there's a lot you can do."

"Carac, I'm sorry for what did, but I don't know what you want from me. There's too little trust between us for anything to happen the way you want it to."

"I know, but we have one common goal, and that's for the horrid, oppressive Din Point that exists now to be gone. You want change for several reasons, but I need Din Point to be gone for me to be able to no longer be called a king, and no longer tied to that failed monarchy."

"I don't think you can help us with that. You killed Kindera's king and queen. You're still a Din Point royal, and I know you had no intention of changing things when you were king. You won't even tell me what's changed now."

"You're forgetting you're still a Din Point royal, too. I won't tell you what's changed now. When your battle is won and Din Point has fallen, maybe I can let you in on the bigger picture." His hands grip my necklace as he undoes the chain. He slips his King's Ring off his finger and loops it around the chain. "Take this... as a promise that I'll do everything in my power to win this war for you."

"What do you want out of this? Are you going to ask for land, for rulership?" I ask.

He clips the necklace back around my neck, his hands not leaving my skin. "I want nothing out of this war except for Din Point to fall and for you to understand that we were born to be a team—and we'll die as one."

The phrase crashes down on my soul. We were born to be a team, and I let him die alone. But now I have a chance, maybe my last, to prove that I believe in him. "I want to be a part of our team again, Carac, but I lost your trust when I let you die, and you lost mine the minute you started to take the side of Din Point's leadership."

"Then you'll restore your trust in me when Din Point falls, and I'll have faith in you once again after this ends, and you learn what I'm fighting for." His hand slips under my chin as his lifts my face and kisses me on the forehead.

"Please, Carac, please make this work. I need you back," I whisper.

"I know. But they don't yet," he says. I lift my head up, wondering who he means by "they." Then Carac takes my arm and sways me to the side.

I feel the water close over me before I realize what's happened. I breach the surface, lifting my head to see Alas and Drítan standing on the rock where Carac stood just a moment ago. I don't know what to possibly say to them. I look around the area to confirm that Carac is gone.

I take a deep breath and dive under the water, to give me time to think of a lie to tell them.

As I finish my story of meeting Carac at the pond, I don't want to look up at the room. I don't want to see Alas's shocked and judgmental stare, or Daymond's distress and the fear in his eyes that reflect on what I've done.

Yet even seeing their faces filled with horror, Carac smiles, leaning back in his chair beside me. He doesn't fear the room.

I silently beg for someone to say something and fill the void. My pleas are quickly answered as the tent-flap moves again. I turn my head back to see who's entered this time.

Ryder stands in the archway. I watch as he reads the room. He gapes at us blankly, not sure if he should convey whatever message he has to deliver to us.

Carac turns his head to see who's entered and not saying anything. Ryder's eyes widen comically as he sees Carac. "Shit," he mutters under his breath. He immediately pivots and whips the flap open again, racing out of the tent as fast as I've ever seen him move. Carac turns his head to me and says, "Excuse me." He stands in a flash and dashed out after Ryder.

"Isadora!" Daymond shouts at me as I rise from my chair.

I tell them all, "I'm sorry," before I rush out too.

Footsteps follow behind me; I glance back to see Alas and Drítan coming with me to see what's happening.

I could have stayed in the tent and answered the mass of questions sure to follow, but I don't want Ryder dead, especially if he came to the room to deliver information. I see Carac catch and then toss Ryder to the ground. The anger that Carac has built up within himself from his murders is all coming out on Ryder. To be fair, Ryder also played a large role in assassinating Carac, and that's not something a friend should do.

A hand clutches my arm. I turn to see Alas. "Isadora…?"

I stop the rest of his sentence as I turn away from him. I watch as Carac says something to Ryder, then throws a hard punch. Ryder doesn't have the time to fear Carac as he throws one in return, the both of them fumbling onto the ground again. Carac isn't using his ability on Ryder, and Ryder isn't making the plants shift, either. They're not trying to kill each other, just even things out.

"You didn't about tell me about this," Alas accuses, frustration boiling in his voice.

"I didn't tell anyone about this," I respond. I can barely concentrate on the conversation with Alas. I don't know where to focus; I can't tell if I should lunge for Ryder and Carac, or listen to Alas in his current state of incomprehension.

"If I had known the Prince of Death was alive, I would have called this whole thing off. I would have stopped this disaster in its tracks," Alas says to me.

"Don't you understand that Carac is the reason we're going to be able to pull this off? Don't you understand that if I hadn't taken a risk with Carac, we would most likely have lost this battle? I'm sorry, I truly am, that I couldn't tell you about Carac. But I took a risk, and it paid off."

"You could have told us. You could have at least hinted at it," Drítan says.

"Out of everyone, you were the one person who suspected this, Drítan—don't think I forgot about the time you told me you knew what my necklace meant. You knew what was going to happen, or you at least had a solid guess."

Alas shakes his head at Drítan and exclaims, "You knew?!"

"I didn't know for sure," Drítan says sullenly, no longer having any arguments to fire back with.

"Look around you," I say with a gesture at the new soldiers on the grounds, who are mostly just watching us argue. "There are new soldiers here. Carac brought them. Bitch all you want about what I did, but it got us a thousand Vaddel soldiers."

"That's still far less than what *we* would have brought," Drítan scoffs out.

"Carac only had to bring us a thousand Vaddel soldiers. They're from the best military in the world. One of their soldiers could easily take out ten of ours." Slight anger at Drítan's questioning comes out in my tone as I say, "And I don't see your troops here."

I free myself from Alas's grip and run to Carac. I grab his shirt collar and pull him back, off the ground and away from Ryder.

"Even after you helped kill me, you went back to Din Point! You're far worse than a traitor!" Carac yells at Ryder before standing up. Carac brushes himself off. He whips the blood off the side of his face with one hand. Blood still trickles, lightly streaming down from his mouth, where Ryder got a lucky blow in.

"Isadora asked me to go back. I did what I had to do after you died," Ryder doesn't hesitate to reply. Carac got a lot more hits in on Ryder than vice versa. His face bleeds heavily, his skin torn in several places. Ryder doesn't even make a move to clean himself up; he knows it will do no good.

"Carac," I plead while stepping in front of him so that he can no longer step any closer to Ryder. "I really need Ryder alive for this, so I'd greatly appreciate if you'd stop beating up my spy."

"Yeah," Ryder shoots back. He's much more confident now that I'm holding Carac back. Ryder tosses his hands in the air. "Don't kill the messenger."

"You think you're a *messenger?*" Carac spits, his body shifting forward as he reaches one hand out.

"*Do* you have a message?" I ask Ryder, while pushing with my weight to keep Carac back.

"You need to do something, send your troops out, whatever plan you have, because Din Point knows you're here and they're coming tomorrow night," Ryder says with a sudden urgency that he must have forgotten he was supposed to have.

I look away from Ryder and grip Carac's wrist, dragging us both forward.

"Take it easy there," Carac nearly jokes. I hurry as Alas and Drítan follow us.

"We need to get Daymond," I yell. He needs to hear this news; he needs to get a plan together *now.* If we don't do something, Din Point will.

CHAPTER 67

Alas POV

T oday, of course, is one of the few days a year that Parten has cold weather. There's no snow on the ground, nor do I think it will fall today. But the air still has a chill to it, leaving a damp, glistering frost that congeals on the tents and plants in the forest.

The weather is neither a good nor bad thing. We have the Xxons on our side, powerful cryomancers, but Din Point may have ice controllers of their own who could put up a good fight if there's snow on the ground or other water nearby. So perhaps this unsettling weather is just nature's way of leveling the playing field.

I was sitting inside the warm white tent that we were planning things in, but no matter how much I try, my eyes no longer want to study that war board. So I've taken my papers outside to read on a small table in the icy air. I still shiver just looking at the frost forming. My skin is concealed in the long sleeve shirt that I'm wearing, and anytime I exhale I see my breath in the air and am reminded of the snow that may come in a day or two.

I could warm myself and the air around me, but don't want to waste the energy.

I stare down at my coffee for a second, before making the decision to down it all in one gulp. I need as much of it as possible to make sure that I don't fall over before the day is done.

I haven't slept well since we got back to Parten. I don't know how the camp's population can be so restful with a battle looming in the morning. Don't they feel the buzz in the air, the silent call for bloodshed?

But this is what Daymond has decided we'll do. He told everyone that the one thing we need to control is when we attack, so we'll start the battle in the morning. I understand his strategy. He didn't know beforehand that we'd have a thousand Vaddel soldiers on our side. None of us knew. So Daymond, the other few generals, and leaders and myself spent the whole night planning a form of attack that revolves around our new fighters.

My eye twitches, just the slightest bit. It's probably from the lack of sleep. I didn't really try to sleep, if I'm being honest with myself. I know once my head hits the pillow, I still won't be able to drift off. Instead, I'd lie there and think of everything I should be doing before the sun rises.

I set down my empty coffee cup and tear my eyes away from my paper as I hear footsteps approaching. The sun hasn't come up yet; it's far too early for that. There's no sunlight to help me see who is coming near.

Eventually, Carac Cavinche walks into my lantern's light.

He's dressed in loose black clothing that's far too nice to be sleepwear, but too informal to for a king or prince, whatever he is, to be dressed in. "Can't sleep?" I ask as he pulls back the chair across from me and sits down in it.

"This is not a night you get any sleep, King Alas." I nod and start to read my papers again. But Carac says sternly, "Put the papers down. I know it's easier sometimes to think your brain doesn't need a break, but you need a clear head before the attack. Give yourself a breather."

I lay the papers on the table face-down. He stares off to the side. I look at his King's Ring, which he still wears even after he's made it clear he wants nothing but for Din Point to fall. My heart races as I try not to move. A part of me wants to know why he wears the ring if he hates the place it belongs to. I let that part of me speak: "Can I ask you something?"

"You can ask, doesn't mean I'll answer."

I take a minute to wonder if it's even worth asking him questions. I can't help but to think about the first time I met him in Isadora's room. He was arguing with her in my own castle. She was terrified, helpless even. She tried to get rid of him, pushing him away instinctively. And now, even after everything, even after what he put her through, the only thing I think she's realized is that her feelings for and her loyalty to him go deeper than we all thought. Deeper than her loyalty to me.

I stare down the Prince of Death, trying not to show in my gaze that I'm studying him. I thought about it before, and still can't stop thinking about how he really could destroy everyone with his ability if he wanted to. Every single person in his path. I'd be six feet under if this sort of ability was given to Lawrence. I, too, would probably have taken advantage of such a power. And yet Carac sits here, across from me, the ruler of an enemy kingdom, in baggy clothes, no crown, with no intention to harm, and is letting me ask him any questions I can think of.

"What changed your mind?" I ask him. "Why are you helping us now? Are you *really* helping us?"

I see him try not to scoff as he sits up and prepares to answer me. He shoves his jacket over himself tightly, looking more uncomfortable with the cold than I am. "I didn't change my mind," he tells me. "I'm not doing this for the sake of seeing Parten succeed or to see you on the throne or to redeem myself in this overall hagiarchy. I'm doing this for Isadora. That's it. I'll probably never admit that to her, but she did something that I should have done long ago, and that was leave Din Point. But before I can leave my title, my promise to that land, and my ties to such a place... I need it gone forever. I need to see it fall before I rise to bigger things."

I lean forward and listen intently to his words. I realize in the moment that this is the most I've ever heard Carac speak. I ask, "And what are those bigger things?"

"Nothing of your concern, King Alas." He pauses for a minute, his mouth clamped shut almost as if he's contemplating telling me those things. "You get to play out this war. You get to write your history, and I'll write mine. And soon, if all goes as we hope, I'll be just a little subplot in your wonderful ruling tale."

"What is it you're holding out on telling us?" I wonder. It's been on my mind since he came to help us with the troops. "I know better than to think that the Prince of Death had some moral epiphany when he died. I know you have something up your sleeve."

"One issue at a time, King Alas."

He's mocking my title, and isn't even ashamed of doing so. I try to brush off his tone and ask, "You knew of Kindera, have connections in Vaddel, and for whatever reason, won't leave Parten alone. I just want to know why, maybe for my own sake." Maybe it's the fact that I can't actually believe he would go to this length just for Isadora.

"Let's see Din Point fall, and then we'll talk. I won't want anything from your kingdom after this, hopefully. We don't have to hate each anymore, King Alas. Well, maybe a bit of hatred is healthy, but we don't have to be blood enemies. We're not so different. You look around at this plan that will soon become blood and tears, and you think we truly have anyone by our sides?

This is a history you write alone. The sooner you understand that, the easier it is to craft."

"But isn't that what you wanted? I always assumed you thought you controlled everything."

"No. I never wanted what was handed to me. Do you think it was nice dying?" He pauses. A breath escapes him, heavily, as if his mouth moved faster than his mind could catch it. "No one prepares you to be immortal. No one tells you that you might feel peace when you die and cling to it desperately, only to have it stripped away. It's the same as no one telling you that you would have to become king all too quickly, that you would have to wear a crown and hate it for a reason that only you can tell yourself. There's been something thrown at us that none of us wish for and don't control."

This strikes a nerve in me. I wear this crown for my kingdom: That's what I want to tell him. But I feel his gaze boring into me, him seeing the secrets that I hold within my crown, the guilt of my brother that has been hiding in the crystals and metal upon my head.

I shudder, turning my eyes away. I don't ever want to tell him the things I'm thinking. Instead, I tell him something he *does* have control over. "If I did die... If it's as you said... I wish to remain dead." I look up and stare at him across the table, his green eyes meeting my brown. The King of Din Point looking at his old enemy. His death meeting my life. "Leave me. If it ever comes to that, leave me and don't bring me back to life."

He doesn't question my wishes. I think he's explained all too well that being alive haunts him now.

He stands gracefully, and with a gesture of his hand says, "I'll do my best."

CHAPTER 68

Alas POV

As the sun rises and the troops breach their tents, I am met by Daymond. He peers straight ahead at the forest that, for some reason, seems just as much our enemy as Din Point. There isn't time to postpone any further, or fulfill our wishes to wait. There's no way to hold back any longer a battle that should have happened long ago.

I breathe out thickly into the air, taking off the crown that I shouldn't be wearing until this day is done. I carefully place it on the floor of my tent. It may not be in the same place by day's end. Isadora also comes to my side, along with Drítan, Era, Ryder, Galen—and Carac.

I dare not to look behind me. I don't want to see the units that Daymond and the other generals have crafted. They've given every soldier a specific position. Every unit has a stance to take and a purpose to fulfill in this attack. Din Point has not yet risen; that's what we're hoping for. We're wishing and praying that Din Point is not yet alert, that we can storm onto their land with just the slightest advantage, hoping that by the time they hear our troops marching, it will be too late.

I hear a rustling behind me, so despite my wishes I look back. A sea of colorful uniforms fills my eyes, like precise brush strokes of color in a painting that's not yet finished. There are the Parten men and women who just ended a war a few months ago and did not yearn to leave for another.

Then there are Oxidence troops, who are all dressed in white, all formal and proper in their stances: soldiers who have not fought by our side, ever, and now are ready to.

And there are the Vaddel soldiers. Thousands of them are in position, wearing dappled green. These are soldiers who haven't fought a war in a very long time, and are overdue to share their abilities.

I wish I could have sat down and had a conversation with every single one of them: to learn their ways, their disciplines that have been crafted over centuries.

I focus on Carac and Isadora for a moment. They may have been bred in the same category: a species that welcomes war, chaos, and battle. A species that has long known battles and has created them. Maybe that's why Isadora subconsciously pushed me into wanting this. She was bred in a society that was spoon-fed those ideals, and she has not feasted until now.

All of these soldiers. Faces that I can't memorize all at once, but wish that I could, so that when some have fallen, I can see the empty spaces and remember who was there. The faces, the thousands of faces that will die today in order to protect and honor a kingdom that fights for what they see as just.

I don't look at Daymond or any of other fellow officers as I say in a hushed tone, "Whenever you're ready, give the command."

I feel a shift at my side, a small hesitation before Daymond moves away. When his presence is gone, I know it's time. Everyone knows it's time.

I launch myself forward. I hear the troops' footsteps trample over the ground.

This is a battle, not a war, I continue to tell myself over and over again. *This is bloodshed, not a bloodbath.*

Everyone advances into the forest. All the paths that we have planned out are being taken. We march in the woods for what feels like far too long. No one speaks; no one wants to say a word.

All that fills my mind is thoughts of what we may meet on the other side. I pray to whatever is out there that we're met in Din Point with an army of age, ambition, ash, color, direction, flower, hair, humor, or sand manipulators... Manipulators who aren't much of a threat on the battlefield. I try to remind myself that most of the world isn't made up of fighters who can manipulate the people I've surrounded myself with. But there's a part of me that knows that there are power manipulators of types I haven't ever meet or even heard of.

Sweat drips down my head as I think of the manipulators I've read of in books. Time, size, power, mind, body, and army manipulators. What if we're up against an army manipulator? What will we do then? How does one of those even control things? Is it just an automatic loss? Do they pit your allies against you, make them turn on each other?

My mind scrambles. I remind myself that the books state that army manipulators don't exist anymore. But they also said that about death manipulators at one point.

If we don't have those sort of powers in our kingdom, Din Point shouldn't either. I hope.

I continue forward, knowing that all manipulators have their own kills, but training and time wins most of the time, and that's what we have on our side in spades.

We march forward for what feels like another hour.

The sun shines brightly through the trees, yet there is no sunrise visible to enjoy. The sky skips over the colors of orange, pink, and red, and has turned right from black to pale blue, the light rising like a room slowly getting lit up by candles. Isadora treads through the forest beside me, maintaining my pace, knowing that this is what Daymond has asked of her. He put his own sister on the front lines.

And Era, along with her brother, is right here with us. Unlike Din Point, the rulers of Kindera and Parten do will not hide behind an army of soldiers. We lead the way.

It feels as if we may never reach their camp, like we won't get close to the capital until morning is over. Maybe Ryder did lie to us about them expecting us to invade. There are no Din Point troops near the border. We're far past the line that divides the two kingdoms.

But now I hear it.

I hear the bustling of a different kingdom. I hear feet shuffling far ahead of us. I stop in my tracks. Carac continues forward, walking a few feet in front of me while the troop that are on our path halt. There is a fear deep in our hearts that tell us it's now; it's happening now.

I don't flinch until I first see the blue of the Din Point uniforms. As I see the first boots that are not our own flash in between the trees, I push forward. And from there, it begins, and I can't do anything to stop it. My feet force me to move, my body telling my brain to do anything to stay alive. People crowd the dense woods. I want to stop and fight by their sides, but Daymond has made it clear that we must reach the capital as soon as possible.

My hands heat the air around me. Isadora, Carac, and I run forward. I watch the crowd with us fade as they get caught up fighting the enemy.

A wall of fighters strikes in front of us. Isadora is the farthest out. She stops running and braces her arms at her sides. She sees it, just as I do: the looks in their eyes that tell us that this isn't a fight they want. The Din Point soldiers aren't fighting us because they have a choice.

Carac tracks ahead. He moves his hand out, makes a swift movement, and takes a knee. The power explodes out of him, and a wall of soldiers fall to the ground. Carac doesn't look up until a split second later, when he rises to his feet again.

I feel Isadora's movements stop. She turns to the fallen soldiers, twisting her hand in the air, calling for whatever water is closest to us. Her knuckles tighten as she pulls with all her strength. Her hand clenches upwards; a small wave of water comes, and before it reaches us, she shoves her hand out and makes the water freeze the fallen soldiers to the ground. I realize then the soldiers aren't dead. Carac just put them down long enough for Isadora to seal them in place.

I don't want to look at the Din Point soldiers any longer. The sound of killing rings out behind us. The soldiers Carac didn't defeat are fighting our troops. The clash of weapons and cries of pain continue to call out to us, beginning for our attention. There are too many Din Point soldiers for me to even guess their numbers. They dash in and out of my sight in all directions.

I catch sight of the castle in the distance—the place we need to reach before we lose too many more of the men who are fighting behind us.

I don't want to know where Ryder and Galen have gone; I just hope they're not caught up too deeply in the fight.

More Din Point fighters approach us, all with their abilities ready. We know now that we can't spare every life. But something is different with this group of soldiers: the way they dash forward at full speed, how their teeth are bared, how they twist their hands while preparing to fight. These things tell us that this unit is ready to kill.

I pull my sword out of its sheath, and the heat I've been building releases into it. The metal blade turns deadly hot, red-orange and murderous. Waves of heat pulse through the air with every swing. The crackling, spitting metal burns every bit of skin I hit.

Two soldiers come at me; from what I can tell, they're not wielding their abilities, they're just skilled fighters. They race at me with swords raised. I send a heat whirl at their faces; they catch it in their breath and tumble down, their throats closing. I don't have to look to my other side, as I feel through the ground another fighter racing towards me. My sword whips out and slices through their weapon.

Carac is in front of me, elegantly wielding his ability. He touches as many soldiers as he can with his hands. Each one he lays a finger on falls dead. I catch a glimpse of how his hand weaves in and under the weapons each fighter tries to use again him. His feet are landing and planting him confidently where he pleases to be, his body taking shape to avoid being stuck as he gets close enough to touch them.

I blaze ahead of him. The death he's harvesting is nearly sucking the breath out of me. I don't have time to wonder how he can even create that sort of energy. As I run, I create another heat wave. I launch it to my right. Four soldiers fall. Isadora stands on the other side of them, and when the heat comes her way, she ducks, making sure that it doesn't consume her, and then she straightens up in a flash. She creates an ice shield and lifts it to her side, protecting both me and her. I see the faint outline of a weapon strike the shield. Her feet come off the ground as she tumbles back from the impact. Isadora then morphs the shield into daggers. She turns and uses the momentum from that movement to launch the weapons at the fighters who struck at her.

I don't let myself watch as Drítan catches up to us. He harvests the energy in the air, and I only hear the gasps of the soldiers that he zaps as I sprint to the castle.

The guards outside the walls don't stand much of a chance against our people. I know there are too many of them to take down quickly, even with all of us. That's why we have the troops; that's where Vaddel comes in. Our only goal is to make it into the castle to cut the head off the snake. Carac leads the way, with Isadora at his side. They know the lay of the land and will take us wherever we need to be. This was once their home, after all.

I hear the collision of the Din Point soldiers behind us as they meet our troops. I pray silently and wholly that Lawrence isn't in the mix, that he isn't dead in this shit-storm. No one can tell who is who on the opposing side. They won't know who they're fighting; they'll just know it's Din Point, and Lawrence could well be caught up in that.

Isadora dashes across a large green lawn. Drítan is the only one who can run as fast as she can, and they don't hold back. Before Carac, Era, and I can even get there, Isadora freezes the glass of the attached greenhouse, so that it has no choice but to shatter. I leap over the broken glass and fallen steel. Carac tramples through the pathway of the garden. There's an exit in the greenhouse that leads us all straight into the castle's marble hallways.

Carac spares none of his energy as he waves his hands, and the guards inside the castle fall before they can even begin to make an advance. I use my ability to melt metal and destroy the doorways that stand before us and wherever Isadora is leading us. She's running us through hallway after hallway. Both she and Carac are searching, looking for the king and queen, finding our call to victory.

And then, finally, we enter into room so large and grand that it seems the Din Point royals didn't even try to hide where they were. A man with hair as dark as Carac's stands. His feet planted on the floor, he moves his hands out to his sides; his hands curl, and he pulls water into the room from holes in the walls. The room begins to fill. Guards shutter the door behind us, making sure the doors seal tightly before closing in on all sides.

Carac breaths heavily, stress lining his brow. I realize why as I look at Isadora; she hasn't moved. She hasn't even breathed, because the King and Queen aren't flooding the room with plain water, they're flooding it with holy water: the one form of water she cannot control.

"Carac? H-how are you here?" the Queen stammers. She watches the water pour in. I look around. It's entering at a rapid pace. They've broken the seal of their carefully hoarded holy water reservoirs. Isadora can do nothing but grips all her existing ice weapons closely. Those few items of regular water may be her saving grace.

Carac doesn't respond to the queen; as he knows that no matter what he says, it won't stop his parents from flooding this room with water.

The king sits and leans forward in his throne. "Carac," he snaps.

"Stop that water," Carac finally responds.

"And you're fighting for them," the Queen says to herself. "You chose them over your own kingdom? Pathetic."

"You two deserve to drown. I ought to kill you myself," Carac hisses.

They don't bother to plead for him to spare them; instead, the Queen threatens, "If you kill us, the water will continue to rise. This is a death even you may not be able to escape."

My heart beats too quickly. It beats so loudly that I can't hear my own thoughts. Drítan focuses on his sister, then launches forward and tries to grip the side of the wall, trying to get to a higher level. In the water, he can't use his electrical power unless he wants to kill us all. I take a step forward; the water is up to my knees. I spread my fingers wide, heating up the water so it at least isn't ice fucking cold.

"Stop the water," Carac yells at his parents. His feet tread through the water as he walks closer to the thrones. "You get nothing out of this! You die with us!"

"And what does that leave? That leaves who we want to remain safe on the *outside* of this room," The King says.

Then it hits me in my stomach: Lawrence.

Lawrence isn't here. They gave their kingdom to him.

What's going to happening if we all die and he's alive? They used him, and set us up to the point where not even Queen Galen or Daymond on the outside can fix this.

Carac's face turns to stone. We all know that we'll die if this room keeping filling up. The water is at my waist, and flows higher with every passing second.

Isadora breaths out so heavily it's like she's screaming. Her head turns, and she looks to me. Fear, true fear, fills her eyes. This is the one form of water she can't control. Her ability is turning against her in a sick, cruel way. I watch as she tries to fight. She tries so hard to move the water back, to stop where it's spilling from, and she cannot. I can't tell if it's tears or holy water streaming down her face as the water rises to our necks. King Argys and Queen Edisa are also taking their last few heavy breaths.

The kind sneers, "What do you think it will feel like, son, for water to kill you over and over again? For you to raise up, for your lungs to feel like they're burning you alive from the water? And you have to see them all dead. You'll just have to repeat that, maybe for an eternity."

Carac whips his head toward his parents. His face drains of color; his eyes flash with fear. I've never seen Carac show fear before. "Stop this!" he screams at them.

The queen lifts her head to a son she's already disowned.

Carac lifts himself up as he treads water and gives his parents a grin. But not even his wicked grin can conceal his genuine horror. "Go to hell," he says, getting in the last word. Carac waves his hand. And I feel it faintly in the room: the shift of life. Carac did it; he ended them in an instant. He killed his parents and every guard in the room. It still doesn't change that fact that the water is nearly to our heads, and we don't have a way out.

Isadora yells suddenly, "Here, swim to me!" I don't hesitate, swimming through the water to her along with everyone else. "Take a breath!" she commands, bringing us in as closely as she can. She pulls from the small icy weapons she has with her, morphing them to regular water. She then creates an ice orb that encapsulates us all, along with our last breaths and the little air remaining in the room.

We sink to the bottom. Only a bit of air remains at the top of the orb, not enough to last long. We probably won't last another full minute before the orb breaks or we run out of air.

I scan the room through the water. I see the door; it's unguarded now.

Maybe, just maybe, I can reach it. If I can, then I can detach the frame with my heat and bend it open so we can all get out, or at least drain the water.

"Let me out," I command Isadora. Her face goes blank, her mouth unmoving. "That door—I can get it open. You need to let me out."

"You won't not make it. Your ability will take too long to open that door."

"This air won't last us long!"

"Wait until someone comes in. Someone from the outside will open that door."

"We don't have the time to wait. No one will come until we've all drowned."

"Someone's coming!" Isadora cries, her voice raucous. "They've got to be!"

"No one is coming!" I yell. Her hands grasp my shoulders. I can see in her face that fear is eating her alive.

"Alas, you won't not make it."

"Let me out!" I scream.

She tells Era, Drítan, and Carac, "Breath in." They all do as she ordered. Then Isadora opens the orb just enough so that

I can exit. More water floods into the orb; they'll probably just have one more breath or two. I swim out into the room, and my hand grasps the handle of the door. I try to heat myself up in this freezing-cold stupid fucking holy water.

The heat pours out, but the frame isn't bending; the door is too thick.

My eyes burn in the water. I look back at the blurry outline of the orb. If I go back, Isadora won't be able to reopen it without losing all the air. My lungs start to ache, demanding air. I turn and force my hands into the door. My body forces me to breath, and I do, water filling my lungs. I continue to push myself, even as I feel my mind fading. I clasp my hands to the door and close my eyes as I begin to feel what the monsters Argys and Edisa were talking about: the darkness, the heat that fills my lungs, as if I'm burning alive in the water.

I don't dare move; the door is bending from my heat now, and it's draining me. It's taking me and my life with it.

That's fine. It's worth it.

Then I feel the door slip. My mind goes blank.

I feel nothing.

CHAPTER 69

Lawrence POV

Where are they?

Where are they? I ask myself over and over as I race through the forest. The slick leaves slip under my feet as I dash over the uneven ground. The light and shadows of the setting sun dance across my skin, fading in and out between the patches of the trees.

Where are Alas and Isadora?

They have to have set up a main camp close to the border in order to spring the attack on us this quickly. We weren't ready, not even close.

But of course, the Din Point royals sent out a declaration of war; they think Isadora killed Carac. Their son is dead. Everyone in the council would go mad if they *didn't* declare war.

Honestly, I probably had the biggest part in them making that declaration. I knew of Isadora and Alas's plan to start a war. Argys and Edisa gladly listened to me, and posted out the declaration the very next day.

Din Point wasn't my first option after my plans were ruined, but they needed a next-of-kin. So I did what I had to: I went to the enemy. I promised them insight if they promised me their kingdom. It wasn't that hard a deal to make.

Once they made me the heir apparent for Din Point, I told them that Isadora expected to have Kindera and Oxidence on her side. Din Point sent out fleets to stop their ships, to cut ties of communication and slow them down in time for us to attack first.

Yet they still went for us first; they attacked when we were still unprepared. In the heat of the moment, Din Point formulated a plan, and I was given instructions from the king and queen. The second we heard Parten coming, I was sent out to take the long way around to try and find their camp, while avoiding the battle front. My main goal now is just to get to the camp. If I get to Alas or to Isadora, I can end this whole operation.

So far, it's working. There's no one around me; I have nothing else to focus on except for my running.

I can still hear some of the soldiers in the distance, a song of weaponry that doesn't seem to ever want to end. I want it to end. By now, most of their troops must have fallen; and if I don't get to Alas, I can at least hope that Din Point's soldiers will eventually.

I push my body onward, running out of breath, my lungs begging for just a moment to recover. But there's no time for that.

Maybe if I get to Isadora first, she'll stop this. She'll yield, and see how she's wronged me. And I will, of course, spare her life.

But Alas—I know Alas will never kneel to me, and he might have brainwashed Isadora so much that she might not kneel either. I'll do what I must if it comes to that point.

Finally, I see their camp: the white tents that shine through the muck of a frosty day grab my attention. But before I can go any farther, I hear a crunch. Not a crunch like you hear when a branch falls in the woods, not something that I could have made myself from running, but the crunch of a branch breaking from someone stepping on it. Someone stepping on it with the intention of getting my attention. I halt, my panting so loud that if there *is* someone in the woods, they'll hear me loud and clear.

Daymond walks into my field of vision, appearing through the trees like he's stalking me as prey. His hands are lowered at his sides; he carries no weapons. At least I have a sword and two knives strapped to my belt. His dark-blue eyes are filled with a gleaming light, as if they've always been ready for this moment. He's someone who was born for war, someone who thrives on the creation of destruction. Just like Alas. This is their prime time, maybe their only time to use their martial skills and knowledge. No wonder Daymond has a look of pleasure on his face.

"I heard they made you the High General," I say to him, my words coming out rough. My hands refuse to shake as I stare him down.

The gold metals hanging from his chest glitter in the dying light. His uniform, which must have been tailored just a few days before, is in perfect condition. Untouched. "I heard they made you next in line for the Din Point throne," he wolfishly echoes. I stiffen my shoulders and can't catch my breath, knowing he's trying to make my choleric tendencies show.

"They did," I say.

"Seems you and Isadora have more in common than I thought. You both dabble in Parten and Din Point affairs far more than you should."

"You were once a Din Point loyalist yourself," I remind him. He takes a step closer to me. I take a step toward him, allowing myself to close the distance.

"I was," he replies, "and then Isadora got all of our heads out of the gutter. Seems she didn't succeed with getting yours out, though."

I don't respond as he takes then another step towards me.

My fists unclench themselves at my side. If he's going to try and fight me, then he'll need to call for water to create weapons, just as Isadora does. In those few seconds of him trying to obtain water, I'll have the greater advantage.

"And the king, your own father—did you kill him because you wanted to be king of Parten, or was it always for Din Point?" he taunts. I roll my shoulders back just the slightest bit as my eyes flicker away from him. "Or maybe it was just to hurt Alasdair? No, no… actually I know what it was: It was a practice round before you tried to take down Alas. You don't think people would have gotten suspicious with two royals dying so close together? Or would you have killed Alas in a different way?"

"Enough," I bark.

He takes three more steps closer to me.

"No, no, you're right. I'm sure you had it all planned out accordingly. Would you have killed first, your mother or Alas? I'm sure you would have had to kill your mother to get the throne…"

"I said *enough.*"

"But then again," he says, turning his heels closer to me. His hands raise to make gestures in the air. "I guess the order of your attempts would be first your father, then Isadora, then Alas, and then your mother? Was that it?"

My mouth clamps shut. My teeth clench down on each other, causing my jaw to tighten, my face to harden, my whole body to stiffen.

"Did you think I could forget about the time you stabbed my sister? Isadora, your wife, your 'love'?"

One moment I'm standing with my thoughts consuming my brain in fury, and the next I'm flinging myself forward. I heave my sword up out of its scabbard and slash, aiming for Daymond's throat. He pivots to the side, out of my sword's path; and as he does, I feel his hands brush my side. He snatches the two knifes I had at my side out of their sheaths.

I turn and swing my sword at him. His hands hold the knives up, crossing them and blocking as my sword strikes them in the middle.

"They always did say your temper gets the best of you at times," he hisses while releasing his hold and jumping back.

I lower my weapon, my hand grasping the metal and heating it up as hot and as quickly as I can. As I do that, he lunges forward. The knives he wields in both hands slash towards one side of my chest. I raise my sword in response and rotate it forward. It cuts the side of his arm, but he doesn't yelp in pain. We dance in tedious, tense movements, each slash barely stopping the other. Daymond has yet to call for any water.

I get myself in position to turn and swing my sword with my whole body. As I do, I watch it go straight for Daymond. Not even the knives can defend against the power my strike carries.

He drops the knife. He raises his arm and grabs my flaming sword in his bare hand.

I remember Isadora's stories far too late. The warning she'd unknowingly given me that told me how their cryomancy was different. How she has the ability to manipulate water and control it, while Daymond has the ability to freeze things on contact.

He has the power to destroy me and my heat with instant frost.

His hand collides with the blade of my sword. A hissing destruction of heat sizzles into the air. I feel the cold climb up my sword and reach my arm. My hand flinches upward, clenching from the intense cold that I'm not prepared for. My arm contracts and fumbles the sword. I exhale in sudden pain, and try to heat myself as quickly as possible. But Daymond has already swept up my sword and wields it now.

The heat that once imbued the metal can't stand against his freezing power.

He kicks me in the chest, knocking me to the forest floor. I try to move, but before I can get up, his leg stomps down. It sends a wave of ice and frost through the ground, spreading outward into the forest so far that I can't see its full stretch. It freezes me to the ground. I lower my head onto the hoarfrost, trying to calm myself down, to think straight.

I need to breath in order to control my ability and get myself out of this situation.

But there's no time.

No time for me to even stand a chance.

I feel the pain before I can even process it.

Daymond has shoved my own sword right through my chest.

My body twitches as I gasp.

I want to ask him to stop, to undo the act, to save me and stop this.

But I can't get the words to leave my lips.

I can't do a thing.

Nothing.

Nothing as the darkness consumes me.

CHAPTER 70

Dritan POV

I sadora's orb shatters around us. The water swallows me before I drift to the exit of the room and collapse onto the floor as the water drains into the hallway.

My hands grasp the marble. I'm soaked; water drips from my clothes, my hair. It floods the castle.

I roll over onto my back. My arm slides over my stomach as my body arches. The misty warm air hits my lungs. I cough up whatever water is still in my throat. I lift my head and squint, trying not to see all the dead bodies that fill the hallway as I force myself to stand.

I immediately search for Era. She's alive, raising herself off the floor. I extend a hand to help her to her feet. I pull her in and tightly wrap my arms around her. She's okay. She croaks out heavy breaths. Her eyes are still watery, and her hands shake.

Isadora and Carac are coughing, also trying to clear their airways.

Isadora's eyes show no relief, not even for a second. Her face is drained of all color as she looks frantically around the hallway. Water drips from her face. Her mouth releases a gasp of sorrow, and she bellows out a raw cry. A punch to the gut hits me as I see what she's screaming at.

She cries at the sight of King Alas, who has not yet taken a breath.

Isadora sprints through the hall to him. He lies face-down. The life has been stolen from his body, leaving nothing but the cold chill of death over his skin. Isadora grips his shoulder, pulling back, trying to find any sign of life. All she's met with as she turns him over is death's cold, silent embrace.

Carac runs after her. He grips her from behind, pulling her back from Alas's lifeless body. Emptiness radiates from her as she weeps. She lunges forward, fighting Carac's hold. He doesn't let her go. Isadora yells, her voice breaking, filled with so much pain that she cannot speak, cannot even breath. She tears herself out of Carac's hold. She collapses on her knees at Alas's side. Her hands move to his chest as she pushes down, trying to revive him. In between her sobs, she counts under her breath.

"Isadora," Carac whispers, as if pleading her to stop.

She continues to count, pressing down on his chest as a form of prayer that the water will escape from his body. I tear my eyes away, no longer able to stomach her grief and Carac's wishes for her to stop. Finally Carac breaks. "Isadora!" he snaps. He joins her on the ground and grips her hands, taking them off the dead king.

"Do something!" she screams at Carac. "Why aren't you doing anything?"

Carac stands, releasing his hold on Isadora. He doesn't meet her eyes; instead he looks down at Alas with his mouth clamped shut. His hand does not reach to fix what he can.

"Carac, you have to do something!" Isadora stands and wails in his face, "Bring him back! Carac, please!"

He does not move; he can't move, I realize. His body is frozen in shock, in horror.

Isadora's hand pushes against Carac's chest. He doesn't move back; he doesn't look at her. Isadora grips his chest and yells at the top of her lungs in agony, "Bring him back!"

Carac's eyes shoot to her in cold, silent fury. Pain fills his throat as he yells, "He doesn't want that! He told me not to!"

"You have to!"

"He doesn't want—"

Sobs fill her throat, cutting off his sentence. Isadora doesn't stop pushing on Alas's chest, her lips quivering so bad and her heart pounding so much that she starts to lose her breath.

I hear my sister starting to weep for the fallen king.

"Carac, please. Please. Please, you have to do something!" she yells again.

"I can't—"

"If you actually cared, even just a bit, you'd do this! Just do this for me, please!"

Carac's fist opens; he closes his eyes and clenches his jaw. He collapses to his knees. He kneels besides the King and doesn't make another movement as he whispers to Alas so softly I almost don't hear him, "I'm sorry."

And then Alas lets out a gasp. His breathing quickens as his eyes open. His hands grasp around him in panic. Carac stand and turns his back on us all. I catch his eye for a second as he glances over his shoulder. He wants nothing to do with this anymore.

Isadora throws her arms around Alas. Her cries of pain turn to happiness as the King looks around in fright.

Eventually, his arms wrap around Isadora. The King has risen from the dead, and with it he now has a new kingdom to rule. And Carac walks away from this with nothing to his name.

CHAPTER 71

Isadora POV

It's been a week since we won the battle. A week since Din Point fell, since Alas died, since Carac ran to the guards after bringing Alas back to life and forced them to wave a white flag in the air. A week since I was so caught up with Alas's death that I didn't notice Carac slip out and end the fighting on the fronts. He put a stop to the fighting, and then immediately got as far away from the scene as possible.

Which makes it also a week since I've spoken to him. I haven't had the chance to thank Carac for the Vaddelian troops. They're the only reason we stood a fighting chance on the battlefield.

I also haven't had the chance to thank him for saving Alas. Really, I owe him apologies more than a thank you for that. Alas hasn't spoken of his experience with death. He hasn't mentioned even a whisper of it. But I couldn't have had him die. He's all we have left to fix the kingdoms; who would have led us if he'd died? Would we let Trinity rule alone? A completely new bloodline?

Maybe it was selfish for me to have him come back to life, but we need him alive. Nevertheless, I still need to apologize to Carac for making him do such a thing against his wishes.

It's been six days since a soldier found Lawrence's body in the woods of Parten, alone and abandoned. I received the news about Lawrence while I was working in the now-fallen Din Point. It's been six days since I was told of Alas's screams of grief for his brother. The tears I shed silently in my room consumed me six days ago, and still the thought of Lawrence hasn't left my mind.

Alas won't speak to me about it. He won't say a word to anyone.

All he's done in the last six days is work: silently work until his brain can't think anymore and he can't feel anything except numbness.

It's been five days since Lawrence's funeral. I flew back to Parten Castle that morning.

Alas didn't tell the public of Lawrence's betrayal; he doesn't want that to be his brother's legacy. He made a public statement about Lawrence's death, saying he died defending Parten in battle, and left it at that. He let the people mourn for their prince.

It pained all of us to hear them say that he died too young, that he was taken from this world too early. The worst part is that all of their cries are true, despite what he did.

Alas held a funeral in private: only their mother, Trinity, and I were allowed to attend.

I remember every detail of that day all too clearly. How the weather was sunny, no gloom overhead. I remember how I saw Alas dressed all in black for the first time in my life. He didn't look at anyone that day. His eyes were filled with a watery sheen that still hasn't left them.

Five days since I've made hours of my day accessible to spend with Alas. Every day since the funeral, I've come to Alas's room when he makes himself available. Most of the time it's just us in silence. The time allows for our thoughts to swallow us whole for hours. One of those times, Alas mentioned to me that he wishes he knew who killed his brother. When the soldiers found him, he was stabbed through the chest, his body stone-cold and shuttered in a layer of frost that the following snowstorm had brought.

Alas just wants a face, a body, a name to connect to his brother's death. I don't know what he'd do to whoever killed Lawrence; it was a battle, and there are always casualties in battle, but the circumstances make it so gray. Regardless, it would give all of us some peace of mind to know who and how.

All I can hear in my mind is the last thing Lawrence said to me. How he, in a spur of anger, screamed, "I killed my father for this!" That's all I have as my last thoughts of him: those cursed last words to me, and then the stabbing.

Yet through all of that, every time I look at Alas, I'm reminded that Lawrence was human. Every time I see Alas's head tilt back to keep the tears away as much as he can, and his leg fidget in the silence, and his eyes drooping after another restless night, I'm reminded that Lawrence was his brother and my husband.

The rush of planning gives none of us any time to cope with his death. It's just a thought we have to carry with us every single moment of the day.

But even through all the pain, Alas is carrying on with his work. He's taken on the rulership of both nations, and is in the long process of reconfiguring the territories and the new people he has to rule. Which makes it four days since Alas split up Din Point. Era and Drítan have returned to Kindera; their apologies play like a record on repeat as they profusely let us know how sorry they are for their lack of troops in the battle.

That's a failing from which they can never truly recover. We were all let down during a time of need, and had it not been for Carac, Parten would have probably been taken over and dismantled, as Din Point is being dismantled now.

Alas hasn't done anything to Kindera in reprisal for their failure, as it was Din Point that undermined us all and prevented their ships from getting to us. Instead, he's opened a trading port with them and with Oxidence. Vaddel has returned to being isolated. Their soldiers left as quickly as they could after the battle. I never even got to say a word of thanks to them.

Alas has been splitting his time between Din Point and Parten to finalize the plans.

He didn't take any prisoners of war, except for the loyalists who refused to comply with the new leadership, and those numbers were very few.

Trinity has been playing a huge role in all this. Her thoughts and power are being used all over the map as she travels to Kindera and Oxidence to learn how to work with them and the people of the former Din Point. Through all of this, she's proven herself to be a key player. She wasn't at the battle, as Daymond had her held back in the castle in case they attacked and needed a person to command a defense.

To my surprise, after all that, Trinity has ceded to Daymond full military power. I haven't seen Daymond since his promotion. He's been up to his throat in work.

It's been three days since Alas asked me to go to Din Point. I can't tell if it was for the sake of having silence in the castle for a few days, since he sent out both Trinity and I, or if he's too stressed and needs me to work here instead of with him for a few days so that he has some consistency in his life by staying in Parten.

Either way, it's given me time to walk through Din Point Castle. When I was last living in the kingdom, I was confined to my room for most of my stay, and now I can roam freely. The castle is mostly abandoned, except for a few groundskeepers and caretakers who linger. Everyone I see in the castle has ditched the Din Point uniform. They wear whatever colors they please. In the last two days, I've found myself trying to make conversation with as many of them as I can. Most of them don't have much to say, just faint smiles to give. They are now getting paid a fair wage, and are not forced to clean the castle just to have a roof over their heads.

I'm the only person actually staying in Din Point Castle now, and the last two days have felt dragging, isolating.

There's not a Ryder near to make my temper rise when I speak with him. And there's not an Xeres to send chills down my spine with every glance. There's no Alas around to make me care, to push forward with a passion. I wish for any of them to be here, to bring whatever good or bad emotions they have to give, just so I can feel something.

That brings me to now: one day since I've stopped feeling much of anything. One day since I've allowed myself to be alone in thought. I've spent every second of the day pacing the gardens, watching the workers rebuild the glass walls I shattered. Other workers are still cleaning up and repairing the throne room where we were trapped.

I return to my room after lunch and watch the rain patter on my window in soft drizzles.

It's the first day of rain Din Point has had in a while. Not snow, not hail or sleet, but simple rain.

I hang my feet over the edge of my chair, passing the time by myself. I grow restless with my thoughts after only a few moments in my room, so I walk to my closet and grab a rain jacket and put on a pair of boots. I find the nearest umbrella and head to the front entrance. I carry myself out into the rain, feeling the brisk warmth of the storm against my skin.

I trudge farther and farther out, walking a few miles along a pathway in the grass that I haven't taken in a very long time. Eventually I have to look down at the earth and watch where I step, as graves now surround me, leaving very little room to walk.

The private Din Point Castle Cemetery: a place where every brisk gust of wind feels like a ghost begging to have its whispers heard. It's a small, condensed necropolis with less than a hundred headstones. Only the royals or people deemed important to the royal family of Din Point are buried here.

Carac stands over a grave that I know well, the only grave in this cemetery with a name I know attached to it.

I walk up to him silently enough that I don't disturb him, but with my footsteps betraying enough sound so that he isn't startled. Our black umbrellas blend together. His eyes don't meet mine. He's wearing his usual all-black clothing, his cufflinks removed from his favorite jacket. I can see the long-sleeve shirt he reserves for rainy days peeking out under his regular shirt. His skin has grown paler in the last week; his hair looks less full, and the bones show under his skin just a bit more. I haven't seen him since the battle.

"Alas told me you were arriving today," I say after a moment. "I figured if you didn't come to see me, you came to see someone else."

I stare down at his brother's grave. Caspian's final resting place.

I haven't been to Caspian's grave since he died, but I've always remembered what it looks like. The dark grey stone, with small, tiny engravements made in honor of his short life. The way that the grave stands out from the others. It's new; it has no cracks in its sides yet, the lettering still clear and well-maintained.

I place my free hand in my pocket and stand a bit closer to Carac to better protect us both from the rain.

"I came to see you, too," he whispers.

"He also told me that you turned down his offer," I say, looking for his explanation.

Alas told me that he offered Carac the same role he gave Daymond. He didn't know what else to offer to Carac; he didn't want him directly involved in political affairs, but after the battle he saw what strings Carac could pull. He wanted Carac to know he has a place, a large one in this new merging of the kingdoms... although Alas also thought a death controller in charge of the military would make a bold statement. But in the letter I got today from Alas, he told me that Carac had said no thank you.

"You turned down his offer as well," Carac contends, his voice smoky and deep. "Plus, I don't think Daymond would like to share his title with me."

I did turn down Alas and Trinity's offer. They asked me to be in charge of communications, to be their ambassador. I would have basically gotten to communicate with all the kingdoms on their behalf. I would have said yes, but it doesn't seem right for me to take any position in the court right now. I was only put up to be princess in the first place because of Daymond's work with the royals. And then I gained power only because of my marriage to Lawrence. It wouldn't be right to take such a high position, not with me only getting that offer because of other people's victories, not with everything going on right now.

All I really want is to have a breather for a while. I've had enough politics and communications with other kingdoms for a lifetime. I'm not ruling out working for Parten; I think I'd really enjoy that, but right now my place is here.

Just because Din Point has fallen doesn't mean everything in the community is fixed. It's going to take years, decades, to rebuild what's been destroyed by the previous monarchy.

"I'm glad you didn't take it so easily," Carac says. A small grin tugs at the sides of his mouth, but quickly fades away. "How is Alas doing?"

"Not good. I don't think any of us is doing as well as we hoped we would after all this, especially him."

Carac nods in response. We stand in silence for a few moments. The rain beats on our umbrellas, creating a rhythm to a dark song. The only thing I think of to ask him is, "Have you spoken to Ryder?"

"Yes. Briefly, a few days ago."

"Did he tell you what he did?"

He looks at me for the first time since the start of our conversation. He winces while lifting his eyebrows and tilting his head, as if asking: *What did he do now?*

I fill him in. "He lied. When he told us that Din Point was ready to attack that night, that was a bluff. He knew Din Point wasn't ready. But he told us a lie to get us moving, in fear that they would surprise us before we attacked." I honestly think it was a brilliant move. If he hadn't lied about Din Point, then maybe they would have cornered us. It could have changed the entire outcome of the battle.

"I'm not surprised; he's quite good at keeping secrets and lying to everyone. Both of us should know that by now." His words come as a backhand compliment. I barely hear the bitterness in his tone that he's trying to conceal.

Carac's eyes go back to the grave. His eye lids close heavily. His free arm tucks under the one holding the umbrella. He lets out a deep sigh as his face contorts. "This is what did it," he says throatily. I raise my head and stare at him with bated breath. "This is what did it for me. I found out they killed him. It was like you said... how you said they wanted me to rule, and they ensured it at whatever cost."

I follow his eyes as he reads the headstone again and again. My stomach drops; I lean forward to hear him speak. This wasn't something I ever wished to be right about.

His eyes snap away and dart to meet mine. "Do you know how fucked up that is? *They killed their own son to make me their puppet.* And I'm not even their blood!"

My mind goes blank; I can't process what he just said. He reads me like a book and in disgust whips out, "*I'm not their real son. I'm not even from Din Point.*"

"What do you mean, you're not from Din Point?" My thoughts jump around rapidly. He isn't from Kindera. Oxidence? The Zenlands? Vaddel? Northwell? Certainly not Parten.

"For the past year, I've been tracking down every little slip-up they made. I've been digging through every piece of history I could find to make sense of what we were all lied to about. They shoved their secrets so far down that no one could find them. No one. They've been lying to all of us, Isadora. Everyone has been lied to."

My eyes trace his face, the way his muscles tense up and his cheeks flush red.

"The Caps. The snowy lands that we all know have no one living there—that's just another fucking cover-up in our world's history. And this one they erased from all the books; they rewrote everything we've ever read. Kindera was one cover-up, one where we at least knew people lived on the island. And some kingdoms knew about Kindera; it wasn't that hard to track down that secret. But this, Isadora, *this* is something not a single living soul in our kingdoms knew about."

My mind falters. My breathing grows shallow in response, not knowing how else to react.

"There are people up there in The Caps. I don't know who, but that's where I'm from. That's where I got this *special* ability from. There's no reason we should have believed the bullshit story they wrote about crossbreeds being a thing. Why would there only be people born every few hundred years with abilities as dangerous as mine?" He lifts his chin, his voice rising an octave, his arms unfolding as he gestures in frustration. "And they kept it a lie for decades! From everyone! Not even my parents knew the whole story. They just took in a kid with the ability to control life and death, and believed the crossbreed bullshit!"

"Carac," I whisper. "This can't be... This isn't... how the hell do you *know?*"

"Because I found their mistakes. Little bits here and there in those stupid books from hundreds of years ago. They rewrote everything very precisely, too precisely, as if they just flung down whatever thoughts they thought would sound nice!"

"Where is this writing? I want to see. I want to read for myself what you've found," I gasp, my curiosity is running wild.

Carac takes a step toward me, pointer finger gesturing in a rapid motion as he points it up in anger. "Burned!" he yells. "Burned to fucking ashes!"

"Burned?"

"And we have Xeres to thank for that! He took everything I had painstakingly collected, all the work I had done, and *burned it* so that there was nothing left except for what I can remember. When I was digging through everything, I found the traces of what had really happened to my brother. The whole fire, the explosion, the way they orchestrated it like a fine symphony that would leave the masses weeping with grief. Not only did Xeres burn it all, but he killed me over it, too."

I don't know what to say. I don't know how to believe him as he continues to spit everything off his tongue like fire. "He killed me, Isadora! He had the ability to manipulate bodies; do you understand what he could have done to all of us? He could have turned my ability against me. He could have made my body fight against my will. People aren't just born with the ability to control bodies in these kingdoms. Xeres, the whole Shade family, were the only ones we ever knew to have such a powerful ability, and we didn't even question it. It's because they were from The Caps! They're members of whatever messed-up breed produces these ungodly abilities. And Xeres sacrificed everything to keep me from figuring the rest out. Everything. The night he used you as a pawn, the night he died, he took everything I had with him."

I think of how Xeres came to me that night. He asked me to kill him; he knew he'd done something that could never be fixed.

He had killed Carac. And just as Carac is saying now, that was the ultimate sacrifice. And it's all over this: The Caps.

"So everyone in the Caps has an outrageous ability? How does that even work, Carac?"

"I don't know, I don't know how many people there are, what they do, how they work, but they're out there."

"Carac…"

"Do you think I'd walk away from the throne over nothing, Isadora? Do you think I'd leave behind my entire life for some weak story? To just tell a lie? There's something out there so much bigger than we expected, bigger than any of us realized." His diction quickens with every sentence. His words fly together in a rant so important that it changes everything I've ever known. "The attack on my castle? That was them. That was all because I was starting to find too much. They blew up that part of the castle, the part with my office, in hopes of destroying everything. Xeres was on their side the whole time!"

My mind flashes back to the attack on the castle. The hundreds of people who ambushed us on that snowy day. The lady in red that Xeres spoke to so easily. He knew her. He knew everything that was going on. Xeres was never touched in that battle; not a single scratch was left on his skin. He told me after the attack that there were people working to see Carac fall, people who wanted him gone much more than I did. I could never have imagined the true meaning behind that conversation.

"That woman who came for us, did you see how the snow stopped falling altogether, how she wielded time at her command?" His voice is breaking in anger. I can see the betrayal playing out all over again in his mind.

And it all makes sense: why he left Din Point so quickly, the way he let everyone think he was dead so he could buy himself some time. He needed to get out of Din Point and the monarchy before they got to him. And now that Din Point has fallen and

Carac has nothing holding him to the kingdom, he can go, he can run with this. He can find the truth.

He was betrayed by everyone. He was lied to his whole life; his parents fabricated everything he ever knew. Even I betrayed him.

"What does this mean?" I ask him, desperately hoping he has an answer.

"It means we figure out what they're doing out in The Caps. There have to be answers out there, something beyond us. I have to get those answers."

I nod; I need time to think through everything he's told me. But Carac gives me no time to process it. He states, "I need to go to The Caps, and I need you to come with me."

"C-Carac," I stutter. I voice my immediate thoughts. "There's so much here—we have so much to do. Now's not the time for me to go. I'll support you in whatever you need. I made the mistake of not being on your side once, and I'll never make that mistake again, but The Caps aren't asking for me; they're calling for you."

He bites down on his lip and shoves a hand into his pocket. His eyes gleam at me, and with the tiniest smirk on his face, he says, "You must."

"What?" I choke out, not sure if I should smile or scream.

"*You must,*" he repeats. "I'm using my last *you must* and making it clear that you must come to the Caps with me." I release a scoff mixed with a breath of anger as I blink rapidly at him. He goes on, "There's no one better to go into the icelands with me than an ice controller. You're the only one I have left to work with, and truthfully, I'm all you have."

The punishing knowledge that he's right fills my head. He really is all I have left on my side. Alas is now King of the combined kingdoms, and he should rule as that; he doesn't need my help anymore, as much as he acts like he does. Daymond has finally found a life and has built it up, and I'll never tear it down again. And Lawrence....

Carac is still here; he still needs me. I still need him. I let myself realize I always have.

I cross my arms and chew on the side of my mouth as I grind out, "You're a prick."

A smile blooms across his face as he looks back at Caspian's grave before turning around. He walks through the rain with airy steps.

"I know," he responds.

I follow him out of the cemetery.

I can see it now so clearly. I can see how his hair flows perfectly with no crown to hold it down. The way his back doesn't stand up so unhealthy straight now. How his eyes have a glow behind them that's running wild with passion and beckoning adventure. He was never meant to be a king; he was never meant to be a royal.

But this; this is something he's meant for. He was always too cunning, too self-proceeding, to unkindly-witted to rule. And while it doesn't make what he did right, and will never fix his past, now he has a place, a job in the world that needs his morally gray ways.

A king should not uncover a whole new history; they should not invade a kingdom that we have never known to exist; they should not control death.

But Carac should. Carac is a whole different breed, and he's just now starting to figure it out.

He's not a king. He's not a prince. He's not a royal.

He is death itself.

CPSIA information can be obtained
at www.ICGtesting.com
Printed in the USA
LVHW011909300122
709647LV00004B/17